# Praise for *New York Times* bestselling author Heather Graham

"An incredible storyteller."
—*Los Angeles Daily News*

"This chilling novel has everything: suspense, romance, intrigue and an ending that takes your breath away."
—*Suspense Magazine* on *The Betrayed*

"Dark, dangerous and deadly! Graham has the uncanny ability to bring her books to life, using exceptionally vivid details to add depth to all the people and places."
—*RT Book Reviews*, Top Pick, on *Waking the Dead*

"[*Waking the Dead* is] not to be missed."
—*BookTalk*

"[A] powerful romantic thriller... This gripping tale strikes a perfect balance between romance and intrigue."
—*Publishers Weekly* on *Night of the Blackbird*

"Heather Graham knows what readers want."
—*Publishers Weekly*

## Also by HEATHER GRAHAM

\* \* \* \* \*

Look for Heather Graham's next novel
**A PERFECT OBSESSION**
available soon from MIRA Books.

# HEATHER GRAHAM

## FLAWLESS

MIRA®

MIRA

Recycling programs for this product may not exist in your area.

ISBN-13: 978-0-7783-1951-1

Flawless

Copyright © 2016 by Heather Graham Pozzessere

The publisher acknowledges the copyright holder of the additional work as follows:

Everyone Goes to Finnegan's
Copyright © 2016 by Heather Graham Pozzessere

For questions and comments about the quality of this book, please contact us at CustomerService@Harlequin.com.

www.MIRABooks.com

**Printed in U.S.A.**

Dedicated to NYC—overcrowded, crazy,
wonderful, diverse,
filled with history, theater,
music, art, architecture
and wonders that can be seen nowhere else.
To the resiliency of
those who live and work
in this great American city.
And to Mr. Korbin Pozzessere,
whose parents,
Derek Pozzessere and Yevgeniya Yeretskaya,
somehow met and fell in love in this
massive sea of people!

# FLAWLESS

# CHAPTER
# ONE

"I'm okay. Really. But I have to tell you what I did. Well, he deserved it, of course," Julie Benton said over the phone.

"What did you do?" Kieran Finnegan asked. So far, she'd only been half listening; Julie's tale of woe had been going on for quite a while now.

Kieran wiped the bar, one eye on her task, the other on the patrons in the pub.

Thankfully, at the moment she could easily work and listen, despite the fact that the object of Julie's venom— her almost ex, Gary Benton—was one of the few other people at Finnegan's on Broadway, the family down-town pub, one of the oldest in the city.

Julie giggled. "He deserved it," she repeated.

Kieran didn't doubt that. She just wished she couldn't see Gary as she was talking to Julie.

She never minded cleaning Finnegan's since it was practically her family home. It was a beautiful old place with finely carved wood, a range of tables and booths, and this classic bar with its array of beer taps and collection of Irish whiskeys. Photographs of the pub through the years hung behind the bar. Beyond was a comfortable dining room, equally rich in wood decor and handsome carving.

They weren't particularly busy at this off-hour of the day, between lunch and happy hour.

Bobby O'Leary was at one end of the bar; although he was an alcoholic long in recovery, Finnegan's was the center of his social life. He was still one of their favorite customers.

She'd given Bobby his standard soda with lime, and he was reading the *Times*.

Two groups of business executives on extended lunch hours remained. Three were at one table, and four—including Gary—were at another. Finnegan's wasn't even officially open. They closed between 3:00 p.m. and 4:30 p.m., according to the sign on the front door, but their clientele consisted mainly of friends and regulars who knew they could come in and receive service with a smile. Both tables had paid their bills and were lingering over coffee. Kieran had served them all their final refills—managing not to spill any scalding coffee on Gary—before she'd started cleaning.

And before Julie had called. She refrained from mentioning to Julie that Gary was at the pub; frankly, she was stunned he'd come in at all. He wasn't wanted here. But he was with Jimmy McManus—a longtime customer and entrepreneur who'd made a fortune in everything from magic mops to designer dog food and Wall Street trading. Jimmy was a great guy with a headful of white hair and a quick smile, taut and fit despite his fondness for a good Irish stout. They were joined by two men who seemed to be friends of Jimmy's. Kieran hadn't allowed herself to run over, grab Gary by the lapels and throw him out on the street. But until the coffee refill, she hadn't gone near the table. Mary Kathleen, a recent recruit from the old country and the love of Kieran's brother Declan's life, had been working the floor. She'd waited on the table, but she'd left at three. Which meant Kieran had no choice except to take over.

The other two at Jimmy's table were men Kieran had seen in the pub before but didn't really know. One was dark and one was pale. They were friendly, polite and dressed in handsome business suits, like many of the pub's clientele, who walked down from the Wall Street banks and firms where they worked.

They all looked richer than Gary Benton, that was for sure. Maybe he was trying to learn how to join their ranks.

Making a point of not looking toward the table, Kieran finished the last of her cleaning and the setup for happy hour while listening to Julie. Now *that* part wasn't easy, and not only because Julie and Gary were in the middle of the sad dissolution of their marriage.

Gary had wanted the divorce. Kieran knew things sometimes just fell apart. It was always difficult and distressing, but in this case, Gary's treatment of Julie had seemed deliberately cruel.

Julie needed her friends, and Kieran felt she had to be there for her.

*Don't look over at Gary. Just listen to Julie*, she told herself. *Yes, listen to Julie and be a good friend.*

And clean up the pub without pouring something over Gary's head. She might not care if Gary ever came back, but she didn't want to drive Jimmy and the others away. Finnegan's wasn't her full-time job, but it was her family's business and important to them all, herself and her three brothers.

Finnegan's was a true Irish-American pub. Her grandfather had bought it from a cousin when he'd come to the United States after the Second World War. It had actually been owned and operated by a Finnegan since shortly after the Civil War. Not only did they have a wonderful bar selection, with excellent beers on tap and high-end call brands, they also offered good pub-style food. People came to eat and drink, but they also came to socialize, to meet up with friends. Sometimes, during off-hours like this, that meant waiting around until the current Finnegan in charge of the place—her oldest brother, Declan, these days—or another family member or server came by.

Although it wasn't her real job anymore, she was always happy to help out at the pub. She had a career as a criminal psychologist now. But she hadn't been working with Doctors Fuller and Miro long enough to conduct an extended phone therapy session with Julie, even if she considered this crisis in her friend's life as something that could lead to a serious mental health issue. Luckily, she had the day off—Dr. Miro was at a conference, and Dr. Fuller had taken a vacation day and ordered the staff—Kieran and the handsome young receptionist and assistant, Jake Johnston—to do the same thing.

"I was calm, Kieran, I swear," Julie said. "You need to understand that. Calm—and clever."

That was good, Kieran thought. Calm. Since Gary had first started his hell-bent attempt to ruin their marriage, Julie had veered from wild rages to copious tears.

Kieran couldn't blame her. Gary had gone out of his way to be hurtful. He'd brought his new girlfriend to their home, made love with her in his and Julie's bed, and somehow the girlfriend had "accidentally" left her panties there. He'd emptied their joint bank accounts and, possibly cruelest of all, told Julie she no longer attracted him sexually. More—he claimed he found her repulsive.

"What did you do?" Kieran pressed warily.

"Well—" Julie giggled again "—you'll be glad to hear I didn't somehow get hold of a gun and shoot him."

"I *am* glad to hear that. So what *did* you do?"

"What *he* did was worse. I went to stay with my parents and left the house to him," Julie continued. "He says he can't stand living with me, but apparently I'm not supposed to leave, either. He called to tell me I'd better get back to feed my damned dogs. He kept them in their crates, hadn't let them out at all! They were starving, Kieran, and covered in their own waste."

Kieran glanced over at the table where Gary was seated. He'd risen with the others now; they were on their way out, which was a relief. She wouldn't feel tempted to inflict bodily harm.

She watched him leave. He was a good-looking man, but Kieran had never been particularly fond of him. There was something...*slimy* about him, in her opinion. His quick, oh-so-charming smile usually meant he was planning something devious. He sold precious stones and jewelry at a high-end store in the Diamond District, and he'd often told Julie he had to take some woman out for dinner or drinks because a big sale was in the offing.

*Slime.*

She and her brothers had tolerated him for one reason and one reason only. Because they loved Julie, their friend since childhood.

*But he'd left the dogs locked in their crates?*

"That's horrible. You should call the police on him. Either that or move out. I've told you to come and stay with—"

"The dogs and I won't fit in your apartment," Julie said.

That was probably true; Kieran's apartment on St. Marks Place was the size of a postage stamp. But she didn't care if she, Julie and the two dogs were all crammed in there. Animal abuse was never acceptable.

"We'd make it work," Kieran told her. "And if he's actually being that horrible, you need to get out of there. I really think you should call the police. There are laws against that kind of thing."

"Oh, I don't want the police involved."

Kieran winced at that. She wasn't fond of police intervention herself, even though her new position would soon have her working with them often enough. While her oldest brother, Declan, had become a completely respectable citizen, her other brothers—her twin, Kevin, and their baby brother, Daniel, who was a whole year younger—still had "friends" involved with various street gangs. They were trying to go straight, but it was easy to fall back into their old ways. She'd had some bad times herself during her teenage years. Like Declan, however, she'd known that things could spiral downward, so she'd gone to college, majoring in criminology and specializing in criminal psychology. In a sense she was paying for her past—and making her past pay.

They'd never done anything *too* terrible. Declan had

made some "deliveries" for the McNamara clan, an Irish family that had challenged the Garcia gang. But after their father's death, he'd decided he was going to be the head of a family that would live and thrive and succeed in NYC. Kevin had hung out with the O'Malley family, really just a loose connection of thugs. High-school stuff. Danny had actually joined the Wolves, another loose-knit group proudly based on the TV show *Dexter*, but without the murders. They stole from those who stole from others, sweeping up their cell phones and hacking their computers in turn. He'd come the closest to being in real trouble when a rival group had caught him and some hackers at the school library and started a massive brawl.

Kieran remembered a time when life had seemed good and normal, even though they'd lost their mother when they were young. Then their father had died almost ten years ago. Declan had been in college at the time, and he'd felt the weight of responsibility for his siblings and to family tradition. He'd gone straighter than an arrow. Kieran, who'd only gotten occasionally involved with computer hacking and a few minor thefts, quickly followed suit, graduating from high school with stellar grades. Declan had made clear to his younger brothers that he had zero tolerance for bad behavior, so they'd realized they had no one to bail them out of serious trouble and struggled to keep their noses clean. They'd been doing that, as far as she knew. The problem with Kevin and Danny was that they both believed in justice—their version of it—even when the law didn't.

"Kieran, are you there?"

"Yes, yes, and I want to hear the end of the story."

Julie laughed softly. "It's good. I promise you, it's good."

A sense of unease began to stir in Kieran. "Julie, just tell me, what did you do?"

"Did I mention that whoever he's fooling around with left her thong in the bed? *My bed?*"

"Yes, I know, and that's deplorable. But what did *you* do?"

"I got over the crying. I don't want you to think I did anything crazy because I was crying hysterically or out of my mind with grief or anything."

At that, Kieran's reaction went from unease to real concern. She looked up, forced herself to flash a smile to Bobby, refilled his glass and asked Julie to hang on for a minute.

She stopped trying to do anything useful; she had to concentrate on this conversation. She headed to the end of the bar, out of earshot of everyone else, and leaned against it. "Julie, *what did you do*?" she asked again.

"I was very nice, actually. His boss called the house, asking if I knew where he was. I said I didn't. Then I went and bought doughnuts and take-out coffee, and brought them down to the store."

That sounded nice so far. In Gary's business, client and coworker relationships were important, because the amounts of money clients spent and the employees' commissions were so high that cooperation literally paid. After all, better that the proceeds were shared than never earned at all. Julie was well liked by Gary's friends and coworkers. She was quick to assist when asked and enjoyed role-playing—pretending keen interest in a piece of jewelry when a possible buyer was studying it. In the process, she'd learned a fair bit about how to judge the quality of diamonds.

But Julie hadn't gone down to the store to be nice; Kieran was certain of that. "Julie, what exactly did you do after that?" she asked.

"I handed out doughnuts. I apologized to his friends and coworkers for the fact that he hadn't been showing up when he was supposed to, and I explained that they'd have to find whatever woman he was sleeping with to know where he was. I saw his boss last. I asked him to save one glazed doughnut with a hole in it so Gary would have a place to put his dick in case one of his new girlfriends got wise to him."

"That was it?" Kieran asked.

Julie giggled. "Oh, no. I want him to *really* hurt."

"So then?"

"Well, then they acted all awkward and said how sorry they were. I just said, well, it was over, and how much I liked all of them, but I wouldn't be able to come in and pose as a potential customer anymore."

"And *that* was it? Right?"

"Well…almost," Julie said. "You have to understand, Kieran. I wasn't stupid about this. I was calm and charming. I'm so ready for all of this to be over."

"And that's good. Close the door. Start fresh."

"You remember, don't you, how I didn't even want to get married right away?"

"Yes, I remember."

"I wanted to go to California and earn my master's. Take some time. He talked me into getting married."

"We all make mistakes, Julie. But back to what you did…" Kieran hesitated. "So you left the shop and that was it," she said hopefully.

"Well…"

"Oh, Lord. Julie, if you wanted to hurt him, you should've just called animal control or the police. I'm sure they would have taken action for what he did to the dogs. You might have gotten him fired just for that. In any case, he would've been in trouble somewhere with someone."

"Trust me, he's already going to be in enough trouble," Julie said.

"And why is that?"

"They're going to find out that the Capelleti Diamond is gone. And Gary was the last one to handle it."

Kieran's heart slammed against her chest. "No! You didn't—did you? Did you steal the diamond, Julie? Tell me you didn't. That's grand larceny! *Did you steal that diamond?*"

"No, don't be ridiculous," Julie said.

"Thank God," Kieran murmured.

"I'm no good at stuff like that! I'd never try to steal anything. I was just setting Gary up. Making sure his boss and everyone there knew he had a *reason* to steal it, what with a new girlfriend and an expensive divorce."

"Get to the point!"

"Well, the point is… I had your brother take the diamond for me. I admit I don't know that many, but Daniel's the best thief I've ever met—besides you, of course."

Craig Frasier headed down the hall to the office of assistant director Richard Eagan and ran into Mike Dalton, who was approaching their boss's office from the opposite direction.

Mike grinned at Craig. "I'm baa-ack!" he said happily.

"Glad to see it." Craig grinned in return and couldn't help asking, "So, how's the ass?"

Mike gave a nonchalant shrug. "Every part of me is doing fine. As for you, you're just a wise*ass* kid," he said.

They'd been partners for five years, and at thirty-four, Craig hardly considered himself a kid. But he and Mike were more than partners; they were friends, as well. Although they could joke about it now, they'd been chasing a suspect in the murder of an up-and-coming politician in the Poconos when Mike was injured. He'd dodged behind cover to avoid a bullet from the Beretta the supposedly unarmed suspect had suddenly stopped to fire and caught the bullet in the left buttock as he took his dive. Craig had taken down their suspect, winging him in his right shoulder. The Beretta had gone flying, and the suspect had been arrested—in pain but alive. He'd provided information on his coconspirators in the murder, and the crime had been solved. It had been a good day for their unit, but Mike had spent several days in the hospital after that, and then a month at home on forced medical leave.

Mike had informed Craig that it was his fine solid ass that had saved the day. An embarr*ass*ing injury, Craig had pointed out, one that had resulted in all the inevitable remarks.

Naturally, even as they teased him, his coworkers were grateful that his injury wasn't worse and that he would easily recover.

"Good to have you back," Craig said, and he meant it.

In Mike's absence, he'd been paired with Marty

Salinger, the new nerd on the block, a by-the-book-
until-the-pages-ripped kind of nerd. Craig had just about
crawled out of his skin every time Marty insisted on
backup when the clock was ticking or refused to make
a move without direct permission.

Craig had made it through some hard situations, situations in which going by the book was no help. He'd
worked undercover in narcotics, and more than once,
fast thinking had saved his life—and the lives of others.

Marty would learn. Sometimes the book was important and gave them what they needed; sometimes,
a good agent was better off making split-second deci-
sions without it.

But hell, Craig himself had learned from Mike. Mike
had been with the agency twelve years; he had experience and resolve. At five-eleven, he was shorter than
Craig by four-plus inches, but he was lean and fit and
determined to stay that way. He and Craig spent hours
training. They both ran, and participated in the various
sports events the agency sponsored.

They both spent long hours at the gun range, too;
shooting skills had to be kept sharp when you worked
in the field.

Mike had been offered desk jobs over the years. He
didn't want them. It would happen soon enough, he'd
told Craig, but he still had work to do making sure he
had Craig trained properly. It wasn't entirely meant as
a joke.

Now that memory made Craig think about Marty.
One day he would probably be a good field agent; Craig
just didn't want to be the one stuck teaching him. He
liked knowing that Mike had his back. He was always

afraid Marty would be checking some manual to see if it was all right before he entered the fray.

Luckily, everything had been straightforward during the weeks Mike was out recuperating. Craig and the new kid had been assigned to a gang shakedown. Intelligence had been good, and they'd made a number of arrests without a drop of blood being spilled.

Craig had recently come off that detail, and with Mike newly returned that day from medical leave, they were being called in to see the assistant director.

"You know what this is about?" Craig asked.

"Not a clue. Hey, this is New York," Mike said. "Could be anything."

The New York State office of the Federal Bureau of Investigation was the largest in the country, and since New York City had such a massive population, most of the agents were assigned to the city and its environs. The New York office had agents assisting with cases across the country. However, since 9/11, the delegation of duties had changed somewhat. There were now special divisions in the New York office that handled practically everything, from fraud and income-tax evasion to organized crime, gangs, kidnapping, murder, terrorism and more. The units worked together to assess a situation and strategize the best approach. After all, as people often said, Al Capone had been brought down not by a hail of gunfire but by the brilliance of an accountant.

Within the different divisions, there was a small group of agents who'd earned a place in one of Eagan's special task forces. Craig and Mike fell into that category, so a trip to Eagan's office was always intriguing. They never had any idea what the assignment might be, except that it was usually in conjunction with another law enforcement agency.

The director's assistant indicated that they should go on in. "He's waiting for you," she told them.

Craig opened the door for Mike. "After you, my friend. I've got to watch out for the elderly and the injured."

"Don't you mean you should step aside for maturity and experience?" Mike said. "But never mind. *You* go first."

"Ah, but I don't want the door catching you in the ass—the back, I mean—if you go in last," Craig said.

"Low blow!" Mike protested.

Craig inclined his head. "Okay, we'll call it maturity and experience." He held the door and followed Mike in.

Richard Eagan was looking out his window when they entered. "Take a seat," he said, turning toward them. "File folders are in front of you."

Eagan was a ramrod of a man. Fifty-plus, he was as fit as a teenager—something he worked at with the same discipline he observed in the office. He was a decent man, but he hadn't kept one of his six wives for more than a year; none of them had truly grasped his overpowering dedication to his work.

Craig knew that because the last two had cried on his shoulder. Marleen, wife number six, had warned him, "Don't let this happen to you, Craig. When you find the right woman, find a balance between work and life. I was all for Richard saving the world. What I didn't realize was that he never meant to save himself."

He knew that Marleen had been genuinely worried about him. Too many casual relationships had lasted only until he was working around the clock again. Truth was, he had his own reasons for not pursuing a serious relationship. He'd actually begun to explain, but then he'd stopped.

*They just don't make them like the one I lost anymore.*

He sat quickly and Mike did the same, and they picked up their folders, scanning the material.

"Jewelry store robberies?" Mike said. "I've been following this on the news, but—"

"There's been a change," Eagan said. "Two thefts in the past two days. And now, two dead."

Craig glanced at him in surprise. The NYPD had been dealing with the rash of jewelry store robberies. Every one of the five thefts that had taken place during the previous weeks had been within the five boroughs of NYC and fallen under the jurisdiction of the city police. Even with the two deaths, it still seemed to be a situation the NYPD should be handling.

"They're killing people now?" Mike asked. "I hadn't seen that on the news."

"It hasn't been on TV yet. I'm having a press conference with the chiefs of police and the mayor in an hour. We've been holding off, pending notification of next of kin. And, of course, to coordinate efforts between agencies."

"We're in?" Mike asked.

"Yeah. State lines and all, since now New Jersey's been hit, too. Twice. Anyway, it's all hands on deck. You two will be lead, but you won't be the only special agents involved. Hell, every law enforcement officer in New York and the tri-state area will be alerted and working on it. The last two robberies took place right over the bridge in Jersey City. The elderly gentleman who owned one of the stores was staying late, doing his books, when he was shot and killed."

"You said there were two murders?" Craig asked, flipping through the folder he'd been given.

Eagan nodded gravely. "There was a murder at the next store that was hit, too. A night manager was there, and a cleaning woman was working in the showroom. She was abducted, then murdered in the alley behind the store."

"What about the manager? Any idea why he was left alive? Did he see anything?" Craig asked.

"He was in a back office. When he came out, they grabbed the woman as a human shield and dragged her away. They shot at him and missed, and apparently were in too much of a hurry to care," Eagan said.

"Video surveillance?" Mike asked.

"Yes, but the thieves wore hoodies and ski masks," Eagan said.

"Are we *sure* that these thieves and the ones who hit the Diamond District are the same?" Craig asked.

"Same MO. Breaking in after closing time, they wear gloves, so no prints. And all the security footage shows the thieves wearing the same disguises," Eagan said.

"But it's *not* the same MO anymore," Craig muttered.

"What do you mean?"

"I mean it's changed," Craig said. "Escalated. Five robberies with no one hurt. And now we have two dead. Seems odd to me that they've suddenly become violent."

"Maybe they got desperate for some reason," Mike suggested. "The pressure of time or whatever."

Craig shrugged. "Maybe these are copycats. Copy-cats who kill."

"Could be," Eagan said. "Get up to speed, see what

you can find. And let's hope to hell we're not looking for two different sets of thieves. Jewel heists are one thing, but murder…"

"What is the matter with you?" Kieran demanded. Her voice was harsh, even though her words were almost whispered.

She wasn't meeting with her best friend and her miscreant youngest brother at Finnegan's. No way could she have done that without Declan getting wind of it. Didn't matter that he wasn't at the bar right now. The customers, the servers, everyone—even the damned walls—seemed to have eyes and ears.

She'd met them at a nondescript chain coffee place down the street from Finnegan's instead.

Daniel looked sheepishly at Kieran, turned to Julie, then back to Kieran. "Julie's like a sister to me," he said defensively. "And her scumbag husband deserves the worst. Kieran, he could've killed those poor dogs, not to mention the emotional crap he's been putting Julie through!"

Daniel was obviously a Finnegan. Everyone in the family had some shade of red hair. Declan's was a medium-reddish brown, Kieran and Kevin were a darker auburn, while Daniel had the lightest coloring among them. Her uncle had once said that visiting the hospital after the twins, and later Daniel, were born seemed pointless, since he'd gone to see Declan and they'd all looked like the same baby.

At the moment Kieran figured she really did resemble her youngest brother. Her expression was pretty much the same. She completely shared his indignation at the man who had hurt Julie in so many ways.

But she—unlike her brother and, apparently, Julie—had acquired some common sense.

Julie had an excuse; she was an emotional mess.

As for Daniel...

The diamond was still in his pocket. Kieran was aware that all three of them were now in on the theft of a flawless stone worth at least half a million dollars.

"Let me rephrase this. What the hell were you two thinking? You're talking grand larceny!" Kieran said.

"But I don't *want* the diamond!" Julie insisted. "I don't intend to keep it. I just want to get him in trouble for stealing it. Or losing it, if his boss feels like giving him the benefit of the doubt." Petite Julie, with her short blond hair and big brown eyes, looked as innocent as a newborn babe as she stared at Kieran. "You know how his store works. Each sales agent is responsible for a certain collection of diamonds and other stones. Any of the associates can show them, but the sales agent has to count and log them in at the end of the day. I just—I just wanted Gary to suffer for a while. I wanted him to sweat it out. When there's a count, it won't be there. He'll be in major trouble. I couldn't care less about the stone itself."

"Oh, God!" Kieran said, sitting back and crossing her arms. "There's been a rash of jewelry store hold-ups. Don't you two idiots see? You're in the same category now."

"Don't be ridiculous. I've never been *armed*," Daniel protested. "I didn't hold anyone up. I just pocketed the stone."

"It has to go back right away—as in *now*," Kieran said. She scowled at her brother. "How exactly did you manage to take it?"

He shrugged. "Well, I said I was there to see Julie's scumbag almost ex—"

"You said that at his place of work?" Kieran asked.

"No, of course not," Daniel said indignantly. "I knew he wasn't in at the time, since he was here. At the pub, I mean. So I asked Neil Davis if I could see Gary's stones in particular—after, of course, acting disappointed that he wasn't there. I know Davis is the king of the lazy asses because Julie's told me about him. He'd just want the sale, and he wouldn't count until the end of the day. I said I'd heard Benton had some great stones that could be set in the design of my choosing and that I wanted to create the perfect ring for my fiancée. And he did the usual jeweler thing—displayed the unmounted stones on a velvet cloth on the counter. Then I told him he had a fleck of something on his chin, and when he turned to the mirror, I pocketed the stone."

"You'll be on a security tape filching that diamond," Kieran said, her heart sinking. How the hell was she going to get him out of this one?

"Don't be ridiculous. I made sure my back was to the camera and that my head blocked it."

"They'll still come after you. They'll go through the security tapes and see that you're the one hiding his face. Neil can describe you, and Gary will know exactly who you are," Kieran said. "Give it to me. I have to get that stone back before they realize it's missing."

"No, Kieran. I'll take it back there," Julie told her.

"Don't be a fool. You have no finesse when it comes to doing anything dishonest," Daniel said. "You'll look guilty as hell, and you'll wind up confessing, saying *you* did it. Gary might have you arrested, not to mention what his boss might do."

"I left the house, trying to give him space to screw anyone he wanted, and what did he do? He nearly killed my dogs!" Julie said, tears rising to her eyes.

"Asshole," Daniel muttered, placing his arm around Julie. "He doesn't deserve you. There *are* good guys out there, and you'll find one, I swear."

Kieran lowered her head, listening to the two of them. They just didn't get it.

"You idiots," she said. "This wasn't just juvenile—it was criminal. Yes, Gary's behaved like the worst and most despicable jerk on earth, but, Julie, if you want to get even, get over him! Finalize the divorce and learn to live a better life on your own. And, Daniel, how could you, you dunce? You've stayed out of trouble for years. You're working. You have a life and a career ahead of you. *Think.* You've risked your whole future. Both of you have to think about yourselves. Forget about Gary. Do you understand?"

They both reddened, nodding their agreement.

"Give me the stone," Kieran said to her brother.

"No, I'll get it back where it belongs," Daniel said.

"No! If something goes wrong, they'll have you on tape twice. I'll go. And you can't go with me, Julie. If Scumbag's there—" She cut herself off. "If Gary is there, I can say I've just come to ask him to start behaving civilly. If he's not there, I'll… I'll let it fall on the floor when no one's looking, pick it up and just hand it over. What you did is serious. I mean years-in-prison serious, grand-larceny serious, you—"

She stopped herself. She wasn't going to call them idiots again.

Even though they were, she'd made her point.

Daniel very casually reached into his pocket and handed her the stone. Casual was the way to do it. She should know. They'd all been proficient at pilfering little things during those difficult early years. Gum, candy—small stuff. Now she understood that they'd been bitter and unable to handle the death of their mother, so they'd acted out.

They'd been good at it. What wasn't good was that they'd never been caught. They hadn't been hauled down to juvenile court, then threatened with their father's wrath and whatever the system could do to them.

"I'm terrified that you don't realize what you did. *Grand larceny.* You could be put away for years and years. Honestly, this is no joke. And no lie—sometimes the sentences for theft are longer than the ones for murder," she said sternly.

They both looked contrite, but what scared her was that they still didn't seem to comprehend just how foolish they'd been. How dangerously foolish.

She pointed a finger at her brother. "You promised me. No more stealing."

"But I wasn't stealing it. I was just...borrowing it for a while."

"My company works with the police," she retorted. "Aside from everything else, think about the position you've put me in."

"You're a psychologist who works with a bunch of doctors," Daniel said.

"Who work with the police," she finished. "You—"

Julie broke in. "It was my fault," she said.

"Yes, in a way it was," Kieran said. "And then again, no. Daniel is responsible for his own behavior. Daniel,

I need you to promise me, once and for all, that you'll never steal again."

"Kieran…" he murmured, glancing away. "This was an exception. I did it for—"

"Daniel."

"All right, I promise." She could tell by the way he looked at her that he knew she doubted him. "Never again. I swear it on our parents' grave."

That, to her brother, was a solemn vow.

"I wonder if they'll even miss it," Julie said. "The diamond, I mean."

*"You wonder if they'll miss it?* A flawless stone worth a half a million or more?" Kieran asked incredulously.

"Like you said, there's been a rash of jewelry store holdups in the city."

"Yeah. Armed men come in and wipe out half a store. Do you think Gary's boss and coworkers wouldn't notice if they'd been held up by men with guns?"

She checked her watch. She had to leave now if she was going to make it before the store closed for the day.

"What do you want me to do now?" Daniel asked her.

"Cover for me at the pub."

"I'll help him," Julie offered.

"No, you won't. You'll go home and walk your dogs. That way Daniel can say I'm dealing with something for you and it won't be a complete lie. Declan will understand." She stood. "And don't you ever—*ever*—put me in this position again." She stared at them hard. "I can't believe what I'm about to do. I'm heading off to *un*steal a diamond."

She turned away. She had to hurry because time was against her now. Pretty soon the staff would be counting receipts and logging the day's sales as well as inventorying the jewelry and stones they'd shown that day.

She prayed she could keep Daniel out of jail—and not land both of them in the arms of the law.

# CHAPTER
# TWO

Wally O'Neill, a civilian tech employed by the FBI, was working with Craig and Mike, viewing the security footage from the jewelry stores. They could have looked at the videos alone, but Craig was glad they had Wally's help. He was a whiz when it came to cameras, computers…anything digital.

The security footage showed that all the robberies had been carried out in much the same way.

Quickly, for one.

Three men—or they looked like men, anyway—in dark jeans, hoodies and ski masks suddenly converged on the door and entered the store. They burst in with guns out. Not one of the recording devices allowed for sound, but Craig was certain that the first man to break in roared that no one had better set off the alarm or someone would die.

No alarms had been set off, but in the last two robberies, people had died anyway.

"Okay," Mike said, "since they're dressed alike, maybe they come from different directions or time it so each one is slightly ahead of the next guy to avoid calling attention to themselves. I mean, half the kids in America walk around wearing hoodies with their heads down and hands shoved in their pockets, but the ski masks are a real attention getter. I'm betting they don't put those on till the last minute."

Mike was probably right about that, Craig thought. In New York City, with crowds everywhere and people walking in every direction, their own agendas in their heads, there would be no particular reason to notice someone dressed like that. And Jersey? Pretty much the same story.

"They don't split up when they leave, though," Craig pointed out.

"There's gotta be a getaway car idling somewhere nearby."

"They committed the murders in Jersey. They're either getting bolder—or they're not the same crew."

"That again," Mike muttered.

"I might be right."

"You might be wrong."

"Yeah, I might be. In fact, I hope I am," Craig said.

Wally cleared his throat. "Uh, guys? What do you want me to do now?"

"Roll the last two," Craig told him.

Wally hit a key and brought up the crime-scene photo from the alley. He quickly apologized. "Sorry, pushed the wrong button."

"It's all right. We're going to have to go over that, too," Mike said.

They all stared grimly at the photo. The woman was

dark haired and wearing a cover-up over her clothing—her way of staying clean while she swept and dusted, Craig thought.

She was lying on her side, almost as if she were sleeping. Except that a pool of blood billowed out from beneath her hair.

Mike looked at his folder. "Ana Katrina Martinez, forty-seven. Small-caliber bullet fired at point-blank range right through her forehead. Cartridge not found and the bullet is still in her brain. The ME will supply it to ballistics right after the autopsy."

Craig felt a swell of emotion. Ana Katrina Martinez wouldn't care what kind of bullet had killed her, and neither would her family. They would only care that her killer was caught. Even dead in a pool of blood, she had a kind face. Craig thought she had smiled frequently in life. "Why her?" he muttered angrily.

"Because someone was a grade-A sociopath with no concern for anyone other than himself," Mike said. "You'd have to be," he added gruffly, "to kill someone just because she was no longer useful. Hell, they were probably still in their ski masks—she couldn't have identified them."

Wally cleared his throat. "Stay with this image or roll the footage?"

"Roll the footage," Mike said.

"So in the city they leave everyone alive," Craig said. "Then they go to Jersey and leave a woman dead in an alley."

"And a man dead at his desk," Mike added.

"I can't help but think it's different perps."

"Just different states. I'll bet you a twenty. No, I'll go a hundred."

"It's a bet I hope I lose," Craig said.

"What are *your* thoughts on the matter, Wally?" Mike asked.

Wally looked up at them with surprise. Craig figured that his expertise was often sought, but not his opinion.

"I've enhanced the footage as much as possible. If they're copycats, they have the clothing and the ski masks down perfectly," he said. "I don't know—I just don't know."

"Let's watch again—then we can start with the interviews," Mike said.

"Whatever you want," Wally said.

"What about the murdered jeweler?" Craig asked.

"You'll see that on the footage," Wally said.

They didn't see the death of Ana Katrina Martinez on the computer screen; no camera had captured that.

They did see the death of the elderly owner of the first store. He looked up, said something and appeared to be willing to do whatever the men wanted.

Then he was shot, and he crumpled over.

Mike looked at the files again. "Arthur Kempler, eighty-four. He owned and managed Kempler's Fine Jewelry for over fifty years. Never had so much as a parking ticket."

"They didn't need to kill him," Wally muttered.

Neither Mike nor Craig disagreed with him.

"Go back to the first robberies," Craig told Wally.

Wally nodded. "Right away."

In the earlier heists, they saw the thieves exit by way of the front door, the same way they had come in.

Only in New Jersey had they used the rear exits, at least so far.

"In those first five robberies—as the cameras show—

they went back out into the street," Mike said. "And they were casual about it. I figure within a few steps they had their ski masks off, and in another few steps the hoodies were gone and no one would have known they'd been wearing them at all. They didn't hide from people—they used them. They melted in with the crowd until they got to their getaway car or the subway and left the area."

Craig shook his head. "Okay, let's look at all the footage again. I'm telling you, these aren't the same thieves."

"How can you be so sure?" Mike asked. "Look at the New York footage. Three of them each time. Walking in and making it all happen fast. Then New Jersey. Same outfits, same number of guys—except in the first one, the bastards shoot the owner, and in the second, one of them grabs that poor woman and drags her out the back door."

"No, go back—go back and look at the height differences. There—look at the first tape. Two the same height, one shorter. Now go to the first store that was hit in New Jersey. None of them are the same height," Craig said. He looked at Wally. "Wally, sorry, run them again. Slow them down."

Wally obliged, and they watched the footage again.

Mike sighed. "How the hell are you seeing that? Maybe they're the same size—or maybe they're not. They could be wearing different shoes, for all you know. The perspective's so crazy there's no way to know for sure."

"I just don't think they're the same. I think the second group are copycats. Except that they kill."

"What's the likelihood of two sets of thieves with

virtually identical MOs starting up at the same time?" Mike asked, exasperated.

"Why not? Some criminal opportunist sees what the first guys are getting away with and figures he'll give it a shot himself. Only he doesn't give a damn about human life."

"Let's watch them one more time, then start interviewing the first cops on the scene, and the staff and customers who were there," Mike said. "Wally?"

"Yeah, yeah, one more time," Wally said. "And I can do comparison ratios—tell you who was and wasn't the same height."

"Great. For now, freeze both of the shots I'm talking about, please," Craig said. "Can you show them to us side by side, split screen?"

As Wally brought up the two shots, Craig heard Mike's phone buzzing. Mike picked it up, and Craig watched his partner's features tighten.

"On our way," Mike said. "Wally, hold tight to that footage. Craig, looks like they're at it again. We have a chance to catch them red-handed and learn the truth. Let's go."

Craig stood quickly, thanking Wally again, and the two men headed out to their car.

"Where's it going down?" Craig demanded as they walked. "What's going on? Did someone trigger an alarm this time?"

"No. No alarm. People are just getting more nervous and, thankfully, more vigilant. They're watching for men in hoodies near jewelry stores. And the thieves are right in the Diamond District this time. Sonny Burke from Atlantis Gems just called in to say he saw three men in black hoodies heading down Forty-Seventh

Street. That place is a smorgasbord for diamond thieves. Damn, they're getting bold!"

"I'll drive," Craig said.

"I'm back, Craig. I'm good. Honestly. I've got it."

"You drive like an old woman. Give me the keys."

Mike didn't argue. Craig was the better driver and Mike knew it. He tossed over the keys.

*This will all be over soon. It will be fixed. Everything will be okay,* Kieran told herself.

She had the diamond; she was appropriately dressed to shop in a jewelry store of the stature of Flawless. The store was in the Diamond District, up on Forty-Seventh, so she'd had a ways to go to get there. She would have chosen a cab with the diamond now in her keeping, but she'd been afraid of getting caught in traffic, so she'd headed for the subway.

She'd been lucky enough to get some traveling in when her father had been alive, but she'd spent the majority of her life in New York City, even attending NYU. She'd taken the subway system all her life.

Today she found herself looking suspiciously at everyone who boarded her subway car. She shifted and moved to a new spot at each stop. If she lost the diamond to a casual pickpocket, all her efforts to save her brother would be doomed. And with technology being what it was, she wasn't certain that there still wasn't some way to prove that he had taken it.

*I'm not his keeper,* she thought to herself.

But, in a way, she was. She'd been the one girl in the family. Her father had been a wonderful man, as proud of his daughter as he was of his sons—and quite ready to open a can of tuna for himself without help. But she had taken on a certain role in the house—different with Declan, of course, because he had her by two years. Like it not, she felt responsible for both her younger brothers, even though she was older than Kevin by a mere seven minutes and her baby brother by only a year.

She'd been "the girl." Spoiled shamelessly, according to her brothers, but...

It seemed girls really did mature more quickly than boys, and continued doing so even as adults.

Nope. She couldn't go by that. After all, Julie had helped develop the idiotic and dangerous scheme.

She arrived at her stop and made it to street level with absolutely no trouble—other than the usual rush of people. New Yorkers weren't rude, despite their reputation, and most of the time they were actually quite pleasant and happy to help anyone who looked lost. There were just a lot of them, and it seemed that everyone was in a hurry to get where she was going. Several people said "excuse me" as they jostled past, and she said the same to several other people in turn.

Once she reached Forty-Seventh Street, she walked along until she saw her destination, Flawless.

She felt sad, remembering how excited they'd all been when Gary had gotten the job. He'd started working there soon after the wedding, just a little more than a year ago.

While the shop—like many others in the Diamond District—advertised Exceptional Quality for Exceptional Prices, it was a high-end and well-respected store. It had been in the Krakowsky family for four generations; landing a job there without being a Krakowsky was no easy feat.

But that was then, and this was now.

In truth, she was glad that she wasn't going to run into Gary today, given her desire to bash him over the head with something. Julie's words had been true. She hadn't wanted to rush into marriage; Gary had. Julie was a video game designer and loved what she did, and she'd wanted to go further in her career. She'd been all set to head to grad school in California when Gary had *begged* her to marry him.

It was ironic.

She was glad that Gary had gotten this job after the wedding. He was friendly with his coworkers, and at that moment she was glad that she didn't know any of them.

She heard the soft sound of the buzzer as she entered the store. The door, she knew, was connected wirelessly to a camera that counted and recorded every entrance and exit made at the store.

There was a large showroom filled with display cases. To her left the cases held diamonds set in yellow gold, to her right were cases with diamonds set in white gold and through an archway beyond there was a small display nook for gems of various sorts set in platinum. Beyond the counter—where some of the finest pieces were displayed—were the offices and the private rooms where salesmen sat down with important clients and served champagne while discussing the merits of the best stones. She knew all this because Gary had once described the setup for them.

She arrived just as one of the salesmen was drawing down the inside shutters that protected the window displays at night. He didn't challenge her entrance, however, but smiled at her.

It wasn't quite closing time; he was just getting ready.

"Good evening, miss," he said to her, smiling again.

"I'm sorry—you're closing," she said.

"Mr. Krakowsky is in the platinum room with another customer—you're fine," he told her.

The salesmen here dressed in designer suits and were perfect gentlemen. This one was in his early forties, she thought, with dark brown hair neatly clipped and a clean-shaven face.

"What can I show you?" he asked her.

"Actually, I was looking for Gary Benton," she said. "Is he working today? He's a friend," she added, almost choking on the word. "And that's why I came—he speaks so highly of the store."

"No, I'm sorry. At the moment it's just me and Mr. Krakowsky. But I'll happily show you whatever you'd like to see."

He was still standing too far from the display cases for her to pull off her sleight of hand.

She smiled sweetly. "I heard you have some exceptional loose diamonds."

"Of course," he told her, grinning. "We *are* in the Diamond District, after all." He offered her his hand. "I'm Matt Townsend. How do you do?"

"Kieran Finnegan," she told him, shaking. "A pleasure."

"The pleasure is all mine," he said. "Come over here, if you will." He led the way to the counter.

He walked around behind it as she followed him, and ducked down to open a safe beneath the counter.

A chill swept through her. She was suddenly terrified that something would go wrong.

It couldn't go wrong; she had to remain calm, act normal.

She looked casually around the shop as she waited. She glanced at the security camera, estimating her brother's position when he had pilfered the stone.

She looked away to avoid suspicion, then looked quickly back at the camera again. Reflected in the lens she could see someone entering the store—another late customer.

*No, not another customer.*

The man was wearing a black hoodie, which shadowed his face. And she couldn't see his face because he was also wearing a ski mask.

And he was pulling a gun from his pocket.

He was followed quickly by a second man—his twin in every detail.

Kieran felt her knees grow weak. She'd read about the recent run of jewelry store robberies, but...

But there were dozens of stores in the Diamond District. Why had the thieves picked *this* store on *this* day?

"Stay down," she said softly to the salesman.

They hadn't killed anyone yet—had they? Even so, there was always a first time.

And when there were guns involved, there was no sense in taking a chance.

No diamond was worth a man's life.

"Stay down," she repeated.

But either the salesman didn't hear her, or he heard her and had no idea what she was talking about.

He rose, setting out a velvet cloth with several uncut diamonds. "Here you—"

He broke off, staring. Kieran's back was to the new arrivals, but she knew Matt Townsend had a clear view of them and the gun—guns?—that was undoubtedly pointed at him now. He stepped back, raising his hands.

Just at that moment, a distinguished-looking older man came in from the platinum room with a young woman in a gorgeous fur coat.

The woman saw the thieves and screamed.

"Shut up or I shut you up!" one of the gunmen said. "You got two seconds."

She didn't hear him. She was still screaming and was clearly hysterical.

Kieran turned to see the first man pointing his gun in the screaming woman's direction, while two others—when had the third man entered?—kept their guns trained on Matt.

Kieran wasn't sure what propelled her—maybe it was the stark raving fear that if he shot one person he would shoot them all—but she wasn't about to let the terrified woman die, much less put them all in the morgue. She hurried over to the young woman and slapped her cheek, then took her face in both hands and said softly and firmly, "Stop. Stop right now. We're going to live. We're all going to live, all right?"

"Smart girl," one of the gunmen said.

The woman had stopped screaming. The older man—Mr. Krakowsky looked at Kieran with what she thought was gratitude in his eyes.

"Take whatever you want," he told the thieves. "We won't move a muscle to stop you or set off the alarm."

"Good call, old man," the second gunman said. "You," he told Kieran. "You look bright, and you're definitely pretty—there's got to be a guy out there somewhere who wants you alive. And you're obviously the type who would really like to see everyone survive here today. So if you listen carefully to my every word, we'll all be able to sleep in our own beds tonight."

She wasn't sure if being called bright and pretty by a gun-wielding thief was a compliment, but there *were* three men in her life who loved her very much: Declan, Kevin and Daniel.

She clung tightly to the concept that everyone would live.

"So, Red," the thief continued, "scoop up those diamonds on the counter. Now. And you, guy behind the counter, get out the other diamonds down there in your safe. The really good ones. And you, Red, you make sure he does it. I want all of them."

"Do what he says," Mr. Krakowsky advised.

"And, Red, watch him, because if you lie to me, Screaming Mimi over there gets it first."

Matt ducked beneath the counter again. He was shaking.

"If the alarm goes off, I shoot every one of you," the thief promised. "I'm a crack shot. Six bullets, only four of you. No problem."

Townsend was far too terrified to hit the alarm. He brought out five velvet cloths filled with loose diamonds and set them on the counter.

"Now, man behind the counter, go ahead of me. Get out your keys so you can open the back door. Old man, you and Screaming Mimi get down on the floor. Come on—move. Time is of the essence."

Everyone stared at him—frozen—for a split second.

"Down," Mr. Krakowsky said, pressing the young woman to the floor with him.

"You," the first gunman snapped to Kieran. "Get those stones and come with me—now."

Kieran stared at him. She wondered whether she

could even move, she was shaking so badly. Some instinct came to her rescue. She swept up all the diamonds while the thief who had done the talking headed to the back with Matt Townsend. A second one moved to stand close to her. Even though she knew that his gun wasn't touching her, she still thought she could feel it.

The third remained near the door, oblivious to the camera, his gun ready.

The thief in charge shouted from the back that the door was open. Kieran stood with the velvet-wrapped diamonds in her hands, frozen once again.

Then the nearest gunman grabbed her arm and turned, walking backward and keeping his eyes on Krakowsky and the other customer as he pulled her down a hallway and toward the back door.

He fired a shot as he walked; she felt the pistol's kick shoot through her via his grip on her arm. The sound was deafening.

She couldn't tell if anyone had been hit or not.

All she knew was that she was being hustled through the store and out the back door.

The alley beside the store had once been an open-air path. It was still a pedestrian passage, but now it was flanked by new buildings—new as in maybe only fifty or so years old—and boasted sidewalk cafés at both ends.

"Move!" the third man shouted, hurrying to catch up to them. "Someone in there must have set off the alarm. Hear the damned sirens?"

Her captor shoved her toward the wall, and all she could do was wonder if they would or wouldn't shoot her in the back.

But before she hit the wall she was grabbed by the third man. "Keep her—we may need her," he said, wrenching her around to face him. His eyes were like chips of blue ice. "If you—"

He stopped speaking for a moment, and she saw his eyes widen. Did he know her? she wondered.

He quickly found his tongue again. "We're going to run, and you need to do everything I say. If you don't, I will fucking blow a hole right through you. Got it?"

Kieran was trying so hard not to shake that she was afraid she wouldn't be able to move. She finally nodded.

"Good. Now run. And don't hold me back. Don't trip, don't falter, don't stop for any reason. Your life depends on it."


The moment Craig brought the car to a screeching halt, double-parking next to a silver Mercedes, he and Mike leaped out. They were already communicating via headsets, ready for whatever they might find inside.

A half dozen uniformed NYPD cops had arrived just ahead of them and were lined up outside the door of Flawless.

Mike produced his badge and said, "FBI. Anyone go in yet?"

"Just got here," one of the cops said.

"We'll take it easy—there could be people in there," Mike said. "If two of you will cover me on the left, I'll take the door. Craig, what are you thinking?"

Craig had been studying the building and thinking about the best way in.

Space had been at a premium in NYC for decades, if not centuries. Buildings tended to be flush against each other, but there were exceptions. In this instance, there was a café at the end of the block, with tables spilling out on a throughway that led to the back of the building. An old archway suggested another narrow alley at the back of the building that fronted the block, an alley that presumably ran between the buildings that faced one street and those that faced the next.

"Going around—there's bound to be a back door," he told Mike briefly and pulled his gun.

He didn't wait for a go-ahead or a reply but moved as soon as he was done speaking.

He heard Mike's voice in his ear. "Hey, watch what you're doing. You need backup, you say the word."

"I'm good, no problem yet," he said in return.

He moved as quickly as he could and rounded the corner. He saw that there was an actual archway on the end of the alley, space enough for some outdoor seating for a chain luncheonette.

There were people at the tables.

"Move!" he shouted, threading his way through them. "Move!"

"What the fuck—" someone said.

"We're moving in," Mike said over Craig's earpiece. "You take care."

"I have backup."

Craig swore softly, running into a chair a man had pushed back.

"Dickhead!" the man said.

"Move—"

"You dickhead!"

"Move. FBI!" Craig roared.

The man moved and then someone screamed and everyone got out of his way.

Craig realized then that he was wielding his Glock.

"What's going on, Craig?" Mike demanded.

"I'm running!" Craig panted.

He tore down the pedestrian alley as fast as he could move.

As he reached the rear of the jewelry shop he could see that the back door was open.

He heard Mike's voice again in his ear. "I'm inside. Two people in here, both okay. One is old man Krakowsky. He said they went out the back and they have a hostage."

"I'm on it," Craig said.

Dammit. The thieves had been there—and they were a step ahead.

He could see people running at the other end of the alley.

Men in black hoodies. And they weren't alone.

Mike had been right. They had a hostage. A woman was being dragged along with them.

At least she wasn't dead on the ground in the alley.

Swearing, Craig cranked up his pace.

As the thieves neared the street, he saw that they were heading to a van that was waiting at the end of the alley, a commonplace white van.

The sliding door was open, the driver obviously waiting for his companions to jump in.

One of the thieves drew the woman out of the way as they reached the sidewalk. Another brandished his gun.

People were screaming everywhere. Some were running; others, too startled to move, stood where they were.

Right in the way of the thieves.

And in his mind's eye, all Craig could picture was

the video of the thieves shooting the manager. And of the dead woman lying in an alley.

"Craig, what the hell are you doing?" Mike demanded.

"I'm on them."

"You're on them how? Wait for backup."

"I can't—I'll lose them."

He could hear Mike cursing.

"Can't talk—running!" Craig said.

The thief holding the woman turned and saw—in the midst of the chaos—that they were being followed. He shoved her into the van and jumped in after her.

Craig practically flew toward the street. The last of the thieves was entering the van, and the door hadn't closed yet. He couldn't fire, though; he could too easily hit the woman or an innocent bystander.

He was going to need both hands, he thought, and shoved his Glock back into the holster nestled into the small of his back. Then he launched himself through the open door.

He pitched headfirst into one of the thieves and heard a cracking sound—the guy's head hitting the far wall.

The driver screeched into traffic, rounding the corner onto the avenue and yelling, "What the hell...?"

His entry had been something like a bowling ball striking the pins at the end of the lane. All three thieves went sprawling. The woman was facedown, and he was somehow entangled with her legs.

"Craig, what the hell's going on?" Mike demanded.

"White van going south on Fifth," he said.

The thief he'd catapulted into was out cold. That left two more, plus the driver.

He heard a cacophony of shouting in the van. And through his earpiece, he could hear Mike cursing Craig beneath his breath between giving orders to stop every white van on Fifth.

Then Craig saw that one of the men was rising and that he had a gun. Craig reacted, rolling the woman onto her back as he struck out with his left foot. He caught the guy right in the jaw, and he stumbled back awkwardly, then fell flat on his rear.

Craig barely missed getting whacked across the head by the third man. But he ducked in time and head butted the man in the gut.

By then the second man was moving again. He lifted his gun and aimed at Craig's head.

He never got the chance to fire.

Craig was astonished—and incredibly grateful—to see that the woman had not only moved, she'd found a tire iron and cracked the thief hard over the head with it. He went down like a brick.

The panel door suddenly slid open. The last of the thieves hopped from the moving vehicle.

The driver suddenly stepped on the gas. Craig looked out the windshield and realized that they'd miraculously hit a clear patch of Fifth Avenue.

Craig knew he couldn't have gone after the thief anyway. The woman was still in the van, and the driver was alive and well.

Now his lead foot on the gas sent both Craig and the woman flying. He landed half on top of the unconscious man she'd hit and half on top of *her*.

For a moment he got a good look at her face. Mid to late twenties, brilliant blue eyes, deep red hair, fine bone structure and porcelain skin.

He got moving again quickly, staggering to the front,

pulling the Glock out of its holster as he went, then pressing the muzzle against the driver's head.

"Pull over. Now."

"Ah, hell," the driver muttered. He added a few colorful expletives, but, as ordered, he pulled over to the side. Craig cuffed him and then went back to cuff the other two, easing their guns out of reach as he did so, swearing inwardly. A takedown wasn't easy when he was stooping over the whole time to avoid hitting his head on the ceiling of the van.

The young woman was getting to her feet at that point, and he realized she was tall enough that she needed to stoop, as well. He met her eyes. They were a stunning crystal blue, almost impossible to look away from.

"Thanks," he told her. "You saved my life."

"I think you saved mine," she said.

"Oh, fuck you both," the driver said. "No one saved anyone. We don't kill people. We're thieves. We don't even use real guns!"

Craig spun around toward him and then bent down to pick up the thieves' guns.

It was an incredibly real copy of a Smith & Wesson. And it was made out of plastic.

He grabbed the other weapon off the floor of the van; it, too, was an excellent copy and, like the first, made of plastic.

"Where the hell did you get these?" Craig demanded.

The driver laughed. "Toy store," he said. "Check that one out. It's a water pistol."

"You idiot. Don't you know that the police would shoot you, whether these were real or not?"

"Police never should have caught us," the driver said.

"Am I hearing this right?" Mike demanded over the earpiece.

Craig wasn't sure how Mike could hear anything, frankly. By now sirens were ripping through the air and police cars were surging around them.

He slid open the panel door, holding out a hand with his badge showing. "Lower your weapons. FBI. The situation is under control."

He looked back at the driver.

The guy wasn't wearing a ski mask or a hoodie. He looked like any other blue-collar worker in a Yankees' beanie and a plaid flannel shirt. He was about thirty-five, Craig estimated. Brown hair, neatly trimmed beard and mustache.

Someone's all-around good old boy uncle, perhaps, come to the big city.

Craig realized that he and the woman were no longer in danger—not as far as this crew went. He regretted the fact that he was now certain he had been right.

There was a copycat group working the streets. With real guns—guns that killed.

He'd won the bet with Mike.

He wished that he'd lost.

Two groups…

And the one that killed was still out there.

# CHAPTER
## THREE

All Kieran wanted to do was escape, but getting away wasn't going to be that easy.

The police and the FBI and everyone else who had shown up where the van had stopped needed to speak with her.

At least half of them were convinced that she needed medical attention.

She *was* somewhat banged up. There weren't seats in the van—the back had been empty except for some tools, including the tire iron she'd used on the thief when he'd had a gun trained on the FBI agent.

Except that it hadn't been a gun at all; it had been a water pistol. However, she didn't feel quite so foolish, because Mr. FBI hadn't known it was a water pistol, either.

Why the hell did companies make such accurate children's toys? Were they trying to help raise the next generation of crooks?

She needed to leave. She needed to get back to the pub before Declan started worrying about her.

But instead she was stuck sitting in the back of an ambulance, wrapped in a blanket and drinking coffee while desperately trying to convince the police and EMTs and whoever else was there that she was fine and just needed to leave.

Finally one cop told her, "Sorry, miss, you're not going anywhere. You're the best witness we've got against these guys."

"But I really need to go to work."

She hadn't seen the agent who had leaped into the van like a fullback since the cops had sounded and he had jumped out again. An officer had helped her out, and then others had entered the van to gather up the thieves, who were now on their way to a police station somewhere to be held for arraignment. She'd overheard the driver, a good old boy with a beard and flannel shirt, inform them that he wasn't talking to anyone until he had a lawyer.

She had turned over all the diamonds to the police—including the one her brother had pinched.

She realized that she was now actively afraid of explaining to Declan what she had been doing. She had promised to work that night, and while Daniel might manage for a few hours, he wasn't up to handling the night crowds.

One of the EMTs came over to her. "You should really go to the hospital for a checkup, just to make sure you're all right. Sounds like you got pretty shaken up in that van."

"I swear, I'm fine," Kieran said, putting a little more pressure on the ice pack pressed to her cheek.

"Everyone who was in there looks as if they've been in the ring with Ali," the EMT said. He kept talking, but Kieran didn't hear him. She was too busy being horrified by the reporters—with cameras—who had arrived on the scene.

She had to get out of there.

She slid off her perch. She'd told her story at least three times: once to a nice-looking man in his late thirties wearing a pin-striped suit, once to an officer in uniform and once to an older man with gray hair and a grim face. They'd said something about statements and the DA's office getting hold of her. Fine. They had her information and they could call her later.

She did *not* want to appear on the news.

As she slipped around the ambulance, hoping that she could just blend into the crowd, she stopped short. The FBI agent who had literally jumped to her rescue was talking with the man in the pin-striped suit she had spoken with earlier.

"The bosses want you to make a statement, Craig," the man in the suit was saying. "They want you to say that the jewel thieves have been caught."

"Mike, they *haven't* all been caught. These guys didn't kill anybody. Don't you understand? *They were running around with toy guns!*"

"Yeah, toys now. How do we know that they weren't packing the real thing before? That they weren't expecting to be caught sooner rather than later and were determined not to go down for murder?"

"Mike, why would they think—"

"Because it's hit the news, Craig. Two people dead—you didn't think that they'd be able to keep a gag on it long, did you?"

Kieran froze where she stood.

Two people were dead?

*Killed by the same thieves who'd taken her hostage?*

She stared at the two men in shock.

"Yeah," her savior—Craig—said. "And I'm telling you, the killers are still out there."

What the hell? Did he really believe that there were more jewel thieves out there, only carrying real guns?

"Just for a checkup," someone said behind her.

She turned. The earnest EMT had followed her and was still trying to convince her to go to the hospital.

He flashed a light into her eyes, his own eyes worried as he examined her. "You need medical attention."

"No, I don't," Kieran said.

She looked away from him and saw that FBI agent Craig—was that his first name or his last? she wondered—was standing only a few feet away, staring at her.

She felt a moment's panic, then remembered that he'd managed to pass the stolen diamond to the police along with the others.

With any luck whatsoever, no one would know that it had ever been in her possession. Thank God she'd managed to give it back, even if not in the way she'd planned.

*Thank God neither she nor anyone else had been killed.*

"Miss Finnegan?" he said.

"Yes," she said. She hoped he couldn't hear the note of guilt in that single syllable. And why should she feel guilty, anyway? She hadn't stolen the diamond. She'd been trying to do the right thing—and she'd been kidnapped for her efforts.

"I'm special agent Craig Frasier," he said, and then he smiled, which changed his countenance entirely. He had high, strong cheekbones and a jaw that appeared to be made of stone. He was tall and dark haired with light eyes that drew her attention and seemed to home in on her like—like truth-seeking beacons.

"I know you've told your story several times, but would you tell it again to me?" he asked her.

"There's not much to tell," she said. "And you were there at the end, so..."

"But I wasn't there at the beginning. You went to the store why? Were you looking for a premade piece or a unique stone you could have set?" he asked.

She looked at him, wondering why guilt had immediately set in. "I went to see some loose stones. A friend of mine was married—still is, technically speaking—to one of the salesmen there. She's interested in buying one of the stones he handles, but she didn't want to see him, so she asked me to go and look at them. It turned out he wasn't working, but anyone can show another salesman's stones. But before I could see them, the thieves came in."

"And had you ever seen any of them before?"

She shook her head. "I still haven't actually seen them. The ski masks, you know. But none of them sounded familiar. I've definitely never seen the driver before."

"Yeah, this is New York, after all," he murmured.

She couldn't help but smile drily. "You mean we all live by the 'don't make eye contact' rule?"

"I'd like you to come in tomorrow and take a look at some pictures of the men," he said.

"Why? You can't need a lineup. You caught them all red-handed." The thief who escaped from the van had later been apprehended by one of the officers.

"I'd still like to know if they look familiar to you in any way."

"I'll come, but…"

"I'll send a car for you," he said. "Around ten?"

At ten she would be working her job at the Midtown offices of Doctors Fuller and Miro.

And she knew for a fact that her employers—whose main work came from police consultations—would have no problem with her helping the police.

She started to look around for her purse, which one of the officers had brought to her. She dug into it and produced a card. She remembered how pleased she had been to have a card with the prestigious names of her employers on it—along with her own.

"You're a psychiatrist?" he asked.

"Psychologist," she said. "May I go now? I have to get back to work."

"You see clients at night?" he asked skeptically.

She shook her head, annoyed to find herself flushing slightly. "I'm a bartender, too. Family. I bartend for the family. I mean, the family doesn't have a private bartender. We own a pub. Finnegan's on Broadway. I'm still helping out there."

She was annoyed with herself for babbling. She didn't know why he made her feel so off-kilter.

*Guilt!*

But she hadn't *done* anything. She'd returned the "borrowed" diamond, for heaven's sake.

But there was something about the way he looked

at her… It was his eyes, she thought, so light against the bronze of his face. She realized that he was tall and solidly built and really good-looking.

She flushed and looked away. Sex appeal wasn't something she should be thinking about right now.

Especially when people had been killed in a situation like the one she had survived.

"You should let them take you to the hospital," he said, "and make sure you're all right. We were flying around pretty good back there." He smiled again, and she was shocked by what it did to his face. His pinstriped suit was rumpled and his tie was askew, so he wasn't looking quite as ruggedly *GQ* as he might have, but his smile made him seem far too…attractive.

"I'm fine. Really. I have three brothers. I've been through much worse," she told him. "Really, I just want to get to the pub."

"I'll get an officer to drive you," he said.

"It's all right. I can hop on the subway."

"Not if you want to avoid the press—which I very much hope you'll want to do," he told her.

"I do want to avoid them, but why do *you* want me to?"

"Police should handle the press spin, that's why," he said. "Stay right there. I'll get an officer to drive you." He pocketed the card she'd given him. "I'll see you tomorrow."

She nodded as he turned and left, then watched as he went over to join two other men in suits who were deep in an animated discussion about something no doubt related to the events of the afternoon. His answer had been logical, but she felt as if he'd hesitated just a shade before answering her. Why?

Suddenly her view was blocked as a uniformed NYPD officer moved to stand in front of her.

"Miss Finnegan? I'm here to drive you home."

She wasn't heading home, of course, but to the pub. She gave him the address and told him where it was. He smiled. "I love that place," he said with a broad smile. As they drove, he told her that Finnegan's was a favorite watering hole for him and a number of his friends—when they were off duty, of course.

He stopped in front of the bar, and she thanked him as she got out. There was an employee entrance that led to the offices, but she knew it would be locked by now, so she walked in the front.

To her shock—and a bit of dismay—the pub was doing a booming business. Mary Kathleen had even come back in for the evening shift. On a Monday, it shouldn't have been so crazy, but it was.

And the first person to spot her was Declan.

Her older brother was handsome and charming and—in her opinion—the best host and barkeep in the world. He looked as if he'd stepped out of a movie as he worked the bar in his white shirt with rolled up sleeves and green brocade vest. But when he saw her, he folded his arms over his chest, a frown settling onto his face.

Danny bounced out to greet her, his eyes wide with warning. But it was too late. Declan was already coming around the bar to confront her. "Are you crazy?" he asked. His tone was furious. "And look at you! You look like you were competing in the mud-wrestling championships!"

She took a deep breath and was trying to figure out just how she was going to explain herself when he threw his arms wide and pulled her into a tight hug. "Thank God you're all right!"

Crushed against his chest, she felt her mind race. *What did he know? What did he think?*

"She's here!" Bobby O'Leary cried. "The woman of the hour!"

"All hail our kick-ass hero!" Jimmy McManus, sitting down the bar from Bobby, lifted his beer glass.

The darker of the two men she'd seen with McManus was there with him. Thankfully, there was no sign of Gary Benton.

Kieran froze, then slowly emerged from Declan's embrace. Everyone in the place was looking at her and applauding.

"What, um, what…?" she muttered inarticulately.

"The television—check out the television," Danny told her, hugging her tightly for a long moment.

Kevin, her twin, had emerged from behind the bar, too, and he also hugged her warmly, whispering, "I know you were just in the wrong place at the wrong time, but if you took chances… I came into this world with you, sis, and if you leave it before me, I won't be able to cope."

"I love you, too," she murmured, then finally got a glance at the TV. A reporter was in the middle of explaining that a brave hostage had helped the FBI take down the thieves. And she was clearly visible in the shot behind him, which showed her seated in the back of the ambulance, a blanket around her shoulders and a cup of coffee in her hand, as an EMT spoke to her. The reporter was still going on about her courage under fire.

Except there had been no courage. There had been no choice.

She smiled weakly, waved a hand and managed a soft thank-you, then dodged behind the bar and ran to the offices in back.

Declan was right behind her, closing the door to the office behind them. She noticed that he'd brought a clean wet bar rag with him and looked at him questioningly.

"You're still wearing a fair amount of dirt. You roll in an alley or something?" he asked.

He was watching her with his arms crossed over his chest again. Even so, she could tell that he was truly grateful to see her alive and well.

She could also tell that he knew there was more to the story.

"You were buying diamonds?" he asked her. "Instead of coming to work?"

She accepted the bar rag from him, sank into the chair behind the desk and studiously scrubbed at her face. "No, and I'm sorry. I didn't think that the bar would be this busy. I—"

The door burst open. Danny rushed in and hurried over to her, dropping to his knees by the chair. "You're really all right?"

She nodded. "I'm fine."

"Oh, my God, when I saw…" Danny sounded sick and shaky.

She patted his red hair gently, reassuringly.

"Kieran, you went there to talk to Gary Benton, didn't you?" Declan demanded.

She went very still, looking at Danny. "Yes," she said.

"Kieran, we all love Julie. She's been our friend since

we were children. I don't like Gary one bit myself, and the way he's treating her is awful. He's a total jerk, and we should all be looking forward to the day when Julie is finally rid of him. I should have expected… Well, he was in here this afternoon, right? You don't need to answer. Bobby O'Leary told me he was. And then you got upset and went to tell him… Well, I don't care what you thought you were going to tell him. It's only by the grace of God that you're alive and well. Kieran—let this be a lesson. Stand by Julie. Be there to listen to her, to hold her hand. Help her make the split final. But stay away from Gary Benton."

"You're right," she said, still staring warningly into Danny's eyes. He opened his mouth as if he was going to admit the truth. She shook her head and looked up at Declan. "You're right. It's just that… He had the nerve to come here!"

"And if he comes again, we have to let him in. And we won't throw him out unless he starts causing trouble or gets in a fight or something—and there's no spitting in his food or his drinks, either. All three of you—you and Danny and Kevin, too are off pursuing careers, which is wonderful. But the bar is my livelihood—and it's all our heritage and what you have to depend on, too, if life doesn't work out for some reason. We will not discriminate against anyone, do you understand me?"

"It's not illegal to discriminate against assholes," Danny said.

Declan shook his head in aggravation. "Danny!"

"Sorry. All right, if the jerk comes in, we won't show him the door," Danny said.

"Kieran?" Declan said.

"Hey, I served him coffee without throwing it on him—or even accidentally spilling a single drop," she said.

"Good. But in future, stay away from him, let someone else take his order. Please," Declan told her.

She nodded grudgingly.

"Now go home, kid—you don't need to be here. Mary Kathleen is on the floor with Danny, and I have the bar. We're fine. Kevin's been behind the bar with me, but as soon as things slow down I'll send him home, since he has an audition tomorrow. So go home. And not to be rude, but I suggest you take a bath."

The door opened again. It was Kevin this time.

"It's slowed down. Maybe the crowd was just waiting to applaud Kieran and now they've all gone home to talk about her. I've got my car, so I can drive Kieran home on my way."

"I can get home—" Kieran began.

"With me," Kevin said.

"Declan said you have an audition in the morning. You need to go straight home and get your beauty rest," she said, smiling. "Although you're beautiful no matter what."

Kevin winced. "Men aren't beautiful!" he said.

"Ouch," Danny said, laughing. "He's a manly man, you know."

"What about you? You have work tomorrow, too," she reminded him. Danny was outgoing, and despite the problems he'd had in the past, he was a keen historian and the tour company he worked for loved him.

"I'm off tomorrow," he said. "Sundays and Tuesdays, remember? I'll help Declan until closing," he assured her.

She looked away, still uncomfortable that they

weren't telling Declan and Kevin the truth but absolutely certain that she didn't want to tell them more than what they already knew.

"Well, in my mind, Kevin, you *are* beautiful!" she said, returning to a safer topic. "And you'll be great tomorrow. Break a leg."

"Thanks. And I'm going to my car now, and you're going with me," Kevin said.

It would be worse to argue than to go along. She said, "Okay, thanks. I could walk it if I wanted to, and I know the subway like the back of my hand, but a ride from my twin will be nice."

Kieran stood, hugged Danny and Declan, and then followed Kevin out of the office through the side door. He slipped an arm around her shoulders as they walked down the street.

"That must have been scary as hell," he told her. "How the hell you didn't lose it, I don't know. I don't think I would have coped as well."

"Thanks—but I think you would have done everything exactly the way I did. We were brought up to do the right thing. Maybe kids remember even more when they've lost both parents," she said.

"We're not kids," he said quietly.

He didn't say anything more until the attendant had brought his car down from the garage nestled in the next block, and then it was only to thank the man and give him a tip. They were parked in front of her apartment before he finally said something else to her.

She moved to get out of the car, but he stopped her.

"Kieran, I don't know what you told Declan, and I don't intend to say another word. But I think there's more to the story of why you were in that store. Something to do with Danny. I don't even want you to tell me—unless there comes a point when you need to for some reason. Danny is *my* baby brother, too, and Julie's also *my* friend. But don't go getting yourself into trouble because the two of them have concocted some wild scheme. You're a therapist now—talk them out of it."

She leaned over and hugged him tightly. "Best twin in the world," she told him. "But I swear with my whole heart, I will not get into any trouble with those two, and I'll make sure they don't get into trouble, either. I'd like to believe that…"

She hesitated.

"That they learned something from what happened to you today?" Kevin asked her drily. "Never mind—I meant it when I said I won't make you say anything. You always keep my confidences, so I don't expect you to break anyone else's trust. But if you run into a problem again, keep me in the loop."

"I swear," she promised.

He nodded and smiled, then watched until she was safely inside her building.

Upstairs, she threw off her jacket and tossed down her bag, then headed into the bathroom to give her face a good scrubbing. When she saw herself in the mirror, she realized stronger action was called for, so she stripped and jumped into the shower.

It wasn't that late when she dried off, feeling like a new woman, but she didn't want to see more of herself on the news, and she was exhausted. She lay down to sleep, but her heart kept pounding. She couldn't deny it. She was worried.

Hiding what she, Danny and Julie had been up to

from Declan and Kevin had proved easier than she had thought it would.

But she was dreading the next day and her time with the FBI agent with the dark hair and deep smoky voice and those light eyes that seemed to look into her with the power of an X-ray machine.

Craig Frasier sat in the office in the near dark, alone except for the skeleton night staff. He'd made Mike go home, knowing that he was being obsessive and not wanting to drag his partner into the pit after him.

He simply didn't believe that they had caught the thieves they most needed to catch: the ones who killed.

The thieves themselves denied it, and their guns had been fake.

But he understood the desire in law enforcement to believe a case was closed, and a lot of people simply didn't want to accept the idea that there could be copycats out there—copycats whose MO was so perfect in every detail…except that the guns they carried were real. The prevailing belief was that there was only one set of thieves who, having established that they were willing to kill to get what they wanted, no longer felt the need to carry real guns and had switched to fakes in order to create confusion and make a case for a lighter sentence if they were caught.

The NYPD had made the arrest. The charges would be up to the district attorney's office. Somewhere the powers that be, whose influence went far beyond his own, were arguing about that right now.

They wouldn't ask his opinion.

But that didn't matter. What *did* matter was whether

there were still killers out there—and he was willing to bet cash money that there were.

He leaned back, rubbing his eyes. He thought about the way things might have ended—and how that too-attractive-for-his-own-good redhead had actually had the sense to do something other than scream and expect the world to save her.

She'd saved his ass—or would have, had the gun been real.

He drummed his fingers on the table, thinking about her. She hadn't wanted any attention from the press; in fact, she had paled at the very mention of it. Strange. Most beautiful women—no, she wasn't just beautiful; she was stunning—welcomed attention. As gorgeous as she was, she could have been hitting the stage or a runway somewhere, a tall, blue-eyed redhead with legs that stretched forever. But instead...

He reached into his pocket for the card she had given him. Fuller and Miro. He knew the names; they and their employees were often called in as consultants. The Behavioral Science Unit of the bureau was in Virginia, and they were called in on the most puzzling or unusual cases, especially when local police asked for help. Otherwise, the New York office often looked to local talent to untangle the psychology of a captured killer or profile one who was still at large.

Therapist. And bartender.

Quite an intriguing combination.

For someone who had such talents—and had saved both his ass and her own—she had acted very strangely.

Almost as if she were...guilty herself.

He mulled over the thought. Then, standing up, he

stretched and walked to the coffee machine in the break room. He needed to go home and go to sleep, but he could use a cup to get that far. The coffee here was wretched; they kept a regular pot instead of investing in pods. But that was all right. Wretched coffee was still better than no coffee.

He lifted the cup to his lips and realized that in the midst of the fray, she'd reminded him of someone.

Of Caroline.

He smiled at the thought.

Caroline had been blessed with that same ability to think on the spot, to behave rationally and, most important, to know when to hold—and when to fight back like blue blazes.

He hadn't really thought about her in years now. And truthfully, she had been nothing like Kieran Finnegan. Caroline had been a petite blonde with hazel eyes and a smile as big as the world.

He felt a dull ache and shook off the thought. He hadn't allowed himself to get morose in years. It had all been so long ago. And yet he knew that when Caroline had died, something in him had died, too. He'd lost the ability to get close to a woman. No matter who he met, no matter how sure he was that he wanted to find something close to what they'd had somewhere along the line, he'd just never met anyone with her fire and humor, charm and...*heart*.

He drained the coffee, returned to his office and turned off the computer. It was time to go home.

And if he thought about it, he was intrigued.

He forced his mind back to the case. Maybe she could help by watching the video surveillance of the deadly robberies and spotting something one of the men she had encountered had done that was different from what was on the tapes.

And maybe he could find out just what she was hiding.

# CHAPTER
# FOUR

The field office was toward downtown on Broadway, not very far from Finnegan's Pub, but, with traffic, Kieran knew it would be a thirty-minute trek from the Midtown offices of Doctors Fuller and Miro. She had barely gotten to work before a black sedan with a black-suited agent—wearing black-framed sunglasses—arrived to pick her up.

She had only just slipped into her own office—a small room not much bigger than a walk-in closet, but at least it had a window—when Dr. Allison Miro came to her door. She was generally a stern-looking woman with her slim, perfectly compact body and short, crisp, iron-gray hair, but that morning she gazed at Kieran with concern and compassion.

"Kieran, dear girl, thank the good Lord that you're all right. When we saw the news…well, we were quite concerned. Anyway, you're a heroine, my dear. We're so proud of you."

Kieran was startled when Dr. Miro walked over to where she stood by her desk and hugged her. It was a slightly awkward hug. Kieran wasn't expecting it, and Dr. Miro was a good half foot shorter than she was. The older woman didn't seem to notice that Kieran rocked back slightly, startled, before hugging her back.

"I'm fine, really, and I'm not a hero, just a survivor," Kieran said.

"Kieran!"

She recognized the deep, rich, masculine tone, and she looked up to see that Dr. Fuller had joined the party. Her employers were a living representation of "the long and short of it." Dr. Bentley Fuller was six foot three, lean and fit, and he could have starred in a "male enhancement" advertisement. He was about fifty—a ruggedly handsome fifty. She knew he maintained his health and physique by religiously adhering to the strict tennis-playing schedule he'd set for himself.

He walked over to her, leaving Dr. Miro sandwiched between them in the cramped space.

The two doctors were not a romantic duo, but they shared the same interests and respected one another's work ethics. Dr. Miro was a grandmother. Dr. Fuller had a lovely—equally tennis honed and perfect—blonde wife. She was a kindergarten teacher, and, in Kieran's opinion, very sweet. She and Bentley were as perfectly matched as a set of Barbie and Ken dolls.

"Thank God you're all right," he said.

She extricated herself from Dr. Miro's hug and stepped back, smiling. "You two deal with some of the most hardened criminals in the NYC system. I managed—with the help of an FBI agent—to escape squirt-gun-toting thieves. Thank you so much for caring. I truly appreciate your concern."

"Of course, of course," Dr. Fuller said. "And you need to go. I came to tell you that your car and escort are here."

"Oh, yes, sorry. I didn't have a chance yet to ask you if I could take the time—"

"You know how much we value our relationship with law enforcement. Take all the time you need," Dr. Miro said.

"Thank you. I'll be back as soon as—" She broke off. She'd been about to say *as soon as possible*. She restructured her reply. "As soon as I've done everything I can possibly do to help."

But what that was, she really didn't know.

Dr. Fuller shooed her out of the office to where her "man in black" was waiting in reception. Jake, the receptionist, wasn't so much as looking at the agent. He was making every effort to look busy. The agent just stood there with his expression impassive and his hands folded behind his back.

He escorted her out, and she saw that his car was double-parked; apparently, for him, that was legal.

He opened the door for her and she stepped in. He was polite without showing the least emotion; she felt as if she had stepped into a movie about alien pod people.

The drive was silent, which made it feel even longer than she'd known it would be.

When they finally arrived, she discovered that no matter who you were, you went through the security screening. As she stood in line she realized that a lot of very normal people worked in the building. Three women in line in front of her were holding their Starbucks cups and chatting as they waited to go through the metal detector; behind her, two men were arguing over the virtues of an iPhone versus an Android phone.

Once through security, she was whisked up an elevator. The doors slid open, and she exited directly into a clean and sparse reception area where a young woman, who had apparently been waiting for her, greeted her then led her down a hall to a small office with a table that held a computer and several sheets of photos.

"I'm Millie," the young woman told her, shuddering slightly. "Sounds ancient, doesn't it? Short for Millicent. I don't know what my parents were thinking. Can I get you anything? Coffee? Tea? A soda or a bottle of water?"

"I'm fine, thanks," Kieran murmured.

Just then Craig Frasier stepped through the still-open door and said, "Morning, Millie. I'd love some coffee. Miss Finnegan, won't you join me?"

"I'll be right back," Millie said cheerfully.

"Thank you," Kieran said, as the other woman left.

Agent Frasier was wearing a suit very much like the one her escort had worn, though he had left off the sunglasses—inside, at least. She was struck again by the man's rugged good looks and masculine appeal. She had seen several men down in the lobby who were tall, honed like steel and handsome. She was starting to think that it was an agency requirement. Or perhaps the job just called for people in good enough shape to jump over fences and coordinated enough to run through a traffic jam.

Agent Frasier smiled at her. "Thank you for coming in," he said.

*Did I have a choice?* she wondered.

"Of course," she said. "My employers understand my need to be here—they are frequently called in to work with law enforcement. They do psychological profiling, decide whether a defendant is fit to stand trial, that sort of thing."

"Yes, I know," he told her, but he didn't elaborate on *how* he knew. She wondered if he'd worked with either of her bosses or if he'd run a background check on her.

"There are three pictures in front of you," he told her, all business. "I'd like you to look at them."

She nodded, sat down and glanced at the photos. They were of the thieves, and they were dressed completely in black—right down to their ski masks.

She looked over at him. "They're in ski masks."

"Yes."

"Okay. I'm not sure why I'm doing this. You've already caught the thieves who took me hostage."

He smiled. "Lift that top sheet. There are four mug shots underneath. Those are pictures of the men we caught last night, minus the ski masks. What I'd like you to do is take the shots from the jewelry store last night—from their security tapes—and line them up with the mug shots. Then I'd like you to compare them with some other pictures I have of a different robbery." He hesitated and then said, "I don't mean to lead the witness, but I don't believe they're the same men."

Millie returned just then with a tray that held a coffeepot, two cups, cream and sugar. Agent Frasier thanked her and asked Kieran how she liked her coffee. She said, "Just cream."

He poured her a cup, added cream and handed it to her. Then he sat opposite her and sipped his own coffee. The room grew very quiet.

At first Kieran felt unnerved. He sat there in silence, leaving her to study the photos, but there was no way for Agent Frasier to be in a room and not be noticeable.

She tried to give her attention to the pictures. The sooner she did what he'd asked of her, the sooner she could leave.

To her surprise, she quickly found herself deeply involved in what she was doing. According to their mug shots, the men who had been arrested the night before were Sam Banner, Robert Stella, Lenny Wiener and Mark O'Malley. She glanced at their faces and the stats on their mug shots, and then at the security stills, comparing carefully. Finally she went through them, pointing. "Mark O'Malley was driving the van, obviously. Looking at height and build, I think Sam Banner was the one who dragged me through the store and down the alley."

Agent Frasier nodded. "All right. Now I want you to compare them to the men from the other robbery."

He got up and moved to stand behind her, then pulled another sheet of photos from the bottom of the stack. "I realize it's difficult, but do you recognize the men from yesterday in any of these other photos? The way they stood? Something else? I can show you some video, too."

She was acutely aware of him behind her. The fabric of his suit, the heat of his body, the scent of his aftershave.

"Uh, video would be great."

He reached over to tap the keyboard. His nails were neatly clipped. His fingers were long, and she was certain that his hands would be powerful.

She swallowed and tried to concentrate.

After a minute, she miraculously managed to do so. She took control of the keyboard herself, running the footage and stopping it when something struck her.

"There," she said, pointing. "That's Sam Banner. You can tell by the way he's standing and by his height."

"All right," Frasier said, "what about this footage?"

He reached over again and cued up a new video.

"No, no, I don't think that's Sam Banner. They stand completely differently. Sam keeps his legs apart. He's angled, almost as if he's casual about what he's doing. This man, he stands straighter, and he's visibly tense. Watch his head move. He's jerky. He looks—"

"As if he's nervous and liable to pull the trigger any second?" Craig asked.

"Yes," she said. "Just my opinion based on my observations, of course," she said, swiveling her chair to look up at him.

He smiled. "Educated opinion, though, right?"

She shrugged. "Honestly, if you asked one of my bosses to—"

"Your bosses weren't in the van with me," he said, and walked back to take his seat.

She'd been about to stand; her work here was done.

But the way he sat, leaning forward expectantly, his eyes probing...

No, she wasn't leaving yet.

"So what were you doing at the store yesterday?" he asked.

She immediately felt defensive, but she tried not to do any of the things that would betray her nervousness. Blinking, wetting her lips...

"A friend works there," she said. "I went to see if he

was there. Well, all right. He's not really a friend. He *was* a friend. Not anymore."

He looked down a moment, a slight smile curving his lips. "Care to explain?"

She shrugged uncomfortably and looked away, but she told herself that was okay. Explaining an awkward divorce would make anyone uneasy.

"Gary Benton was—is—married to a close friend of mine. They're going through a very nasty divorce. I went to see him to remind him that they were adults and that…" She felt herself stiffen, but she was so angry at Gary that she couldn't help it. "She went out of town to give him space, and he locked her dogs in a crate and didn't feed them or let them out the whole time."

"She should have called animal control," he said.

"The logical answer, of course, but she was too upset to think straight, and—" She paused and looked away again. "She went to the store and said some pretty awful things. I went to ask him to stop being so nasty and trying to upset her. But he wasn't there and, well, you know what happened next."

He seemed to believe that. "Well, thank you again for your help," he told her. "I'll get you back to work."

"Thanks," she said.

He rose. She kept sitting.

He smiled at her. "I meant that literally. *I'll* get you back to work."

"Oh! Okay, thank you."

She stood quickly, dismayed to feel herself blushing.

She felt his hand at the small of her back as he politely ushered her out.

She told Millie goodbye and passed another half dozen men and women in well-tailored suits as they left the building, walking past the line where people were still lined up, chatting as they waited to pass through security.

She noticed an interesting group waiting their turn. They weren't in suits and didn't look at all like members of the FBI.

"Who are they?" she asked.

"A teachers' group," he told her.

"Oh?"

"They're going to take a class in keeping schools safe."

"I didn't know the FBI offered anything like that."

He flashed her a smile. "We're a friendly crowd, not the enemy," he said.

"I wasn't suggesting that. I just never thought of the FBI as being so…open-door," she told him. "Practically warm and cuddly."

"Well, that depends on who you are and what you're up to," he told her.

A car was waiting for them. Double-parked again, she noticed. Craig Frasier seated her before walking around to slide into the driver's seat himself.

"In a city full of very different crimes, I find this to be an especially interesting case," he said as he drove.

"I think it's a terrifying case," she said. "Men holding up jewelry stores and killing people, but making it look as if other people are the killers."

She realized from his expression, which had hardened as she spoke, that he was accustomed to dealing with people killing people. That had to be difficult. Then again, she had known when she took her job that she would be dealing with criminals whose behavior made her brothers' previous escapades look like child's play.

"Actually, I was referring to you," he said.

"Me?" She prayed there was no fear—or guilt—in her voice.

"Bartender by night, assistant crime fighter by day."

"I'm a psychologist, not a crime fighter."

"A therapist."

"Yes."

"What sort of cases have you handled?"

She took a breath and shrugged. "I haven't been in the role that long—I'm pretty fresh out of school. But so far I've spoken with a woman regarding a competency hearing. And I was asked to speak separately with a husband and wife suspected in the death of their newborn. That one was very sad."

"Life can be sad," he said wearily. "And you're a bartender on top of all that?"

"It's a family business," she said. She winced. Did that make her family sound like the Mafia?

They'd reached her office, she realized. He had the car in Park and was ready to hop out and open her door for her. Professional courtesy? Was he always like that?

"Thank you," she said quickly, opening her door. "I appreciate the ride back."

"Thanks for your help," he told her.

"Of course," she said quickly as she stepped out of the car, then bent to look back in at him. "Um, goodbye."

"Goodbye, Miss Finnegan. And my thanks again."

She closed the door and hurried toward the building. When she got upstairs, she was grateful to discover that both her bosses were in consultation. She hurried to her own office and began to write up her report on the parents she had interviewed the other day. Both were heartbroken; in her opinion, neither had in any way been responsible for the death of their child. It was sad, as she'd told Agent Frasier, but infant deaths still occurred through no one's fault. She was convinced this was just such a case.

Eventually her bosses finished their consultation and came in to see her, quizzing her about her visit to the FBI. They both seemed pleased that she'd been consulted.

"If you're needed again, you just go right on over, Kieran," Dr. Miro said.

"We always help whenever we can," Dr. Fuller assured her.

She smiled weakly. "Of course."

They left a few minutes later, and Kieran realized she'd worked through lunch and the day was nearly done.

Craig spent most of the rest of the day reinterviewing everyone he could get hold of who had been at any of the robberies. The prosecutor, Julian Smith, wanted to charge the men they'd caught with the murders, and they finally got together to discuss that with him late in the afternoon. Craig, Mike and Eagan argued against bringing charges, showed him the security footage, brought up Kieran's insistence that the tapes showed two different men and emphasized that the men in custody had been caught with toy weapons.

Smith was a hard-ass, though. He wanted to throw everything at the defendants that he could possibly throw. On top of that, the media was already calling them murderers.

Everyone in the city wanted the crime spree to be over.

"They were toy guns!" Craig said, slamming the table with the flat of his hand. "Even a public defender will be able to make that case. Give us some time to work this."

"Toy guns this time, real ones the last," Smith said. "You could have been killed, Agent Frasier. I'd think you'd want them locked away forever."

"And *I'd* think *you* would want them charged for the appropriate crimes," Craig said.

"Yes, well, real guns or not, there are laws—" Smith began.

"Gentlemen, gentlemen!" Eagan protested, raising a hand. "Smith, give my men time to work this. You're going to want all available evidence and witnesses concurring about the facts, aren't you?"

Smith finally left in a huff after agreeing to give them more time. "But not too much," he'd said threateningly.

It was nearly seven o'clock after a damned long night and day.

Mike was heading to the hospital for a checkup. One of the perks of being FBI was that doctors bent their schedules to see you after hours. Craig offered to tag along, seeing as he had no plans for the night.

"Hell, no," Mike told him. "Leave me alone. Let me be grouchy and crotchety tonight, go in, go home and then hit a bottle of Scotch and my bed. You should go do something fun. Shake off this job for a few hours."

But when he left the building at last, Craig wasn't ready to go home.

And he wasn't sure why, but he found himself heading for Finnegan's on Broadway.

Maybe he *did* know why. Kieran Finnegan intrigued

him. She'd been helpful, pointing out body language he might not have noticed himself.

But she'd also been nervous. Nervous just because she'd been in an FBI office?

He doubted that.

He had a feeling she was still hiding something. So what the hell was it?

Had she somehow been in league with the thieves?

He relived the previous night in his mind. It didn't seem likely, though he couldn't say it wasn't possible.

It certainly seemed like a coincidence that she'd even been there. She had a day job, and though he doubted she worked two jobs every day of her life, she'd been slated to work at the bar that night. He knew from the NYPD report he'd read through that she had her own apartment near St. Marks Place. Not right next to the pub, but not much of a subway trip, either. On a beautiful day and with a little time, she could even walk it easily enough.

But if she *was* involved, what was his plan? Come right out and ask her what the hell she was acting so guilty about in the hope she would confess?

She would hardly admit to being guilty, so that wouldn't do anything except raise her suspicions and make it even harder for him to figure out what was going on.

He would have to take a more indirect approach. Luckily for him, Finnegan's was known for its food as well as its hospitality and selection of beers on tap.

Couldn't hurt to get some dinner.

Old double wooden doors with frosted, etched glass faced Broadway, the sidewalk in front protected by a green-striped canopy overhead. Inside there were a number of booths to the right and a few more to the left, tables filling the rest of the room, and a long bar lined with taps at the rear. The place was busy with the dinner crowd and a number of cocktail-hour stragglers. He quickly saw that Kieran Finnegan was there, standing behind the bar and talking to a waitress. A tall man with dark red hair was also working behind the bar—one of her brothers, he was certain.

He started to head that way, then chose a booth that gave him an unimpeded view of the bar instead. He watched the action for a while. Another tall man, this one with lighter red hair, was working the floor along with two young women.

Before long one of the women headed to his table. He didn't think that she was a Finnegan. She was petite and blonde, with lively blue eyes and a quick smile. "Hello. Welcome to Finnegan's. What can I get you?"

He was in an Irish pub, so he figured why not order Guinness on draft? He asked for a menu, as well.

"Special tonight is fish-and-chips. Really good," she told him.

"Then forget the menu. I'll have fish-and-chips."

She brought his beer quickly. He thanked her and sipped it as he continued to people watch. A group of young women seemed to be holding a baby shower. Business executives filled several of the tables. An older couple sat and ate a quiet dinner; the bar stools were mostly filled.

When his food came, he thanked the waitress again. "So this is a family business, huh?" he asked.

"Yup, and the Finnegans are all working tonight. That's Danny on the floor there, Declan and Kevin behind the bar—and Kieran is back there, too."

"Are you related, too?" he asked her.

She laughed. "Actually, I'm the only one—well, be-sides the kitchen staff—who isn't a Finnegan or almost one. That's Mary Kathleen O'Shaunnessy over there," she said, pointing. "She's Declan's fiancée. And I," she told him brightly, "am Debbie Buenger, an old family friend. I went to school with Kevin and Kieran—who are twins, by the way. Anyhow, enjoy the fish. Our food is great, so if you haven't been in here before, you're in for a treat."

"I don't think I've been in before—and I'm pretty sure I'd remember. I have a lot of friends who love this place, though."

She gave him another of her charming smiles. "What's not to love?" she asked, and moved on.

The fish was delicious.

At least at first glance, Finnegan's seemed to be ev-erything a pub was supposed to be. He couldn't help but allow his mind to consider the possibility that there was something going on beneath the surface, though, since there had definitely been something off about Kieran Finnegan both last night and today. Were they laundering money? Raising funds for the Irish Repub-lican Army? He doubted that. The violence seemed to have dropped substantially in Ireland since just about the time the Twin Towers had been hit.

What, then? Was there an illegal poker game in the back?

He'd nearly finished his meal when he paused, tak-ing a sip of his beer, to stare at the bar again. Kieran happened to look up at just that moment and see him. She was visibly startled.

She also looked guilty—again.

She stared at him so long that Debbie—waiting in front of her with a tray of shot glasses—had to say something to stop her from pouring as whiskey started sloshing over the rim of the glass she was filling.

Kieran looked away quickly, flushing, and reached a bar rag. She said something to Debbie, who smiled and replied cheerfully.

Within a few minutes Kieran came around from behind the bar and walked over to his table.

He liked the way she moved, almost in rhythm with the music of the Dropkick Murphys playing in the background.

For a minute, he thought she was going to demand to know what he was doing in her bar and ask him to leave.

But she just looked at him, puzzled and uneasy.

"Agent Frasier," she said after a long moment.

"Guilty as charged."

"What are you doing here?" she asked.

"Eating."

What did she think he was doing there? He would love to know.

"Oh," she said. "Well. Um, I hope you're enjoying your dinner."

"I am. Very much."

"It's only pub food, nothing gourmet."

"I love pub food," he said blandly, curious to see where she would take their conversation. He didn't have to wait long.

"Are you watching me for some reason?" she asked him.

*Was he?*

She was certainly a pleasure to watch, with her long, long legs, blue eyes and fiery hair. But he doubted that saying as much would please her any more than would giving voice to his suspicions that she was keeping something from him.

"Actually," he heard himself say, "I wanted to talk to you again but figured I'd wait a bit. You seemed to be pretty busy when I came in, and I was hungry anyway."

"Being busy is a good thing for—for a business," she said.

He smiled. "Yes, of course. But I was wondering..." He paused, surprised that the right approach came to him so quickly. "The thing is, the prosecutor wants to charge the men from last night with murder, but I don't think they're the killers."

"Yes, I know. I spent the morning studying video footage, remember?" she said, smiling for the first time since she'd come over to his table.

"I'd like to get you to Rikers so you can speak with the men. They were held in lockup last night, but they were arraigned on grand larceny today. The prosecutor wants to add homicide charges right away. I'd like to counter him with more than grainy video, toy guns and my own gut feeling. Would you come with me to talk to them?"

She seemed surprised—and relieved. And still uncomfortable.

"Um, sure."

He saw the taller bartender heading in their direction. One of her brothers, but which one?

The question was quickly answered.

"Declan Finnegan," the man said, holding out his hand.

There was a definite family resemblance, at least in

height and coloring, Craig thought, rising to offer his hand. "I'm Craig Frasier. Special agent, FBI."

"Pleased to meet you, and thank you for keeping Kieran safe and sending her back to us. Your meal is on the house. The least we can do," he added, when Craig started to protest.

"Kieran did extremely well on her own. She's quite competent in a tough situation," Craig said. "And thank you, but I need a bill. We're not allowed to accept gifts, not even a meal."

Her brother shot Kieran a frown, but he didn't object. "I'd love to hear more about what happened last night. If you've got some time, come on up to the bar when you've finished your dinner."

"Will do," Craig promised.

Kieran's face grew a full shade paler. "Great," she said, not quite managing a smile. Then she turned and walked away.

Her attitude made him even more certain that something was going on, whether at the pub or just with her, and he was going to find out what.

Things had gone from bad to really bad.

There was Craig Frasier sitting at the bar. And there were her brothers—all three of them—chatting with him as comfortably as if they'd known him all their lives.

Danny didn't have the sense to realize that a federal agent might, at any moment, ask him questions he might not be prepared to answer. Honestly, her baby brother could be so oblivious.

She forced a smile each time she passed by them, determined not to be drawn into their conversation. But she couldn't help overhearing, and she realized after a little while that they were talking about city politics, local sports, music and theater, and the newest exhibition at the Met.

By about eleven, the place was almost dead quiet. It was a Tuesday night, and only some regulars were hanging around along with a smattering of tourists, all nursing their last drinks before their night's rest and the workday or the exertions of touring the city come morning. Both Debbie and Mary Kathleen had called it quits earlier; the chef and his staff were cleaning up the kitchen, and Kieran knew there was no reason for her not to join her brothers and Craig Frasier.

Declan slipped an arm around her when she walked over, studying her with pride in his eyes.

"We heard you kicked butt yesterday," he said.

She shrugged and admitted, "I wouldn't have had the chance if Agent Frasier hadn't burst in the way that he did."

"And you're still helping with the investigation, huh?" Danny asked.

"Um, yeah. I guess so," she said.

"Immeasurably," Craig said. "She's very observant about people."

"Sounds like her," Kevin said. "She was always psychoanalyzing us as kids. She had us pretty well nailed, too."

"I'm sure Agent Frasier doesn't care about my childhood, and it's getting late," she said, embarrassed.

"And I have an early call," Kevin said. "Time to go."

He'd gotten the job he'd auditioned for. She wasn't exactly sure what he was doing, but it had something to do with being a singing potato chip.

"Wanna take me home on your way?" she asked her brother.

"I'm not going home. I'm sleeping at your apartment," he told her. "Early call, remember? And I didn't drive in, because I didn't want to deal with finding parking in the city."

"How about I get you both home?" Agent Frasier asked. "I have a car."

"Oh, really, that's okay. We can hop a train," Kieran said.

"Works for me—thanks," Kevin said, ignoring her.

"You two get going now," Declan said. "Danny and I can close up. I have the weekly pro cleaning crew coming in tomorrow, so there's not much for us to do tonight anyway. And thanks, Craig."

So she was calling the guy Agent Frasier and her brothers were on a first-name basis with the man.

She forced a stiff smile. "Well, thanks. I'll get my things."

Kieran didn't have to make small talk. Kevin talked all the way. Apparently Craig had expressed interest in Kevin's career, and now Kevin was telling him how grateful he was that he had the family pub to fall back on. So many actors had trouble making it in the city because they couldn't find jobs to keep them going while they went through the arduous audition process.

They reached St. Marks and her apartment quickly; the traffic was light that time of night. She managed to jump out of the car before anyone could offer to help her. Her brother and Frasier exchanged goodbyes, and then Frasier told her, "I'll pick you up here tomorrow around eight thirty."

"I need to talk to my bosses. I know they won't protest, but—"

"Don't worry. My boss will take care of that," he told her.

"C'mon, time for bed," Kevin said. "Early morning for both of us."

Her apartment was directly above a Japanese restaurant and karaoke bar. Someone was warbling their way through "Don't Stop Believin'," and the sounds of laughter and conversation drifted all around them as they climbed the steps to her place. She loved her apartment, so she didn't mind that a bit of noise seeped up every night. It was one of four units on this floor, and there were eight more on the two floors above.

She loved her whole neighborhood, where there were still stores selling unusual items—crafts, imports—along with those carrying the usual T-shirts and souvenirs.

"I wonder if I should pop down and try a few numbers, get some practice in," Kevin mused, more to himself than to her. "Nah, I should get to sleep." He paused as she used her two keys in their respective locks. "You okay?"

"I'm fine, why?"

"You're so quiet. That FBI guy you're working with seems great. You're lucky—damned lucky—he came along."

"Yes, especially when I shouldn't have been at the store at all. You're not going to point that out?"

"I'll let Declan keep the paternal thing going. You know you shouldn't have been there without me telling you. But listen, I love Julie, too, but you've got to draw a line. Let her cry on your shoulder, but stay the hell out of the shenanigans between her and Gary."

"He could have killed those dogs," Kieran said indignantly.

Inside now, she closed the door and double-bolted it, then headed to the living room closet. She took out the guest bedding while Kevin unfolded the sleeper-sofa. Her place was fairly small—only her bedroom, a tiny nook she used as an office, the kitchen and the living room—but it had been an incredibly lucky find. It had a private bathroom off her bedroom and a guest bathroom to the left of the kitchen, off the dining area.

Her sleeper-sofa was the only modern piece of furniture she had. The rest consisted of odds and ends and period pieces: an art deco buffet she'd found at an estate sale, a Duncan Phyfe love seat she'd found in pieces at a bric-a-brac shop and had reupholstered, and more. Her walls were covered with framed movie posters and prints of old masterpieces.

"Care if I keep the TV on while I fall asleep?" Kevin asked.

"Not at all. I'm accustomed to noise," she reminded him, smiling.

"So what's your beef with Craig?" he asked, surprising her.

"I don't have a beef with him."

"Then what's your problem?" he asked.

"I don't have a problem."

"Okay then, what are you afraid of?"

"I'm not—"

"I'm your twin."

"Yeah, and you and Danny have checkered pasts," she reminded him.

He started to laugh. "You think a guy who chases *killers* for a living gives a damn about our little past transgressions? He's looking at the bigger picture." He sobered, turned sympathetic. "If you're afraid working with the Feds is going to put you in danger, you should bow out of the investigation."

"Afraid? They caught the guys."

"But did they catch all of them? That's the real question, isn't it?"

Yes, it was. And she was certain they *hadn't* caught them all.

She waved a hand in the air. "Kevin, stop worrying about me and get your beauty rest. You need it to be a singing chip. I love you—good night."

She headed into her bedroom. She was suddenly deeply tired.

She was almost asleep when she heard Kevin's sleepy voice. "Who is it?"

She sat up and looked at her bedside clock. Almost one o'clock. Was he rehearsing lines?

Hurriedly crawling out of bed, she went to her bedroom door and peered out.

Kevin was standing by the door, puzzled.

"What's going on?" she asked.

He shrugged. "Thought I heard someone at the door. Guess not. There's no one there now, anyway," he said. "But I could have sworn I heard someone playing with the lock." He shrugged. "Sorry I woke you. Probably just some drunk from downstairs looking for a place to crash."

"Probably," she agreed.

She gave him a quick hug and reminded him to get his beauty sleep.

She went back to bed. But then she began to wonder.

*Had* someone been trying to get into her apartment? Not just any apartment, *her* apartment?

And if so…

Why?

She tried to be logical. Kevin had to be right. Some drunk had just wandered up from below. It wasn't an unheard-of occurrence, as she knew firsthand. They ran a pub, after all. Most of the time people more or less knew their limits, and when they didn't, Declan refused to keep serving them.

But alcohol was a moneymaker. Not every establishment was as careful as Finnegan's.

And yet…

She tossed and turned, glad that her twin was in the living room and that she had not one but two serious dead bolts on her door.

# CHAPTER
# FIVE

They headed over from Queens on the three-lane Francis Buono Memorial Bridge, known unofficially as the Rikers Island Bridge.

She'd never been to Rikers Island before, either, though her employers had been there often enough.

"You been here before?" he asked, as if reading her mind.

She shook her head.

"It's pretty amazing. Inmates may be held here pending trial. Maybe their attorneys couldn't get them bail, or maybe they couldn't pay it. Or they might have been sentenced to under a year. Anything longer, and they'd be in prison. Rikers is a jail."

She nodded, pretty sure that she'd more or less known that.

"How many inmates?" she asked.

"At any given time? More than thirteen thousand, but with guards and staff, including civilian employees, there may be as many as twenty thousand people on the island—even more on some days. It's like a city unto itself."

"You've been here before, obviously."

He nodded. "Too often." He glanced her way. "This whole place is a mess. You've got New York prosecutors, federal prosecutors, even Jersey prosecutors, working here. But we're the ones charged with getting and presenting evidence. Any prosecutor's success always comes down to the evidence and statements—and ideally confessions—we can give them. Of course, they're also the ones who make the deals in spite of that evidence."

"Yes, I know," she said. "I just haven't been here before."

"But this is what you do, right?" he asked. "Work with criminals."

"So far I've only dealt with people who *might* be charged," she said. "And usually the situation is sad. I think I told you—I talked with a couple suspected of killing their baby, but the expert physician who was brought in agreed that the child simply stopped breathing. Crib death. Not smothered, poisoned, ignored… I write a lot of reports," she added. "Interview witnesses. It's amazing how people can be in the same place at the same time and see completely different things."

"Because everything is perception," he said. "Everything we see is filtered through the way we perceive it."

"And here I liked to think I went to school for something useful," she said.

He laughed. "I didn't mean to suggest that you didn't. Your help with the crime-scene footage was pretty amazing—you saw a lot that I didn't. But that more or less proves my point."

"Will their attorneys be present?" she asked.

"No, oddly enough, I think they actually want to talk. They seem to want to convince us that they might be thieves, but they're not murderers."

They arrived, headed through security and then went on to the building where the suspects were being held.

They went through another security check, where Craig turned over his gun. He seemed to know the guard who escorted them to the room where a man in jail coveralls was handcuffed to a table, waiting for them to arrive.

Kieran realized that it was the driver, Mark O'Malley. He looked at Craig Frasier with deep distrust and eyed *her* suspiciously, as well. She was still surprised that he hadn't asked that his attorney be present, then realized that while he might want to prove his point, he might not be at all certain that he really trusted them, so he would prefer to keep things somewhat off the record.

"Ah, so it's Black Widow and the Hulk," he muttered, looking away and shaking his head. He hesitated and then said in a hurt tone, "You were there. You know we didn't stash any real guns anywhere. You *know* that! They want our blood. Yes, we robbed people, but we never killed anyone."

There was a seat opposite O'Malley, and Craig Frasier indicated that she should take it. He remained standing, then took a step back.

"What?" O'Malley asked him. "You're antisocial?"

"I'm just here to watch out for Miss Finnegan. She's here to listen."

"*Miss* Finnegan?" O'Malley stared at Kieran. "You're not with the Feds?"

She shook her head, studying O'Malley in return. He was young—late twenties to early thirties. He wasn't a bad-looking man. He had the air, though, of one who had come from nothing, who had scratched his way up since birth and dreamed of something better. Blue-eyed, blond-haired…in another world he could have been a California beach bum.

"You weren't a plant in the jewelry store?" O'Malley asked her.

She shook her head again.

He started to laugh. "Well, hell. Done in by a girl shopping for diamonds!"

Except she hadn't been a girl who'd wanted a diamond; she'd been trying to get rid of one.

"I'm a psychologist," she said.

"A shrink, huh?" O'Malley asked.

"Psychiatrists are shrinks," she said. "I'm more like someone you…someone you talk to."

That brought a pained smile to his lips. "Yeah? Could have used you a few years ago. Not much to talk about now, is there? My family has pretty much disowned me, and I have a baby for a lawyer who wants me to confess to what I didn't do… A little late for talking, I guess."

"Not at all. If you really didn't kill anyone, then you shouldn't confess to it," Kieran told him.

"You know what we were carrying," he said. "But some district attorney wants to charge us with first-degree murder, though I don't get the first-degree part at all, something to do with the laws about armed robbery. Not that it matters. I swear, we didn't kill anyone. And I was always in the car."

"I'm pretty sure that, in the car or out of it, you can all be charged, since the murders occurred during the armed robbery and you were part of the robbery," Kieran said.

"Except we weren't armed. And we didn't kill anyone. Someone is imitating us."

Kieran didn't agree or disagree with his words; whether he and the others could prove themselves innocent of the murders, she didn't know. "At the moment, not many people believe that theory. You *appeared* to be armed, after all. Anyway, I'm not a lawyer, and I'm not here to argue the law. I'm here to talk to you, and if you didn't kill anyone, then I'm also here to help you. I'm one of the few people open to the idea that you didn't," she added softly. "I suspect that there really is a copycat group out there," she said. "Unless *you* were copying *them*?"

He shook his head emphatically. "No, we were first, hitting stores with our toy guns and stealing, but leaving everyone alive. Our biggest fear was being shot by a guard or caught by the police, but no matter what, as you saw, we couldn't shoot back." He leaned forward. "I'm telling you, someone out there was hoping we'd be caught, that they'd get away with what they were doing because we'd been taken in." He let out a deep sigh. "I've already written pages explaining every detail of the robberies we did plan and carry out. That child they gave me for a lawyer has them all. Someone has to prove we didn't kill anyone." His shoulders sank, and he glanced over to where Craig Frasier stood, legs slightly spread, arms folded across his chest, silent and unreadable. "I don't suppose the agent over there thinks I might be telling the truth."

"That agent is your best hope of the truth being accepted," she told him.

He brightened. "You said 'accepted.' So that means you really do believe me?"

"Yes, I tend toward believing you," she said.

"They won't hit up another store now," he said. "They won't—not for a long time. Not until we're tried and convicted for their crimes."

"I'm sure the authorities have ways to find them whether or not they strike again," Kieran said. She looked over at Craig Frasier.

He glanced at his watch. "We need to let Mr. O'Malley go now," he told her. "Is there anything else you'd like to ask him?"

Mark O'Malley stared at her, clearly ready to give her any information she asked for.

"I think we're good," she said.

Craig nodded toward the guard at the door. As he walked over to uncuff O'Malley and lead him away, she walked toward Craig and asked, "Are we done?"

A smiled cracked the stone of his features. "Not by a long shot. We've just begun. There are three more men."

And so the afternoon went on. She interviewed the other three men; each time the story she heard was the same, except for the details of each man's participation in the robbery.

Each man swore passionately that they'd never killed. They had carried toy guns and no other weapons at any time. It was one thing to steal, another to kill. They had a certain code of honor, she realized as she spoke with them. All three men were deeply rooted in one form or another of religion, and all three had had a religious upbringing. In their minds, God forgave a man for taking from another who had too much, but he didn't forgive the taking of a life.

Through every session, Craig Frasier stood a few feet behind her, tall and stoic, expression unwavering, arms folded across his chest. He heard everything that was said, and she knew that he was close enough to step in if there was the least hint of trouble.

There wasn't. The men seemed almost baffled that anyone could think them capable of murder.

When the day was done at last and it was time to leave, they signed out and headed back across the bridge. As they drove, Frasier asked her, "What do you think?"

"I don't think any of those men killed anyone. In my opinion, you do have a copycat group out there. There must be a way to prove that forensically. There must be computer programs that compare height and body characteristics. I pointed out what I saw, and if I saw it, it must be obvious via computer comparison."

"Yep. And I have a man on it. So far the charges against them are only for the attempted robbery. There are huge arguments going on above my pay grade. These men, as you know, claim that all their robberies were in the state of New York. The powers that be are arguing over whether they should face federal or state charges, or both. We're executing search warrants on their homes, and we'll see what those yield. In my gut, I know that the killers are still out there," he told her.

"If you're so convinced," Kieran said, "why do you need my opinion?"

"Verification," he told her. He turned and looked at her. "No matter how things go down, you'll be called in to testify, you know."

"Yes, I know."

Kieran was uneasy, wondering why, even though he was driving, she felt as if he were watching her suspiciously, seeing how the reminder that she would have to appear in court would affect her.

She looked out the window. She could picture the scene. She would be sworn in, agreeing under oath to tell the truth, the whole truth and nothing but the truth—even though the prosecutor might well ask, *Why were you in that jewelry store?*

*I went to see someone I know who works there.*

*Is that the truth?*

*Yes.*

*Allow me to remind you that you're under oath.*

*All right, all right! I was returning a diamond my brother and my best friend stole. But they didn't really steal it. They were just borrowing it.*

*And this "borrowed" diamond was in your possession?*

"Miss Finnegan?"

"What?" She turned to look at Agent Frasier, startled.

"We're here," he told her.

"Oh! Ah, thank you."

They were parked in front of the offices of Fuller and Miro.

"No, thank *you*. I mean it. Thank you for your help."

She knew she should get out of the car. That this would be the last she would see of Agent Craig Frasier, at least until the trial. And when that happened, the thieves were going to be the ones in the hot seat, not her.

She moved to get out of the car, but she was too late. He was already out of the driver's seat and coming around. He opened her door, and she scrambled out as quickly as she could. For a moment she was standing on the New York street just staring up at him. He was a foot away, but that was too close. The man was built like steel and seemed to tower over her, and while she wanted to run, she also wanted to reach out and touch him and find out if he was still somehow flesh and blood, despite the way he looked at that moment. His eyes were on her, and she was drawn to return his stare, as if he were somehow compelling her to. The man was almost impossibly attractive. She certainly didn't meet people like him every day. She found herself feeling sorry about saying goodbye, despite the way he seemed to be using X-ray vision to peer into her mind. Something stirred within her, and she wished she could meet him again in the pitch-dark, could simply touch him, feel him and...

Her fantasies moved in a very dangerous direction, as in hot, wild, wet sex, and she felt her face turning every shade of red.

She had to get away.

She reached out a hand to shake his. "Well, goodbye," she said awkwardly.

She felt the length of his fingers curling around hers and the solid strength in his hand. And he smiled.

A smile that seemed to say that he was sure she was guilty as hell of *something*.

"Goodbye, Miss Finnegan," he said. Then he headed back around the car to the driver's side. She watched him, knowing she should turn and head into her building.

He paused right before he slid into the driver's seat.

"I'm sure we'll be seeing one another again," he told her with a wave.

She did turn and flee then.

She had to forget him, forget her guilt, forget the whole situation.

And forget her totally inappropriate—and quite frankly, embarrassing—fantasies.


"So, how did the assessment go?" a deep, gruff and familiar voice inquired.

Craig looked up. He had been in his office with Mike, the two of them studying the manifests of stolen property and comparing them to the items stashed by the jewel thieves, and retrieved by the police when they executed their search warrants.

That Eagan was looking in on them—rather than summoning them—was somewhat surprising.

"Your trip to Rikers with Miss Finnegan. Did it help you any?" Eagan asked.

Craig nodded. "Her conversations with the suspects reinforced my belief that there's a second gang out there—one that copycatted our guys, but with real guns and killing."

"You going soft on the guys you picked up?" Eagan asked him. "Because you lived? I mean, that's a good reason, but I want to make sure that's not the *only* reason."

"When have you known Craig to be soft?" Mike asked.

"Hey," Craig protested. "I told you from the get-go that it looked like two groups. I'm waiting on the guys in Tech. They're making comparisons of the footage from the different locations. But study the footage again, sir," he told Eagan. "Miss Finnegan pointed out a lot of differences in the way the men stood, in their body language—I'll be happy to show you."

"I've looked at that footage so many times now that I'm all but blinded," Eagan said. "Here's the problem—the DA's office isn't on board with there being two sets of thieves. They want to go for federal prosecution and maybe even the death penalty. They want this over with, and they're going for the big win. That's a hell of a big bill for the Justice Department."

"And it's crazy," Craig insisted. "Look, I'd happily throw the federal book at the murderers, but only if they really *are* the murderers. But what's that saying? 'It's better that ten guilty men go free than one innocent man is wrongly convicted'? Something like that, anyway. William Blackstone, I believe."

"Very big-picture of you, buddy," Mike said. "Especially when a majority of the city is screaming for blood, afraid someone here's going to get killed."

"That doesn't make it right," Craig said.

"I didn't say that it did. I'm just seeing it from the point of view of the victims' families and playing devil's advocate," Mike told him.

"Neither of you is a prosecutor," Eagan told them. "And neither am I. If you feel strongly, get out there and prove the existence of the second gang. In the meantime, I'd like to speak with Miss Finnegan myself. After today she's both victim and consultant."

Craig glanced at his watch. "I doubt she's still at her office. It's almost six. Only underpaid federal employees with no real lives work all hours of the day."

Eagan grinned. "I feel the need for a Guinness. Want to join me?"

Craig wasn't sure if he was eager or loath to join Eagan. The woman was going to think he was stalking her.

Maybe not a bad thing. She was hiding something from him, and he needed to know what it was.

"I could use a beer," Mike said, watching Craig, a light in his eye betraying the fact that he was amused.

"Well, there's two of you, then," Craig muttered.

"She's a lovely young woman," Mike told Eagan.

Craig groaned. "What the hell. It's true that I have no life. Oh, yeah. And that I'm horribly underpaid. Let's go get a beer."

Leaving the offices of Fuller and Miro, Kieran paused on the sidewalk. She didn't need to head to Finnegan's tonight; Declan didn't expect her to work all day and then all night every night of the week. And this was Wednesday night, traditionally slow. But she didn't feel like going home, so she headed for the subway.

The term *rush hour* could mean almost anything in New York City. It now extended far beyond the morning going-into-work and early evening getting-off-work hours.

As she walked the block and a half to the subway entrance, she thought about the city. She loved her hometown. She knew that, once upon a time, there had been signs at a number of businesses that read No Irish Allowed. But now, some of the finest St. Patrick's Day festivities in the country were right here in New York. Everyone came to the Big Apple. The Statue of Liberty was there, the very symbol of America to many. Immigrants from all over the world had met prejudice here, then become accepted as Americans here, and it was still one of the most wonderful melting pots to be found anywhere. New Yorkers had a reputation for being rude, and there was the standard joke about not making eye contact. But New Yorkers weren't rude; they were just trying to get from point A to point B on an island that was sometimes filled with more than twenty million people.

And, of course, when you had millions of people running around, you were bound to get a bad element now and then. Muggers, thieves, rapists and murderers. And yet, for a city the size of New York, she thought that the police did a damned good job. Crime was very much on a downward trend.

Just outside the subway entrance, Kieran saw a woman with a map in her hand looking baffled. She paused to offer her assistance. The woman looked at Kieran warily for a moment, and then smiled with relief and admitted she was lost. Kieran was able to direct her to the A train. She thanked Kieran, then walked away with a wave and a smile. Kieran hurried down the stairs to catch her own train.

The subway platform was filled with all kinds of people: businessmen in suits and carrying briefcases, women leaning on the uprights to change from their work heels into their "getting around" sneakers or sandals. Several women in burkas were herding a group of children and trying to keep a safe distance from the edge of the platform. She could hear the distinct Southern accent in a nearby woman's voice as she chatted with friends about a play she had seen the night before. A group of uniformed Catholic-school students was milling nearby, talking about homework assignments.

A foursome of high-school boys was hanging out at

the edge of the platform, laughing and cutting up. At least half the people there looked bored and tired and ready to be home. It was going to be a crowded train.

She stepped closer to the tracks. As she did, she noticed a man in a dark hoodie standing some distance away. She couldn't see his face; his head was down and he'd pulled the hoodie low over his forehead.

She felt oddly uneasy and wondered why; she'd passed dozens of people in hoodies on her way to the train.

It was spring. Hoodies were perfect for spring, just enough when there was a chill in the air, not too much when the sun was warming things up.

She forced herself to stop looking at the man and pulled out her phone. She found a group message from Kevin to her and her brothers to say that his shoot had gone great. The director had mentioned using him for a new cola ad he was shooting soon.

She texted back that she was proud and delighted.

When she looked up, the man in the hoodie was gone.

She turned in the direction the train would be coming from and saw light, a sure indication that it was on its way.

It was then that she felt someone behind her. She wasn't sure what had alerted her, but she could tell that someone was there.

She stepped quickly out of the way, edging between a rabbi and a teenage Goth.

She heard a scream.

When she turned in that direction, she saw that someone was falling.

Onto the tracks.

And the train was practically there.

It was a teenage girl wearing a Catholic-school uniform. Her backpack had gone flying, and she was down on her knees.

Kieran didn't think. She simply reached out to help the girl. People were screaming and shouting directions, but she ignored them as the girl looked at her with grateful eyes and grabbed her hand.

Kieran pulled hard, the train's roar loud in her ears. The girl flew through the air, falling back on Kieran, knocking her over. Several people — who had tightly gathered first to board the train and then to help with the rescue—fell, as well.

The train shrieked to a halt.

Kieran heard shouts from all over.

"Hey! What happened?"

"Is anyone hurt?"

"That girl was nearly killed!"

Kieran felt as if she was being crushed beneath the weight of all the people on top of her. They were trying to disentangle themselves and get to their feet. As soon as she could move, she scrambled to do the same. As she tried to stand she realized that her skirt was hiked up around her hips. She quickly pulled it down, then accepted the hand of the rabbi, who had a look of concern and admiration on his face.

She thanked him quickly, then looked around. There was still chaos everywhere.

"She was pushed! That kid was pushed."

Someone from the transit authority had arrived. Then, as if they'd called on some kind of warp speed, police were flooding the platform.

Kieran wanted out. She tried to back away and

bumped right into an officer—tall and powerfully built and intimidating in his crisp uniform.

"Hold on, miss. You're the one who helped her up, aren't you?" he asked.

"I gave her a hand, that's all," Kieran said. She wanted to disappear. The situation was nerve-racking.

"She's a hero!" someone cried.

"Hey, she was on the news the other night. She helped catch those jewelry thieves!" someone shouted.

Her face flooded what must have been a brilliant shade of red.

"Please," Kieran said to the officer. "I have to get out of here."

"Sorry, but I can't let you go till we've talked to you about what you saw. Hell, we have to close the station, talk to everyone who might have seen anything. People are saying a man pushed her onto the tracks just as the train was coming. Is that what happened?" he asked.

"I don't know. It's rush hour," Kieran said. "There were tons of people, jostling and pushing and... I don't know."

"Did you see anyone suspicious?" he asked her.

She started to speak, but the words froze in her throat.

Was she obsessed with men in hoodies now? She'd seen that guy, and then he'd disappeared. And *then* she had been certain that...

*That he was behind her.*

And then that girl had fallen. Or been pushed.

"This is New York. What do we consider suspicious?" she asked.

The way the officer looked at her, it seemed that he considered *her* to be suspicious.

"Anyone acting strangely? Agitated, intense…something other than tired and ready just to get on a train and get home," the officer said.

She couldn't say. No, she just didn't want to say. She was afraid that she'd become paranoid, convinced that men in hoodies were chasing her everywhere.

Which meant, of course, that she was afraid of at least 10 percent of the people walking around the city.

"You're the girl from the jewelry robbery, aren't you?" he asked. "I saw you on TV."

She nodded. "Yes," she said, looking at him and deciding honesty was the best policy. "And that's why I'm hesitant to say anything. I'm worried that I'm just being paranoid because of what happened that night. There was a man on the platform walking around in a dark hoodie with his head down. I saw him, but then I looked away for a second, and when I looked back he was gone. And then I had the feeling someone was behind me, and I was afraid it was him. So I moved away from the edge of the platform, and the next thing I knew, that girl was on the tracks. Please, may I go?"

"Not until we've taken your statement."

She felt her phone vibrating in her pocket. She pulled it out, looked down and winced.

It was Declan. She sighed and said, "Mind if I take this? It's my brother. God knows, this could be on the news already, and I don't want him worrying."

The officer nodded and stared at her expectantly. Apparently she wouldn't be having this conversation in private.

She smiled and answered.

"Hey, kid, what's up?" he asked her. "You don't have to work the bar tonight. You know that, right? You probably had a long day." She was relieved to realize he hadn't heard anything about the subway incident.

"I actually was on my way there, but there was an accident on the subway."

"You're okay?" he asked anxiously.

"I'm fine. A girl fell onto the tracks—" no way was she telling him the girl might have been pushed "—and I was right there, so I helped her up, and now I have to give a statement. Are you being slammed? Do I need to hurry?" she asked, looking pointedly at the officer.

It was growing apparent to her that the old saying was right: no good deed went unpunished.

"Craig is here with his boss, who wants to meet you. Are you sure you're all right?"

"Absolutely," she told him.

"Where are you? Maybe one of these guys can get down there and help you out," Declan said.

Her blood seemed to drain away. Without thinking, she said, "No, Declan, *no*. We can't have them getting that cozy with us."

"Huh?"

She didn't want to explain her statement, and the perfect out suddenly occurred to her, not to mention it could keep her from being there all night.

"Yes, send someone down." She told him where she was, then smiled at the officer as she hung up. "The FBI is on the way," she said sweetly.

"I don't care if God is on the way," the officer said. "I need your statement."

She forced herself to keep smiling. The man's badge said that he was Officer Kurtz, but she decided to try thinking of him as Officer Friendly. "I just gave you my statement," she said.

He pulled out a pad of paper. "I need it again. From start to finish."

Kieran looked around. Other people were speaking with different officers. Emergency med techs had arrived and were speaking with the girl who had fallen onto the tracks; they had her on a gurney. The crowd had thinned out. Apparently some people had already escaped the scene. Others were talking loudly and almost enthusiastically about their experience.

Kieran took a deep breath. "I don't know what happened. The platform was crazy crowded, but it was rush hour, so I didn't think anything of it. I was people watching, and then I saw a man in the hoodie standing over there." She pointed. "Like I said, I looked away, and when I looked back he was gone. I had this feeling that he'd come up behind me—I don't know why, I just did—so I moved away between a rabbi and a woman dressed like a Goth. The next thing I knew, that girl was on the tracks and everyone was screaming. I don't know what else to tell you. I didn't see what happened to her, only that she was down there, so I reached for her, and the next thing I knew, I was on the floor with her and a bunch of other people on top of me."

He nodded, taking notes, and then said, "Your name is Kieran Finnegan, right?"

"Yes. How do you know that?"

"I told you. I saw you on TV. Couldn't miss hearing about you, to tell the truth. Didn't you notice that the press were in love with you?" He looked over her shoulder. "And speaking of those vultures, here they are. Whatever... Can you sign this for me? And put your phone number and address there, please."

She scribbled her name and the information he had

requested, trying to look over her own shoulder at the same time.

The media had indeed descended.

She wasn't sure how they'd gotten in—the police had cordoned off the entry and were letting people go as they finished speaking with them, but they weren't allowing anyone else in—yet somehow the press had made an appearance.

She could only imagine what the closing of this one line was doing to traffic and commuters citywide. Most people took incidents like this seriously. Still, there would be those who were sure they were only being inconvenienced because an idiotic girl had been playing around and managed to land herself on the tracks.

But…

She *hadn't* been fooling around, just chatting with friends. And then she'd come close to being killed.

"How am I going to get out of here?" she murmured aloud. The last thing she wanted was the press descending on her. It wasn't that she was so humble, she realized. She just didn't want the attention, certainly not now. And not for instinctively doing what anyone would have and reaching out a hand.

Especially when maybe, just maybe, she was the one who was supposed to have wound up on the tracks.

"Miss Finnegan, in all honesty, they're here to report that sometimes, things have a happy ending. And imagine! It's you again. The city has an angel. That's the spin I'd give it, anyway."

"Trust me, I'm not an angel and I don't want to be one. If you could—"

"I can't stop the press from reporting the truth," he said.

"No, but can you get me out of here?"

Thankfully, she didn't have to rely on his resources. No sooner had she handed back the signed report than she was stunned to see a group of men coming toward her.

Danny was leading the charge, but right behind him she saw special agent Craig Frasier, the older man she'd seen with him the night of the robbery and another man, perhaps fifty—Craig's boss?—white-haired, but lean and fit, as if he worked out with the same determination as Dr. Fuller.

She doubted, however, that this man stayed so fit by playing tennis.

How the hell had they gotten there so quickly?

None of them was panting or sweating—certainly not Danny, who was unfortunately used to running hard since he'd had to do it so many times in the past, generally while running away.

She quit questioning the situation as Danny stepped aside and the white-haired man showed his credentials to Officer Friendly, who had stepped forward, as if to stop them coming near her.

"I hope you have all you need from this young woman," the white-haired man said in a tone that said the response had better be yes.

"Yes, sir. I have her signed statement," Officer Friendly replied. "If she's with you… We may need her again, but we know how to reach her."

"Excellent. It seems our timing is perfect. We'll see the lady out. Thank you, Officer. Miss Finnegan, shall we?"

Kieran wasn't sure whether to be embarrassed, thrilled, smug—or more worried than ever.

Before she knew it, she was back up at street level

and suddenly aware of how the foursome had gotten there so quickly. A black sedan awaited them on the street, guarded by a beat cop.

"Thanks, Reggie," Craig Frasier told him, opening the rear passenger door and ushering her in.

Danny entered from the other side, and she ended up wedged between her brother and Frasier, with the white-haired man driving.

And as he sat next to her, those ice-chip eyes of his on her, Agent Craig Frasier murmured softly, "Miss Finnegan, you do seem to have a talent for finding danger. Just what is it about you?"

# CHAPTER
# SIX

"Miss Finnegan, I'm sorry, but there wasn't time for introductions in there," the white-haired man said. "I'm assistant director Richard Eagan. I'm not sure if you two have met yet or not, but—" he nodded at the man beside him "—this is special agent Michael Dalton, Craig's partner. I hope we didn't drag you away against your will. I know the press were eager to talk to you. Saving the day twice in one week is news, even in New York."

"Proud of you, sis," Danny said, nudging her. "You saved her from a grisly death." He shuddered, murmuring, "Even thinking about it..."

"Thank you," she said. "I'm pleased to meet you—and very grateful for the rescue. I just happened to be closest to her. Anyone else would have done the same." She was acutely aware of Craig Frasier by her side—and equally aware that he was still watching her with suspicion.

"We heard some of what happened on the way over—

news travels at the speed of light today. Or sound," Eagan said. "Or internet…waves or whatever they are. You're probably tired of talking about it, but what exactly did happen down there?"

"It was a typical rush hour," she said. "I don't think people mean to push and shove. And most of us are wary and keep a safe distance from the edge of the platform. I think there was just a—a surge in the crowd because the train was approaching."

She felt Craig Frasier's eyes on her. She was lying, of course. But after what had happened the other night, how could she say she'd seen a man in a hoodie? That he'd made her nervous, so nervous that she'd moved away into the crowd?

And that she was afraid maybe *she* was the one who was supposed to have fallen on the tracks?

She didn't want him to think she was paranoid.

But, she realized, given how suspicious he was of her, he was bound to read her statement to the police. Feeling as if special agent Craig Frasier could actually read her mind, she decided on a few sentences of honesty that she hoped wouldn't sound paranoid or, worse, delusional.

"The officer asked me if I saw anything suspicious. I told him that I saw a guy in a hoodie," she said, "and then I looked away and he was gone when I looked back up. I don't think he pushed the girl, though, even though people were saying *someone* did. I think he just made me nervous because of the other night, and it worries me. It's spring. Lots of people wear hoodies this time of year. I didn't see anything, so I just don't know."

That was the truth. How did the man manage to

make her feel so off-kilter, even when she was telling the truth?

She couldn't help but look Craig's way. Yes, he was watching her assessingly.

They pulled up in front of the pub just then, and Eagan pulled into a no-parking space, then tossed a permit of some kind onto the dash.

They all got out, but before they could even enter the building, Declan and Kevin rushed out, followed by a half dozen of their regulars and even a couple of curious strangers.

Kieran wanted to sink into the pavement. Once again she was hailed and cheered, grabbed and squeezed by her brothers. Mary Kathleen, with her huge green eyes and bright red hair, was right there with Declan, hugging her between them. Bobby O'Leary had actually left his seat at the bar for her, and even Jimmy—who she was pretty sure spent more time at the pub than he did working—came out to embrace her. Then again, Jimmy had made enough money so that he didn't have to work anymore if he didn't want to. He worked, he told her once, because he had to, or lose his mind doing nothing.

Tonight, he was with the paler of the two men from the other day, a tall man with hair so blond it was almost white. Nordic, she thought. He hugged her, as well.

Chef Rory O'Bannon, an Irishman from County Cork, and his two grill cooks, brothers Pedro and Javier Marcos, came out and took turns hugging her and praising her bravery. They'd all been with Finnegan's for over five years and were like extended family. Pedro had once told her cheerfully that he and Javier were from the very south of Ireland, a nod to their Puerto

Rican roots, though the brothers themselves had been born in the Bronx.

It seemed to take an hour before all the hugging was done and she was seated in a back corner—despite her insistence that she was fine and more than capable of helping out—surrounded by Richard Eagan, Michael Dalton and, of course, Craig Frasier.

Dalton was a nice guy who watched her with a combination of amusement, admiration and curiosity. Frasier watched her as suspiciously as ever.

After a few minutes of casual conversation, Eagan turned serious. They were there, he told her flatly, because he'd wanted to meet her.

"Your timing was perfect. I can't believe you got to me so quickly," Kieran said.

"Craig drove, though I insisted on the siren. He's one hell of a driver. Traffic's always at a dead stop somewhere in this city. I'd hate to be emergency services. They must dream about traffic at night," Eagan said.

*Does that mean you dream about vicious killers?* she wondered but refrained from asking.

Her hopes that once she'd met Eagan, the three of them would drink up and leave were quickly dashed when they started asking about the menu.

"I'm starving," Eagan told her. "No time for lunch today—nonstop meetings. What would you like for dinner, Miss Finnegan?"

"Dinner?" she asked blankly.

"A meal one eats at the end of the day," Craig said lightly, smiling. He looked down quickly—smirking, she was certain. He was undoubtedly aware that she wanted them gone. "I've had the fish-and-chips," he told Eagan. "It's excellent. Tonight I thought I'd try their shepherd's pie."

"Sounds good. Shepherd's pie it is," Eagan said.

Danny was waiting tables tonight, and Kieran had been keeping an eye on him. Time and again she'd seen him point her out, beaming with pride.

She silently cursed whatever fate had made her the one standing closest to the girl.

Danny seemed to realize that the men were ready to eat and arrived to take their order. She didn't feel up to eating anything and told him she would order later. The way he smiled at her made Kieran realize he'd completely forgotten that he'd stolen a diamond—or borrowed it, as he insisted—just a few days back.

She wished she could do the same.

In a way, it was nice that he was proud of her.

In another way it was terrifying. How could he forget? These men were FBI!

Danny took their order, and just as he left them, the door opened. As if just to put the icing on the bizarre cake that the night had become, Kieran saw Julie stand there for a moment looking around. Seconds later her friend saw her and raced over to the table.

Ignoring the three men, Julie stared at her and gasped, "Are you all right? It's all over the news, that poor girl in the subway... My God, it could have been you. Thank God you were there to save her! But are you sure you're all right? First the other night, and now this!"

"Julie!" Kieran snapped quickly, praying her friend wasn't about to start spilling her guts about "the other night." "I'm fine. These men are from the FBI. Craig

Frasier, Mike Dalton and assistant director Richard Eagan."

Julie looked as innocent as Daniel had. Apparently the two of them still didn't understand the gravity of what they'd done. Now she took the time to look around the table, her eyes widening. "Oh. Um, nice to meet you. I didn't mean to be rude a minute ago. Kieran is my best friend...has been since we were kids. Anyway, I heard what happened, and I was so scared." She stared at Kieran. "You haven't been answering your phone."

"Sorry, I didn't hear it ring. You know how loud it gets in here."

"That's okay. I called Danny, and he said you were here," Julie said, then looked suddenly embarrassed. "Sorry. I'm sure you're talking about something official, so I..."

She was met by a chorus of "No, not at all" from the three men, who all stood up to offer her their chairs.

Julie took one. Not, unfortunately, special agent Craig Frasier's chair, but Mike Dalton's, leaving Craig between the two women.

Kieran didn't know whether to be relieved or worried that he now had two targets for those suspicious eyes of his.

"Julie Benton," Craig said, sitting again. He smiled, but to Kieran it looked like a predator's smile. "Your husband is employed by the store where Kieran was taken hostage, isn't that right?"

Kieran frowned. Had she said Julie's last name? Maybe. She didn't remember. But if she hadn't, then... did he know?

Ridiculous. He probably knew everything there was to know about the store by now; he'd helped foil the robbery, after all. He undoubtedly knew the names of everyone employed there, along with their spouses, and he'd probably seen pictures of them, too.

She tried to breathe normally.

"Almost ex-husband, I'm happy to say," Julie said, mincing no words. "And a wretched human being. It's too bad that he wasn't there when the robbers were."

Craig turned to Kieran. "Didn't you say you stopped by hoping to see him?"

"I didn't know he wasn't working at the time," Kieran said.

"Ah," he murmured.

"Shepherd's pie, twice over, and a fish-and-chips," Danny announced, swinging by and smiling at the agents as if they were old friends. "Sis, you really do need to eat. Did you decide what to order yet? Julie, my love, what can I get you?" he asked.

"Nothing, Danny, thanks. I already ate," Julie said.

When Kieran shook her head and told him she wasn't hungry, he shot her a questioning look but didn't push it. "Well, then, I'm off. Gentlemen, another ale anyone?"

"No, thanks, early day tomorrow," Craig said, speaking for all of them.

Just then Mary Kathleen called to Declan in her high, sweet brogue, "Declan! Turn up the telly, please."

A handsome young reporter with gel-slick hair and a plastic smile was in a hospital room with a pretty blonde girl lying in a hospital bed.

"Ron Jacobs here, coming to you live and covering a human-interest story with a very happy ending. This is fifteen-year-old Shirley Martin, the young survivor of tonight's incident or, as some are calling it, attack on the tracks. I hope you're doing well, Shirley. All of

New York is pulling for you tonight," he said, moving the microphone toward her face.

She really was a pretty girl, and the whole city really would be cheering for her, Kieran thought.

Shirley smiled tremulously. "I'm fine. They're just keeping me overnight as a precaution. I'm just so grateful to be alive."

"Of course, of course. Now, tell me, did you fall—or were you pushed?"

"As I told the wonderful officers who helped me," she said, "I don't know. There's always so much pushing and shoving on the platform, you know? I could hear the train, and the next thing I knew, I was on the tracks and a woman was reaching down to help me. I'm so lucky and so grateful she was there. Whoever she is, she's an angel. I'd love to meet her and thank her in person."

"I'm happy to tell you, Shirley, that your angel is New York City's own Kieran Finnegan. I'm sure she's out there somewhere, maybe watching this very broadcast." He addressed the camera. "We'd love to meet her, too, so, Kieran, if you're out there, give us a call."

Shirley Martin smiled and said straight into the camera, "Please call. I plan to finish high school, then go to NYU for their performing arts program. I intend to act in film and on Broadway. Thanks to you, Miss Finnegan, I'm alive to get my shot."

She smiled broadly again, and Kieran had to wonder if they hadn't practiced their "live coverage."

Once again, as everyone in the pub broke into whistles, toasts and applause, all Kieran wanted was to crawl under the table.

She felt her face burn, but she forced a smile and waved.

Then she felt Craig Frasier's face close to hers, very close, as he whispered to her, "What's the matter? Aren't you enjoying your fifteen minutes of fame?"

She turned to look at him, dismayed. And apparently he saw honesty in her face at last.

"I'm sorry," he said. "Really. It's just that—well, most angels *would* want their moment of fame and the thanks of an entire city."

"Anyone would have done it," she said almost desperately.

"Actually, no. A lot of people would have jumped back or panicked, afraid they'd be pulled down. You need to give yourself more credit for your quick thinking and competence. But then again, I've seen you in action. Now, you've saved two people... Angel."

"I saved *you* from a water pistol," she reminded him, and suddenly she couldn't take it any longer. "Julie, gentlemen, if you'll all forgive me, I really need to go home and crawl under the covers."

"Of course," Julie said, looking guilty, as if she were personally responsible for Kieran's need to escape.

Which in a way she was, Kieran thought.

The men stood, and Kieran couldn't stop herself from glancing over at Craig.

He was looking over at Kevin, who was standing by the bar, a towel in his hand. She could have sworn that the two men exchanged a look, and that her brother nodded.

In two seconds Kevin was beside her. "You ready to head home?" he asked.

"Yes." She couldn't keep a tinge of suspicion out of her voice.

"Cool. I'm ready when you are."

"You coming with me again?"

"Another shoot in the morning," he said. "We'll catch a cab. You've had a long day."

"I'm done eating," Craig said. "I'll drop the two of you, then swing back for Mike and my boss."

It seemed agonizingly long to Kieran, though it was only a few minutes, before they headed out to the street. Declan had to hug her, then Danny, and then half the pub again. But finally she was in the car next to Craig with Kevin behind her, headed toward St. Marks.

"You know it will be a few days before people leave you alone, right?" Kevin asked her.

"What do you mean?" she asked, glancing worriedly back at Kevin.

"You're the girl of the moment," Kevin said. He looked out the window, as if searching for hidden paparazzi. "Reporters, bloggers, anyone looking for an audience is going to try to interview you. I guess people don't know you're a *Finnegan's* Finnegan or the place would have been crawling with reporters."

Kieran leaned her head back and groaned softly.

"Don't worry. It will end soon," Craig assured her. "The press is fickle. They've already forgotten about the other night, and they'll move on again as soon as there's a new sensation or a juicy scandal."

"Must be something going on at the karaoke bar," Kevin said, sitting forward to peer out the windshield as they drew close to her building. "Reporters, I bet. The wolves are congregating."

"Great. Everyone knows where I live. How is that?" Kieran asked.

"Easy enough information to find," Craig said.

"I can't believe this," she said, falling back on the

seat and staring ahead. What if she didn't go home? She could sleep on a sofa at the office. That would be fine.

"What do you want to do?" Kevin asked her.

"Back to the pub, to a hotel, my office—anywhere but here," Kieran said.

Craig kept driving past the clump of reporters milling on the sidewalk.

She hoped the karaoke bar would at least get some extra business from curiosity seekers drawn by the men and women of the media with their cameras, notepads and microphones, then staying to sing.

Craig pulled over about five minutes later, near Cooper Union and about a block off Broadway.

"Where are we?" she asked.

"My place. We'll hang out here for a bit. Maybe I can get you home unnoticed in a few hours," Craig said. "If not, I have an extra bedroom and an office with a sofa. Plenty of room."

"In New York City?" she asked incredulously, staring at him.

"I bought my place right after the housing collapse about ten years ago," he explained briefly. "Anyway, make yourselves comfortable."

"What about your boss and your partner?" Kieran asked.

"I'll give them a call."

"You're going to make your boss call a cab?" She was incredulous.

Craig shrugged that off. "We're sworn to protect and serve. That comes first."

She wasn't sure that protecting a woman from the press fell into that category, but Craig Frasier seemed completely comfortable with what he was doing.

He found a place to park on the street, quiet except for the faint sounds of music and revelry from a horror-themed club on Broadway. While making his call, which seemed to go fine, he led them to his building door, unlocked it after quickly sifting through his keys, then led them down a hall.

The building was beautiful, dating back to the deco era. Everything was well maintained, and crown molding and arched doorways gave it a charming look. The lone elevator appeared to be hand run, a unique, glass-enclosed vestige of the past, but Craig started up the stairs and they followed.

His loft was incredible. It must have been several thousand square feet, with half walls separating it into rooms. The kitchen stretched into the dining area, which stretched into the living area, with the other rooms off to the side.

At the far end of the living area, a large-screen TV hung on the wall, surrounded by shelves that were filled with books, games, CDs and DVDs in seemingly random order. That slight messiness surprised Kieran; she would have expected an FBI agent to be somewhat anal about keeping everything in order.

The couches and sofa were old leather pieces, comfortable and inviting, and there was a fireplace to the side with another couple of chairs, then the dining area, with a simple wooden table and six chairs. The kitchen was fairly new.

"Guest room is the first door there, my office next and then my room," Craig told them.

"I'm going to crash, sis," Kevin said to her. "I have to be a bouncing ball of dryer fluff in the morning."

"I thought we were just staying a little while to

see if the press would give up and I could go home," Kieran protested.

"Bouncing balls of dryer fluff need their rest," Kevin said.

"Don't they also need to shower and brush their teeth?" she asked.

"I can set an alarm for 5:00 a.m.," Craig said. "We'll all get up, and I'll take you both to your place, Kieran. That should give you both plenty of time to get ready for the day. Meanwhile, make yourself at home. You're welcome to shower here, of course, and I may even have an extra toothbrush or two in the bathroom cabinet."

"Kieran, it's the best plan," Kevin said, his tone serious. "Unless you want to give the vultures what they want, get over it."

"Fine," she said with a sigh. "You want the guest room or the sofa?"

He laughed. "You're the girl. You get the guest room."

"You're my twin, and you know I don't care about stuff like that."

Kevin put his hand over his heart. "Mom might be looking down," he said, "and she would never forgive me if I stole the guest room." The genuine emotion behind his joking words made her feel a tremendous swell of affection for him, a measure of the strength of their sometimes difficult family bond.

"Okay, well, good night," she said, heading toward the door Craig had indicated. Nearly there, she paused and looked back at him. He was still regarding her with what looked very much like suspicion. "Thank you," she said. "I really don't think this kind of hospitality is in your job description."

"We serve where we can," he said.

He continued to stare at her, making her feel as if both sparks and chills were taking turns running through her bloodstream and into her very bones.

Why couldn't she have wound up sharing that getaway van with an older agent, a fatherly type, someone who didn't...

Didn't do this to her.

She smiled weakly and disappeared into the guest room.

It was nice—neutrally nice. Smallish, with a wardrobe rather than a closet, a dresser, period seascapes on the walls and blue bedding. She set down her bag and sat on the bed, awkward and uncomfortable for a minute, but also very aware that she was exhausted from the tension and worry of the past few days.

Just what she needed. Her miscreant brothers getting buddy-buddy with the FBI.

She could hear Craig and Kevin discussing the contents of the shelves by the flat-screen TV. The next thing she knew, she heard the muted sounds of a video game being played. So much for Kevin getting his rest, she thought.

Frustrated and completely confused, she made herself lie down. To her amazement, she immediately began to doze, even with the noise.

As she felt herself fading, she realized, to her dismay, that she could sleep because she felt safe.

Why this sudden need to feel safe? She'd lived in the city her whole life. She loved her job, the pub and having her own apartment.

But that was before someone had tried her apartment door, before she'd felt she was being stalked by a man in a hoodie and a girl had ended up on the subway tracks moments later.

The next thing she knew, she was waking groggily with special agent Craig Frasier knocking at the bedroom door, telling her that it was 5:00 a.m.

Craig went in to work early—ridiculously early—after he dropped off his guests and stopped by a diner for breakfast.

He pulled out the reports he'd been working on, sheets and sheets of eye-witness statements and forensics from the diamond thefts. Glancing at the clock impatiently, he rose at last and headed for the tech department. To his surprise and pleasure, he found that Wally O'Neill was in his office, or rather, his cubicle.

"Hey," Wally said, after nearly dropping his coffee cup, startled by Craig's appearance so early in the day. "I was looking forward to seeing you. You can tell the bosses that you were right. They were in too much of a hurry to put a bad situation behind them."

"Tell me more," Craig said.

"I've finished my analysis, and there are definitely two sets of jewelry thieves out there. To be fair, I'm not surprised you and Miss Finnegan were the only ones who saw the differences because they're not obvious. The guys you caught are five-nine, five-ten, six foot even and six foot one. The guys from the Jersey tapes are six even, six-one, six-one and six-two."

"Great work, thanks," Craig said. He wasn't pleased or relieved; he wished he'd been wrong. At least he'd saved innocent men from a murder charge, but that meant the killers were still out there. "Have you sent the info up to Eagan yet?"

"Emailed it to him...marked urgent. If he's in, I'm sure he's seen it."

"Are you analyzing the video surveillance from the subway last night?"

"Not officially—NYPD are handling that. But Eagan managed to get it to me."

"May I see?"

"Sure. And in my opinion? That kid was pushed."

"Show me," Craig said. He dragged a chair from the next cubicle to join Wally at his computer.

The footage was grainy and only caught so much.

"I backed up pretty far before the incident," Wally said. "I was looking for that guy in a hoodie from the Finnegan woman's police report and several of the witness statements."

"And?"

"I found twenty guys who could be him."

"Great," Craig muttered.

"Wait, wait—I'm not your go-to man for nothing," Wally assured him. He paused the footage. "Guy in a hoodie here, guy in a hoodie there. But they look up, they look around, they look at their phones. Now..." He unfroze the frame and images went by. Then he stopped the film again. "Guy in a hoodie here. Head down all the time. Dark hoodie, either black or dark gray. Watch him—never looks up once."

Craig studied the man as he paced the platform, then found a place by a pillar and lounged against it.

He was in a position where he could watch the stairs, see who was coming down. And still, it was impossible to see his face.

"There's Miss Finnegan," Wally said, pointing.

Craig looked, and there was Kieran, coming down

the stairs in her work suit. She smiled and apologized to someone as they brushed shoulders, then merged into the crowd. He saw her look around and frown and then take out her phone.

He saw the people on the platform, teens, uniformed schoolgirls, a rabbi, several Muslim women, everyone waiting, some patiently, some less so, edging forward.

Everyone edging forward.

Kieran looked up from her phone and appeared to be searching for someone.

The guy in the dark hoodie had shifted. He'd joined the throng, moving in more and more closely, filtering his way between people until he was directly behind Kieran. And as if she sensed someone there, she moved away from the edge and closer to the rabbi.

And then the girl fell.

Had the guy in the hoodie pushed her?

Or had he, like those around him, just surged forward?

He saw the chaos that ensued, the girl on the tracks and Kieran—right above her—reaching out. The girl scrambled up with the aid of Kieran's hand, almost leaping onto the platform as if her life depended on it.

Which it did.

After that it looked as if all the pins in a bowling alley had been struck, with people falling here, there and everywhere. They'd all been pushing to get on the train, and then some had tried to help Kieran, while others had apparently gotten caught in the crush.

"Looks like our Miss Finnegan is a true hero," Wally said. "What are the odds on that? The same woman who came in here to help winds up saving a life a few days later."

*What were the odds?*

Had the man in the hoodie been aiming for Kieran Finnegan and accidentally pushed the wrong girl?

"Thanks, Wally," Craig said, glancing at his watch. Mike should have arrived by now. He was going to head up and have a talk with his partner and then assistant director Eagan.

He was attracted to Kieran Finnegan, and if he had any sense, he would step out of the picture entirely. Of course, he couldn't do that now without explaining himself.

Besides, he was still suspicious of her.

She was holding something back, and he needed to know what it was, needed to know if it impacted the case or not.

Had she been in on the thefts somehow? She'd known that there were two separate groups of thieves at work. That could indicate that she was connected to one of them. On the other hand, if she was connected, would she have shared what she knew, what she saw?

He was of two minds. The first possibility was that she knew something. And because she knew something, the killers saw her as dangerous.

Or she was innocent, but for some reason the killers were afraid of her anyway. In that case…why?

Either way, he was certain the woman was in danger.

And he had to keep her safe.

Doctors Fuller and Miro had joined Kieran in her office.

"We're so proud of you," Dr. Fuller said, brandishing his *GQ* smile. "So proud."

"The thing is, you really should grant an interview,"

Dr. Miro said. "Our phone lines have been ringing off the hook."

Kieran winced. "People are bothering you *here*? At work?"

"Yes, but the real point is that you did a good thing," Dr. Fuller said. "Of course people want to know about it."

Kieran shook her head. "Please, please, I'm trying to keep a low profile and just lead my life. I can't function like this."

"Don't be silly," Dr. Fuller said. "This is New York. Celebrities walk down the street daily, and they function just fine."

"You're not at that level, so you have nothing to worry about," Dr. Miro added. "A brief interview or two, everyone gets to feel good about their city and then the moment passes. There's so much bad in the world. If you do an interview or two, you'll make people feel good for a change. Trust me, it's for the psychological good of the city."

"May I think about it?" Kieran asked.

"There's not really time for that, I'm afraid. Or not entirely. You don't have to speak to anyone if you don't want to, but the girl you saved—Shirley Martin—has been released from the hospital and is on her way here. We've arranged for limited media access, and the police are providing security," Dr. Miro said.

Kieran wished she'd thought to call in sick and considered claiming illness now.

But a second later Jake rushed in. "They're here. You really are a big deal, Kieran. Way cool."

Despite every instinct inside her screaming that she should run, she wound up out in the crowded reception area, where Shirley Martin—adorable, but quite clearly determined to make this a step on her path to fame and fortune—thanked her, as did a very attractive young man who was an assistant to an assistant at the mayor's office. To Shirley's credit, Kieran thought she was sincerely grateful, but she also played up the fact that she had almost died and seemed to think she might as well make use of the terror she had endured.

Kieran reiterated yet again that any decent human being would have offered a hand.

Eventually they all left, but not before she was given a huge bouquet of flowers from the attractive assistant to the assistant and a repeat of the heartfelt thanks of her city.

Jake, Dr. Fuller and Dr. Miro beamed at her.

"Um, do we have any real work to do today?" Kieran asked.

"I have to be over at Rikers in an hour," Dr. Fuller said.

"I have a deposition," Dr. Miro said. Then she sighed. "Come on, Kieran. Just let us bask in the knowledge that we hired you, and that makes us good judges of character."

"Thank you," Kieran said. "And?"

"And what?" Dr. Fuller asked.

"What would you like me to do?"

"Oh, right. You're going to be interviewing a young woman who's out on bail," Dr. Miro said. "She's coming here under police escort."

"What did she do?"

"She pulled a Lorena Bobbitt," Dr. Fuller said. "Hacked it off in the middle of the night. Husband is alive, and it's been sewn back on. We need to know if there was abuse, or if she was just pissed off because he was sticking it somewhere else."

"Dr. Fuller! How professional," Dr. Miro chastised.

"Hey. It is what it is," Dr. Fuller said. Then he looked at his Rolex. "She's not due for another few hours, and *you* are due an extended lunch."

"Thank you," she said. "I'll just take it in my office."

There was no way in hell she was going out on the street right now. She was going to text Kevin, since he would be bouncing around in his commercial shoot right now and wouldn't have his phone on him. She was going to tell him that he was picking her up at the end of the day. She wasn't leaving this office alone.

Great. Now she was paranoid about leaving work.

When Jake was back in reception, the doctors had returned to their offices and she was alone at her own desk at last, she sent her text and sat back.

Free time. She actually had free time. She could pull out the book she'd been reading, the newest in a fantasy series she loved. No, she'd lost the concentration to read.

She just sat at her desk and wondered again if the man in the hoodie had pushed that girl last night—and if he'd intended to push her instead.

And if so...

*Why?*

# CHAPTER
# SEVEN

Craig and Mike spent the day going over witness reports and video from the robberies, convinced that the killers were still out there. Biding their time.

They were probably waiting to hear that the four men who had been caught were being charged with murder.

Late that afternoon, Eagan had called a press conference and reported painfully that the police were still actively seeking the persons who had robbed two jewelry stores in New Jersey and murdered two people. He asked for vigilance and warned that the people they were seeking were armed and highly dangerous, but he also asked people not to panic.

Craig was about to call it a day when Mike appeared in his office doorway.

"You gotta see this!" Mike said.

"What?"

"News replay. You can pull it up on your computer. Search for 'New York City's superhero.'"

Craig typed, and up popped Kieran in the ultramodern foyer of the offices of Fuller and Miro, surrounded by people and standing next to the girl she'd saved the night before. She was calm and polite but brief in her answers, all the while looking as if she wanted to be somewhere, anywhere, else. The interview, such as it was, ended, and the reporter turned to the camera. "There you have it, folks. A new motto for the city of New York. 'Any decent human being would offer a hand.' Words we should all live by here in the Big Apple."

After that Kieran got flowers, and Shirley Martin informed the reporter that she'd been asked in for several auditions and was sure she was on her way. She was clearly relishing her fifteen minutes, while Kieran was quite clearly shrinking from hers.

"She looks miserable, doesn't she? The good thing is her fame is about to dim. Eagan's revelation that we haven't caught the killers after all will take precedence."

"Yeah, that's a good thing." Craig knew he didn't sound convincing.

"What's wrong?"

"I don't know, Mike. Did you watch the subway footage?"

"I did. With you, remember? And, yes, we all wonder about the guy in the hoodie."

"But was he intending to push Kieran Finnegan?"

"Why would he have wanted to do that?"

"Maybe he thinks she knows something."

"Like what? Sure, she was there when we caught the thieves, but what would that have to do with the killers who are still out there?"

Craig shook his head. "I don't know."

"Think maybe the killers are mad because they know

it's partly down to her that we know they're still out there? Eagan said in his press conference that our computer techs acted on a tip from a witness when they proved that the men we have in custody didn't murder anyone. It's pretty obvious that she's the witness he meant. Still, I don't see why anyone would be after her for that."

"I just have a hunch, you know?"

Mike shrugged and then smiled. "A hunch? Or more?"

"What do you mean?"

Mike laughed. "Hey, the freakin' air sizzles when the two of you so much as look at each other."

"Don't be ridiculous," Craig said, immediately defensive.

"She saved your life."

"It was a water pistol."

"Might not have been." Mike smiled. "Hey, what's not to like? The woman's gorgeous *and* smart, and she's given the whole city a motto to live by."

"She's a victim and a witness," Craig said.

"And you're worried about her. Not a bad thing. And we're investigating, though I'm not sure how we can stretch our investigation to include Finnegan's on Broadway."

"There's something, Mike. Something she's hiding. Hell, maybe it's something to do with that pub."

"You're suspicious of *her*?"

"Not suspicious, exactly," Craig said. "There's just… something."

"Then go get her, dude." Mike looked at his watch. "Quitting time—and tomorrow's going to be a long one."

In the morning they would be going back to Rikers and interviewing the four thieves again. They'd try to discern if one of them might know who had gotten wind of them, and how, and decided to imitate them, with lethal consequences.

"Yeah," Craig said, rising. "I'll do that. I'll go get her. She may need rescuing again."

"From evil forces."

"I don't think the press likes to be referred to as an 'evil force,'" Craig said. "But, yes, I'm going to go and rescue her from the press."

In her quest to fulfill her life's dream, Shirley Martin was thrilled with her moment of fame.

In her quest to fulfill *her* life's dream, Kieran was plagued by it.

Officers escorted Tanya Lee Hampton to Kieran's office exactly on time. Kieran introduced herself and welcomed the woman, ready to let her talk, but also ready to ask questions that might uncover any underlying truth Tanya was unwilling to reveal.

Things didn't start off well.

Tanya was dark haired, young and pretty—and voluptuous. She eyed Kieran curiously as she sat down. "You're her!" she said.

"Her?"

"The 'Subway Savior.'"

"Yes, I'm afraid so," Kieran said ruefully. "Are you uncomfortable speaking with me?"

"Hell, no—it's exciting." Tanya's eyes widened. "Did you leap right down onto the tracks? Could you hear the train coming? Did you, like, throw her over your shoulder or something?"

"I gave her my hand, just like any decent person would have done."

"Yeah, I guess," Tanya said, sighing and sinking back into her chair. "I guess a decent person wouldn't have hacked off her husband's tallywhacker, huh?"

"Why did you do it, Tanya?"

Kieran was surprised when the woman's demeanor changed. She'd been almost nonchalant, even rebellious, at first. Suddenly something was different.

"Tanya?" she asked softly.

Tanya just shook her head. "I couldn't take it anymore."

"Take what? My report says that he was seeing other women. Do you mean you couldn't take the fact that he cheated on you?"

"Whatever," Tanya said, looking away.

"So that *wasn't* it?"

The woman winced, looking down. Then she met Kieran's eyes again. "It was big, you know. Like…huge. He loved to brag about it."

"I see," Kieran said.

"No, no, you don't," Tanya said, and of course she was right.

And then Kieran suddenly knew. "He hurt you with it, didn't he? With sex. Did he force you?"

Tanya looked startled. "Yeah, and I know it's rape if a guy forces his wife. But…"

"But?"

"It wasn't just that," Tanya said, sounding as if she was barely breathing.

"What?"

"It was the things—the things he did with it." Tanya was silent for a long moment, looking near tears. "The

places…on me…he forced it. I couldn't bear it anymore.
I couldn't take it. I couldn't leave—no job and two kids.
And I couldn't—I couldn't take the pain. I'm not stupid—I'm not well educated, but I'm not stupid. I know
this makes it look like I am, but… I knew that I couldn't
do anything crazy, that they'd take me away and then
my kids would be left with… But I wasn't thinking
when I did it. I just looked up after he made me bleed
again, and he had a knife in the room to peel an apple
he was eating in bed after and I… I just picked it up."
She fell silent again. "I never thought there would be
so much blood. And he was screaming and screaming,
and I…" She stopped speaking and lifted her shoulders,
let them fall. "I called 911." She shrugged again. "I hear
they sewed it back on and that he's going to live to brag
another day. And I'll go to jail for the rest of my life."

Kieran hesitated. She wondered why she'd chosen
this work. It was so hard to see the suffering in others.

"Tanya, what happened to you—what was happening—needs to be brought to the judge's attention. My
report is intended to help your lawyer. He or she will
bring up the information about the way he was abusing you. I don't mean to give you false hope, but—"

"Oh, my God, no!" Tanya said, her face turning scar-
let.

"No—what?"

"People will know! They'll know…what he did to
me."

Kieran was amazed that the prospect of others' opin-
ions could sway Tanya's resolve to fight for herself.

"They *should* know," Kieran said. "Why would you
let this happen to someone else?"

Tanya was thoughtful. Tears sprang into her eyes.

"My kids… Does that mean maybe I'd get my kids back?"

"I'm not a lawyer. But, as a therapist, I can assure you that telling the truth is what you need to do right now, and that if anything will help you, it's the truth."

As if taking Kieran completely at her word, Tanya launched into a flood of truths. By the end Kieran was surprised the woman hadn't put the knife through her husband's heart, though she didn't say anything like that to Tanya. She assured her that she would write everything up and put it into the hands of her attorney.

For once, Kieran thought after Tanya had left in the company of her police escort, her mind wasn't on her own situation. She typed away furiously, consulting her notes frequently and occasionally replaying part of the recorded session.

She had no idea how long she'd been working when she was startled to feel a presence behind her, though she'd never heard the door open.

She spun around and nearly gasped when she saw who it was.

Special agent Craig Frasier.

Moments after Craig arrived, Jake arrived at her door escorting Kevin and Julie.

"Looks like we were all of the same mind," Kevin said, looking at Craig. "You here to help my sister escape unscathed, too?"

Craig nodded.

"Thank you. All of you," Kieran said. "Are there… people out there on the street, or have I been worrying for nothing?"

"This is New York. Of course there are people on the

street," Kevin teased, but he sobered quickly. "Yeah, a few. One guy's lounging against the building, smoking a cigarette, but I don't think he really smokes."

"How do you figure that?" Julie asked.

"He keeps coughing," Craig said. "There's a woman, too."

"Is she coughing, too?" Kieran asked him.

"No. She's holding a microphone and her news van is down the street," he said. She winced, then looked at him hopefully, as if, he thought, she expected him to have an answer for her.

And, actually, he did.

"I tracked down the building superintendent. We can leave through the service entrance, then follow the alley out to the next street over. My car is on Park Avenue."

"Thank you!" Kieran leaped up and grabbed her bag and coat. Suddenly she seemed to remember that she'd been working, so she quickly shut down her computer. "Ready," she said.

The super was a nice guy. He had a heavy accent and had told Craig he was from the Ukraine. He was more than willing to help Kieran and kept bowing slightly toward her, making her flush and thank him over and over again.

They left through the delivery door, and as they made their way through the alley, out to the next block and then down to Park, Kieran kept her head low. He couldn't help but think that with her height, especially in heels or shoe lifts, her head down and covered in a hoodie, she could be a match for one of the killers they'd caught on camera.

That was ridiculous. His heart—and the powerful sexual attraction he felt for her—fought against it.

She seemed in a lighter mood than she'd been in the previous evening. Maybe she was hoping that tonight would pass without a hostage situation or a subway mishap. And maybe she even felt a little warmer toward him; he had, after all, helped her make her escape.

"Where am I taking you?" he asked, once they were in the car. "Did you want to go straight home?"

She hesitated, then said, "Finnegan's, please. It gets busy on Thursday nights."

"You're going to be in for it even if the press haven't connected you to the bar yet," Kevin warned her. "The city has a new motto, after all. 'Any decent person would lend a hand.' Funny how that's taken precedence over the fact that you helped catch a gang of jewel thieves. Not to mention that, thanks to you, Miss Shirley Martin is now receiving offers from agents. I waited weeks to see some of those people, you know."

"Don't be bitter, Kevin. She did have a few seconds there when she was certain she was going to die," Kieran said.

Kevin shook his head. "I'm not bitter. That's the way the acting business works. Of course, if you decide to do another interview, you might want to make sure I'm with you so you can let the world know I'm the subway savior's twin."

Craig looked at Kieran, wondering how she would take her brother's words.

"Will do," she promised. She was sitting next to him in the front; Kevin was in the back. Craig saw their amused gazes meet in the rearview mirror.

Twins. He'd heard they could sometimes read one another's minds.

He decided he should spend more time with Kevin.

He was certain there was more going on here than he knew, and Kevin might be able to help him figure it out.

And if he was wrong, and Kieran was on the up-and-up?

Then Kevin might be able to offer some insights into the most fascinating woman he'd met in years.

He hadn't been sure whether he was going to drop her off at the bar or accompany her inside, but when he saw the open parking spot right near the pub, he considered the decision made and slipped into it.

Kieran looked his way as he started to open his door.

"You're coming in?" she asked.

"You may need a quick escape. Besides, I have a yen for fish-and-chips. And since I'm a horrible cook and your chef's fish-and-chips are delicious…"

"And you have such a nice kitchen, too," she said, quickly stepping out of the car.

Kevin grinned as he and Julie joined them on the sidewalk. "Come on in… The place will be hopping."

Kevin wasn't kidding, Craig thought as the sounds of energetic conversation, along with the strains of a lively jig for violin, flute and drum, wafted out the door. He noticed that the outside menu board mentioned that Thursday nights offered Irish music from five until ten. No wonder there was a crowd.

"Ah, by the saints and sinners, she's arrived!" someone called as Kieran passed through the door. Craig was behind her, and he almost bumped into her when she stopped suddenly. He enjoyed the moment; the top of her head came to just beneath his chin, and the smell of her hair was pleasantly arousing.

"Sorry," she said, and started walking again.

Declan rushed out from behind the bar, grinning.

"Any decent person would lend a hand?" he asked her. "That's all you have to say about what happened in the subway?"

The song ended and the music stopped. "Ah, Declan, she's here, eh?" called the man with the fiddle. "Ladies and gentlemen, three cheers for our own Kieran Finnegan!"

People shouted her name, applauding.

"Thank you," she said loudly, ducking her head to hide her embarrassment. "Was that a jig? Don't let me stop you."

The violinist grinned, picked up his instrument, and the music took flight again.

"You're looking lovely as always, Kieran," Declan said. He looked past his sister to Craig. "Nice to see you again. Have you made yourself my sister's guardian?"

"Maybe," Craig said with a shrug. "She's been incredibly helpful to us, so we want to make sure she can get around easily."

"And he likes the food," Julie said.

"As any sane man would," Declan said. "Well, I'd better get back to it."

"You slammed behind the bar?" Kieran asked him.

"I'm doing all right. You sit and relax with your friends—and our layabout brother," he added, looking at Kevin.

"You need me?" Kevin asked.

"No, we're good. Danny is helping out on the floor."

"I'm too restless to sit," Kieran said. "I'll help out." She turned to the others. "Forgive me, but I've got to keep busy."

And with that, she headed toward the bar.

That was all right, Craig thought. Kevin and Julie

were ready to sit and have a meal, so who knew what he might learn.

"I'm so glad you're looking out for Kieran," Julie told him as they sat.

He had more or less steered them toward a small booth right by the bar. He could keep an eye on Kieran, see who she interacted with, without being obvious about it.

Meanwhile, he was curious about Julie, since it was her soon-to-be-ex husband who worked at the jewelry store where the theft had taken place. Kieran had said she'd only been there because of Julie.

"She's been very helpful with our case," Craig said. "She was there that day to see your ex-husband, right?"

"He's been behaving like a real bastard," Kevin said.

It looked to Craig as if Kevin was staring at Julie distrustfully, as if he was worried what she might say.

But Julie didn't seem to notice. She turned to Craig and said, "He nearly killed our dogs! Well, *my* dogs now. I have a pair of rescue greyhounds. Benji and Sally. They're so sweet and so beautiful, and he locked them in their crates and left them without food or water."

"You should have called animal control. It's illegal to abuse animals," Craig said.

"I didn't want them taken away. I just wanted them to be okay. As soon as I got back I gave them food and water, bathed them and washed out their crates. But I was still so *mad*."

"And since Kieran's degree is in psychology," Kevin said quickly, "she went to the store, hoping to see Gary and talk him into behaving like an adult."

"You can't even imagine everything he's done," Julie murmured.

Craig was afraid he was going to hear about all of it.

He was half listening to Julie go on about how badly Gary was behaving and watching Kieran at the same time. He wondered if she'd taken her bartending expertise and used it when working on her psychology degree or if she'd used her interest in psychology as a bartender. Whichever. She was good with the customers—many of them obviously regulars—friendly and efficient without disrupting their private conversations. She spent a fair amount of time talking with an older man at the bar who seemed to be drinking nothing but soda and lime.

But suddenly everything about her changed. She stiffened, and her smile froze.

She appeared to be reacting to a group who'd just approached the bar, two men and a young blonde with huge breasts and a very low-cut blouse that displayed them to their best advantage.

Silicone, he thought.

The younger of the two men was tall, but not overly so. He had wavy dark hair and wore a well-tailored dark blue suit. His arm was draped casually around the woman's shoulders, his hand dangling near her breasts. The older man had slicked-back silver hair and looked like an aging athlete; he was equally well dressed in a designer suit. They were talking and laughing as they waited for their turn to order.

Suddenly the young man looked up and saw the way Kieran was looking at him. He jerked his head, as if to indicate that he was with the older man and had no choice but to be there.

*Gary.* That had to be the nasty almost-ex, Gary Benton. His assumption was proved true when Julie looked up and let out a gasp. Kevin grasped her hand, either to comfort her or to keep her from leaping to her feet and attacking.

Kieran stepped around from behind the bar to speak directly to the trio.

He couldn't hear their conversation over the music, but the older man was nodding, while the younger man had reddened and was clearly unhappy.

The blonde woman tossed her hair back petulantly.

"The nerve! How could he come in here?" Julie said, her voice thick with unshed tears. "And with his... bimbo!"

"Just calm down, Julie, please," Kevin said. "We can't throw him out—there are laws and all—though, believe me, we'd be happy to kick him out if we could."

Danny, working the floor, had noticed the trio, too, and was moving in their direction.

"You stay here with Agent Frasier, Julie," Kevin commanded as he rose, then hurried to cut off his brother.

"You really can't give him a right jab to the jaw, Julie. You don't want me to have to cart you off for assault, do you?" Craig said, trying to make her smile.

She stared at him with sad brown eyes. "Would you really arrest me?"

"I'm an agent, not a cop, but I'm still sworn to uphold the law," he told her. He took her hand and held it tightly. "Look at me. Just...talk to me. Tell me, what do you do for a living?"

"Huh? What?" Julie asked.

He smiled. "What kind of work do you do?"

"Oh, I'm a game designer."

"A game designer? That sounds exciting. What games?"

"I, uh, work with a team. I guess our most popular game is 'Dargon the Dragon Slayer.'"

"One of my favorites," he assured her.

"You play video games?"

"Love to play. When I can, that is." While he'd been talking to Julie, he'd still been watching Kieran, her brothers and Gary and his friends.

Kevin had blocked Danny before he could reach the threesome and was talking animatedly to his younger brother.

Declan, oldest and clearly the master of the house, had just entered from the back room, rolling a keg. He stopped to watch what was going on.

Kieran was still talking earnestly to Gary and his companions.

And it seemed her strategy had been successful because the men were leaving. The older man was shaking his head, and now Gary looked angry as well as embarrassed. The woman tossed her hair petulantly again.

They were on their way to the door when Gary saw Julie. For a moment he looked at her with loathing. Then he noticed Craig, and his eyes widened, his mouth tightening. He shook his head and mouthed the word "Bitch."

He didn't actually say it *to* Julie, but it was said just loud enough for her to hear.

Craig rose, staring him in the eyes. "Friend, that kind of language isn't appropriate."

He knew he had the man by several inches, and Gary, too, seemed to realize that Craig was taller and bigger and undoubtedly tougher all around.

The older man urged Gary Benton away, and the three of them left the pub.

Craig saw Declan breathe a visible sigh and start

rolling his keg again. Someone at the bar called out that they were getting parched. Kieran hurried back behind the bar.

Julie's hand trembled in Craig's. Then, suddenly, she rose and threw her arms around him. "Thank you. Thank you so much."

He disentangled himself gently. "It was nothing. But you have to learn to ignore him."

"I know, and believe me, I've tried," Julie whispered. "He just keeps sliding the knife in deeper and deeper."

He wished he knew what to say to that. "Try feeling sorry for him," he suggested.

"Sorry? For *him*? Why?"

"Because he's so messed up that he isn't able to behave any way except badly. And because he's clearly incredibly stupid if he left a woman as sweet and pretty as you."

"Thank you. It's just scary to suddenly be alone."

"Julie, I know you've heard all this, but the right person is out there. You'll find him. Like I said, you're pretty and sweet, so learn to like yourself. Then you'll know when a guy like Gary is just being a jerk."

He flushed suddenly, aware that Kieran was standing beside their table.

He fought bad guys; he wasn't a therapist. Was she going to think he was an idiot for trying to give advice?

But she was smiling at him.

"I keep telling her that. Maybe she'll believe it coming from you," she said.

He shrugged and said, "How come no one's been by to take our order?" He looked at Julie and whispered with a wink, "Service kind of sucks here, huh?"

"Just part of the charm," Kieran assured him. "Don't

worry. Rory, our chef, knows you're here. He's sending out something special."

He saw that she was smiling as she turned and headed back toward the bar. A moment later Chef Rory O'Bannon himself came out bearing three plates. His best Guinness pie, he told them. He was a big, florid man, but not overly heavy, perhaps forty-five or fifty, with a quick smile.

"The finest you'll have this side o' County Cork," he assured them. Then he frowned suddenly. "You're not one of those vegetarians, are you, sir?" he asked Craig.

"Not at all, and this looks delicious," Craig assured him.

"And you, missy," Rory said, looking at Julie. "You're as lovely as the dew on the Emerald Isle. Don't be letting that damned fool steal another moment of your happiness."

"I won't," Julie promised, "and thank you."

Rory tipped his head and left.

Craig assumed Kevin would be coming back. To his surprise, he glanced over to the bar and saw Kieran hand her bar towel to her twin and head back over to the table instead.

"It's really stew in a pastry crust," she explained, sliding onto the seat next to Julie.

"I've actually had Guinness pie before," he assured her. "Not as good as this, I'm certain, but I *have* had it."

Julie turned to Kieran. "What did you say to him? To get him to leave, I mean."

"I actually appealed to Jimmy McManus, the man he came in with," Kieran said. "I said that you were here this evening and feeling a bit down, and then I asked him nicely if they might go somewhere else for the evening."

"Jimmy's a decent guy," Julie said.

Kieran looked across the table to Craig. "Thank you. I saw what you did." She smiled. "All you had to do was stand up. Good show."

Craig shrugged, a little uncomfortable. "I just asked him not to use certain language. My mother taught me never to suffer fools. And my dad came from a very tall family of Highlanders. Height always helps."

"You were wonderful," Julie breathed.

Kieran looked down at her plate—hiding a little smile, he thought. She also seemed glad to have the attention on him rather than on her.

"I have to say, Rory was right. This *is* the best Guinness pie this side of County Cork," Craig said.

An attractive young couple approached their table just then, apologizing for interrupting, then telling Kieran how proud of her they were.

Thirty seconds after they left, an older woman came by, saying, "'Any decent person would lend a hand.' Nice, Kieran. I don't know what this city is coming to—girls being pushed in subways, men killing people who don't even fight back over diamonds. Diamonds! Just rocks. Wretched things. I hope they catch those bastards soon."

"We all hope so, Lorna," Kieran said.

The woman bade them good-night and left, but only after studying Craig curiously.

"I should have introduced you," Kieran said to him. "How rude of me. I'm sorry."

He shook his head. "No, I'm glad you didn't. I'd just as soon stay anonymous. If you do introduce me to anyone, just use my name—say I'm a friend. Tell people you're with the FBI and suddenly they're afraid to say anything."

He thought he saw Kieran color a little. "Only the guilty ones," she said.

Julie smiled. "Hey, see the three guys over there at the far booth? Grooving to the music? They're some of New York's finest. This place is always filled with cops. New York has a lot of Irish cops, you know. Irish descent, at any rate."

"You're Irish, too?" Craig asked her.

"My dad," Julie said, rolling her eyes. "I was a Jameson—no relation to the whiskey Jameson's, I'm afraid."

The white-haired man who seemed to be a fixture at the bar with his soda and lime suddenly rose and came over to them. "Mind if I join you for a spell?" he asked, his brogue rich.

"Of course not," Kieran said. "Have you two met? Bobby O'Leary, this is my friend Craig Frasier."

"Frasier, eh?" Bobby said.

"Yes, sir, how do you do?" Craig shook the man's hand.

"Scotsman, eh?"

"My father's father, yes."

"You're that FBI agent."

"Yes," Craig said.

He was always in control, Kieran thought. But she saw his mouth tighten a bit and realized he wasn't pleased that he was known to be with the FBI.

"Saw you on the television with Kieran here. Scary thing. She's precious to us. Glad you were there for her."

"Actually, sir, she saved me."

"From a water pistol," Kieran said quickly.

"Still, we had no idea we weren't dealing with killers," Craig said.

"I think I was just functioning on adrenaline. Besides, I have a feeling you would have Rambo-ed your way out of the situation eventually," she told him.

Bobby wagged a finger at them both. "You be careful now, you hear? This is no joking matter. Those killers out there are real. Now you, sir, you're trained for this. Kieran, you may be a hero, your face plastered all over the papers, but you take care, lass, take great care. There's no Finnegan's without you, you know."

He rose to leave them.

"Bobby's one of our oldest customers," Kieran said.

"He's quite observant," Craig remarked.

"He's been in recovery for years," Julie added.

"Must be hard, spending as much time in a pub as he does."

"Pubs aren't just bars," Kieran said. "Pubs are meeting places."

"Whoa, I wasn't attacking the place!" Craig said, lifting a hand. "This is my new favorite hangout."

Her smile faded. She looked uneasy.

Julie didn't notice. "Rory outdid himself tonight," she said. "This is delicious."

By the time they were finishing, the pretty young Irishwoman, Mary Kathleen, Declan's red-haired fiancée, came hurrying over to them.

"Julie, I know you've been wanting to move, and I have the perfect solution for you," she said, flushing with pleasure.

"What is it?" Julie asked.

"My flat," Mary Kathleen said. "I'm never there." She glanced over at Kieran, blushing, a pretty sight given the fairness of her skin. "I'm with Declan all the time. Me toothbrush is there, you know? My place allows dogs. There's a wee bedroom and a parlor, and a nice big kitchen. You and the pups would be gloriously happy there."

"Oh, I couldn't!" Julie said.

"You could," Kieran told her. "It's perfect for you. It's right by the fire station on Reed Street, a great neighborhood, very safe."

"I can help you get your things in the morning, if you can take a few hours off work," Mary Kathleen said. "In fact, you can come home with me tonight and we'll get started packing up me things."

"Won't Declan be upset you're not going home with him tonight?" Julie asked.

"He'll be thrilled—he was the one who came up with this idea," Mary Kathleen said.

"Where are you living now?" Craig asked.

"At the apartment Gary and I still share," Julie said. "We avoid each other as much as we can. He ignores me and the dogs, I ignore *him*. We try to come and go at different times. I wanted to move in with my parents temporarily, but their building doesn't allow dogs. I haven't found anything else I can afford, and Gary refuses to leave."

"And you're not afraid Gary will…try something?" Craig asked.

"Oh, Gary is hateful, but he's not violent," Julie said. "He says things, but he's never touched me or hurt me physically in any way."

That could change in a split second, Craig knew.

"Go home with Mary Kathleen tonight," he said. "Please."

"But the dogs..." Julie said.

"We'll go get the dogs right now," Kieran said, rising. "I'll borrow Declan's car."

Julie paled. "What if he's there tonight—after this?"

"I'll take you," Craig said decisively as he stood.

*What the hell was he doing?* He was getting far more involved than he'd intended. He'd meant to keep watch over Kieran. He hadn't meant to become a member of the damned extended family.

"Oh, no, we can't ask you to do that," Kieran protested.

Her protest suddenly solidified his determination to help when only a moment ago he'd been wishing he'd never spoken.

"Let's go," he said.

A few minutes later he was driving down Broadway to Canal and planning to cut over to the West Village.

# CHAPTER
# EIGHT

It wasn't a long drive at all, but the whole time Craig kept wondering what the hell he was doing.

He wasn't a by-the-book guy in the sense that Marty was; he was by nature careful and thoughtful. He made sure he knew what he was doing, and when he chose a direction and moved forward, he always had a reason.

This was crazy.

He wasn't a therapist.

Or a bodyguard.

And yet he had wedged himself into the middle of a nasty divorce.

But what the hell else could he have done? As Kieran had said, any decent person would lend a hand.

He was glad that she was along for the ride, too. He was still inexplicably on edge about her after watching the surveillance tapes from the subway.

As he drove, he couldn't stop keeping an eye out

for people in hoodies. Unsurprisingly, there were lots of them.

Julie's apartment wasn't too far over from Kieran's place. She and Gary had the basement of a beautiful old brownstone. Craig remembered reading that the basements of the nineteenth-century row houses had originally been servants' quarters.

The apartment might once have been the servants' quarters, but the servants had been given plenty of space. And Julie Benton had a flair for decoration. The walls held animation stills from her work, charming dragons and medieval fantasy sorcerers, knights in battle and more. There were collectible superhero action figures here and there, and plenty of twenty-first-century comforts. The television screen looked to be a good seventy inches; the cabinets surrounding it were filled with high-end sound equipment, controllers, remotes and more. Modernist lamps and mirrors completed the decor.

"My place is nothing like this," Mary Kathleen said.

"Most of this is mine, but I'm not allowed to touch it. Everything is part of the divorce now," Julie told her. "I don't care about any of it, though, just my babies!"

Her babies, of course, were the dogs, Benji and Sally. Benji was a brindle male, Sally a cream-colored female.

Craig waited by the door while Kieran and Julie took them down the street for a walk, then accompanied them back inside so Julie could pack.

In the end, other than dog supplies, her packing consisted of nothing but a small bag of toiletries and a change of clothing. She was clearly anxious to leave.

Craig soon knew why. Just as they locked the door

behind them and stepped onto the sidewalk, Gary came down the street.

He was weaving slightly, as was the blonde next to him, the two of them somehow holding each other up. When they reached the house, however, and Gary saw Craig standing there, he stopped dead, forgetting his companion. "What the hell is going on here?" he demanded.

Craig didn't let Julie answer and he didn't allow Gary any closer, immediately stepping between them. "Animal control," he said drily. "We're taking the dogs."

"Tell him, Gary!" the woman said. "Tell him that he'd better not have touched even one of your things."

Gary straightened his shoulders, but it was obvious he was no more eager to get into a fight now than he had been back at Finnegan's.

"You better not have touched anything," he warned, but he didn't make any move to back up his words.

Julie stepped to Craig's side and glared at his date. "And you'd better not touch anything of mine—like my bed!"

Craig had a feeling things were about to get ugly.

But Kieran grabbed Julie's arm and looked at Gary. "We're leaving, Gary. No more whining dogs to ruin your special moment."

"Yes, let's go," Mary Kathleen urged.

"Come on, honey," Craig said, slipping an arm around Julie's shoulders.

That made Gary's jaw drop. "You're with—with *him* now?"

"Let's go," Craig insisted.

He led her down the sidewalk toward his car. Gary and the blonde stepped aside, Gary still looking stunned.

"What the hell is that?" Gary cried after him. "Your fucking harem?"

Julie tensed as if she was about to turn and confront Gary, but Craig kept her moving and helped her into the car.

With the dogs. Two sizable greyhounds. Sweet—but big, they sat in the backseat with Mary Kathleen and Julie, but one of them kept licking his ear. He liked dogs, but that was a little too personal.

Eventually they reached Mary Kathleen's place down by the Reed Street fire station.

"You went above and beyond," Kieran told him as they all got out of the car. "Thanks so much for getting us here and dealing with Gary. You don't need to give up the rest of your night, though. You should go home."

"Are you going to stay here tonight, too?" he asked her.

"No, but I can grab a cab."

He shook his head. "Not on my watch," he said softly. "It's late—there's barely any traffic. Come on, I'll see you home."

She hesitated, then acquiesced. Everyone said goodnight and thanked Craig for his help. Even Benji and Sally seemed happy to be there, wagging their tails nonstop.

"You were a lifesaver tonight," Kieran told him as they drove.

"It was nothing."

"Making Gary believe you're with Julie? That will have him think twice."

"Frankly, I'm amazed Danny hasn't belted the guy yet. All of you seem to be very close."

"Our dads were best friends," Kieran explained.

"We've known each other since we were born, I'm pretty sure. She's like the other girl in the family. And," she added, swinging around slightly to study him, "she's not only gorgeous, she's smart and talented."

"Brakes on there," he said.

"She's not your type?"

"I don't have a type."

"Seriously, thank you. I've tried to talk Julie into getting out of that place since her marriage fell apart three months ago. I know there are smart lawyers out there, but the idiots they've hired have warned them that the other one will clean them out and the division of property will become a nightmare if they don't hang in until their court date. But..."

"But?"

She shrugged and glanced at him, looking uncomfortable. "But I've seen what can happen when a marriage turns toxic. Today at work I interviewed a woman who—according to one of my colleagues—'pulled a Bobbitt.'"

"Ouch," Craig murmured.

"The guy is going to live and, of course, rip her to shreds in court. I've told my bosses that she suffered terribly at his hands, but claiming self-defense when she was the one wielding the knife is going to be hard."

"Makes me even happier I was able to help Julie get away from Gary."

"He's never been violent, just cruel. But who knows what people will do? I don't think the woman I interviewed was ever violent before she suddenly picked up a knife and whacked off her husband's...you know. I guess there's only so much anyone can take. Gary's already nasty, so if he started thinking Julie was persecuting him or cramping his style… Well, let's just say I'm glad we won't have to find out," Kieran said. She flashed him an awkward smile. "Funny. I'm a psychologist—I'm supposed to know so much about people, but the more I learn, the less I seem to understand. Please don't tell my employers I said that."

"If you felt you knew everything, you wouldn't be any good at your job," he told her.

When they reached her apartment, he once again got lucky and found parking on the street, and this time the media weren't lurking nearby. "I'll see you upstairs."

"I'm fine. I can see myself up."

"No. You know I can't let you do that."

"Your mother taught you that you always have to walk a woman to her door?"

He laughed. "I'm FBI. I've seen too much."

"I think I've seen too much, too, and in less than a week." She frowned. "And now everyone knows that the thieves you caught the other night aren't the killers."

"True."

"Maybe they'll lay low."

"I hope so. That will give us time to see if the guys we caught can help us figure out where at least one of them met the copycats, because the killers know too much. They didn't only study what our guys were doing—they had some kind of inside information to be able to copy them so completely."

Kieran shuddered lightly. "Thank God the original thieves were at the store the other day."

He nodded, then walked her past the entry to the karaoke club and to her door, then up to her apartment. When she opened the door, he followed her in before she could close it.

"I'll take a look around," he told her.

"I had the double bolts on," she said.

"Very sensible," he assured her.

He noted that Kieran had a number of stuffed toys and collectible models on display; she was clearly an admirer of Julie's work. There was a family crest on one wall, along with a Celtic cross. Other walls held a combination of photos and paintings of New York, the Rockies and Ireland.

"Nice place," he said.

"Thank you."

He wasn't sure what happened then. He would never be sure.

She was standing against the wall, watching him. Her hair was slightly tousled, a swath of deep fire-auburn falling across her forehead.

"You don't have to do this," she said. "You can't— you can't watch over me every second. I mean, I appreciate what you've done. Julie really needed help. I don't. I'm strong. I can manage."

Something in her words pushed all his buttons. He found himself directly in front of her, arms out, hands on either side of her head, almost yelling.

And he *never* yelled.

"What are you—a complete fool? *You* don't need help. *You're* so tough. Well, you're an idiot. No one is safe against a determined killer."

"Why would anyone want to kill me?" she demanded.

"I don't know!" he said. "Why don't you tell me?"

"Tell you what? I don't know why anyone would be after me."

Their eyes met and locked.

"There's something going on with you."

There was something going on with her, all right. All he wanted to do was kiss her, hold her, get closer to her....

"Something..." she repeated.

And then, to his astonishment, she let out a little cry—maybe self-disgust?—and moved against him. He didn't know if he kissed her first or she kissed him, but their lips met as she pressed her hands against his chest.

The kiss deepened and deepened, until at last he broke away. His breath came fast and strong; his voice was harsh as he said, "This is wrong on a thousand levels. You're a witness, involved on a case I'm actively working."

But he didn't move away. He still had her pinned against the wall, leaning toward her, his face a tense mask of anguish.

Kieran could still feel the kiss, almost as if his lips continued to touch hers. His body was close enough to hers to send his heat swirling around her like invisible steam. She could see the tension in his muscles.

She knew all she had to do was nod. Say yes. Or say no.

And he would move.

She realized that on some level she had known from the first time they met, even in the middle of what might have been a deadly situation, that she wanted him. The last remaining iota of logic within her screamed that she needed to run.

But everything else screamed that she wanted this moment, this time together, no matter what was to come. The part of her aching to touch him, to feel him touch her, argued that she could handle this. She could handle the truth and the lies…and him.

She knew she was lying to herself, but it didn't matter; none of it mattered. She reached out and touched his face, marveling at the planes and angles of his jaw. She met his eyes…chips of blue ice, she had once thought them. Now they were like blue fire, and when they touched her, she felt a slow burn inside, one that promised a blaze as strong and sweet as the soul could imagine.

"Wrong," he murmured.

"Maybe," she agreed.

But she moved closer to him, slipping her arms around him, pressing her lips to his.

For a moment he fought the urge to return the kiss.

But only for a moment.

And then he took over, his kiss powerful and sure, deliciously wet and deep, and she wondered if she would ever get enough of his mouth. No, she would never be sated….

She would always want more.

As she did now.

*Wrong*, he'd said.

It couldn't be.

It felt too right.

He was still kissing her as he shed his jacket, letting it fall to the floor. Still kissing her as he tugged at his tie, tossing it aside. She applied her fingers to the buttons of his shirt just as he reached to undo them himself. Their eyes met, and they smiled, then laughed, and turned their attention to their own clothing. His shirt fell to the floor, and then he paused, reaching to the small of his back for the gun he kept there in a leather holster. She stepped back.

"I'm not a proponent of everyone in the world running around with a gun," he said. "But in my line of work, it's a necessary evil."

She stared at him. "I was just waiting for you to put it down," she said quietly.

He held it awkwardly for a moment.

"On the bedside table," she suggested.

"I'm staying?" he asked.

"See me through until morning?"

"I won't leave you," he said.

"It wouldn't be at all professional to leave me in danger," she told him with a smile, then was immediately sorry she'd said the word, knowing he already felt it was unprofessional for him to be here.

She turned quickly and headed toward her bedroom, letting her blouse drop to the floor as she went. A part of her was afraid he wouldn't follow.

But he did.

In her room she kicked off her shoes, slipped out of her skirt and wished she'd worn stockings for once instead of panty hose. She sat on the bed so she could peel them off.

She was startled when she found him dropped down to his knees by the bed. His eyes met hers, and he slid the panty hose slowly from her legs. She watched him, feeling her breath catch, her arousal rise. He was shirtless, and now she had time to revel in him. He was everything she'd imagined, broad in the shoulders and chest, all lean muscle, perfect in every detail. His lips dropped to her kneecap, and she trembled in surprise. He looked at her again, then pushed her back on the bed,

kissed her knees and her thighs up to her bikini panties, then teased there, too, tasting her through the silk
before removing them and rising to strip off the last of
his own clothing.

She shuddered wildly in his arms, certain she'd never
been so aroused in her life. He kissed her lips, and
she felt the pressure of his erection against her flesh.
She ached to feel him inside her and wrapped her legs
around him, arching to meet his thrust as he entered
her. She wasn't very experienced, didn't fall easily into
intimacy, but she was certain it would be impossible to
find a better lover. He began to move, slowly at first,
each movement awakening a wilder urge inside her...
throughout her. In moments she felt as if there was nothing more important in the world than what was happening between them, nothing that could be more sensually
explosive than the feel of him inside her.

She felt as if she were riding a wickedly sweet roller
coaster, rising to peak after peak, everything simultaneously real and surreal. She was overwhelmingly
aware of the scent of him, the feel of his naked flesh, the
heat that burned between them. Suddenly she climaxed
more wildly than she had ever imagined possible. She
felt him shudder violently, and then he held her for a
long moment before he fell to the mattress beside her,
arms around her still. No matter what was to come, she
thought, she would never regret the night.

They lay in silence for several minutes—probably
necessary since she could barely breathe, much less
speak. He pulled her close to the slick dampness of
his body and smoothed her hair before he spoke again.

"Whatever my punishment might be, I'll accept it
gladly," he said softly.

That roused her from the cloud of mist and magic that had surrounded her in the aftermath of their spontaneous union. She rose up on an elbow, staring at him. "I'll never say anything," she promised vehemently. "I'd never risk your job."

That drew a smile from him, and he reached up to touch her hair with something like reverence. "I don't kiss and tell, either, Miss Finnegan." He laughed. "And I certainly have no intention of risking the mighty wrath of the brothers Finnegan. Not that I'd ever deceive your brothers. But do you honestly think that I'll ever be able to look at you and not feel, not remember, what just happened between us? As far as my feelings for you go, I don't intend to deny anything, just to be careful enough so that no one decides I need to be reassigned."

She frowned at that. "I understand that I'll be called as a witness when the thieves you caught that night go to jail, but the case doesn't really involve me anymore." She bit her lower lip. "You're looking for the copycats now, and they don't have anything to do with me or Finnegan's. You've been great, helping me after the whole subway thing, but that's not an FBI matter, is it?"

He didn't answer, and that scared her.

"You don't really think I'm in danger, do you?" she asked.

Again he held silent, but only for a moment that time. "No," he finally said.

She didn't feel convinced. "You only escorted me home to protect me from reporters, right?"

"Yes, of course," he said, pulling her back down to his side. As she lay there curled against him, he spoke again. "And no," he said softly. "Or… I'm not sure."

"Craig…"

He smiled suddenly. "You've finally used my first name."

"It finally seemed appropriate—really appropriate."

His smile deepened, and he said, "Let's just say I'm suspicious by nature and leave it at that," he said, pulling her closer.

As much as she liked the feel of her naked flesh next to his, she pulled away. Her bedroom light was off, but she hadn't closed the door and they were bathed in a glow from the other room. That was enough for her to see that, just as he had tried to reassure Julie earlier, he was trying to be casual now and not arouse her fears.

"There's something else, isn't there?" she said.

He let out a long breath and rolled to his side to look her in the eye. "Let me do the worrying, okay? You just be careful. I studied the video surveillance footage from the subway. I watched the guy in the hoodie you told the cop about. The footage is difficult to follow, but he does move around, just as you said. And he did end up behind you just before Shirley Martin started screaming and ended up on the tracks."

"Oh, my God," Kieran breathed. "I felt that he was there, but I didn't want to believe it. Do you think that means something? I mean, people move around on the platform all the time. Do we even know for certain that Shirley was pushed? You've taken the subway. People always surge forward when a train is coming."

"They do," he agreed.

Craig tried to concentrate on her words, on the potentially life-threatening situation.

But at this moment, he knew they were safe.

The light from the hallway created a halo of fire

around her hair, turned her flesh to porcelain and highlighted her exquisite beauty. And the way she felt against him…

"Trust me, believe in me," he said, and pulled her closer.

His lips found hers. His hands slid down her porcelain flesh, but it wasn't really like porcelain at all. It was silk; it was warm and vibrant. She touched him in return, and soon they were making love again. The problems of the world seemed far away. It was as if they had entered a time warp, moved into a different dimension and existed in their own intimately urgent universe.

But, of course, eventually they were forced to come back to earth.

"I just can't live like…this. I can't be afraid of every man in a hoodie I see."

He pulled her close. "Let's worry about that tomorrow. Right now we need some rest."

"Did you set an alarm for five again?" she asked him.

"Seven."

"A little better," she said, curling close. He held her, staring at the ceiling. He tried to remember the last time he had lain so with a woman and felt this way, but he couldn't.

"Wrong," she murmured.

"Very wrong," he said. "But sometimes it's good to be wrong."

He saw the slight curve of her smile as she lay with her head on his chest. He kept an arm around her, feeling every little thing, the way her hair fell across his chest, the pressure of her body, the feel of her long, long legs.

He stared at the ceiling.

Oh, yeah, this was very wrong. And he had every intention of going on being wrong.

He felt her relax as she finally slept.

Eventually he drifted to sleep himself.

Craig's alarm never had a chance to go off; his phone rang at 6:37 a.m.

It was Mike.

"They struck again, Craig. In New York this time. Vintage by Victoria, an antique place with a valuable jewelry collection, in the Diamond District. Meet me there." Mike hesitated just a fraction of a second before speaking again. "They robbed the place, and they killed again. Vic was part of the cleaning crew. Aw, Jesus, Craig, she was just twenty-two, emigrated from Romania six months ago. Welcome to the American dream, right?"

Kieran finished up her notes on her interview with Tanya Lee Hampton earlier than she'd expected.

She'd been at work since 7:30 a.m., and somehow she'd even managed to concentrate on her job.

At first she'd had a hard time focusing, lost in her natural human sympathy for the woman who had been killed. She didn't know the woman, of course, but her untimely death still hurt, and without the distraction of work, her thoughts now turned back in that direction.

*Any decent person would feel that pain*, she thought, then laughed drily as she realized she was practically quoting her suddenly famous phrase.

But someone out there had lost a daughter, a lover, a sister....

She thought the killer deserved the death penalty

himself and hoped that he would be tried in a jurisdiction that allowed it, though she wasn't sure what requirements defined a death-penalty case.

The murder must count as inhumane, right?

Didn't people give up any claim to humanity when they took a life?

She gave up trying to solve that dilemma on behalf of the world, or even in her own mind, as her thoughts turned to the cataclysmal change in her own life.

Today was Friday. She'd only known Craig Frasier since Monday. She'd slept with him last night.

On the one hand, she'd deserved a night of incredible sensual pleasure. She barely remembered the last time she had even gone on a date. She'd been busy with school and her new job and, over the past three months or so, being a support system for Julie.

She'd been attracted to Craig from the beginning. He was, frankly, an Adonis. She realized that her attraction to him had caused her to react self-defensively and against her own interests, as when she'd told him just how wonderful Julie was.

She smiled to herself. He was the type of man who could have posed for the kind of calendar women hung on their walls—or hid in a drawer.

He was courteous.

And employed. She remembered when her dad had warned her never to date a guy who was unemployed.

He was educated, smart, caring....

*And an FBI agent.*

One she hadn't even known for a full week.

What the hell had she been thinking?

Okay, maybe she was taking things a little too seriously. After all, even if Julie spilled the information that Danny had "borrowed" a diamond and Kieran had been there putting it back, what would he do? What *could* he do?

Arrest Danny?

There was no proof of any crime; the diamond was back where it was supposed to be.

Would he despise her?

Was that her real fear now?

She told herself that it wasn't, that she was really afraid he would look into Danny's juvenile records and discover what he—and Kevin, too—had gotten up to in their younger years.

Face it, she was still afraid of what Danny and Kevin might do. After all, Danny hadn't realized that stealing a diamond made him a felon, even if he had done it for what he saw as the right reason.

She felt a little chill run through her.

She liked Craig, really liked him. And sex with him had been amazing. She tried to convince herself that she could have it all, hot nights with Craig and her brothers' safety from punishment for the sins of the past.

The click of her office door reminded her that she'd come in so early because another jewelry store had been hit and another person had died.

And that a man in a hoodie might have pushed a girl into the path of an oncoming train—and that perhaps she was the one who'd been meant to meet a grisly end on the tracks.

Dr. Miro entered the office, smiling, and Kieran breathed a sigh of relief.

"Kieran, hard at work as always, I see. Did you know you're still all over the news? 'Any decent person would lend a hand.' Everyone's saying it now. And of course," she added wryly, "you really did lend that young woman a hand. The media will get to that eventually, I'm sure. Meanwhile, you're certainly giving this office a lot of great press."

"I'm so glad," Kieran murmured, wishing the media would just stop talking about her. "I've finished my notes on Tanya Lee Hampton. She was abused for a long time before she finally turned on her husband. I think we need to help with her defense."

"Then we will." Dr. Miro sat in the visitor chair and took the file Kieran handed to her. She skimmed through it, her lips pursing, then looked over at Kieran.

"I agree," she said. "How is she going to look on the witness stand?"

"Her attorney needs to thoroughly prep her. But I believe that if she lets go and reveals her emotions along with the truth, it will serve her well."

"Good. I'll speak with her attorney, but you should be prepared to take the stand yourself."

"Happy to," Kieran assured her.

"On another note," Dr. Miro said, folding her hands on her lap, "we've had a call from assistant director Richard Eagan of the FBI."

"Oh?" Kieran said, suddenly feeling guilty.

He knew! He was calling her to tell her to keep her hands off his agent.

She told herself that was ridiculous.

And, of course, it was.

"You heard about this morning?" Dr. Miro said, shaking her head. "There's been another robbery, and another murder."

Kieran nodded.

*I heard about it before 7:00 a.m.*

Dr. Miro went on. "Eagan was very impressed with your work on the robbery you were caught up in, and he'd like your help again as his agents continue interviewing the men from the other night."

"I've interviewed them once already, and I said I didn't believe that they were the killers, which has now been established," Kieran said.

"They're looking for something different now."

"Where and when one or all of them might have come in contact with the killers," Kieran said.

"You *are* intuitive," Dr. Miro said, sounding impressed.

"Ah, yes, intuitive," Kieran said, deciding not to explain that she really knew because Craig had told her so.

"Eagan seems to think that you're the woman for the job of interviewing them again. Apparently they were all more comfortable and talkative with you than with his agents, so he'd like you to talk to them, see if you can find the connection between them and the killers," Dr. Miro said, patting down her short gray hair as she rose. "I wanted to let you know an agent will be arriving to escort you back to Rikers."

An agent?

Craig Frasier?

Kieran looked at her cell. He hadn't called her. He had driven her to the office that morning, and he hadn't left until she was inside with the door double-locked since it was too early for anyone else to be there.

But he'd been distracted, grim. No surprise. As soon as he left her he was on his way to the scene of a crime.

The murder of a twenty-two-year-old woman.

These people killed without blinking, and she couldn't help but be afraid that she was on their radar.

After all, she'd been on the news after the robbery, and then she had been the "any decent person" to lend a hand to the girl on the tracks.

The girl who might have been there in her place.

She sat at her desk and began jotting down questions she might ask the thieves that afternoon.

It suddenly seemed more imperative than ever that the killers be caught as swiftly as possible. So many lives might well be at stake.

Including her own.

# CHAPTER
# NINE

As long as he had been in the field, Craig still had a tough time when it came to viewing victims of violent crime. It was hardest to bear when it was a child, when the crime had been particularly heinous or when torture had been involved—even when death had been a blessing after torture had been inflicted.

Maria Antonescu lay in the narrow little alley behind a row of jewelry stores, faceup. She'd died with her eyes open; they seemed to mirror shock and confusion.

*Why?*

She lay on her back, knocked down by the impact of the bullet.

Death had been quick, at least. They'd shot her straight through the heart.

Young, so young. Pretty, a little bit round, and working as a cleaning woman to stay in the United States. They'd checked immediately to discover if any of the other stores that had been held up used the same service, but none did.

Craig felt a momentary rage rip through him; he couldn't begin to comprehend the callousness that allowed these men to kill people as easily as they swatted flies.

He hunkered down by the body. Despite his feelings, it was necessary. The medical examiner was there; he'd determined time of death to have been between 11:00 p.m. and 1:00 a.m.

"Her equipment was packed, vacuum back in the closet, along with her brooms and mops," Craig said, looking at Mike, who'd been waiting for him at the scene and had stayed with the ME. "She was almost finished here. If she'd left five minutes earlier, she'd still be alive. The owner's been using the same cleaning service for over twenty-five years. All diamonds are locked in the vaults at night, and all workers—his own staff and contractors like Miss Antonescu—are bonded. That's why she was allowed to work through the night with no one else present. They've never had an incident before. The alarm never went off, so she must have shut down the system while she was working."

"Or she turned it off because she was on her way out," Mike said.

"Either that, or…" Craig murmured.

"Or?"

Craig hesitated. The dead girl was stretched out before him, that look of horror still in her eyes.

"Or she was involved and she let them in."

"But how the hell did they know the combination to the safe?" Mike demanded. "She wouldn't have known that, and the cops who were first on the scene said it hadn't been forced."

Craig shook his head. "That I don't know," he said. "What I do know is that they dragged her out here and…" He rose to demonstrate what he thought had happened. "My guess is someone had her by the arm, forced her out the door and pushed her forward. Then someone else shot her at point-blank range. With something powerful. A .44 Magnum, I suspect."

"New gun. The others were killed with a .45," Mike commented.

"Different shooter?" Craig suggested.

"Please tell me you don't think we have *another* copycat group."

Craig shook his head. "No, I don't think you'd get another group together like this—organized and cold as ice, and all willing to kill hostages who pose no threat. It's true, I don't want to admit the possibility. But also, logic backs me up."

He nodded at the medical examiner, who assured him that Maria Antonescu would be a priority case.

"Anybody find her cell phone?" Craig called.

Someone called out, "No cell."

"Let's take a walk through the store again," Craig said to Mike, and headed to the still-open back door.

The display windows were still blocked by the heavy shutters that were pulled down every night, and the front doors were locked.

The showroom was filled with glass cases. Two rooms stood off to the side, private spaces where special clients could be taken, and past them, a hall with three offices. The safe was set into the wall between two of the offices.

In the back was the diamond cutters studio, behind that a storage area, and a small room with a few chairs, a microwave and a small refrigerator—and the door to the alley.

Like the other stores that had been held up by the copycats, the rear exit led to a small alley that was open at both ends but was too narrow for vehicle traffic. This particular building dated from the end of the nineteenth century, but even then, no carriage would have been able to navigate the alley.

"These thieves definitely know the layouts of the neighborhoods they hit," Craig said to Mike.

Detective Peter Mayo had overheard their conversation and walked over to join them. "You think?" he asked.

Craig liked Mayo, who was with the major crimes unit. The years he had spent in the unit showed on his deeply creased face. He was nearing sixty, probably nearing retirement. Craig was going to be sad to see the day Mayo left the force.

Mayo was a true old-style detective. He was grateful for any help received from computers and technicians, but he always said that people perpetrated crimes and people had to solve them.

He hadn't been sarcastic when he spoke, and now he was looking at Craig thoughtfully.

"The original group wasn't as careful about alleys. There weren't any at the first two stores they hit. Each time the killers have struck, there's been an exit onto an alley," Craig said.

"We're sure we know who did which stores?" Mayo asked.

Craig nodded. "We can see differences in height and build on the surveillance tapes."

"Yeah, I read that in the reports," Mayo said. "Just wanted to make sure you agreed with it. I've been assigned lead on this now that the killers have hit the city, along with my new partner, Joey. Not sure you know Joey. I was working with Liz Grable, but she decided to take early retirement and live out her golden years sailing the world with her husband. Can't blame her. Joey's a little wet behind the ears, but he's a good kid. Still, gotta train him before I retire myself."

Mike laughed. "I know the feeling."

"You're just a kid yourself," Mayo said lightly, though his face was so creased, it was hard to tell a smile from a frown.

"So what are you seeing?" Mayo asked, returning to business.

Craig and Mike went over their earlier conversation. Crime-scene techs were everywhere, looking for prints, for fibers—for anything. The NYPD had cordoned off the street. Neighboring business owners were out on the sidewalk, simultaneously complaining that they were losing business for the day and thanking God that it hadn't been them.

"This place is owned by a Harry Belvedere," Craig said. "I'm going to have a conversation with him now." He hesitated. "My gut says this has to be an inside job."

Mayo nodded. "Because the safe wasn't hacked? Yeah, someone knew something. You take Belvedere. I'll take Joey and start with the employees. Five of them, not counting any other cleaning crew who've been here recently. The dead girl…that look in her eyes. Can't believe she was in on it, but who knows."

Mayo went off, leaving Mike and Craig to head into Harry Belvedere's office.

Craig almost wondered if you had to be a distinguished-looking older man to own a diamond store.

Belvedere was wearing a pin-striped suit, pink shirt and gray vest. He had steel-gray hair cut short and combed back.

He was sitting at his desk doing nothing, just staring ahead into space. The uniformed cop who had been watching over him nodded briefly to Mike and Craig, then left them alone with the owner.

"Mr. Belvedere," Craig said quietly.

The man didn't respond.

Craig said his name again, louder this time.

Belvedere winced and looked at him at last. He seemed pained to have been brought back from wherever his mind had taken him.

"That girl… I only saw her once or twice. She started late, but sometimes I was still here. She had another job in the afternoon. Wanted to make enough to stay in school," he said.

"She knew the code for the alarm system?" Mike asked.

Belvedere nodded. "I've used Clean Cut Office Services for twenty-five years. Their people are bonded." He hesitated. "And there's nothing out at night. The stones are all moved into the safe. I change the combination frequently."

"You must tell someone, write it down somewhere," Craig said.

Belvedere shook his head, a humorless smile curving his thin lips. "No. I have ten grandchildren. I use their birthdates. Different kid each time, no order to it."

"Who knows you do that?" Mike asked.

Belvedere shook his head. "No one. Not even my kids, and they're not local anyway. My son is career army, deployed to the Middle East, and my daughter is with the Red Cross. She's in Haiti right now. The grandkids are scattered across the country."

"So if something had happened to you, no one would have been able to get into the safe?" Craig asked.

"They would have had to contact the manufacturer," Belvedere told them.

That was impossible, Craig thought. Someone must have known something.

Belvedere sighed. "That poor girl. I found her, you know," he said softly. "I want to do whatever's necessary. I want to help her family. I want to see that she's buried."

"I'm sure that can be arranged," Mike told him. He and Craig glanced at one another. They didn't tell him that they suspected Maria Antonescu had let her killers in—whether accidentally when leaving or on purpose.

"We need you to help us catch her killer," Craig said. He handed Belvedere a piece of paper. "I think no matter how discreet you believed yourself to be, you said something somewhere that eventually led to the killers being able to figure out your code. If you could give us a list of friends you've talked with, of places you've been in the past couple of weeks, that could be very helpful."

Belvedere nodded and picked up a pen.

Craig watched as the man wrote, then took a look at

the list he handed over. Belvedere had attended a gala at the Kennedy Center, seen a Broadway show, dined at a dozen restaurants.

One in particular stood out.

Finnegan's on Broadway.

Jake knocked on Kieran's office door, calling out to her. He didn't wait for her to respond, just popped his head in.

"FBI's here for you," he said cheerfully.

Given everything with her brother and the diamond, she couldn't help feeling a twinge of unease, as if the FBI was there to take her in, not just talk to her.

She rose as Jake opened the door wider, expecting Craig.

But it wasn't Craig.

It was assistant director Eagan himself.

"Assistant director," she said. She managed a smile. "Whatever's going on must be important to get you to leave your office."

"This is…" He trailed off, took a breath and said, "I'm here to take you to Rikers. I'll keep an eye on you while you speak with our thieves."

"Of course," she said, wondering why she suddenly felt as awkward as a newborn filly. "Let me just grab my jacket and my bag. Oh, and my notes."

"Cheerful sort," Eagan said, after Jake sent them off with a big smile and a bright "Good luck!"

"Sometimes too cheerful. But Jake is great. He sets people at ease."

Eagan had come for her in person, but he wasn't doing the driving. A car waited for them on the street.

* * *

Since this was Kieran's second time at Rikers, she knew the procedure.

Soon they were through security and seated in the same stark visitors' room as last time. In a few minutes, the first of the thieves, Sam Banner, was sitting across the table from her. Eagan—just as Craig had done before—stationed himself a few feet away, leaning against the wall, arms crossed over his chest, watching.

They'd been allowed to question the men without their attorneys present because the questions didn't involve their own charges and nothing that was said could be brought up in court.

"Hi, Sam," Kieran said.

"You're back," he said, sprawling into the chair, looking over at Eagan, then back to her. "I thought the computer proved we weren't murderers. Plus I heard there's been another murder."

"That's true," Kieran said.

"So what do you want from me? We were telling the truth. You know that." He gave a little shudder. "Although the other inmates were afraid of us when they thought we were killers. Now… I guess we gotta get used to prison life anyway, huh? We may not be killers, but I guess we're in for a while."

"I would imagine," Kieran said. "Armed robbery."

"With squirt guns."

"The point is—"

"Yeah, yeah, we've all talked with our lawyers," Sam said.

"Sam, here's the thing," she said flatly. "The killers are following what you guys did to a T. That means they know a lot about you and your MO."

"Yeah," he said glumly.

"Think about it. How could they have known? How did they know how many of you were involved? How did they know what you wore and how you operated once you were inside a store?"

He looked at her blankly. She was pretty damned sure that he hadn't even thought about that before.

"Huh. I don't know. The news reports? They showed actual footage of our robberies."

"Okay, let's start here. Girlfriends, boyfriends. Any of you have one and talk about what you were doing?"

"No. Never. That was the thing—say nothing. Not to your girl, your mother or the priest in the confessional. That was the agreement we had."

"Okay, let's try another angle. Where did you meet to plan your jobs? Where did you talk about what you were up to?" she asked. "Did you meet in public? At someone's apartment?"

"The gym, sometimes. Franchise place downtown on Broadway. They keep the music too loud for anyone to overhear. And other places, too. Bars and restaurants. Never the same one twice. At the end of a haul, we'd pick a place to meet next."

"You're sure no one breathed a word to a girlfriend, a sibling, a mom or dad, a best friend?" Kieran asked.

"We're all each other's best friends," Sam said gravely.

"If you think of anything at all, will you ask someone to get hold of me?" she asked him.

"Will it help me get a shorter sentence?"

Kieran couldn't answer that.

Eagan spoke up. "It might. It might also be the decent thing to do, since people are dying. The victim was practically a kid, nice girl, twenty-two years old."

Sam nodded. "Yeah. I'll make sure I get ahold of you," he said huskily.

"Sam, can you do something else for me?" Kieran asked.

"Yes."

"Make a list of all the places you guys talked. Every place you can remember."

"Will do. Without asking for anything," he said quietly.

Sam Banner was taken out and Robert Stella was brought in. The questions were the same, and the answers were just the right amount of slightly different to assure Kieran that Robert Stella was just as perplexed, and that the men hadn't planned or rehearsed what to say if they were caught. She asked him to write up the same list of places, hoping he might remember at least one Sam had forgotten.

Next up was Lenny Wiener. Everything went the same way with him, too.

Last in was Mark O'Malley. He looked at Kieran and shook his head. "You're back."

"I am."

"I know that you're the one who clocked my buddy in the van," he told her.

"It seemed necessary," she said.

"Pretty good hit."

"I have three brothers."

He grinned at that. "Irish women. They're tough, huh?"

"Irish-American," she said.

"It's all the same. Something of the old country comes

with us," he said. "I wasn't born there, but my mom… what a tyrant, God rest her soul."

Kieran smiled. "I think mine was an angel. I was just ten when she died."

"I'm sorry," he said. Then he frowned, looking at her. "Finnegan? You any relation to the Finnegans that run that place down on Broadway?"

Kieran felt a strange, creeping sensation shiver through her and tried to keep her unease out of her expression. She wasn't sure why she felt so uneasy. The pub was well-known, so it wasn't a crazy question, and yet…

"Family owned," she said.

He nodded and looked away. "Cool place," he said. "Real Irish bands—or at the least bands playing actual Irish music. Not everyone brings in the real thing anymore." He looked at her and grinned.

"So you've been to Finnegan's?" she said, filled with tension.

"Just a few times."

"Is it by any chance one of the places the four of you met to plan a job?"

"No, no. We were there once, but just celebrating. I'd been before, and I brought the guys with me. Just for the music, you know?"

Apparently even jewel thieves loved good music.

"So where did you do your planning?" she asked him. "Tell me what you can remember, but I'm going to ask you to write down anyplace you can remember for me, too."

"Sure," he said, and he looked up at Eagan. "It'd be nice if maybe that helped us at trial."

Eagan glared at him.

"Whatever!" Mark said, taking the hint and shutting up. "Offhand…" He paused to think, then rattled off the names of five restaurants, three dives and two expensive places.

It was time for the guards to take him away. When he was gone, Kieran sat silently at the table for a minute.

"Thank you, Miss Finnegan," Eagan said, joining her. "I think they talk to you more easily than they would ever talk to an agent."

She nodded.

"You're upset," he said.

She looked at him. "They've been to Finnegan's."

He smiled and sat down across from her. "You know, most New Yorkers have been to dozens of restaurants at least once."

"You're not concerned."

"He said that they didn't do any of their planning there," he reminded her.

"But…what if they did say something? Anything? Any little thing?" She hated the thought of Finnegan's being involved in any way. Hated to think what an investigation of the pub might turn up about her brothers.

"Then whoever the killers are, they could have followed them out and kept an eye on them from there. But most likely they overheard them somewhere else," Eagan said.

"You're just trying to make me feel better. And I know now you'll have to investigate Finnegan's up the wazoo," she said softly.

He shrugged. "We follow up on all leads," he said.

"Of course. And it will be good, I guess…."

"Good to know someone is watching?" he asked.

She nodded.

"Don't be ashamed of being afraid, Miss Finnegan. You're not stupid, and only a stupid person wouldn't be a little bit afraid. Come on. Let's head out. I'll drop you back at work," Eagan said, then looked at his watch. "Nope. I won't drop you back at work. Where would you like to go? Home, where you can lock the door and relax for the evening? I'll make sure the cops keep an eye on your place."

She nodded. "Thank you. But it's Friday night. If you wouldn't mind taking me to the pub, I'd appreciate it."

"Great idea," he said, smiling. "Friday night. Time for fish-and-chips."

"Do you really think that the guys we're looking for were all dressed up in their finest for some gala?" Craig asked Mike.

"Who knows?" Mike said. "Belvedere suggested another half a dozen places. And we need to get on Maria Antonescu's friends and family here in the States. Between us and the NYPD, we're following up on every possible lead, just in case someone working at one of those places saw something."

Craig nodded. Mike was right. There was no way in hell the two of them could be everywhere themselves, and in fact, as soon as they finished up with their current interviews, he would be heading to Finnegan's.

Their first stop was incredibly hard and painful. They had to speak with Maria's aunt, a woman who looked to be about eighty, spoke English poorly and could barely stop crying long enough to talk to them. In the end, she wasn't any help, either. Maria was a good girl. Maria had no friends and no lover. Maria worked.

They managed to make her feel just a little bit better, assuring her that Maria would receive a good Christian burial, thanks to Mr. Belvedere.

Craig asked her about computer access. She didn't have one herself, but Maria had owned what sounded like some kind of tablet, and yes, she'd had a cell phone. She took both to work with her.

Craig and Mike looked at one another. Maria's murderer had been smart enough to see to it that both her tablet and her cell phone disappeared.

"Probably at the bottom of the Hudson River," Mike commented.

Craig thought that was about right.

Since she had been unable to give them any additional leads, their next visit was with Sylvia Mannerly, the CEO of Clean Cut Office Services.

Ms. Mannerly, Craig was certain, hadn't cleaned anything herself in years.

Her nails were perfectly manicured, her hands soft—as soft as the limp handshake she gave each man before asking them to take a seat in her spotless office.

"I can't tell you how devastating this loss is to all of us," she said. "Maria was a dream employee. She was so hardworking. Her clients loved her."

"I believe that," Craig said.

"How can I help you?" Ms. Mannerly asked them, suddenly no-nonsense. She might have been devastated, but her manner said she was also a busy woman. She folded her hands on her desk and leaned toward them. "What can I do?"

"We need a list of every place she worked in the past month, no matter how briefly," Mike said.

"And," Craig added, "we need anything you can give us about her friends. Boyfriend's name, if she had one. Anyone she might have been close to."

Ms. Mannerly frowned. "Maria was the victim. Why are you investigating her?"

"We're not suspicious of her, if that's what you're worried about," Craig said evenly. "We're just trying to find out if she saw anyone strange hanging around. Anyone who might have asked her to meet him after work."

"She went home after work and went to bed," Ms. Mannerly said icily.

"Everyone needs friends," Mike said.

The woman might have continued to freeze them out—perhaps afraid for what an investigation might mean to her business—but suddenly the sound of a truly anguished wail came from the foyer.

Craig quickly stood and walked out to see what was going on, followed by Mike and Sylvia Mannerly.

A pretty woman of about thirty and of possible Hispanic or Middle Eastern heritage had crumpled to the floor in front of the receptionist's desk, crying.

"Alicia, Alicia!" Sylvia Mannerly said quickly, stooping to draw the girl to her feet. "My poor dear, control yourself."

"It's true? Maria is dead?" Alicia asked, looking around with tear-filled eyes.

"Yes, I'm afraid so," Craig said. "She was your friend?"

Alicia nodded. "The best. A good person."

"I've told them that," Ms. Mannerly said primly.

"What was she like outside of work?" Craig asked gently.

Alicia told them at length about just how good Maria had been—always happy to meet up with others at the end of their shifts, even pitching in if there was still work to be done. She loved café lattes and watching the ducks in the pond in Central Park.

"You see?" Ms. Mannerly said. "The girl was a saint."

It was obvious to Craig that they weren't going to get what they needed with Sylvia Mannerly standing there. "Ms. Mannerly," he asked, "is there a place where we can speak quietly with Alicia—alone?"

Miss Mannerly's lips pursed and she stiffened. But, apparently realizing that they were FBI and she had no choice, she led them to a conference room.

They got Alicia seated with a box of tissues and a glass of water. Mike sat next to her, and Craig perched on the table.

With a little encouragement she started talking. They learned that she was Alicia Rodriguez, and that she'd come to New York from Puerto Rico when she was twelve. Like Maria, she was working hard to make her way through college.

"I can see how much Maria meant to you," Craig said, "and we're very sorry for your loss. That's why we need to catch the people who took her life and make sure they face judgment for what they've done. Maria's not the only one they've killed."

Alicia blew her nose loudly and nodded.

"Did Maria have a boyfriend?" Craig asked.

She looked up at him, startled, then quickly looked down. Too late. It was obvious that Maria had been seeing someone she shouldn't have.

Mike glanced at Craig. "Who was he, Alicia?" he asked very softly.

"I don't know his name," Alicia said, sniffling. "And I never met him. She only saw him a few times."

"What can you tell us about him? Where and when did she see him?"

"She only saw him when she got off work. That's how I know she only saw him a few times, because she'd go see him instead of meeting up with the rest of us. He plays in a band or he's a bartender or something. He would get off work right around when she finished. They'd only meet for an hour." Alicia shook her head. "But I know he would have loved her if they'd had more time. She was nuts about him."

"And you know about him because she told you about him?" Craig asked.

Alicia nodded and almost smiled. "She said that he saw her on the subway one day and followed her. She tried to ignore him, but he was so nice that she started meeting him. Just for an hour late at night. And then she'd go home, because she couldn't let her aunt know about him. Her aunt didn't want her dating. She wanted her to get through school, and Maria didn't want to disappoint her."

"She met him on the subway," Craig repeated. "Between her home and the Diamond District?"

Alicia nodded and blew her nose again.

"Do you know anything else about him?"

Alicia shook her head. Then she said, "I just remembered! I did see him once. From a distance. I was meeting her after she saw him because I was going home with her. We were going to the museum the next day. I met up with her at the Rose and Thistle. It's a little place not far from her house."

Thank God it hadn't been Finnegan's. He didn't like

the idea of criminals hanging out there—so close to Kieran.

"Can you describe him? If we set you up with a forensic artist?" Mike asked.

"I only saw the back of his head as he was leaving. He was pretty tall. About six feet, maybe? And he had dark hair. Very dark hair."

"Thank you, Alicia," Mike said.

"Can you remember anything else Maria told you about him?"

"Yes. He loved pubs. He told her once that he hated the whole club scene. He loved friendlier places, like pubs."

Mike and Craig looked at one another.

"Did Maria ever mention a downtown place called Finnegan's on Broadway?" Craig asked.

Maria frowned. "I'm not sure. But if it's a pub, he would have liked it. She said he loved the downtown area. He told her it had character. Trinity and St. Paul's, the area they used to call Five Points. Wall Street. He was smart, she said. He loved architecture and history."

"But she never told you his name?" Mike asked.

"I guess she wanted it to be a secret, something special because it was private. We called him Mystery Lover."

*Mystery Lover. Great.*

"Let's backtrack for a minute. When you saw him, did he turn at all? Do you remember what he was wearing?"

"Oh, yes, of course," she said.

"Well?"

"Jeans. He wore jeans. And sneakers. Jeans and sneakers."

"And? How about his shirt?"

"I don't know. I told you, I just saw him from the back. I couldn't see his shirt. He was wearing one of those jacket things. You know, a hoodie."

# CHAPTER
# TEN

The pub was being slammed.

Only natural, since it was a Friday night.

Eagan sat at the bar next to Bobby O'Leary, the two of them talking away over their club sodas and lime. Soon they were both eating fish-and-chips—and still talking.

Declan had all the screens above the bar and around the pub tuned to the news. It was impossible to miss the reports on the jewelry store holdup that morning, along with the sad fact that a young woman had been killed.

As she headed into the storage room to replenish the bar-brand whiskey, Kieran nearly smashed right into Danny. She paused, unable for a minute to hide the worry that had been tearing at her.

"They were in here, Danny. They were in here!"

"What? Who?"

"Those thieves, the ones who were caught when I was trying to put the diamond back. The FBI think the copycats—the killers—eavesdropped on them and learned about their MO by listening to them in public places. And they were *here*."

"Wait, whoa, you don't know that the killers were in here, right?"

"No, but…"

"So calm down."

"Danny, I'm scared."

"You were taken hostage and nearly killed in the subway. Being scared is normal."

"No, it's more than that. I'm scared for *you*. Danny, could anyone have heard you and Julie talking about 'borrowing' that diamond? Do you think—"

"I think you're paranoid."

"I'm scared. I'm scared for you and for the pub."

"Hey, is something wrong?" Declan asked, coming through the door and stopping dead when he saw the two of them.

"No, just running out of whiskey out there," Kieran said quickly.

"I'm back here for a keg," Danny said.

"Thanks, both of you, for staying on top of things," Declan said. "It's a zoo out there tonight. Go figure, someone gets killed and the world needs to drink." He hesitated, then added in a heartfelt tone, "Thank God, Kieran, that the thieves who grabbed you weren't the killers."

"Don't I know it," she said, grabbing a bottle at random. Rum, she saw, not whiskey, so she put it back, grabbed a bottle of whiskey instead and quickly headed out.

If she'd thought that would make things easier, she'd been mistaken.

Eagan was no longer at the bar.

That was because he had taken a seat at the booth closest to the bar, along with Mike Dalton and Craig Frasier.

Craig did seem to have a way to home in on her. She saw him the minute she emerged from the stock room and found herself staring at him like a deer caught in headlights.

Why was she so damned panicked?

And also glad he was there, filled with memories, warm at just the sight of him...

But mostly panicked.

He smiled at her. For a moment she could think of nothing but the night they'd shared.

And then she wondered about his smile.

Was it a suspicious smile? Even a little grim?

But he was sitting with Eagan. He knew where she'd spent her afternoon.

She wondered what his day had been like, then immediately realized it must have been awful. He must be feeling like hell.

"Kieran, girl, did you forget me?"

She snapped back into motion, hurrying to give one of their regulars, Nathan Worth, a Scotch and soda.

The night became a blur. Every member of the Finnegan family was working, along with Mary Kathleen and Debbie Buenger. Pedro had left the kitchen to the chef and his brother so he could bus tables, though more people were drinking than eating.

A local Irish band began to play at 8:00 p.m.

But even then, Kieran could overhear bits of conversation as she worked.

A group of young women talked about a wedding, then moved on to the murder during the morning's robbery.

Business execs discussed stocks and then the poor girl who had been killed.

A few people danced on the little bit of empty floor in front of the low stage. And then they, too, started talking about the robberies and the most recent murder.

She began to think the night would never end, and, of course, it wasn't even due to end until late, or was that early? On Fridays they stayed open until 2:00 a.m., and they were generally busy until the last moment when, according to their license with the city of New York, they were required to stop serving and usher people out.

Even more people than usual didn't want to go home that night.

Some left, of course. Eagan was gone by ten. Mike called it quits around midnight.

But Craig Frasier stayed.

He didn't hog the booth, though, but made his way to the bar, where he was quickly engaged in conversation. Not only with customers, either.

He talked to Declan.

Kevin, and even Mary Kathleen, Debbie and Pedro. And Danny.

And he was still there when last call came.

Nervous—because on the one hand she kept imagining him naked, while on the other she pictured him declaring that the pub was a den of iniquity where thieves met to plan their nefarious deeds—she forced herself to go up to him at last.

"You're really a trouper," she told him. "Working all day, then staying here all night. You don't have to do this, you know. I have brothers."

"I know. But I needed to be here."

Her hands were resting palms down on the smooth wood surface of the bar. Now he ran a finger over the back of one hand, sending a shock of sensation through her.

"Uh, okay, thank you," she said, her words almost a whisper. She looked around, but they were pretty much alone; everyone else was busy, customers gulping their last drinks, staff cleaning up and trying to get out and go home.

"You're thanking me?"

"Yes, of course."

"For?"

"Last night, this…" That sounded wrong, she thought, and tried again. "I meant thank you for caring, not for the sex. No, wait, I don't mean that I don't thank you for the sex. It was great. *You're* great. But more than anything I appreciate the fact that you're concerned for my welfare. But you're working a case. You can't be so concerned with me that you're not…on it."

He smiled. "Oh, don't worry. I'm on it."

That sounded ominous. Unsettling.

"We're closing up now," she said softly.

"Yes, I know, and I'm waiting."

She leaned forward. "To make sure I'm safe?"

"Let me stay with you tonight," he said, his finger playing across the back of her hand again.

She needed to say no.

Instead she nodded. "Yes."

"Good night, Kieran!"

She turned to see that Bobby O'Leary was leaving. Leave it to Bobby. He didn't even drink—and he was closing down the pub.

"Night, Bobby!" she called, pulling her hand away from Craig's touch and waving.

Declan was heading around the bar. He seemed to accept Craig being there as perfectly natural. "Are you seeing my sister home?" he asked.

"I'd planned to. Figured you must be worn out after a night like this."

"I am, but you must be worn out, too. The city is in an uproar, and you're caught right in the middle of it," Declan said.

Craig smiled. "But *I've* had a relaxing evening, meeting a lot of interesting people here at the bar."

Mary Kathleen came up just then and sat on the stool beside Craig, sighing as she let her head fall. "Brilliant night, but, oh! I'm beyond exhausted."

Kieran hadn't even had a chance to speak with her almost sister-in-law. "Did everything go well with you and Julie?"

"Aye, the girl's a love!" Mary Kathleen said, lifting her head and grinning. "Quiet as a mouse, she were. Slept well, then woke up and headed over to her old place for whatever she might need most. Figured we'd get a list of the heavier things, and the boys can go get them on Sunday morning, when this place is actually closed for a spell. For the moment she's fine—happy as a lark. She's working from home the next few days, hangin' with the pups. And what angels they are, too. Never knew I wanted a dog till now."

"I'm not so sure a pub keeper and his wife have time for a dog," Declan said.

"No harder than babes, and I assure you, we'll be having a few of them," Mary Kathleen said.

Kieran was relieved to find herself actually smiling.

Raising his voice so his brothers, who were still bus-
ing the last of the tables, could hear, Declan called out,
"Thank you—no, bless you all. Couldn't have handled
tonight without you. Now go home. Get out. I need to
lock up."

Kevin and Danny stopped and headed to the bar,
staring questioningly at Kieran and Craig.

"You're good—go home. Kieran has an escort," Declan told them.

Kieran couldn't tell whether Danny was looking at
her with a strange expression or not.

"Well, great," Kevin said. "I'm off. I plan to sleep
late tomorrow. I'm totally wiped. And I'll see to it that
this reprobate gets home, too." He punched Danny play-
fully on the shoulder.

"Night all," Kieran said.

"And, you two, you need to get out of here, too," Declan said to her, with a nod toward Craig.

Kieran reached under the bar for her bag and jacket.
With Declan making shooing motions behind her, she
rounded the bar and joined Craig. He didn't touch her
as they walked to the door together and he opened it
for her.

His sedan was just down the block. They walked to
it quickly, without speaking. She took a quick look over
her shoulder as they went.

"Do you think we're being followed?" he asked her.

"What?" she asked in turn, her brow knitting in confusion.

"You were looking around."

"Just wondering who else was out this late," she said.

He nodded and opened the car door for her.

As she slid inside, she wondered what the night was

going to be like. He was being so silent suddenly, and she knew that she herself was tense.

Why hadn't she said no when he said he wanted to stay the night? Why hadn't she protested?

Why had she been so afraid to speak up? And exactly what was she so afraid of tonight, here with an FBI agent by her side?

"Eagan really likes you," he told her, pulling into the street.

"I'm glad. He seems so…normal. I mean…for a boss."

He smiled at that. "He *is* normal, just obsessed with work."

"And you're not?"

He shrugged. "We have shifts, we're allowed to have lives, but it does turn into an around-the-clock type of thing a lot of the time. So," he said, changing the subject back to her, "how do you feel the interviews went? Eagan said you were upset that the thieves had been to Finnegan's."

"Wouldn't you be, if it were *your* family's business?"

"Hey," he said, "every crook out there has dined all over town. The only difference this time is that usually management never knows about it."

She turned in the seat to look at him. "Did you learn anything today?"

"It's an ongoing investigation."

"Oh, so you can't tell me?"

He was silent.

"Great! I'm supposed to tell you everything, and in return you get to keep me in the dark."

He let out a sigh. "We're investigating a number of leads."

"That's a stock line if I've ever heard one," she told him.

"But a true one."

He glanced at her, and for a moment she thought she saw suspicion in his eyes. A moment later his expression held nothing but concern.

"How about we talk about this in the morning?" he suggested.

"So you're still staying?" she asked.

He'd found street parking down the block from her place and was maneuvering into the space.

"That's up to you," he said, expertly sliding between an old Honda and a shiny new Acura.

"Oh, God!" she snapped. "Stop this! Do you want to stay? I actually wish I didn't want you to stay, because you're driving me crazy. It's up to both of us."

"It's up to you," he said evenly, "because I know I want to stay. Obviously, if you don't want me to, I won't. I'll lie awake all night—"

"Worrying that a killer is after me?" she interrupted.

"That," he said with a shrug, a small smile on his lips, "and remembering what it was like when I did stay."

She held very still for a moment.

Hadn't she been bright enough at some point during the day to think that she really needed to put the brakes on their relationship?

*Relationship?*

It was Friday night. Come Monday she would have known him for a week.

A niggling unease feathered along her spine.

*If she made it until Monday.*

She determined not to let fear influence her.

"I'm not sure yet what the hell this thing between us

is," she said, looking forward and not at him. "But yes, I want you to stay."

He exited the car quickly, then hurried around and opened her door.

He didn't give her much room; she almost slid into his arms as she got out.

"I'd like to think it's a relationship," he said. "Sexual attraction along with something more. I like, admire and respect you. In fact, I find you absolutely fascinating." He grinned slightly. "I'd like to think of myself as sexually appealing, especially to you—and, of course, I hope you find me intriguing."

"I'm not sure whether I want to kiss you or deck you," Kieran told him. She was already a little breathless; her knees didn't seem to have much staying power. She laid a hand on his chest and asked, "Really? Can this really be a relationship? We only met on Monday."

He moved closer and whispered against her ear, "Yes, but don't you think we're getting to know one another very, very well, even if it is quickly?"

Yes.

She smiled and nodded, and decided that, at least for tonight, she was going to live with the uneasy feeling of an FBI agent coming too close to their daily lives.

*Relationship.*

So far, she thought, they'd tumbled together in a van and then, in an entirely different way, in a bed. Was that a relationship?

It didn't matter.

"Let's go up," she said huskily.

As they passed the karaoke bar, someone was warbling out a Rolling Stones number—very badly, but with a great deal of energy and happiness.

"One day," Craig murmured, "I'm going to have to go in there."

She smiled, feeling his hand at the small of her back as they climbed the stairs.

"You enjoy karaoke?" she asked, slightly incredulous.

"Can't sing a note, but yeah, I love a karaoke bar. Do you know the owners?"

"Yes, and they're a lovely couple. He's Chinese and she's Japanese. A lot of their customers sing in Japanese and Chinese. Their food is very good, too."

"That's got to be a date night sometime in the future," he said.

*Date?*

Didn't a date always follow sleeping together?

At her door, she undid the double locks. As soon as they were inside and she'd resecured the dead bolts, she turned and found herself in his arms. As breathless and turned on as she was, she pulled away, suddenly embarrassed.

"I—I need a shower," she murmured. "Too much beer, whiskey and white sauce. And," she added drily, "sweat."

"As you wish," he said.

She stripped hastily, leaving a trail of clothing for him to follow as she hurried into the shower.

And follow he did.

She felt his arms around her and heard him whisper in her ear, "Lots of soap, hot water, steam…"

His voice trailed off. For a brief moment she winced, imagining what he might have said, considering the way his morning had started off.

*So much blood.*

She turned in his arms. The day had been long and difficult for both of them. And now, somehow, despite it all, they were one another's reward for enduring, for making their way through those endless hours.

Sharing a shower with him was wonderfully sensual.

Steam…

Soap…

Slippery lather, lips and kisses and hands everywhere…

And then laughter when she dropped the soap and they both reached to get it, clunked their heads together and staggered. She nearly fell into the exposed pipes.

He caught her, and with one look into each other's eyes, they mutually agreed that their shower was done.

Which was fine.

Because there were towels whose softness became erotically charged as they slowly dried each other while walking slowly into the bedroom, where, lips locked once again, he angled her backward until the backs of her knees hit the bed. She fell onto the mattress, and he came down atop her in a tangle of towels. They wriggled out of the towels and into one another, breathless, whispering incoherently and touching clean, hot flesh.

*Relationship…*

Could it really be?

Or was it sex…the circumstances…the world of wonder he'd seemed to open?

For these moments, at least…

Sex.

He was a practiced lover, balancing arousal and tenderness with a fire that quickly escalated into passion and urgency. She felt his lips everywhere, intimately, his hands caressing her, and the size and heft of him against her seemed to make her skin spark with something electric. She moved against him and with him, and felt the delicious waves of heat rise within her until she climaxed with such a surge that it seemed the night literally broke into stars. She lay beside him thinking that there were so many secrets between them, it ought to be impossible to feel so close, so much as if they were one, if only for those moments, and yet she *did* feel close, closer than she'd ever felt to anyone else.

He held her gently in the aftermath of what had seemed so wickedly wild and urgent. But, she reminded herself, there seemed to be multiple facets to him on every level—the stoic agent who loved gaming, so strong and serious, then filled with laughter when a bar of soap fell.

She could fall in love with a man like that....

Oh, no, no, no.

*Like* was fine right now.

*Lust* was definitely in the picture.

He rose up on an elbow to look down at her. "You're remarkable," he said.

She flushed. "I'm not at all sure that's true. But," she added, touching his face, "I'm very happy you feel that way."

As if by mutual agreement, they didn't talk about the day, about jails, criminals, victims or diamonds.

They murmured little nothings to one another.

They made love again. And finally, ridiculously spent physically and mentally, they fell asleep at virtually the same time.

Once again, however, they were woken by the strident sound of Craig's phone.

He answered it, listened tensely and turned to her.

"You have to go?" she said. "Not another—not another robbery and murder?"

"We have to go," he told her.

There was something in his voice. Something that frightened her.

She sat up, tension filling her. "One of my brothers?" she asked in a whisper.

He shook his head, and relief filled her. Then he spoke, and her relief drained away.

"No, not one of your brothers. But I think you're going to want to come with me. It's Bobby O'Leary."

Her heart seemed to stop. "He's—" She couldn't bring herself to say it.

"He was attacked last night. Just the other side of the block from Finnegan's, by the old St. Augustine's Church. I'll drop you at the hospital on my way."

Craig met up with Mike at the crime scene.

The police had roped off the area, and a crime-scene unit was searching it.

People gathered around but then, realizing there wasn't a body or anything else exciting to be seen, moved on quickly.

The crime scene was the small remaining parcel of churchyard that belonged to St. Augustine's of the Fields. While not as old as Trinity and St. Paul's, St Augustine's was, in Craig's eyes, both beautiful and fascinating. At a time when what was now downtown was pretty much the entire city and Wall Street was the site of a real wall built to protect the original settlers, the little church of St. Augustine's was actually in a field, thus the name.

There were no graves left in the little yard. While a

few revered priests rested in coffins inside altars inside the church, those consigned to the graveyard had long ago been moved out to a Catholic cemetery in Queens.

The churchyard still retained some beautiful sculptures, though. There were a Madonna and Child, a huge winged angel of victory, a weeping cherub and more. A few little concrete benches sat about, making the area, inside its two-foot stone wall, a peaceful, if small, place for contemplation.

Detective Mayo was there, standing just inside the low stone wall. Craig and Mike flashed their badges to the men in uniform guarding the area, then passed through the narrow wooden gate—though they could have stepped over the wall—and joined him.

"I called you in on this," Mayo told them, "because I pushed myself in on it since it happened so close to Miss Finnegan's family pub. I know you guys don't usually show up for a mugging. Hell, *I* don't usually show up for a mugging, since sadly, as we all know, a mugging in Manhattan isn't considered a major crime. But given that Kieran Finnegan has been unwittingly involved in two recent crimes and works at the family pub sometimes, I thought you two would be interested."

"Good call," Craig said. "Not to mention Bobby O'Leary is an acquaintance—almost a friend, I guess," he said, glancing at Mike.

"A friend," Mike agreed. "We spent a lot of last night talking with him." He looked at Craig. "When did he leave?"

"Right at closing," Craig said. "The very tail end of the night. The streets were almost empty, a few cars and cabs on the road, some people still out, but it was quiet."

Thinking back, he could easily see how a mugger could have emerged from the shadows to attack Bobby.

"My sense is this," Mayo said. "Someone knew when the pub closed and that O'Leary tended to stay till the bitter end. Our mugger waited here, in the shadows, behind this wall. O'Leary wouldn't have been worried about anything—probably walks this same way most nights of the week. Thing is, I doubt your usual mugger hides out in an old churchyard hoping someone will go by. I think Bobby was targeted."

"He's hanging in, right?" Mike asked.

"Tough old bird, so yeah, he's hanging in," Mayo said. "A crack to the head—forensics already told me he got a beating with a piece of wing broken off that angel over there—and some major bruising. The mugger might even have left him for dead. Anyway, Father Christopher—over there, on the church steps—came in about five this morning and found him. He called 911 right away."

Craig looked over at Father Christopher. He was a young priest, somber as he watched the action around him.

"Kaley, what ya got?" Mayo called, addressing one of the young women in a crime-scene coverall.

She rose from the patch of grass she'd been inspecting and headed their way.

"I don't know if what we've got helps much. We've found gum stuck under all the benches, not to mention on a few angels. Some candy wrappers, some beer cans…going to be hard to prove anything based on what we're finding. I'm pretty sure the attacker wore gloves, anyway. That piece of angel wing has blood on it, but it's going to be the victim's. There are no prints on it at all. We already tested. If he didn't wear gloves, he wiped it clean."

"Of course he did," Mayo said, shaking his head.

Craig looked from Kaley to the small churchyard.

"Okay," he said, "so Bobby O'Leary was walking down the street. The attacker, maybe even more than one, was waiting behind the wall—probably in the shade of that massive cherub over there."

"That's my thought, and it looks like it, the way the grass is trampled," Kaley said.

"Then the mugger grabbed Bobby and dragged him over the wall," Craig said.

She nodded. "Yep. Scrape marks on the stone."

"And then the bastard bashed him," Mike finished.

"Exactly." Mayo nodded grimly. "Like I said, this was a planned attack."

"Do you think the mugger meant to kill him?" Mike asked quietly.

"In my opinion, yes," Mayo said. "That broken wing was one wicked weapon. If they'd struck him just a bit differently, he would be dead. You see why I called you. And," he added, "the kicker is, Bobby O'Leary was found with his wallet in his pocket with all his credit cards and a couple hundred in cash."

Kieran hurried straight up to see Bobby. He was in the critical care unit, though, and she was stopped by a nurse before she could enter the hallway to his room.

"Are you family?" the nurse—Emily, according to her name tag—asked.

Kieran found herself glad that this woman was like a bulldog when it came to protecting her patients.

"Yes," Kieran lied quickly. They were *like* family,

and in the circumstances that would have to be good enough. "I'm his niece."

She didn't know why she'd added that; the lie she'd given would have been sufficient. Bobby really didn't have family, and at Finnegan's, people became family.

"He's in and out of consciousness and there's a cop waiting to take a statement from him—assuming he's ever able to give one. He's in pretty serious shape. I'm not allowed to give details—you'll have to talk to the doctor for those. You're not to distress him in any way. I've told the cops that, too. His life comes before anything else. You understand me?"

Kieran nodded, and Emily escorted her down the hallway.

There was a cop seated before the door, a copy of the *New York Times* in his hand. He stood as they approached.

"Vic, this is O'Leary's niece. She may sit there and hold his hand. If she starts to bother him in any way, shoot her." She winked.

"I promise not to disturb him in any way."

"Good. I try not to shoot people in hospitals," the cop told her. Then he winked, too.

Bobby was almost as pale as the sheets. His head was wrapped in what looked like a white turban.

She sat next to him, staring at the array of monitors attached to him and the IV that flowed into his veins.

Poor Bobby.

How the hell—*why the hell*—had this happened to him?

His eyes were closed. She didn't try to speak to him. His hand lay on the white sheet. She saw the gnarled old flesh and the spattering of liver spots. He had long fingers, calloused from a life of hard work.

She slipped her fingers around his and held his hand with no pressure, but with what she hoped was reassuring warmth.

She was sure he didn't even know she was there.

Then he squeezed her fingers.

She looked quickly at his face. His eyes were still closed.

But he had responded to her.

She sat back, grateful that he was alive. She was happy just to sit there and stay with him.

She heard a commotion in the hall and recognized Danny's voice.

She rose, still holding Bobby's hand, and tried to signal the police officer. "My brother. Um, Bobby's nephew!"

A moment later Danny was there. "He's—he's hanging in?" he asked anxiously.

She nodded.

Danny went to Bobby's other side and carefully took his other hand. A moment later, he looked at Kieran with relief. "He squeezed."

"Yeah," she said softly.

It wasn't long before Declan and Mary Kathleen arrived, and then Kevin. That was okay. They were family; even Declan had come in with the lie on his lips.

Poor Nurse Emily was having a fit. Only two people could be in the room, and that was that. And so they rotated, two of them in with Bobby, the others drinking coffee and pacing the waiting room.

Hours went by.

A doctor came in at last and spoke with them. Bobby

had a skull fracture; the big fear was water on the brain. He and the rest of the team wanted to wait before taking further steps. They would only operate if it was Bobby's only chance, because the operation came with serious risks.

"What can we do?" Kieran asked.

"If you're the praying sort, then pray," the doctor told them.

"We're Irish. We're good at that," Danny said. He looked over at Kieran, his expression anguished. "We're great at praying—and guilt," he said softly.

She felt her stomach flip.

Did Danny know something about what had happened to Bobby? Or, worse, about the robberies—and the murders?

# CHAPTER
# ELEVEN

Richard Eagan called an emergency interdepartmental task force meeting that morning, laying out flatly what they knew, what might be circumstantial, what they surmised—and what every law enforcement agency in the city needed to be looking out for.

The FBI, the US Marshals Service, city and state police, and Homeland Security were all involved.

Craig wasn't sure if he was glad to be appointed—with Mike—as colead on the investigation, seeing as they didn't seem to be getting anywhere.

Except Finnegan's, he thought unhappily.

And, of course, he was left to field questions such as, "What are we supposed to do? Stop and question anyone who's wearing a hoodie?"

After the Q and A, he wrapped up with an overview of what he *did* want everyone to do.

"Watch for individuals in hoodies behaving in a suspicious manner. I want the surveillance footage from all the robberies shown at every agency, so every man and woman out there is aware of who and what to look for. We're also posting twenty-four-hour surveillance in the Diamond District and at a rotating selection of jewelry stores across the city that carry high-end diamonds. We're working on a theory that the killers stalked the foursome that we apprehended last Monday in order to learn and copycat their MO. We have a partially complete list of places where the original thieves met and did some of their strategizing, places where the copycats might have eavesdropped on them. We'll have people at these locations, too, questioning staff to see if anyone noticed something that might help us, then cross-referencing that information looking for repeat customers, so to speak. We've already collected a massive amount of information, and you'll all have access to those files."

Mike said a few words next, and then Eagan spoke again when he was done. Everyone filed out a few minutes later, leaving the three FBI agents alone in the room.

Craig didn't wait to consult with the others; he pulled out his phone and dialed Kieran's number.

She didn't answer.

He dialed the hospital and found that there had been no change in Bobby O'Leary's condition.

He realized, as he hung up, that his director and partner were staring at him. "Checking on O'Leary," he said.

"Could have nothing to do with any of this," Eagan said.

"But it does. Somehow, I know it does," Craig said.

"Can we really afford to work off our guts on this one?" Eagan asked.

"Can we afford not to?" Craig asked in response, feeling a little desperate because he hadn't reached Kieran.

"All right, I guess I need to trust you on this. You're a good agent, Craig. You and Mike are a crack team, which is why I put you on lead. Follow the evidence *and* your gut wherever they take you. Just solve this thing," Eagan said.

He left the conference room. Mike and Craig were left alone.

"You really think the killers hang out at Finnegan's?" Mike asked.

"I think something is going on there."

"Think the Finnegans are involved?"

"No!" Craig protested, knowing even as he spoke that he sounded defensive.

They couldn't be.

Or rather, being honest with himself, he didn't want them to be.

Craig sat up suddenly. "I just thought of something."

Mike groaned. "Oh, God, what does that mean?"

"We worked a lot of different units, both of us, before landing here."

"So?"

"Come on."

"Where are we going?"

"My place."

"For?"

"A change of clothes."

Mike arched a brow.

"And faces. A change of clothes—and faces."


The Finnegan family was good at allotting tasks to make sure everything was covered, especially in times of crisis, Kieran thought.

Declan, in his role as eldest, created a schedule.

Danny had to work that day, but when he was done being a tour guide he would head back to the hospital.

Finnegan's opened at 11:00 a.m., but Rory, Pedro and Javier would have the kitchen going early, Debbie Buenger would open the bar and Mary Kathleen would join her to make sure opening would be covered. Declan himself would be there by eleven thirty.

Kieran would leave the hospital in time to make it to the pub by around twelve thirty, when the lunch crowd got going, and Kevin would stay at the hospital until Danny arrived. Once Kevin got to the pub, Kieran would return to the hospital and stay as long as they let her. Moving forward, Danny would be a floater and either stay at the hospital or come to the pub, depending on which seemed more important on the day.

At one point, as Kieran sat next to Bobby, nearly drowsing, she felt him squeeze her hand again.

Her eyes flew open, and she saw that Bobby was looking at her. He managed a weak smile and his lips were moving.

"Thank you," he said, and he closed his eyes again.

She looked across the bed at Kevin, who was staring at her.

"Did I just hear that?" he asked.

"Yes!" she said excitedly. "He spoke."

Kieran rose, easing her hand from Bobby's, and headed into the hall, looking for a doctor. She found Nurse Emily, who told her that even momentary consciousness was a very good sign, but they had to be patient. With luck he would wake up again soon.

As the lunch hour drew near, Kieran rose to leave.

Due to her recent experience in the subway, she opted to take a cab and made it to the pub without incident.

Saturday crowds could be a strange mix.

The pub was closer to downtown than not, so the business crowd that flooded the pub on weekdays wasn't around.

Saturday nights tended to be very busy, with tourists and random locals on top of their regular patrons.

The regulars all knew Bobby O'Leary and would understand that the Finnegan siblings had taken on the duty of watching over him.

When Kieran came in, she saw that Declan or someone had asked Julie to help out; she was wearing an apron and carrying a tray filled with frosty ales.

Julie saw Kieran walk in and paused with her heavy tray. "How's Bobby? Any change?" Her tone was worried.

"I think he's a little better. He opened his eyes for a minute and spoke," Kieran said.

One of the regulars overheard her, and in seconds her words were echoing through the entire place.

"Bobby is a fighter, that he is!" someone called out. "Three cheers for Bobby."

Cheers and applause filled the air.

"This really is an amazing place," Julie said, smiling. "In a city made up of neighborhoods, Finnegan's just might make this area the best."

"I'm not about to disagree, Now, where am I needed?" Kieran asked, smiling.

"You're always a godsend behind the bar, you know that. But," she said, lowering her voice, "if you and your brother don't mind, I'd love some help here in the bar. Mr. Krakowsky is here."

"Krakowsky?" Kieran said blankly.

"Gary's boss, Simon Krakowsky." She nodded in his direction. "I don't think Gary would have arranged to meet him here after the last time he came in, but I'm still worried he'll show up. And Mr. Krakowsky loves you. You saved his store, after all, running after those guys and jumping into that van."

"I didn't run after anyone, much less jump into that van. I was dragged at what I thought was gunpoint," Kieran protested.

"Whatever, he adores you. He's told the world about you saying 'Any decent person would lend a hand.' But he's still Gary's boss, you know? Please, I don't mind helping at all, just please don't make me wait on him."

"Where are Mary Kathleen and Debbie?"

"Running their butts off over there," Julie told her, nodding toward the dining room.

The bar area held five tables, while the dining room held twenty, along with the stage.

"Gotcha, not a problem," Kieran said. "Just let me set my things down."

Declan was behind the bar, moving at the speed of light. Kieran set her jacket and bag beneath the bar, explained Julie's request to her brother and headed to Simon Krakowsky's table, passing several tables on the way.

Austin and Libby Anderson were at the first—regulars. She flashed them a quick smile. She didn't recognize the two men at the second table, both long-haired and bearded, one in classic John Lennon wire-rims, and both wearing T-shirts advertising a band called Resurgence. A guitar was propped up next to the one with the longer beard. She'd never heard of the group, but New York was overrun with up-and-coming bands—and, of course, plenty that would never make it at all.

She reached Simon Krakowsky's table. He was eating alone, but she could easily understand Julie's fear that he might be joined by one of his employees, specifically Gary.

"Mr. Krakowsky," she said, smiling as she stood beside him. "How are you?"

"I'm just fine, Miss Finnegan," he said, nodding gravely. "Largely thanks to you, of course."

"I'm happy that you feel that way, but, really, I was a hostage and simply went into self-preservation mode."

"Maybe, but your quick thinking might have saved our lives."

"We were being held up by men with water pistols," she reminded him.

"I heard that on the news, but you didn't know that as it was happening."

"Self-preservation," she repeated. "But thank you. Are you dining alone today?"

He nodded. "Felt the need to be surrounded by good people," he said. "Even if I'm on my own. I heard about your friend being mugged. I'm so sorry. I don't know what this world is coming to."

"There's still a lot of good in the world, Mr. Krakowsky. And Bobby's hanging on. I believe he's going to make it."

"I'll pray for him," Mr. Krakowsky said. Then he shook his head. "Seems like just yesterday that I was in here with friends and the world felt safe."

"The world has never really been safe," she said.

"*My* world was safe. Humdrum, day in, day out."
He was quiet for a moment, then pointed to the bar. "I
was in here with my friend Harry Belvedere. Do you
know Harry?"

"I might. I'm not sure."

"He owns Vintage by Victoria. He named the place
after his late wife."

Kieran paused, frowning. "That's the jewelry store
that was just held up. And it's where…"

"Yes. Where that poor young girl was killed."

"You two were in here together?" she asked him.

"That's what I just said. I had a shipment of stones
coming in from Africa—clean stones, by the way. I always check. I'm not a broker for any bastards making
their money off blood diamonds."

"I believe that you run a very ethical business," Kieran assured him. "But you were *here*, talking about
diamonds?"

"Harry needed some stones to restore a piece of estate jewelry. He specializes in antique jewelry. He's
devastated. That poor, poor girl."

"Yes," Kieran said. She felt frozen in place.

She'd known the thieves had been in Finnegan's.
Now it seemed that the killers might have been here,
as well.

Listening. Stalking her family's clientele. *Picking
their next target.*

She was heartsick—and furious. How dare they sully
Finnegan's, where everyone was welcome, where hospitality meant everything.

"I know. It's horrible," she said.

Mr. Krakowsky nodded gravely, and then smiled,

nodding to someone across the room. Kieran turned to follow his gaze. He was looking at Julie.

"I probably shouldn't be saying this, but… Gary is a good employee, but I have to question his intelligence. Julie is one of the loveliest women I've ever met. Divorce is hard, but marriages do fall apart. Still, there are ways to conduct yourself and ways not to. The man is an idiot, leaving her for some of the women I've seen him with recently." He met her eyes. "I hear you asked him to leave the pub the other night."

"I did," she said firmly.

"I told him the same thing, said he needs to have the good sense to stay out of this place. He's tight with Jimmy, though, and I guess this has been McManus's watering hole since your dad was running it."

She'd been there too long, and she was starting to feel her anger at Gary growing all over again. She had to shake off the way she was feeling and do her job.

"Look at me," she said with forced brightness. "Standing and chatting in the middle of the lunch rush. I'd better get to work or I'll hear about it from my brother later. What can I get you today?"

"I'm sorry. Selfish of me to monopolize you. A stout, please—surprise me with which. And that chicken pot pie thing your chef does so well."

"Coming right up," Kieran promised him. She poured and delivered his stout, then headed back behind the bar to help, since it would be some time before his food was up.

She found herself pausing to look at the two musicians. They were scribbling on music paper, apparently working on a song. Their half-full beer glasses and empty plates sat in front of them.

She walked over to pick up the plates. "Can I get you anything else?" she asked.

They both looked up at her.

"No, thank you," said the full-bearded one, who she noticed had dark eyes versus his friend's green ones.

She nodded and stepped away. Something about them seemed odd. And vaguely familiar.

Surely she would have noticed them if they'd been in before.

Maybe she was going overboard looking for anything suspicious.

Besides, bearded men always looked suspicious. Or creepy.

At least they weren't wearing hoodies.

She put the empty plates in the bin under the bar and went back to work.

Every time someone came in and wanted to talk about Bobby, it seemed the rest of the place wanted to drink a toast to his recovery.

Around three thirty, Kevin came in. He assured her that Bobby was stable and his vital signs were good. A new nurse, Molly, was on duty, and she had been more forthcoming than steely-eyed Nurse Emily.

"Did he open his eyes again?" Kieran asked her brother.

He shook his head. "Maybe he's waiting for you," he said, smiling.

"I'm going to stay there tonight," Kieran said.

"I figured. I'll be there early in the morning," he told her.

She said goodbye to Declan and the others, then noted that Mr. Krakowsky was still there and that Jimmy Mc-

Manus—minus Gary Benton, thank heavens—was at the bar.

Kevin saw her out and safely into a cab.

When she returned to Bobby's room, an officer she hadn't met yet was on duty, as well as the new nurse. The officer seemed aware that she was coming and rose to open the door to Bobby's room for her. She thanked him as she entered.

Danny was in a chair beside the bed, holding one of Bobby's hands and apparently dozing. He heard her arrival, though, and blinked and yawned, then smiled at her.

"Any news?" she asked.

"No news is good news," he told her. "They took him out for some scans a bit ago. One of the doctors will be back in soon."

She nodded and took up a seat across the bed from her brother, taking Bobby's other hand and squeezing it lightly.

Nothing at first.

Then she was certain she felt a slight squeeze in return.

"Everything okay at the pub?" Danny asked her softly.

"Yes," she said, then hesitated. She wanted to talk to him openly, wanted to tell him what Simon Krakowsky had told her.

But she didn't want to have that conversation over the body of a friend who was fighting for his life.

"Yes, everything is fine," she said. "I guess we should be quiet and let Bobby rest, huh?"

"No, the doctor who came in before they took Bobby

out for his scan—Dr. Huang—told me that we should talk all we want, to each other and to Bobby."

"Oh?"

"Yes, he might hear us on some level, and it might help draw him back to consciousness."

"Oh, well…great."

She still didn't want to talk about the pub, though.

"So how was your day?" she asked him. "How was your tour group?"

"Fantastic," he said. "A bunch of college kids. It always seems so strange to me that people come to New York City to shop or go to Broadway shows, but they never come downtown. They don't see Trinity and St. Paul's. They have no clue that the Dutch settled New Amsterdam in 1609 and that the English didn't take over the colony until 1664. They don't know that the British held the city during much of the Revolution, or even that it was the capital for a while. They know nothing about Washington being here, about—" Danny stopped abruptly and gave her a wry smile. "Sorry. I just love this city so much."

Kieran grinned. "I love the city, too, Danny."

"Of course you do." He sighed. "I'll never get rich, of course. Leading tours. But I truly love it, and I hope I get to do it forever."

"Of course you do. And you know every little nook and cranny of it, too," she said.

Her own words suddenly disturbed her.

Yes, her brother knew the city. Knew every neighborhood, every street and every alley.

She was immediately furious with herself. Her brother was no killer.

"Our building has been there since 1833," she reminded him.

He nodded. "Built as office space, a landmark back then at four floors. And a Finnegan opened the first pub there in 1845."

"We're remarkable," she said, smiling.

She felt Bobby squeeze her hand and quickly looked down at him.

His eyes were open, and he was looking at her again. She thought that his lips even twitched into an almost-smile.

He spoke, his words raspy and barely a whisper on the air.

She couldn't make them out and looked over at Danny, a question in her eyes.

He smiled. "He said we should keep talking."

Bobby's eyes fluttered shut. She could have sworn that almost-smile was still there, though.

"So, who are you taking where tomorrow?" she asked.

As Danny rattled on about his plans for the next day, she half listened.

And half worried.

"Everyone looks pretty normal to me," Mike said.

Craig lowered his head, grinning. His partner looked anything but normal himself, with his neatly trimmed beard and mustache, and green contact lenses.

"They *are* normal," Craig said. He was watching Krakowsky. The older man had stayed at his table by the bar all day, and he didn't seem about to leave.

Then again, he and Mike were still there, too.

It had taken just about all his resolve not to get up

and leave when Kieran did. He was afraid, he realized, of her even being on the street alone.

Which was unreasonable, he knew.

He and Mike had watched customers come and go—or come and stay—throughout the day, many of them people they'd seen on previous visits.

He'd overheard snatches of Kieran's conversation with Mr. Krakowsky, and he was more convinced than ever that both sets of thieves had been here, either to share information or pilfer it.

As the afternoon wore on into evening, they saw many if not most of the pub's regulars. The man who had been with Gary Benton—he heard Declan greet him as Jimmy McManus—was there with friends, luckily not including Gary. They sat where they could see one of the screens and watched a college baseball game.

"I thought your girlfriend had us pegged there for a moment," Mike said.

"My what?"

"Kieran. When she walked by, I thought she was about to ask us what the hell we thought we were doing. She would have figured it out if she hadn't left."

"Maybe."

"What was that accent you were doing, anyway? Slavic-Hispanic?" Mike teased.

"My best Romanian," Craig said. Then he went still.

"Krakowsky has company," he said.

"Oh?" Mike murmured, turning his head surreptitiously.

It was Harry Belvedere.

The two men hugged in greeting. Then Belvedere sat down, and the two talked quietly, leaning in head to head.

"Probably commiserating," Mike said.

Craig nodded. "Comparing notes on being robbed?"

"Not much to compare. Krakowsky got back his jewels and no one was hurt. Belvedere lost his best pieces, and worse, a woman was killed."

"The point is," Craig said quietly, "they're here together now, so the odds are they've been here together before. And I'm betting *both* groups of thieves have been here, too."

"Awfully coincidental that they were apparently all here at the same time. Think our bad guys could have been tipped off by someone near and dear to the pub?" Mike asked.

Craig shot him an unreadable look, then started to rise.

"We're leaving?" Mike asked.

"I think we've found out everything we can here, at least for now. And I'm more and more convinced that Maria Antonescu, intentionally or otherwise, abetted the robbery that led to her own murder. We have to ID the guy she was dating, her secret lover."

"And we're going to find him by...?"

"Actually, I think he's here. Maybe not here right now, but I think he's someone we've seen in here before. We need to change clothes and head back to Clean Cut Office Services."

Mike groaned. "It's Saturday. You really think Ms. Mannerly is going to be there?"

Craig nodded. "I do, because I'm going to call her and tell her to meet us there. Though there's another stop I want to make first." He signaled for their check. Julie handed it to him with a smile and not even a whiff of suspicion.

Not bad, Craig thought, for a guy who hadn't gone undercover in years.

"Hey," Mike said, just as Craig was laying down money for their bill. He nodded toward the door.

They both stood there as assistant director Richard Eagan walked in and headed straight past them to the bar.

Craig and Mike stared at each other in surprise, but they managed to contain their laughter until they were out on the sidewalk.

Toward midnight, Kieran made Danny leave.

After all, he had a tour to lead in the morning.

He protested at first, but she finally convinced him that she was just fine. She was in a busy hospital, and a cop was sitting right outside Bobby's door.

Once he was gone, she watched Bobby hopefully, looking for signs of returning consciousness. She hadn't understood everything Dr. Huang had said, but the overall prognosis was good. There was no water building up on Bobby's brain, and the swelling was going down.

It was about thirty minutes after Danny left that Bobby opened his eyes, looked at Kieran and smiled.

"Angel," he said.

She flushed. "Oh, Bobby. Please. You know me well enough to know I'm no angel."

He started to say something, but she could see it was an effort for him.

"I don't think you should be talking too much. I'm just so glad you're awake. You really took a wallop on the head. Did you see who did it?" she asked anxiously.

He winced. "A large cemetery cherub with a bat? Ah, lass, no. I was walking—sober as can be, you know that—and suddenly it felt like I was flying. Except that I was scraping stone. And there was a big man there, aye, a big man. I'm pretty sure he was dark haired, but it was a chilly night. He might have been wearing some kind of a cape. You know—like Dracula." He was quiet for a moment. "He wasn't alone, either. Someone said, 'He's a goner, and I never even got to ask him,' and I don't think you'd say that unless you were talking to someone else. So...did they rob me blind?"

She shook her head. "They didn't take anything, Bobby."

"They didn't, eh?"

She couldn't tell whether he was surprised or not.

As if to himself, he murmured, "What do they think I know?"

"What are you talking about, Bobby? Who are 'they'?"

He shook his head. "I don't know. But they must have been there in the pub at some point that night, and they must have been after something more valuable than my wallet. I remember old Krakowsky—you know, Gary's boss—bragging about his new shipment of stones. There were a bunch of jewelers in there that day. They thought they were so discreet, but I sit at the bar and I hear a lot. But," he added, "not enough, I think."

Kieran heard footsteps in the hall and looked up to see Craig standing outside the room with Mike, speaking with the policeman guarding the door.

Bobby suddenly gripped her wrist in a fierce hold, shockingly strong for his condition.

She turned to look at him. His features were tense.

"Don't tell them anything, not yet. You can say I've

opened my eyes a few times. I'm not ready to talk, do you understand? I'm not ready."

Bobby's grip fell away as he relaxed his features and closed his eyes.

Seconds later special agent Craig Frasier walked in.

# CHAPTER
# TWELVE

Craig left Mike in the hall, talking to the officer there, as he entered the room. The latest report was that Bobby O'Leary had yet to reach full consciousness, though the doctors said things were going well.

Kieran was sitting by the old man's bed, her fingers curled around his hand where it lay on the covers. She was leaning down, resting her head on the bars of the bed, as if she had been resting. He saw that she was sitting in a chair that could fold down into a bed, and something told him that she was planning to use it, stay for the night, keep her eye on Bobby and hold his hand.

"Anything?" he asked her softly.

Her long dark auburn hair seemed especially vibrant tonight, falling over the white sheet. She lifted her head, and her eyes were especially blue in the harsh lighting.

"I think he's doing well. The doctor said there's no sign of water building up on his brain, no swelling." She glanced down at Bobby, and Craig thought she sounded a little uneasy when she spoke again. "He's opened his eyes a few times, but it never lasts."

"Good to hear. I've been calling in all day, but all I got was 'no change, stable condition.' I'm really hoping he's going to be able to help us out."

"Do you think he saw anything?" she asked. "If he was attacked from behind…"

"He may still be able to tell us something. Even if he couldn't see his attacker, he might have noticed something. Like the scent of soap or aftershave," Craig said. "Or maybe he heard something, his attacker's voice, the way he breathed…something. You never know. All we can do for now is hope."

"It was probably some random thing," Kieran said. "Wrong place, wrong time."

"Or it might have been someone who knew he spent his days in the pub and thought he might have heard something or know something," Craig said.

"Do you really think so?" Kieran asked. "It seems strange that…that someone would go to such lengths to attack Bobby, of all people. I still think it was a robbery like—"

"Nothing was taken."

"Maybe the mugger was interrupted. Maybe a taxi went by, or even a cop car."

She sounded defensive, Craig thought. And that wasn't good.

"Kieran, don't you want this solved—no matter what?" he asked her.

"Of course!"

The door opened, and a nurse walked in. She looked Craig up and down and nodded—with approval, he hoped—and then turned to Kieran. "Honey, you want some bedding for that chair?"

"It's not necessary."

"You might as well. You need to sleep, and we have monitors all over Mr. O'Leary. If anything happens, we'll know at the nurses' station."

"In that case, thank you," Kieran said.

The nurse left, and Craig smiled at Kieran. "I figured you'd be staying," he said softly.

"Of course."

"Listen, we really need to talk to him, and as quickly as possible," Craig said. "You'll call me if he wakes up and is coherent?"

She didn't look at him as she nodded.

"Well, then," he said softly. "I'll see you in the morning."

She still didn't look up.

Because she was lying to him. He knew it. What he didn't know was why.

Or just what, exactly, she was lying to him about.

Kieran wasn't sure if Bobby O'Leary was still faking it at that point or if he was really out of it again.

Whichever, he didn't speak anymore that night.

Molly brought sheets, a pillow and a blanket, and Kieran did her best to settle in and sleep for the night.

Time seemed to tick by very slowly as she found herself unable to sleep. She lay there and thought about everything that had happened. She wondered what Craig knew that he wasn't telling her.

She worried about Daniel.

He would *never* kill anyone.

But was he involved, even unwittingly?

When she wasn't worrying, she was remembering the events of two nights ago.

Thinking about Craig.

Every time she should have backed away, she'd been incapable of doing so. She genuinely cared about him.

Or was it pure physical attraction?

Something in the underlying scent of his skin that sent her mind reeling and made everything else in her ache with longing?

Angry with herself, she groaned, then tossed and turned and finally caught a few minutes' sleep every so often, waking up every time a member of the medical staff came in.

At seven, when she woke up for good, she was surprised to see someone peeking in the door, and it wasn't one of her brothers or even Mary Kathleen. Julie had come.

"Hey," Julie whispered softly, tiptoeing in. "How are you doing? How's Bobby doing?"

"Well, I think," Kieran whispered, trying to get her "bed" back into chair mode as quietly as possible. She almost managed it, but the sheets got tangled in the mechanism and she had to start over. "Sorry, Julie, just give me a minute here. There's a chair on the other side of the bed, if you want to sit down."

She finally righted her chair, bundling the sheets to the side. When she turned, Julie was holding Bobby's hand, Bobby was awake and they were both grinning at her.

"Bobby!" Kieran said. "You're good?"

"Ah, why does everyone misuse that word? If I said I was, it would mean I was without sin, or maybe out there in the world doing something good for someone.

Now, am I well? Yes, feeling much better, lass, especially knowing you were there beside me, watching over me during the night. Thank you." He turned to Julie. "And you, too, of course."

"I just got here," Julie said with a grin. "You have to give me some time to do some *good*."

Bobby's smile faded slightly, but he forced it back into place. "Where are those wretched doctors? When are they going to let me out of here?"

"Bobby! You're in critical care, so you're not going anywhere right now," Kieran told him firmly.

"They have any decent food around here?" he asked.

"I'm not sure if you're allowed to have food yet," Kieran said.

"No food? Now how will I be healing without something substantial in me belly, eh?"

"There's good stuff running through that IV line," Kieran said.

"I'll go out and ask about breakfast," Julie said.

"Now that, my lass, would be doing a body some *good*!" he said.

When Julie left the room, he turned to Kieran, and spoke swiftly and fiercely. "I'll tell those coppers what happened when I walked down the street, but don't you repeat anything else I said. I'll call you a liar, do you understand me? You're not to repeat anything I said."

"Bobby, if you know something—if someone at the pub has been threatening you or anyone else in any way—we have to tell the cops, and the FBI, too," Kieran said.

"If I actually knew something, don't you think I'd say so and have the bastards locked up?" Bobby asked, staring at her very seriously. "Lass, I'm an old man, alone in some ways but not in others. Wife gone, never blessed with wee ones, and I can't even be having me a pint o' stout now and then, but I *like* living. I *love* my life. I think someone out there thinks I've heard things I shouldn't. Thing is, I don't know what I've heard. Don't know why they didn't shoot me, except that wouldn't look much like a mugging now, would it? Stupid bastards forgot to steal my wallet, though." He pointed a finger at her. "I'll be talking to Declan. Meanwhile, don't you be in that pub alone. Don't any of you be in there alone."

He had her curious, but also frightened, really frightened.

She couldn't ask him anything more, though, because at that moment, Julie walked back in.

"Liquids," she said.

"What?" Kieran asked blankly.

"Bobby, they're starting you on liquids. Clear liquids," Julie said.

"Liquids, eh?" Bobby said. "That's something, I guess."

"The nurses are changing shifts right now, but there's a lovely aide who's going to come in soon with apple juice. You hold that down and you get broth, and if that goes well… Jell-O. And then maybe you get to eat."

"Our Sweet Lady Mother and Jesus be praised," Bobby said. "Broth, did you say? Why, my mouth is just watering already."

"Behave," Kieran told him. "You'll drink your apple juice first and love it, and then we'll talk about broth."

"Aye, Miss Finnegan," Bobby said. "Whatever you say."

Julie had been standing with her hands behind her

back. Now she produced a cup with a spoon in it. "I brought you ice chips," she told him.

They all laughed.

"Maybe juice won't be so bad," he muttered, once his dry, cracked lip had been soothed.

A new nurse came in, Jarrod, tall and fit, with a quick smile and easy manner. He was pleased to see that Bobby was doing so well. He was there to take Bobby for another scan, but he expected positive results, given how alert Bobby was.

Bobby told the nurse about his desire for a Danish.

"If all goes well, you can have one in a few hours. Ice chips were good?"

"As sweet as me Sainted Mother's tit," Bobby said.

Jarrod grinned, glancing at Kieran and Julie, then left, telling them that Officer Clayton was on duty outside the room and would be happy to know Bobby was doing so well.

Bobby's smile faded the minute the three of them were alone in the room again. "I suppose the lawmen will be here any minute with their questions. Aye, and that's fine. I'm up to talking now."

No sooner had he finished speaking than the door opened. An aide was there with a plastic pitcher of ice water and a glass of apple juice. She warned Bobby to drink slowly.

The minute she was gone, Officer Clayton walked in, a nice young guy in his early twenties, and told Bobby how happy he was to see him doing so well.

As soon as he left, Julie said, "I guess everyone is hoping you can help catch the guys who hurt you, Bobby."

"Don't you think that I'd like them caught?" Bobby asked softly.

A technician came and rolled Bobby down for the promised scan; Julie and Kieran stayed in the room, looking worriedly at each other.

"This is really terrifying," Julie told Kieran.

"Yes," Kieran said, wondering if Julie suspected that Finnegan's was somehow connected to the jewelry store robberies.

Julie leaned forward. "Kieran, you be careful. You're always coming and going at odd hours, and you never think to be afraid, no matter how late it is."

"I'll be careful. We all will."

Julie's eyes brightened. "Not to mention now you've got an FBI guy in your corner."

"What?"

"Oh, Kieran, please. Maybe you two think you're acting cool, but there's something in the air when you're together. Something good. Are you sleeping with him yet?" She read the truth in Kieran's eyes. "Oh! You *are* sleeping with him. Don't look as if you just ate a pack of peppers. I'm not judging."

Julie stopped speaking. Her eyes had wandered to the door. Kieran looked in that direction, too.

She wished she could crawl under Bobby's hospital bed.

Craig was back, and Mike was with him.

If such a thing as spontaneous combustion existed, Kieran was pretty sure it would have happened to her at that moment. She felt as if she was burning up and knew her face must be an unbecoming shade of crimson.

Mike was one good guy, she realized. He was pretending that they hadn't heard a thing, though she knew that both men must have heard at least the tail end of Julie's speech.

"Good morning, Kieran, Julie," Mike said. "We were relieved when we heard that Bobby is doing so well."

"He's out for a scan," Julie said quickly.

"Yes," Craig said. "We heard from the officer outside." His eyes turned to regard Kieran. They were frost blue, betraying nothing. "Why don't you two go down and get some coffee, maybe even breakfast?" he suggested. "Detective Mayo is going to be joining us in a minute, and we need to talk to Bobby when he comes back."

Julie was instantly on her feet. "Oh, yes, coffee," she said, a little too much enthusiasm in her voice.

Kieran stood. "Of course," she said.

She had to walk past Craig. He was the epitome of an FBI agent, crisp and clean in his dark blue suit. As she got closer, she realized that he must have showered recently, because his hair was still damp. She wanted to reach out and run her hands down the fabric of his suit or trace the freshly shaved contours of his face.

She managed to flee the room quickly, Julie at her heels.

"I'm so, so sorry about embarrassing you that way," Julie said.

"It's all right," Kieran said.

"I still feel terrible. And now his partner knows, too. I hope I didn't get him in trouble."

"It's all right," Kieran repeated. "Really."

"But it's true, right?" Julie said. "You *are* sleeping with him."

They were standing in front of the elevators, surrounded by both visitors and staff, and Julie wasn't exactly whispering. Embarrassed, Kieran said, "Julie, keep it down. Please."

"Sorry," Julie said, lowering her voice. "It's just that being in the middle of a divorce, I guess I'm living vicariously through you. The way he's built, is he like that...everywhere?"

"Julie!" Kieran protested again as they stepped into an elevator with a half dozen other people.

Julie grinned and made a motion that indicated she was zipping her lips.

On the ground floor, they headed for the cafeteria. Kieran realized that she'd spent half of yesterday at Finnegan's with a chef who worked wonders with every dish he created and she hadn't eaten a thing. She'd been in such an emotional whirl that the thought hadn't occurred to her.

It shouldn't now, with danger seemingly everywhere, but it did.

A few minutes later—armed with eggs and toast and the largest cup of coffee available—she joined Julie in a booth. She nodded curiously at the three to-go cups of coffee sitting in the center of the table.

"I thought the guys might want coffee when we go back upstairs," Julie said. "But right now I want to know everything. How did it happen? And when? Do your brothers know? Was it like a fantasy? Did he drive you home, then sweep you up the stairs? Or were you at his apartment?" Julie giggled. "It wasn't on a table in the storeroom like in *The Postman Always Rings Twice*, that old movie we just watched on Netflix, was it?"

"Julie! I never said that I was sleeping with him," Kieran protested.

"But you are—whether you said it or not. Now that we have an in with the FBI, maybe he can arrest Gary."

"Julie, Gary has to do something that warrants an arrest," Kieran said.

"He's done plenty to warrant an arrest," Julie said. "Think about my poor dogs."

"And when he was abusing the dogs, *you* should have called the police," Kieran said.

Julie waved a hand in the air. "They wouldn't have done anything. They'd have told me to call animal control, and animal control might have tried to take Benji and Sally away from me. I couldn't take that chance."

"I'm afraid someone can't be arrested just for being a jerk," Kieran said.

Julie's hands were wrapped around her coffee cup, as if for comfort, and she was staring down at the dark surface. "No," she agreed softly, then looked up. "But, Kieran, I like him. I like your guy. He was so nice to me at the pub the other night." She giggled. "A harem! Gary thinks Craig has all of us. That's too funny. He's actually jealous, even while he's bringing his bleached blonde bimbo into our apartment and sleeping with her in my bed."

"It *is* your bed. Get it back."

Julie shook her head. "I don't want it back. Ever. I'd always think of it as filthy." She sighed. "Look at me. I'm a horrible person, teasing you and moaning about Gary when Bobby is still in the hospital."

"I think Bobby is going to make it. I really do," Kieran said. "Think we should get back up there? The guys probably prefer their coffee hot."

Julie nodded, and they headed out.

* * *

Back upstairs, they discovered the hall had become a busy place in their absence. A new and different doctor was there and entered the room as they approached. The officer on duty was alert in his chair, and Declan and Danny were leaning against the wall, waiting for their chance to see Bobby. Inside the room, Craig and Mike had been joined by an older man who appeared to wear years of trial and weariness on his face, and the three of them were talking with Bobby, who was back in his bed.

"What a good sister," Danny said, helping himself to one of the cups of coffee Kieran carried.

"Nice of you," Declan said, taking one from Julie. "And one for Officer Hunt here. Thanks."

Kieran looked at Julie, who shrugged.

"I'll head back down for more," Julie said. "You know, for the guys in the room who are actually working," she added lightly, then headed back toward the elevator.

Declan turned to Kieran and said, "Bobby's last scan came out really well. Lots of medical jargon that I didn't understand, but the upshot is that he's out of the danger zone. He'll be moved to a different room this afternoon and kept another day or so, and then he can leave."

Officer Hunt smiled at her. "I'm not surprised you've stayed with your friend. 'Any decent person would lend a hand,' right?"

Kieran smiled weakly. It wasn't that it was a bad motto. She just hadn't really wanted to be a creator of mottoes.

Or recognized so easily by strangers.

Especially men in hoodies.

Bobby, she reminded herself, had not been attacked by a man in a hoodie. But even Bobby seemed to believe that he'd been attacked by someone who'd been in Finnegan's.

"We're *all* still worried about him," Danny explained. "Who knows whether this is over or not."

Kieran felt a knot forming in her stomach. So much for the eggs. She met her brothers' eyes. "You think someone was really after Bobby? That it wasn't a random attack?" She spoke in a normal tone, seeing as Danny had already included the officer in their conversation.

"Who knows what happened?" Declan said.

As he spoke, the door to Bobby's room opened, and the doctor left. Mike and Craig joined them in the hall, followed by Detective Mayo.

Introductions were made, and then Declan asked, "Was Bobby able to help you at all?"

"Well, if tall, dark and wearing a vampire cape helps, yes," Mike said.

"There was more than one person in on the attack," Craig said.

"Coffee!" Julie announced, joining them and handing around the cups.

"I've seen you before. You come into Finnegan's now and then," Declan said, addressing Mayo.

"I do indeed," Mayo agreed, nodding to Declan and glancing over at Craig and Mike. He shrugged. "My family hails from County Mayo, Ireland. My great-grandfather was one of the many who headed to New York in the middle of the nineteenth century during the great potato famine. Finnegan's is like a touch of the home I never knew. And," he added, "cops love the place."

"We do have plenty of cops around," Declan agreed.

"Well, pleasure, and I'll be moving on," Mayo said. "Craig, Mike—we'll keep in touch," he said, then headed down the hall. He paused to turn back and lift his coffee to Julie. "Thank you," he said.

"Pleasure," she assured him.

Declan looked at Craig and Mike, his expression serious. "I don't like it," he said. "I don't like it one bit." He shook his head. "It's no secret that we really do have off-duty cops in the place all the time. You'd think people would know that and misbehave somewhere else."

"One would think," Danny murmured.

Declan looked over at his sister. "Kieran, go home. You worked all week. You were caught up in a robbery on Monday and then involved in that subway thing two days later. Last night you slept here at the hospital. Go home. Get some sleep. Julie, why don't you go with her? I have a few free hours to hang here, and Danny can stay until tonight."

"Danny has to work today," Kieran said.

"But I can be back for tonight," Danny said.

"I just got here, and I had plenty of sleep last night. I can help out here or at the pub, wherever you need me," Julie said.

"There, you see? Everything is covered," Declan said. "I'll just see you home and—"

"Declan, I know how to hail a cab. I've lived in New York my whole life," Kieran reminded him.

Declan hesitated, and Kieran realized that her brother didn't want her leaving alone.

Craig quickly stepped in. "Mike and I can take Kieran home, see that she's bolted into her apartment."

"Thank you," Declan said. "Now get going, sis. You need a break."

"Declan, I'm all right," Kieran said.

"No, you're not. You look like hell, like you slept twisted in a knot."

"Someone needs to stay with Bobby tonight," she said stubbornly.

"I can sleep here," Julie said. "I'm mostly working from home now anyway."

"We'll see," Kieran said. "I may be back. But right now I'm going to tell Bobby goodbye, if you'll excuse me."

She still felt a little embarrassed around Craig and Mike, but they'd offered their help and she knew she had no choice but to accept it.

She moved quickly past them and into Bobby's room. Leaning down, she gave him a kiss on the cheek, and then met his eyes and whispered, "Bobby, if you know something—anything—about something going on at Finnegan's, you have to tell the cops."

"If I actually knew anything, I would," he told her. "You leaving?"

"Not if you don't want me to."

He smiled at that. "Lass, get out of here and quit fussing over me. Let me have some rest."

She smiled. "I'll see you soon."

"That you will, lass, that you will."

Declan entered the room just then and greeted Bobby cheerfully.

"You're in responsible hands now," Kieran told Bobby. "I'll see you all soon."

Declan caught her before she could leave. For a moment he held her in a tight embrace. "Be careful," he warned her. "Make sure your door is locked and bolted."

"Yes, sir," she assured him, heading out.

"See you all later," Kieran said to the group gathered in the hall.

Danny looked over at her. "Call me if you get cabin fever. And don't leave your place without at least one of us in tow, okay?"

"Don't forget, I'm here, too," Julie said.

"Thanks," Kieran called, leaving.

Craig and Mike stepped up and flanked her, as if instinct allowed them to fall into protective formation instantly.

As they waited for the elevator, she tried to appear nonchalant. Tired and nonchalant.

She couldn't help but wonder just how much the two men had heard of what Julie had been saying.

Had Mike already known that his partner was sleeping with her?

Had Craig talked about her? Said something like "Hell, yeah, nothing like an auburn-haired bartender," with Mike replying along the lines of "Nice piece of ass, my friend, nice piece of ass."

No. They wouldn't talk like that. She didn't know why she was so certain of it, but she just was. They had class.

Like her brothers. She'd heard them talk among themselves often enough. They could tease, they could even make the occasional off-color remark. But they weren't...crass.

Gary Benton, though. *He* was crass.

She mentally shuddered, just thinking about the man.

The elevator came, interrupting her thoughts, and a few minutes later the three of them headed out to the street.

It was a perfect spring day, and their car was parked just down the street, its official decal protecting it from tickets and tow trucks.

Craig opened the front passenger door for her, but she hesitated. "Mike, you can ride up here. I'll just be hopping out when we get to my place."

"I like the backseat," Mike said, rolling his eyes. "You've driven with him, right?"

"You should drive so well, old man," Craig teased him back.

She didn't want to make a scene. She just wanted to get home and retire to the comfort and tranquillity of her own bed.

No, forget tranquillity. Her bed would only make her think about the last time she'd slept there.

Maybe she could just nap on the couch.

Craig drove quickly and competently. "Any new insights?" he asked her.

Kieran immediately felt fearful at his words because now she knew Finnegan's was involved.

But not any member of the Finnegan family!

"I wish," she murmured. "What about you? Oh, yeah, you can't tell me or you'd have to kill me."

"Ongoing investigation," he said.

"All I know right now is that I'm really tired and that I'm really, *really* grateful Bobby's going to be okay."

Mike leaned forward, his head between Craig's and Kieran's. "Bobby say anything to you?"

"Other than that the guy who attacked him seemed to be wearing a vampire cape?" Kieran asked.

"Yes," Mike said.

She shook her head, feeling as if she was lying when she really wasn't. She just wasn't telling them everything, that was all.

"We're all worried," she said honestly. "We have diamond buyers and sellers and jewelry store owners as customers."

"Like Mr. Krakowsky, Gary's boss," Craig said.

She nodded. "Like Mr. Krakowsky," she agreed.

Sunday morning traffic was light. They were at her place in no time. She started to get out of the car, but Craig was there before she could set foot on the sidewalk. She looked up at him as he reached to give her a hand.

She hesitated and then took it.

Mike was out of the car, as well, but only to take the front seat now that she was out of it.

"It's broad daylight on a Sunday morning," she said, and managed a rueful smile. "We should be at church. On Sundays Finnegan's opens with a traditional roast at one, and we only serve a limited menu. We have a lot of good Catholics among our clientele," she told him. "Of course, this is New York. We also have a rabbi who comes in, and pretty much every other religion, even atheists and—"

"You're babbling," Craig interrupted. "Let's get you up to your apartment."

Craig didn't follow her in this time. He was all business, with his sunglasses and FBI-sanctioned suit.

"Lock yourself in," he said, then waited to be sure she followed his order.

She started to, but he suddenly put a hand on the

door, stopping her. "Kieran, call me. Please, call me if you think of anything at all that might be helpful."

"Of course."

"And keep your door locked and bolted."

"I will."

That time he let her close it, but she knew he was still waiting in the hall as she slid both the bolts.

Then he was gone.

And she was alone.

# CHAPTER
# THIRTEEN

Sylvia Mannerly was almost too easy to read, Craig thought.

She was terrified that her company was going to wind up looking bad, that maybe Maria had been into something illegal, which had led to her death.

But through Ms. Mannerly they'd found another contact—Jilly Bowen, a young woman from the Bronx who had been friends with Maria Antonescu. They hadn't managed to reach her the night before, and today she seemed scared to be talking with the FBI, but she agreed to meet him and Mike at a coffee shop in the Diamond District.

Jilly was young, only a girl. Maybe nineteen. She wasn't sure what she wanted to do with her life and had started with Clean Cut Office Services right out of high school. "I have the Manning building. No diamonds to steal," she said. "God! I can't believe what happened to Maria. She was so nice, and she worked so hard. All she

cared about was work and school. Not me. I'm stash-
ing away my savings. I'm going to backpack through
Europe before I decide on school or anything else. But
Maria...she had a goal. Very little fun. Until..."

Her voice trailed off, and she looked nervously from
Mike to Craig.

"Until?" Craig pressed gently.

Jilly let out a sigh. "You can't tell her aunt!"

"We already know about her secret lover," Mike said,
smiling. "And not to worry. A young woman seeking the
companionship of a young man is a pretty natural thing."

Jilly smiled at that. "Joe," she said softly.

"You know the guy's name?" Craig asked, surprised.
From the way Alicia Rodriguez had fallen apart, he'd
been sure she must have been Maria's best friend.

But she hadn't known the boyfriend's name.

Jilly nodded. "She didn't tell me on purpose. She was
on the phone with him, and she was a little upset. I heard
her call him Joe and say something just wasn't right."
She stopped speaking, and her eyes widened. "You can't
believe Maria was in on the robbery! She would never
have done anything like that. You didn't know her. She
was the most ethical person I've ever met."

"We're not casting aspersions on Maria," Craig assured her. "Okay, so tell me, did you ever see Joe?"

Jilly shook her head. "I'm sorry."

"You said she talked to Joe on the phone."

"Yes, her cell phone. Didn't you find it?"

Craig shook his head.

"I can't believe Miss Mannerly didn't have a con-
niption fit when she didn't get it back," Jilly said. "We
all have company phones. Cheap pay-as-you-go things.
Miss Mannerly gets them for us, and we'd better an-

swer them at all times when we're working. She's a jerk. Cheapest service, hardly any data, no games, no watching the latest movie trailers. I'm surprised she didn't demand that you find it and give it back to her. Don't get me wrong, it's not a bad place to work. We're paid a decent wage, and we even have insurance. But, boy, she's a tigress when it comes to the rules."

"Not always a bad thing," Mike said. "Though she does sound pretty tightfisted."

"She's just careful with the company's expenses," Jilly said, softening a little. She shook her head. "You should have known Maria. She was wonderful. She'd help anyone in a pinch." Tears filled her eyes. "I heard that Mr. Belvedere is going to have a funeral for her?"

"When the body is released," Craig said.

"He sounds like a nice man. Maria liked working for him." Jilly sighed. "I need to go. I work Sundays for a few hours. Is there anything else? You can call me anytime if you think of something. I'd do anything to help catch Maria's killer." She shivered. "I still can't believe they just shot her that way, point-blank."

"Unfortunately there are a lot of terrible people in the world," Mike said. "Thank you for your help."

"You're welcome," Jilly said. "It's all just so scary, you know?"

She looked nervous.

"We can drive you to work," Craig said.

"You don't have to do that. It's only a few blocks away. And if Joe *was* somehow involved, it's not like I've ever seen him. Oh, God! Do you think that's possible? Maybe he got her to disarm the alarm so he could come in and wait for her, when really he was planning to…to…"

"We've considered that as a possibility, yes," Craig told her. "Come on, we'll drop you off."

"No, thanks. I'd rather not be seen with the FBI. Just in case anyone's watching, you know?" she told them.

"As you wish," Craig said.

When she was gone, Mike said, "Damn. This means dealing with Mannerly again."

"We have to find out why she never mentioned the phone," Craig said. He drummed his fingers on the table. "I don't like this at all. I think Bobby O'Leary was attacked because someone thought he knew something. I'm afraid for this girl, for Alicia Rodriguez, and everyone we talk to now because our killers could think they know something, too. Mike, I think that means we're getting close to something."

"Yeah. Too bad we still don't see what it is."

Craig agreed with that. "Joe," he said thoughtfully.

"Yeah, what a great clue. A tall, dark-haired guy named Joe running around New York City," Mike said glumly.

"We have more than that," Craig said.

"We do? What's that?"

"A tall, dark-haired guy named Joe running around New York City—and possibly frequenting a pub called Finnegan's on Broadway," Craig said. "It's only an assumption, but with Bobby being attacked and everything else that's been going on, it's a fair one, I would say."

By three o'clock in the afternoon, Kieran felt that she was going stir-crazy.

She'd actually managed to doze on and off for several hours and she felt rested, but also as nervous as a cat on a hot tin roof, as the saying went.

She tried to make herself look at things logically. To utilize every bit of training she'd had since she'd decided to go into psychology.

Not to mention calling on all her time in the field—more or less—as a bartender.

She didn't want to die. She liked living. She loved her brothers and wasn't sure they would actually make it to old age without her.

But it was also ridiculous to think that she couldn't go down a flight of stairs to a busy street and hail a cab to go somewhere.

She was surprised, in the midst of her argument with herself, to receive a call.

It was Dr. Fuller, and he sounded impatient. He must have been called off the tennis court, she thought.

"Kieran, it's Sunday, and I'm sorry as hell to bother you," he said.

"It's all right. I'm not doing anything important," she said. "What is it?"

"Dr. Miro actually tried to deal with this, but…it's a woman you were doing an assessment on for us. She's at Rikers."

"Oh?"

"Tanya Lee Hampton. You know. The one who cut off her husband's penis," Fuller said flatly.

"Yes? Is something wrong?" Kieran asked worriedly. Had she made a poor assessment? Had the woman knifed someone in the cafeteria?

"She wants to see you and only you."

"She does?"

"Her attorney called me. She's very upset, and she won't tell anyone why. Only you."

"All right. What do I do?"

"Nothing. I'm sending a car for you. The driver—William Buell, he drives for us all the time—will call when he gets there. Mrs. Hampton's attorney will be waiting for you when you arrive."

Reprieve! She could go out and no one could fault her for it. She was being picked up at her door and going to a place where dozens of officers would be keeping watch.

"I'll be ready," she said.

In twenty minutes she received the call from William Buell. She'd seen him before, though he'd never actually driven her.

Along with working with the police, her bosses often worked alongside defense attorneys representing the very rich, enabling them to be very rich themselves. Buell, she was pretty sure, was Dr. Fuller's private driver.

He was on the sidewalk waiting for her when she came down. "Miss Finnegan, good afternoon. Lovely day for a drive. Too bad we're going to Rikers."

"Not to mention we're both working on a Sunday."

He laughed and let her into the car.

He was a talkative man and entertained her with stories about his son's Little League games as they drove.

As Dr. Fuller had said, she was met by Tanya Lee Hampton's public defender, Joan Terry, a dark-haired young woman with a harried expression and frizzy hair who reminded Kieran of a schnauzer. But she turned out to be highly professional and dedicated to her often thankless job.

"I don't know what's going on," she told Kieran, as

they jumped through the metaphorical hoops involved in entering the facility. "She was insistent that we reach you. I kept telling her that I'm the one who'll be defending her in court, so she has to tell me anything that can affect her case, but she begged me to get hold of you. I've read your report, and you will help us, won't you?"

"Yes, of course," Kieran said.

She was led to a small room similar to the one she had been in twice before, just in a different section of the jail. There was a door with a window, a table and two chairs.

"A guard and I will be right outside," the attorney told her.

"I'll be fine," Kieran said.

Tanya Lee Hampton was waiting for her. She didn't say a word until the guard and her lawyer were outside the door.

"Thank goodness you're all right. And thank goodness you're here," Tanya said then.

"Forget about me. How are *you* doing?"

Tanya shrugged. "My sister is trying to come up with bail. This isn't a great place, you know." She leaned in closer. "Dr. Finnegan, I think you're in danger."

Kieran was stunned by her words, but said by rote, "I'm not a doctor. Please, just call me Kieran."

"Kieran, you were great to me. You were the first person who actually listened to my side of the story. I don't want anything to happen to you."

"Thank you. I don't want anything to happen to me, either. Now tell me what you're talking about."

"It's something I overheard, and I can't let anyone in here know about it or know that I might pass something on if I overheard it. You won't say anything, right?"

"I'll keep this in confidence, yes, though I'll have to give some explanation to your attorney," Kieran said.

"I'm afraid of dying here, if anyone finds out I said something," Tanya said.

"We won't let that happen," Kieran said.

*Was that the truth?*

She prayed she wasn't lying and nodded encouragingly at Tanya.

"Okay, I was at dinner, and I heard these other women talking, only I couldn't see them because there was a big concrete column between us. I heard them talking about the chick in the subway, laughing because the girl who went down on the tracks is probably going to get famous and all. And then they started talking about *you*."

"By name?" Kieran asked.

"Actually, they called you 'the Irish broad.'"

Kieran shrugged at that. "Okay, go on."

Tanya took a deep breath, then let it out slowly. "The one's boyfriend was the one who did it! She was whining because he was supposed to get good money for it, too. But he didn't get paid 'cause he pushed the wrong person. He was aiming for you and blew it."

Kieran nodded slowly, feeling chilled but not shocked. She'd sensed that the man in the hoodie had been after her.

Thankfully, whoever wanted her dead had hired an inept assassin.

Whoever wanted her dead...

Yes, someone wanted her dead.

She tried not to shrink into herself with fear.

"Tanya, I think what happened in the subway is connected to several murders. Can you tell me anything else at all?" she asked, amazed that her voice wasn't trembling.

"Oh, God, I'm so sorry, but I can't. I'm a coward. But I've got kids, you know? I should have moved closer and tried to hear more, but instead I waited until I knew they'd gone."

Great. There was no way to question every woman at Rikers. Besides, whoever it was would only stare at them blankly and lie anyway.

Not to mention that it would put Tanya in danger.

There was *one* thing she could do, she thought.

"Tanya, I'm going to get a Good Samaritan to post your bail. I'll do it as quickly as possible," she promised. She hesitated, then asked, "Did you hear anything else? Anything at all?"

Tanya was reflective, her brow knit into a frown. "Yeah, there was one more thing," she said finally. "But I didn't really get it."

"What?"

"You work at a pub, too, right?" Tanya asked.

"My family owns a pub, yes."

"That makes sense, then," Tanya said. "Whoever she was, she said her boyfriend knew what you looked like. The people who were supposed to pay him pointed you out one night. At a pub."

"I can't even begin to understand what *you* don't understand," Ms. Mannerly said indignantly. "Why would I worry about a phone when a woman was dead?"

"We need all the information you have on that phone," Mike told her calmly.

"Why? I've already had it turned off."

"Because that phone has disappeared, but if it turns

up again, we'll have something to go on," Craig said, smiling pleasantly.

The smile was almost real.

He was grateful as hell that *he* didn't work for the woman.

"All right, all right, I suppose that makes sense," she said. She pulled up a spreadsheet on her computer and rattled off the phone number, the service provider and where all her employee phones were purchased.

They thanked her, and as soon as they left her office, Craig put through a call to Wally, their top civilian tech, and gave him all the information. "Can you get anything from that?" he asked.

"Probably not much. I can tell you when it was last used and maybe get some call records. I'll do my best," Wally promised, then was quiet for a moment. "You know this is Sunday, don't you?"

"Yeah, I know," Craig said. "I owe you one, Wally." When he hung up, he looked at Mike. "We really need to find Joe."

Mike nodded. "We need to find out everywhere she went with Joe and anything her friends know about where he's been, then check out every damned Joe in the place."

Craig nodded. "Maybe those phone records will help. I'll tell you one thing, though."

Mike looked at him questioningly.

"We go back to Finnegan's ourselves," Craig said.

"We need to ask Declan for all his receipts."

"No, we'll get Mayo to do that," Craig said.

"Why?"

"Because we're going back as Ian Stone and his drummer buddy, Nate Ellsworth," Craig said.

Mike looked at him suspiciously. "You think something at Finnegan's isn't what it appears, don't you?"

"Yes, you know that."

"Do you suspect one of the family?"

"No, I don't."

"Of course you don't. Not when you're sleeping with Kieran Finnegan," Mike said. "You've got to get past that, buddy. You don't know what's going on there, and you need an open mind."

"I *am* past it. I never let my personal feelings interfere with the job, and you know that, Mike." Craig was surprised that Mike hadn't yet mentioned what they'd heard from Julie Benton.

Mike shook his head. "You need to be careful, buddy, really careful. Now, me? I believe in her. I think you found a frickin' pot o' gold. She's smart *and* beautiful, but you still need to watch out."

"Mike…"

"Yeah, yeah, you're a pro. I know. Listen, do we really have to wear beards again? And those flipping contacts?"

"Yes, Mike, we do."

"She's going to see through you," Mike said.

"Bull. I worked undercover for years. Eagan didn't even recognize us, remember?"

Mike laughed. "Yeah, but you're not sleeping with Eagan."

Kieran assuaged Tanya's attorney by making up something about Tanya telling her additional and very personal details of her marriage, things the woman wasn't comfortable talking about to anyone but her.

She promised that she would put everything in a revised report.

She managed to get out of Rikers quickly, despite the fact that Miss Terry insisted on seeing her to the gates, apologizing all the way for having brought her in on a Sunday.

As soon as Kieran was back in the car, she asked William Buell to drive her to Finnegan's.

Yes, that was where someone had pointed her out to the man who had tried to kill her. But, she reasoned, no one was likely to try to kill her there—at least not during business hours.

She went back to wondering why someone wanted her dead.

If someone was trying to kill her, it had to be because he or she thought she knew something. The problem was, if she did know something, she had no idea what it was.

They'd tried to kill Bobby, too, and presumably for the same reason. And given that he was pretty much a full-time barfly, it was in fact reasonable to think he might have overheard something.

But what?

She had to talk to Craig. This was getting serious.

Of course, Craig already suspected something was going on at Finnegan's. She could tell that he was suspicious of the clientele—and her family.

Maybe even of her.

No, he couldn't be. He'd been with her when she'd been taken hostage. Then again, maybe he thought she'd been some kind of plant, and then the wrong set of thieves had shown up.

Maybe he was even sleeping with her to try to find

out what was going on. Maybe he even expected to hear her whisper the truth when she was asleep.

She told herself she was being ridiculous. Even paranoid.

All she knew for sure was that at that moment she needed to be at Finnegan's, needed to be with her family, the people she could always count on.

And where she was afraid someone she loved might be inadvertently involved in everything that was going on.

Buell let her off directly in front of the door and Kieran hurried inside.

The place was relatively quiet.

The pub always did a traditional roast from 1:00 p.m. until closing, which was midnight on Sundays. People came in at random times all day, and when she arrived, half the tables were full. She saw Mary Kathleen right away.

Her brother's fiancée was in bright spirits; she knew that Bobby was doing well, so as far as she was concerned, all was right with the world.

"Kieran! I didn't think you were coming in today," Mary Kathleen said. "You must be worn to a frazzle, working all day, then sleeping at the hospital. Why didn't you go home?"

"I needed company, I guess," Kieran said. "And I had to talk to someone for work, and since they gave me a driver, I thought that I'd just get dropped off here."

"Work on a Sunday?"

"No rest for the weary," Kieran said lightly.

Mary Kathleen looked at her worriedly.

"No, no, I'm not really weary," Kieran said quickly. "It was just something that needed to be done today."

"Well, Declan's behind the bar, Kevin is doing books and Debbie and I are doing fine out here on the floor. Why don't you get something to eat? You're starting to look a wee bit pinched."

"I'll say hi to Declan and maybe ask Rory for something, and then I'll head back and see if Kevin wants some company," Kieran said, smiling.

Her brother frowned fiercely when she walked up to the bar.

"I told you to get some rest," he said with a scowl.

"And I did. I just wanted company, that's all."

"All right, you can help out if you want. I need you to pull all the credit card receipts from the past three weeks, and then I need you to see if any of them were paid by a man named Joe or Joseph."

"What?" she asked, wondering if she'd heard him correctly.

"Detective Mayo is on his way—says they have a lead on a guy named Joe. I need you to go through our receipts and see if you can find him."

"They think that someone named Joe is involved in all this and has been here?"

"That's what I gather."

"If Joe were a crook, wouldn't he pay cash?"

"Possibly, but then again, maybe he's a stupid crook or just thinks we'll never get onto him."

"Okay," she said, turning away from the bar.

A married couple from the old country who had been coming in as long as Kieran could remember were seated in the first of the bar tables. The second was empty. Jimmy was sitting alone at the third. The two musicians from the day before were seated at the fourth, talking animatedly over their Sunday roast.

"Kieran!" Jimmy called to her.

She walked over to his table. "Hey, Jimmy."

"Bobby is doing well, I hear?"

"He's going to be fine."

"Ah, now, that's a relief," Jimmy said. He looked at his watch. "It's so irritating when people don't show up."

"Someone is a no-show, huh?"

"Yes, but enough of my bad mood. You look quite professional today," he said.

"I ended up working today," she said. "Your beer is empty. Want another? Or maybe a coffee?"

"Irish coffee," he said, as if he'd come up with a great idea.

"I'll be right back with one," she told him.

"That will be great. I'll drink that, and then I'm done waiting." His eyes widened. "Damn!"

"Damn what?"

"I forgot. I'll bet that's why he's not here."

"Why who's not here?"

"Gary Benton. I forgot—I'm sorry. You asked him to stay away. Although, don't you think that's kind of silly. Sometimes marriages don't work out. Doesn't mean people should be banned from the best pub in town."

"We haven't told Gary he can't come in here. We've just asked him to have some decency and stay away when Julie—who, quite frankly, he's treating very badly—is here, which, I admit, is often."

Jimmy shrugged. "He said she had a fit because he forgot to feed her dogs. That's not exactly a hanging offense."

Kieran decided that it wasn't worth trying to explain how he'd left the animals in their own filth and without food or water, much less that he'd found it amusing to leave other women's panties in Julie's bed.

"I'll get you that Irish coffee," she told him.

She was in the area, so she decided to check on the married couple and then the musicians after she brought Jimmy his coffee.

"Can I get you anything?" she asked.

"No, we're good, thanks," said the one with the full beard.

There was definitely something odd about the man.

Could he have something to do with the robberies? Or the murders?

Was he watching her, waiting to hire another contract killer to do her in?

She smiled. She hadn't really heard him speak much before, but now she had an opening. "You have an interesting accent," she told him. "Where are you from?"

"Georgia," he said. "The country, not the state."

"Well, welcome to Finnegan's."

She walked away, still disturbed.

Then she reminded herself that they ran a pub. She didn't have to like every customer. And it was unlikely the two men were involved in any way with the robberies or her own troubles. For one thing, she'd never seen them before yesterday.

Still…

She was telling herself to forget them when she saw that Jimmy had left his table to speak with them. Strange, but hardly proof of anything.

She headed back to the office, where Kevin was seated in front of the computer. He looked up at her and shook his head. "We need help."

"That's what I'm here for," she said.

Kevin eased back in his chair. "I'm trying to get the quarterly taxes ready for the accountant," he said. "And I just got a call. A commercial for a dating service. I get to be a real person in this one. With a hot date," he added. "I don't even have to audition. But I feel guilty saying yes when Declan asked me to handle this. And now we're all looking after Bobby, too—which is a pleasure, of course."

Kieran smiled and sat down in the chair across from him. "It's the curse," she said. "Feeling that you were born guilty. The Irish-American curse, and it affects all thirty-five million of us with Irish lineage. Did you know at one time in the 1860s a quarter of the population of the city was Irish?" She grimaced. "I listen to Danny too much, huh? All that trivia rubs off." She squared her shoulders. "Okay, how can I help?"

"The pub does well. I know that at first, after Dad died, Declan was careful not to hire anyone because we desperately needed the income ourselves. But now…we have to hire more help. You and Danny and I all have other jobs, and I'm worn out, frankly. I don't know about your social life, but I'm glad about this commercial, because that's all the dating I'm going to be doing for a while."

She smiled. Sure, Kevin was her twin. But he was tall and smart and considerate, not to mention good-looking. He could have a dozen dates a week if he wanted to.

"We'll talk to Declan," she said. "I'm sure he'd be fine with hiring a few more people."

Kevin laughed. "Trusting anyone outside the family is not in our big brother's nature," he reminded her. "Hiring even one more server is going to be torture for him." He took a deep breath, then met her eyes, his expression serious. "I'm not sure he should be trusting family, either."

She stared at him. "What are you saying?"

"Everything that's going on," Kevin said quietly. He lowered his head. "I pray Danny isn't involved."

"Danny would never be involved in murder," she said.

"Not intentionally. You're right on that."

"I should call Julie and check on Bobby," Kieran said.

"I just called. He's in a new room, out of critical care. Julie and he are doing fine, and there's still a cop outside his door."

"Good," she murmured. Yes, good. Things were going well on that front.

There were other problems, though, other situations that could possibly be solved. Situations that also seemed to revolve around the events occurring far too close to them and Finnegan's.

There was the problem of possible danger to Tanya, who had risked a great deal to speak with Kieran.

She didn't want Tanya to end up in a hospital like Bobby—or worse.

She considered suggesting they could all pool their resources and put up bail for Tanya Lee Hampton. But that didn't seem like a good idea anymore, not with so much already going on with her family and the pub and their financial concerns.

But she knew who else might be able to help Tanya.

"I'll be back. I need to make a phone call," she told Kevin.

Outside in the hall, she looked through her phone

contacts, hoping she had a number for Simon Krakowsky. To her relief, she did. She must have gotten
it from Julie or Gary at some point. She was afraid it
might be the store phone, but it went straight through
to him.

Now she just hoped he felt grateful enough for her
help catching the thieves that he would be willing to
do her a personal favor.

She identified herself, and he immediately said how
pleased he was to hear from her. She drew a deep breath
and explained her call.

"She really needs help, and I know she'll appear at
her trial and that you'll get your money back. I'd stake
my reputation on it. In fact, I *am* staking my reputation
on it," she told him.

"I'll take care of it—anonymously," he promised her.

"That easily?" she asked.

"Absolutely. I owe you," he assured her.

"You don't owe me," she told him.

"Then just think of me as a humanitarian. Either
way, consider it handled."

She thanked him and rang off, then headed back into
the office. "Day job," she said to explain her absence.

"I rest my earlier point," Kevin said.

She nodded. "Point taken. For now, I have to start
looking for Joes," she said.

"Joes?"

"Yep. Declan told me to go through the receipts and
find anyone named Joe or Joseph."

"Okay. Go for it."

She booted up the second computer and had already
found eleven possibilities when there was a knock at the
door. It was Declan, escorting Detective Mayo.

She handed Mayo the list of what she'd found already. She'd annotated it with all the information she had, adding a note if it was a regular, even about how old they were and what they did for a living, if she knew.

"Excellent work," Mayo said. "And I've brought my laptop, so if you'll log me on, I can help."

Declan left them to it, and for the next hour the three of them worked in near silence, except for the occasional pertinent comment.

When they finished, she printed out the results for Mayo, who folded them up and tucked them in his pocket.

"Thank you," he said. "Wish I could stay for dinner, but there are a few other places in the city I want to look in on for myself," he said. "Do some more investigating of my own."

Kieran frowned. Something was definitely going on. Clearly Mayo wasn't the one in charge of this investigation.

Kieran walked him to the door.

"Take care, Miss Finnegan," he said with genuine concern. "I mean it."

"I will," she promised. Then she headed back to the bar, where she saw that Jimmy was still seated with his two new friends.

She stopped by their table. "Can I get you anything?"

"We're fine," Jimmy said. "I'm just talking music with these two fine fellows."

"Great," she said, leaving quickly.

She found Kevin at the bar talking to Declan.

They both looked up at her, and Declan said, "Kevin is going to go with you to your apartment, and then he'll hop the subway back to his place."

She looked at her twin. "You're not going to stay over?"

He shook his head. "I have to get some things at my apartment."

"Then it's senseless for you to see me home," she said. "I can just get a cab."

"Not alone," Declan told her.

Normally she would have argued with him, would have assured him that she knew which areas were safe and which weren't, and that she knew how to watch out for suspicious people and stay out of the shadows. After all, she was a native New Yorker.

But things were different now that she knew someone wanted her dead. She could have told one of her brothers.

But they would have called in the cops, not to mention the FBI, and she would have been putting Tanya in danger, besides.

"Okay," she said simply.

By the time Kevin opened the pub door for her, she was worried that she might be putting her brother in danger, as well. Maybe she *should* say something. No. She had talked to Tanya in confidence.

But this was her brother....

She sensed something, and turned to see the two musicians getting up and starting toward the door.

Following her.

She stepped out to the sidewalk, and then something snapped in her and she spun around, nearly slamming into the musician from Georgia. Without stopping to think how crazy she sounded, she demanded, "Why are you following me?"

"Kieran!" Kevin protested.

But suddenly she knew. It wasn't anything in the way he looked.

It was his scent. The faint yet sensual scent of the aftershave he wore.

Her eyes widened, but she managed not to blurt out his name, something in her mind warning her that it might not be safe.

"You bastard," she muttered.

"Kieran!" Kevin protested again.

A cab pulled up just then to let someone out, and she spun around, raced toward it and practically leaped inside, shaking.

Special agent Craig Frasier had been spying on her family—on *her*—just waiting for one of them to give themselves away.

# CHAPTER
# FOURTEEN

"Kieran, please, let me in."

Craig stood outside her door, aggravated and yet kicking himself. She was no fool, and she'd jumped to at least part of the right conclusion the minute she'd figured out who he was.

He didn't know what had given him away. He'd changed his voice, and he knew his accent had been good, not to mention his disguise was worthy of the big screen.

And yet somehow she had seen right through everything.

When she didn't answer he said, "Kieran, I'm going to start suspecting a lot more than you think I do if you don't talk to me."

That did it. The door swung open. She stood there in her stocking feet, hair streaming around her shoulders, eyes shooting off sparks of fury.

"I can't believe you!" she snapped. "The whole time,

you were only there to watch my family, thinking you were going to trip one of us up. What, do you think I was with the jewel thieves that night and they were all so stupid they forgot I was their partner and took me hostage? Or maybe you think Declan's the bad guy. Yeah, Declan. He just pretends to work his ass off running the pub. He really meets with master criminals and the KGB and the IRA and you name it, ready to tear down the political infrastructure of the world."

"Kieran—"

"Or how about Kevin? Screw acting. Maybe he's really a drug dealer when he's not figuring out the best way to rob a bank."

"Kieran—"

"I know! It's Danny. One look at him, and you just know he's a vicious killer."

"Kieran, stop it!"

He stepped forward, forcing her back into the living room, where she flew at him, ready to beat her fists against his chest. To his amazement, she seemed to deflate the minute she touched him.

He wrapped his arms around her, but she pulled back, walking away from him.

"You have no right to suspect my family," she said. "I can absolutely guarantee you that my brothers would never, ever be involved in anything that hurt people."

"Did I say I suspected your brothers—or you—of anything?" he asked her.

"No, but…"

"Are you worried about what your brothers might be caught up in?"

"No!" Kieran protested. *"No!"*

"Are you worried about yourself?" he asked quietly. "Or even Julie?"

She turned away and walked into the kitchen, taking a bottle of Jameson's from the cabinet. She poured a liberal portion into a glass.

He smiled. He'd never seen her drink and doubted that she did so often. Few bartenders imbibed on a regular basis, probably because they saw the effects of too much alcohol on a regular basis.

"Were you going to offer me one?" he asked.

"I don't know. Aren't you on duty? Aren't you always on duty?"

"No. Well, a lot of the time, yes," he admitted. "But not now. I've never been on duty here, with you, Kieran," he said quietly.

For a moment, he thought that she believed him as something softened in her eyes.

"Suit yourself," she said, pushing the bottle toward him.

He found a glass and poured himself a shot. A small one. He lifted the glass to her.

"I swear to you, I don't know what crazy ideas you've got in your head, but you're wrong. I'm not in disguise because I'm after your family. What I believe—and with good reason—is that Finnegan's has been used as a meeting place by both sets of thieves, the ones you helped us catch and the copycats who are still out there. I was there in disguise because some people already know me there, and who's likely to talk about their criminal plans if they think an FBI agent might overhear?"

She swallowed her whiskey straight, set the glass

down hard and stared at him. "Why didn't you tell me what you were doing?"

"You might have inadvertently given me away."

"Really. So you think I'm an idiot?"

"Kieran, stop right there," he said, his voice quiet but authoritative. "I didn't want to put you at risk, that's all. I think you're far more afraid than I am that someone in your family is somehow involved in this."

"Don't be ridiculous. As if any member of my family would ever try to kill me," she snapped.

He paused for a moment, studying her. "So you think someone *was* trying to kill you?"

She nodded, but then her temper flared again. "If you don't take off that ridiculous disguise, I can't talk to you."

"Fair enough."

He turned and headed for the bathroom, searching through his pockets for the spirit-gum remover. He looked at himself in the mirror over the sink as he methodically metamorphosed from musician to lawman. Contacts first. The wig was easy, the facial hair less so. As he worked he noticed that Kieran had poured herself another shot of whiskey and was leaning against the door frame, sipping as she watched him.

He could tell that she was furious without even looking at her. The air vibrated with the angry heat emanating from her.

She reached over at one point for a tuft on his chin he hadn't reached yet. He started to thank her, then realized she wasn't pointing it out as she ripped it off, leaving the skin underneath stinging.

"Missed a spot," she said as she retreated back to the doorway.

He went after her, grabbing her shoulders. "Look, I get it. You're angry. But I don't think you're mad because you think I'm after your brothers. I think you're mad because I actually fooled you. And I'm sorry, but this is what I do, especially when people are dead and I want to bring their killers to justice. No matter what I feel about you, I swore an oath, and I owe the dead the best I have. And if you can't deal with that, I'm sorry. Meanwhile, I fully believe that someone wants to kill you, I just don't know why, but my best guess is that they think you know something that's a danger to them. And maybe you do and just don't know yourself what it is. As for your family...dammit, Kieran, if there's a reason why you think I'm after them, a reason why you think one of them might be involved—even unintentionally—tell me now."

He realized he was gripping her shoulders too hard and released them.

She stared up at him. "I have already told you—no one in my family would have anything to do with robbing anyone, much less murder."

She turned and walked away.

He thought about following her, but he decided to give her some space and headed back into the bathroom to finish removing his disguise.

That spot on his chin still smarted. He rubbed it gently. No doubt about it, she was strong.

When he finished, he found her sitting on the living room sofa beneath a watercolor of the Brooklyn Bridge, staring into space.

"Kieran?" he said.

She looked up at him.

"I can leave if you want. I'll stay nearby, maybe out

in the hall, and keep an eye on your place. But I don't want you to feel as if I'm crowding you."

"Don't be ridiculous. I would never make a government agent sit in a hallway all night," she told him.

He sat on the sofa, too, but not so close as to touch her.

She didn't look at him.

"What aren't you telling me?" he demanded, aggravation getting the better of him.

She did turn to look at him then. "Did you find out anything while you were in disguise? Did you overhear something that might help?"

He hesitated. He and Mike thought they were onto something. Jimmy had told them that he'd been bringing business associates into the pub. Men who were looking to invest, but smart enough to want to know the details of their potential investments. He'd introduced them to Krakowsky and a few of the other diamond brokers. That was exactly the kind of info both sets of thieves would have been interested in, too.

"I think Jimmy knows the thieves. I also think he doesn't know that he knows them," Craig said.

He was surprised when, instead of pressing for more information, she changed the subject.

"So what makes *you* think that I'm in danger?" she asked.

He hesitated. "I watched the video surveillance from the subway. There's nothing in the footage that proves anything one way or the other, but the guy in the hoodie *did* seem to be following you." When she didn't say anything, he frowned and said, "Now tell me why *you* think someone's after you."

She inhaled slowly, staring at him. "You have professional reasons why you can't tell me certain things. Well, I have a profession, too, and I often speak with people in confidence. I have no information that would help you identify whoever's out to get me, even if I were to break a professional confidence. All I have is something my…client overheard."

"Kieran, I don't know what you think your obligation to your client is, but if you're holding back information that could help stop or solve a crime—"

"I'm not!" she snapped, cutting him off.

"I wish you'd reconsider and tell me what you know."

"Oh, so my professional obligations aren't as important as yours since I'm not some hotshot FBI agent? I already told you, I don't know anything that would help solve the crime, and whether you think I'm worthy or not, I will not betray a professional confidence. You have your secrets, and I have mine."

"Like your brothers' sealed juvenile records?" he asked.

She froze. "How dare you?" she said angrily, leaping to her feet and staring down at him. "They never did anything that truly hurt anyone else. They turned the tables on a few bullies, stole candy a few times. They never used violence, much less a weapon. They were a bunch of kids who suddenly lost their mother and started acting out. My brothers are good people, Craig Frasier. And if you try to go after them, I can promise you a fight."

"Good people—and good thieves," he said, smiling slowly. "Here's the thing. I'm a government agent. I need a warrant if I want to search a place. I need to go by the letter of the law. But I sure would love to see

Jimmy McManus's phone without leaving a paper trail. Like I said, good people and good thieves."

"You want one of my brothers to steal Jimmy's phone?" she asked, confusion replacing the anger that had animated her features only a moment ago.

"I would never say that. I *could* never say that," he told her.

To his amazement, she suddenly smiled. "Piece of cake. You don't even need my brothers for that. In fact, I'd rather not tempt them. It hasn't always been easy, keeping them on the straight and narrow. Well, except for Declan. He's purer than the driven snow."

"What are you saying?"

"I was always the best thief in the family," she said. "I'll get that phone for you. Tomorrow night, if you like. I don't think Jimmy has missed his five o'clock Guinness in a decade."

"It *would* be interesting," he said, "if he happened to lose it and you happened to find it."

"*Interesting* is my middle name," she said. Then she turned and headed into the bedroom.

He stayed on the sofa, considering his options.

A moment later she poked her head out of the bedroom doorway. "Are you coming, Agent Frasier? You're welcome to the sofa, of course. As I said, I'd never be so rude as to leave you in the hallway, but if you're here to watch over me…this is where I'll be."

He knew he should say something, but the fact that she was naked had him too stunned to speak.

He rose and started for the bedroom, then turned back to double-lock the front door.

That done, he realized that he was more than a little shaky.

She meant too much to him. And that was dangerous.

The thought made him careful. He made a point of setting his Glock on the bedside table and folding his jacket carefully. Then his arousal got the better of him and he began to disrobe in haste.

She was lying naked on the sheets, hair spread out on the pillow like a dark angel's wings.

He slid onto the mattress beside her, held her, felt the warmth of her body envelop him.

He was in deep.

Way too deep.

Anger, passion, confusion, need, chemistry...they all seemed to combine that night. They made love urgently, then gently, then urgently again. In the end they lay spent and exhausted in each other's arms, drifting in an otherworldly afterglow, wondering whether what they'd shared had simply been sex done right, or whether their feelings came from someplace deeper and more powerful than pure physical passion.

She curled against him, and he thought about all the things he could say.

*I care about you so much...*

*You're so beautiful...*

*I think I'm falling in love...*

He didn't have time to say anything, because Kieran spoke and suddenly the magic was gone and reality was back in charge.

"What's up with Joe?" she asked. "Why does Detective Mayo have me looking for customers named Joe?"

He held her more tightly, picturing Maria Antonescu dead in the alley just outside the store.

"The dead girl from the last robbery, Maria Antonescu...she was seeing a guy named Joe. And," he added almost unwillingly, "we think Finnegan's is one of the places where he hung out. We're trying to ID him. Any idea who Joe might be?"

She shook her head. He felt her hair shift against him as she lay with her head against his shoulder.

"I went through our credit card receipts from the past few weeks and gave everything I found to Detective Mayo. I even gave him all the information I could on the men I knew. The thing is, lots of people pay cash. Or they're with other people and someone else picks up the bill. Even if you follow up on every Joe I found, there's no guarantee you're going to find the Joe you're looking for."

He rubbed his chin; it still smarted. "We'll find him," he said with complete certainty.

"Are you sure that girl's boyfriend was involved?"

He nodded. "As sure as we can be. Maria must have turned off the alarm. There was no evidence of a break-in."

"How do you know he gave her his real name?"

"We don't, but we have to follow every lead."

"Every lead," she repeated. "With most of the leads leading to Finnegan's?"

He hesitated, about to deny it. But his gut told him it was true. *Enough* leads pointed to Finnegan's that he had no choice but to assume the place was connected somehow.

Not to mention his undercover work that day had paid off big-time.

*Joey, yeah.* McManus had said he knew a Joey, and the guy seemed to be a real player. Smart man, wanted to see where his money went, wanted to understand all the ins and outs, whether they were talking stocks, gold—or diamonds. There was a distinct possibility he was Maria's Joe.

Craig trusted Kieran; he believed in her. He was worried about her safety. And he meant to use her talents, even the illegal ones.

But he still couldn't tell her everything he knew.

"I just realized," she said suddenly. "Mayo was there today and he didn't recognize you, did he?"

"Neither did Eagan when he saw us yesterday," Craig said.

She punched him lightly on the arm. "Don't you ever do that to me again—ever. Because I'll know. I'll always know it's you."

He didn't doubt that she would. He pulled her close. "I won't."

"Because you don't want to deceive me—or because I'll catch you anyway?"

"Both," he told her honestly. "Kieran, I am what I am."

"An agent first and always."

*No, not really,* he thought, *or I wouldn't be here.*

He pulled her closer, stroking her hair tenderly. He felt her body ease, felt her breathing grow rhythmic as she dozed.

It took him longer to sleep. And when he did, he dreamed that something was whizzing toward him through the air. Something moving faster than sound, faster than the speed of light.

But he was trying to catch it anyway. Catch it before it reached Kieran, who was standing directly in its path.

He realized then that it was a bullet.

And that no matter how fast he ran, he would never be able to stop it.

He woke drenched in sweat, frozen for a moment as he realized that they were both safe in her bed, in her apartment. She was still sleeping soundly in his arms.

And he knew that he had to make sure that bullet was never fired.

Kieran was never sure just how Craig always managed to see that things were arranged for her so easily—and apparently via telepathic communication. In this instance, she found Mike Dalton standing at her door just as it was time for her to go to work.

"He may be younger and cuter," Mike told her, nodding in Craig's direction, "but I'm your man this morning."

He wasn't in his usual suit; he was more casually dressed in jeans, a plaid shirt and a windbreaker.

"My man?" she asked, looking from one man to the other.

"I have to meet with Mayo this morning," Craig said. "Mike will stay with you this morning, and this afternoon he'll be spelled by another agent, Marty Salinger."

"Marty is kind of a pain-in-the-ass kid, but he's a good agent," Mike assured her.

"I have twenty-four-hour bodyguards?" she asked.

"Someone did try to kill you—we're all agreed on that," Craig said.

"I didn't say there was anything wrong with it," Kieran told them, and smiled in unexpected relief. It was nice to feel protected. "In fact, I like it."

"Good," Mike said enthusiastically. "In that case, Miss Finnegan, shall we?"

"I'll see you tonight," Craig told her. "And you'll know it's me—whether it's me or not," he promised.

She didn't argue with him.

"Could we stop by the hospital to see Bobby?" she asked Mike as they walked down the stairs.

"Your chariot awaits, Miss Finnegan. I'm at your disposal," he said. "No problem with getting to work late?"

"I helped with a situation yesterday, so I'm sure they'll comp me the time."

Once they were in the car, Kieran excused herself to Mike and put a call through to the office to ask Jake to explain to their employers why she was going to be late.

Dr. Miro took the phone from Jake almost immediately. "Kieran? I gather you'll be in late today."

"Yes. I hope it's all right."

"You take all the time you need. I just heard from Tanya Lee Hampton's attorney, and Tanya is out on bail, reunited with her children for the time being. You did that, didn't you? How on earth did you manage it?"

Kieran looked over and saw Mike's curious eyes on her. Dr. Miro's voice seemed to be exceptionally loud; he could probably hear her. "I, um, know some good people," she told Dr. Miro. "Of course, if she doesn't show for her court date, I'll be down one friend."

"She'll show. I have no doubt of it. I understand you have to redo your report?"

Kieran winced at that. She'd hated lying to Ms. Terry, but she'd had no choice. Now she had to deal with the consequences of that lie.

"I just need to add a few more details," Kieran murmured.

"Fine. You take all the time you need this morning. If you can give me that finished report by this afternoon, that will be fine," Dr. Miro said.

"Of course," Kieran agreed.

Mike was still watching her as she hung up. She glanced over at him. "A client my bosses took on pro bono. Dr. Miro is passionate about helping abused women."

"So why is she the one in jail?" Mike asked.

"She, um, she cut off her husband's penis."

"And *she* was the abused one?" Mike said, startled.

"No, she was arrested for that. She called 911 right away. Saved his life *and* his penis."

"How…nice," Mike said.

"Believe me, if you knew what he'd done to her, you'd applaud what she did."

"I don't know about that, but I'm sure you deal with some pretty awful stuff," he told her.

"So do you."

"Yep. But sometimes we get to make it right." He grinned at her and nodded toward a neon ticker tape on the building they were passing. "'Any decent person would lend a hand,'" he said.

She groaned. "Why couldn't I have thought of something else to say?"

"You saved a woman's life."

"Only fair, since it turns out I was the intended victim," she said. "Trust me, I'm no hero. I just reacted without thinking."

Mike smiled. "Hey, courage is a strange thing. It's stupidity, not courage, to put yourself in danger without considering the consequences. Courage, as we've all heard, is doing the right thing even when we're afraid."

She grinned at him.

"What?" he asked.

"You and Craig are pretty stupid," she teased.

He grinned back. "Yeah, I guess," he said. Then he

studied her again. "I'm glad my boy has found you. I hope that, as stupid as he may be, he's smart enough to keep you."

Kieran stared back at him, a little uncomfortable all of a sudden, but also glad that she'd earned Mike's approval.

"Thanks," she said simply.

They had reached the hospital by then, and he pulled up in front and started to get out of the car.

"Oh, Mike, we can't park here," she began, then cut herself off. "I keep forgetting. You guys can park anywhere."

"Just about," he told her cheerfully.

She noticed that he stayed close to her as they walked inside, and she smiled. Stupidity, maybe. But of the nicest possible kind.

These guys were willing to take a bullet for her.

She prayed that it never came to that.

Craig went home for a change of clothes and then headed into the office. He reported in to Eagan quickly, then hurried down to Wally's office.

"I have something for you," Wally said, picking up several sheets of paper. "Something, but not enough, I'm afraid. I have the numbers Maria Antonescu called and the numbers of the people who called her. She called her aunt at least once a day. She called Sylvia Mannerly twice a day. These numbers here…" He paused to point out several lines highlighted in pink. "…are her coworkers. I checked them all out. They're legitimate, phones like hers, cheap with pay-as-you-go plans. There is *one* number from a different no-contract company, but the phone was purchased with cash." He grimaced as he looked at Craig. "The phone is no longer active. It was only used to dial Maria. There's no way to trace who owned it."

"Do you know where it was purchased?"

Wally nodded. "A pharmacy in Tribeca."

"Let me have the address. I'll see if I can find out anything."

Wally brightened. "I can hack into their system and find out which salesperson sold it."

"Wally," Craig said, shaking his head, "no hacking—not from a government office, anyway. I'll head down there and hope the manager is a good guy. Thing is, those people probably sell these phones fairly frequently. I doubt anyone will remember who he sold this particular phone to."

"I'm sorry," Wally said. "Wish I could have given you more."

"You may have given us everything we need," Craig said. "We'll just have to find out."

Craig headed to Marty's office before leaving. "Hey," he said, and Marty looked up at him hopefully. Craig felt a moment's regret for being so hard on the kid; Marty had wanted to be an agent since he was a kid and just wanted to do well. Yes, he was dedicated to doing things by the book, but most new kids were. They had to get their feet wet before they could realize they had to think on their own sometimes.

He realized, though, that he wasn't afraid of having Marty watch over Kieran.

Marty would die for her.

That was by the book.

He didn't believe, however, that whoever wanted her dead would hire someone to do something like shoot her in the middle of the street. That would make it too obvious that someone had been after her. The killer, Craig was pretty damned sure, didn't want her death associated with the diamond thefts in any way. The killer believed that so far he and his cohorts were getting away with what they were doing—and the frustrating thing was that they were.

They wouldn't complicate that by getting caught knocking off someone who might have heard something that could threaten them. They would want her death to look random, accidental, unconnected to the case she'd gotten herself caught up in.

"Sir, can I help you?" Marty stood up eagerly.

"I need you to guard Kieran Finnegan later today. You wearing a vest?"

"Not at this moment, but I can put one on if you need me to. You think someone might try to shoot Miss Finnegan?"

"No. But I want you prepared just in case." He ran through his plan for Marty's afternoon.

Marty nodded. "So after work I get her to Finnegan's on Broadway. And then...?"

"You hang around until Mike tells you to leave. He'll be there by seven or so."

"Yes, sir," Marty said.

"Marty, you don't have to 'yes, sir' me. We were partners, and we're still coworkers. Just call me by my name."

"Yes, sir," Marty said.

Craig shook his head.

"I mean Craig. Is it all right if I hang around and eat there?"

"Sure."

"Great, thank you."

"Do you need the address?" Craig asked.

"No, thanks. I've been there a few times before."

Hell, everyone had been there but him, Craig thought. How had he missed the place?

He left the office and headed to Tribeca, where the pharmacy manager, John Rowe, was quick to help him. He pulled the receipt from the records on the main computer, and he was even able to tell Craig who had sold the phone because each employee had an ID number that was associated with every sale.

The employee in question, however, wasn't in, and Rowe was unable to reach her by phone. She was due in to work at 4:00 p.m., so in the interim Craig returned to the office to go over his notes on everything they knew—and everything they didn't.

He decided to return to Rikers Island, and asked Eagan to pave the way for him.

Even with Eagan wielding his considerable power, Craig ended up standing by his car for an hour before he was let in. This time, he asked to see all four men together. That caused a further delay. They had different attorneys, and getting them all to agree to an interview was no easy task. Craig finally got them to agree by pointing out that finding the killers could only be a plus when their own clients went to trial.

Eventually, they were all arrayed before him at a table, each prisoner with an attorney at his side.

Sam Banner, Robert Stella, Lenny Wiener and Mark O'Malley all stared at him with matching looks of suspicion.

"First," Craig said earnestly, "I want to thank you sincerely for seeing me. I'm not condoning what you did—squirt-gun larceny is still larceny—but you didn't kill anyone. If you ask me, you should all be furious that these killers imitated you so well that they were convinced that if you were caught, you'd be tried for their crimes, as well."

The foursome looked at one another.

O'Malley stepped up as their spokesperson. "We've talked to you, we've talked to the cops and we've talked to Miss Finnegan. We would gladly tell you who the killers are, but the truth is, we don't know."

"And," Stella added angrily, "we don't know how they knew our exact MO, either."

"None of you spoke to anyone else about any of this?" Craig asked.

"I swear on my mother's bones," O'Malley said solemnly.

"All right, you've given us a list of places where you met, but now I need more lists from you. Friends, family, even acquaintances you bump into on a regular basis. Anyone with whom something just might have slipped."

O'Malley's attorney pointed out that they weren't required to do any such thing and that it could even work against them, then recommended silence.

Craig didn't blame the attorney; it was the man's job to protect his client.

To his relief, though, O'Malley didn't take the advice. He looked around at the others. "I say we do our best to help nail the bastards."

The others nodded.

"When do you want these lists?" Wiener asked.

"I'll wait," Craig said quietly, and motioned for a

guard, who arranged for pens and paper. He tried not to fidget impatiently as the men worked on their lists.

At one point he excused himself and put through a call to Mike, who was in the process of changing shifts with Marty. They arranged to meet at the pharmacy to see what they could find out about the mystery phone.

Finally, with the four lists in his hand, Craig left Rikers. He felt a growing urgency as he wove through traffic. As he drove, he used Bluetooth to call Wally back at the office and, keeping one eye on the traffic and the other on the pages propped on the steering wheel, dictated the names, many of which were duplicates, from the lists.

He arrived at the pharmacy a few minutes after 4:00 p.m. Mike was already there.

"Marty all settled in?" Craig asked.

"He is. He's a good kid, you know, and he's going to be a good agent. Yeah, he's by the book. But he'll watch over Kieran like a hawk. And since I suspect you're interested, Bobby O'Leary is doing very well. He's starting to champ at the bit. He's missing his bar stool at Finnegan's."

"They're not letting him out of the hospital for a few days, right?" Craig asked. At the hospital, with a cop on guard at all times, Bobby was far safer than he would be out on the streets.

"Until the end of the week," Mike told him.

*Until the end of the week.*

Some cases took months, others took years. And now all Bobby had was a few more days of relative safety.

He didn't voice his unease; he knew Mike was as aware as he was of the difficulty of such a short timeline.

They were standing at the back of the store when a

door between athlete's foot medications and heating pads opened and the manager stepped out. He saw Mike and looked questioningly at Craig.

"My partner," Craig explained, and he introduced the two men.

"Yes, of course. Would you like to come into the office? Bailey Headley is on her way to speak with you."

They had barely entered the small one-desk office cluttered with samples, from condoms in bright yellow wrappers to children's toothpaste decorated with popular television dinosaurs, when Bailey came in. She was in her midthirties, mixed race, a pretty woman sporting a multicolored Afro.

Craig produced his badge and thanked her for seeing them.

Her eyes widened. "Anything I can do," she assured him.

"We realize we're taking a stab in the dark here, but a little less than two months ago you sold a no-contract cell phone for cash. We're hoping against hope that you remember who bought it, since very few people use cash these days," Craig explained. "I know it was a while ago, but..."

Bailey frowned, and then she gasped. "I do remember."

"You do?" Mike asked, stunned.

"A complete asshole! That's why I remember," she said. "Plus it was the only phone I sold that day."

The manager, standing behind her, said, "Now, Bailey, we don't talk about our customers that way."

She turned to look at him. "Not in front of them, but I'm trying to help the FBI."

Apparently, that made it all right, because Rowe shrugged and backed off.

Bailey gave her attention back to the two agents.

"Seriously, *such* a jerk. So demanding, making all these special requests for time and data, and all for the cheapest phone we carry. It took forever, and then not even the courtesy to say thank you. Boy, did I wish I hadn't been behind the phone counter that day."

Craig glanced quickly at Mike.

"Was he a tall, dark-haired man?" Mike asked.

"Man?" Bailey said, surprised. "It wasn't a man. It was a woman."

# CHAPTER
# FIFTEEN

Despite the fact that someone wanted her dead, Kieran reached the end of her workday and counted her blessings. The biggest, of course, was that she was still alive.

On top of that, she'd been to see Bobby, and he was doing great.

She'd managed to rewrite her report and make it seem that she had added to it when she had really only rearranged a few lines.

Tanya Lee Hampton, according to a call from the public defender's office, had been reunited with her children, and while the state was still going to press charges, her husband had said that he wouldn't testify against her in court. Why such a man had suddenly decided to act in a decent manner, Kieran wasn't sure. Apparently all he wanted now was a divorce, which Tanya was happy to give him.

She shut down her computer, picked up her coat and purse, and joined Marty Salinger, who'd been reading magazines in the reception area. He flushed at being caught reading the newest *People* magazine, but she just smiled and didn't say a word.

Marty was a likable guy, and she was glad not to be alone. She knew that both Mike and Craig carried their weapons in waistband holsters in the small of their backs; Marty wore a vest, and his holster and gun were on his hip, visible when he rose to set down the magazine.

"Hey," he said. "You're ready?"

"I am, thank you," she said, and couldn't help glancing at the magazine.

He glanced at her and then flushed again. "I love movies, and I don't get a lot of leisure time."

She smiled. "Did you read about all the Hollywood remakes coming up? So ridiculous. Some of those movies shouldn't have been done once."

His face brightened. "You're so right!"

Jake rose to say goodbye, and she got the feeling that he and Marty might have done some talking, since Jake was a movie buff, too.

"Me first," Marty said, stepping out into the hall ahead of her. He kept her behind him all the way to the car.

He had a little trouble getting out of the parking space, but she pretended not to notice.

"Sorry, I don't get a car too often," he told her. "In all honesty, this is only my fourth time on guard duty. I do work in the field, but the older, more experienced guys get most of the real action. I'm on my way, though. I got to partner with Craig when Mike was out recuperating."

He said that with the same kind of pride a contender for an Oscar might have felt.

She smiled. "Congratulations."

"Mike has twenty-four years with the Bureau, and Craig has over a decade."

"They must like their jobs," she said.

"It's not a job," he said seriously. "It's a way of life."

They reached Finnegan's, and of course he gave her very explicit instructions on how she was to exit the car and allow him to block her as they walked in.

She looked around.

Declan and Kevin were behind the bar, and Danny was working the floor with Debbie and Mary Kathleen.

Jimmy was at one of the bar tables…with Gary Benton. She stifled a groan. The other tables were full, too, and the bar itself was crowded.

It was a typical happy hour, but on a Monday, it would thin out soon enough.

"See anything out of place?" Marty asked.

She shook her head.

"Okay, good. But don't forget, I'm still on duty," he said gravely.

"Okay," she said, looking around. The only empty seats were in the dining room. "I'm going to go help out behind the bar. Want to watch me from there?" she asked, pointing to one of the tables.

"I'd rather hang around the bar, where I'll be close by in case I'm needed," he said. "You have any nonalcoholic beers?"

"Of course," she told him, smiling, "but we also have coffee, soda and iced tea."

"I should look like I'm drinking," he decided. "Nonalcoholic beer."

"All right."

Declan looked up as she walked behind the bar, then stowed her purse and jacket.

"Who's the kid?"

"FBI agent," she said.

"Kind of young," he said.

"We're not exactly old," she reminded him.

He grinned. "You have a point. And I'm glad he's with you."

"He's okay. Not quite Mike. Or Craig."

"No, I guess not," Declan said, turning his attention back to the glasses he was washing, but she could see him grinning.

Apparently everyone knew that something was going on between her and Craig.

"Gary is here," she said.

"I know." Declan looked up at her again. "He came and asked me if it was all right. I said since Julie was at the hospital with Bobby tonight, it was okay."

"He should really find somewhere else to go," she said.

Declan sighed. "Look, anytime Julie is here, we'll ask him to leave. What do you want me to do? Ask Jimmy McManus to find another place to hang out, too?"

"No, but…"

"We're a pub, Kieran. I know he treated her like crap, but plenty of people like him, and I don't want to turn this place into Julie's camp versus Gary's. Just let it go for tonight, okay? Stay away from his table. Debbie's been waiting on them. You don't need to go near him."

"Okay," Kieran said. "Okay. For tonight."

She looked over at the table and saw Gary looking straight back at her.

Suddenly he said something to Jimmy, then rose and headed toward the door.

He turned back to stare at her one last time, and then he left.

She decided it was time to have a chat with Jimmy.

And steal a phone.

Bailey was hugely helpful, and the more she described the customer, the more the woman sounded like someone Mike and Craig knew.

They exchanged a look as Bailey spoke.

Short brown hair.

Tall.

Perfectly manicured nails. Bailey said she'd admired the bloodred polish on the customer's long nails until she'd begun to think the woman intended to scratch her eyes out with them.

"Lots of women have short brown hair," Mike said. "And are tall."

"Bailey, would you mind working with a sketch artist?" Craig asked. "Mr. Rowe, I know that Bailey just got to work, but—"

"If she's needed," Rowe said, "she must go. And you'll receive your full pay for your shift, Bailey."

"Thanks," she said, sounding surprised. Then she turned back to Craig and Mike. "I'm ready to go whenever you are," she said.

She picked up her jacket and purse, and they headed out of the office into the store.

Craig heard the soft whizzing sound in the air and knew exactly what it was. And why.

Someone had seen Bailey going into the inner office with them. Someone had been watching, knowing Bailey just might remember who'd bought the phone. Someone had been keeping tabs on their investigation.

"Down!" he shouted, just as shelves of toilet paper exploded in a ripple of white snow.

Someone had fired a gun, a gun with a silencer.

He covered Bailey Headley's body with his own while he drew his Glock. Mike was up first, ducking and running down the aisle.

"Shit!" Mike shouted.

By then Craig was up, too, and he saw Mike heading out to the sidewalk in pursuit of the shooter. Meanwhile people were screaming, and Bailey was lying facedown on the floor, repeating over and over, "I don't want to die, I don't want to die, I don't want to die!"

"He's gone—the shooter is gone," Craig said quickly. "Dial 911!" he ordered Rowe, who was standing just outside the office door, shaking in shock. "*Now*, man. Do it! And get Bailey into the back!"

Then Craig was on the move, chasing after Mike. Mike was dogged and fast, but Craig was grateful he was faster.

Outside, people were already milling in fear, asking questions, looking as if they didn't know which way to run.

Craig got a glimpse of Mike sprinting toward the cross street and raced hard in that direction.

He entered an alley just in time to see Mike disappear behind a delivery truck. He hopped over a box of garbage and followed.

Mike was standing in the alley ahead of him, looking up at the various fire escapes behind the buildings. His Glock was raised, but he was looking in the wrong direction.

Craig saw the shooter; he was on the opposite side of the alley, high on a fire escape. He had his gun trained on Mike.

"Mike!" Craig roared.

Mike dropped just as the shooter fired. The bullet slammed into a wall.

"Drop it!" Craig ordered, his own gun aiming upward.

The shooter's gun turned toward him.

Craig had no choice but to fire.

The shooter catapulted down from the fire escape to land with a heavy thud on the broken pavement of the alley.

Mike got to his feet, and they both hurried over to the body.

The dead man had been wearing a hoodie, but the hood had fallen away as he fell, and Craig gasped.

He knew that face.

No time to worry about that now. He hunkered down to feel for a pulse, while Mike called in the shooting.

No pulse. The man was dead. He'd bled out from the hole in his heart.

It occurred to Craig suddenly that it had all gone down by the book. He regretted the fact that he'd had to kill the man.

Because he knew him. He'd seen him before. Several times. At Finnegan's. With Jimmy.

It seemed obvious. He'd been at the pharmacy to kill Bailey Headley before she could give anyone a description of the woman who had purchased the phone.

The sound of sirens filled the air.

He hung his head. It would be hours now before he could leave. Hours before he could get to Finnegan's.

And he had never before felt such an urgency to be there.


Kieran didn't have to wait for the news to hear about the shooting.

Marty filled her in.

He was proud to be on duty all night, watching over her and the pub. Although, as he was quick to assure her, he wasn't alone.

Detective Mayo had sent in several officers, two in uniform and two in plain clothes. The two in uniform were there to be imposing. The two in plain clothes were there for backup.

She had to admit she was worried, though also hugely relieved that Craig and Mike were all right. But, she reminded herself, she had promised to steal a cell phone.

Even with the place filled with cops and Marty there watching her, stealing Jimmy's phone was, as she had promised Craig, a piece of cake.

She sat at the table with Jimmy for a few minutes while he told her about stocks and bonds.

She didn't know much about either one and had no real idea what he was talking about, but she pretended to pay attention.

His phone was sitting on the table. She was easily able to lean toward him on an elbow as if fascinated by what he had to say, and ease it off onto her lap.

She could always say she had found it on the floor, but she doubted it was ever going to come to that. People lost phones at Finnegan's all the time. She was pretty sure that Jimmy had left his on the bar more than once.

But after Jimmy had left and with his phone tucked safely in her pocket, they all stopped to watch the news and suddenly it all seemed so much more immediate and terrifying than when Marty had told her about it.

She found herself shaking with relief when the reporter on the scene emphasized that no one other than the shooter, who had died at the scene, had even been injured.

"Live by the sword, die by the sword," a customer at the bar murmured.

Others echoed the sentiment. If a guy was shooting at innocent people in a pharmacy, it was probably a damned good thing that he'd gotten shot instead.

A lot of people left after that, and it turned into a quiet night. Kieran didn't want to leave, so she decided to take advantage of all the empty tables to start scrubbing them down with the special polish they used to protect the wood.

She was on the third table when she found scratches that annoyed her. She tried to polish them out at first, then realized that they went too deep, that someone had written on a piece of paper and pressed down so hard that the impression had gone through to the wood.

"Idiots," she murmured to herself. "Would they do something like this at home? I don't think so."

But just as she realized that they were going to have to sand the table to even out the surface, she paused. She'd seen Jimmy here the other night along with Gary and the two unknown men—the dark guy and the Nordic-looking guy.

She hesitated, then headed back to the office and found paper, a pencil and a heavy jade paperweight, before returning to the table. The impression was so faint that she hoped the paperweight would give her the pressure she needed to make it readable.

She almost crashed into Marty; she'd forgotten that he was there, watching over her.

"Please don't go off without telling me," he asked her.

"I'm sorry. I just needed something from the office."

"Just tell me when you're going to disappear, okay?"

"I'll tell you next time, I promise."

Marty nodded, apparently appeased, and she hurried back to the table. She realized that he was watching her closely and tried to appear nonchalant about what she was doing.

It was trickier than stealing a phone, but she managed to make it appear that she was trying to remove a spot, when in reality she was rubbing the paper into the indentations with the paperweight. A faint impression began to emerge on the paper, and she began to use the pencil to capture what had been written.

She almost couldn't believe her eyes when something legible began to appear.

It was an address, but she couldn't quite make it out. At first she thought it said Forty-Second Street.

The Theater District?

Then she realized that the number was a forty-seven. The address was on Forthy-Seventh Street near Fifth Avenue.

The Diamond District. And to the best of her knowledge, it was a store that hadn't been hit as yet, not by the water-gun-wielding thieves—or by the killers.

She fumbled, reaching into her pocket for her phone. She dialed Craig, but the call went straight to voice mail.

The same thing happened when she tried Mike's phone.

She knew there were at least four policemen and one FBI agent in the pub, but still...

As she sat there, Declan came over and told her to go home. "Have your agent take you—and make sure he stays with you."

She looked at her brother. "Declan, this is getting too scary. What about you and Danny and Kevin? I'm beginning to be afraid for all of us."

Should she tell him what she'd just found?

That could put him in danger, too.

Or it could mean nothing. Maybe some idiot had been writing down the address of a place to buy a ring for his fiancée.

Somehow she doubted that.

"Don't worry. Debbie's already gone, and the rest of us are going home soon. Danny, Kevin, myself and Mary Kathleen, the four of us will go to my place. We'll be a little tight, but we'll be fine," he assured her.

"How long?" she murmured. "How long can we do this? How can you run a business when you're worried all the time that something awful's going to happen?"

"Something has to give. And," he reminded her, "I'm good at taking care of myself."

It was true, she knew. When they'd been kids, Declan had been able to win them all the toys they wanted at every street fair. Even then, he could shoot with precision. And nowadays he had both a gun permit and the gun to go with it.

She nodded.

He grinned. "I'd make you come, too, except I think you're in even better hands."

"Marty Salinger?" she asked him, surprised.

"The FBI," he said, smiling.

She knew he meant Craig. And that he assumed Craig himself would join her as soon as possible.

So much for brothers being overprotective. All three of hers seemed to think that whatever was going on between her and Craig was fine and dandy. They liked him. Really liked him.

What wasn't to like?

Still…

She found it a little perplexing that they'd never once so much as questioned his intentions.

"Okay," she said. "Maybe I should go to the hospital. Julie might want to go home."

"No need. She's settled in there for the night," he told her.

"How do you know?"

"She called Danny."

"Oh," Kieran murmured. She rose to go, but Declan took her arm to stop her.

"Whatever that kid tells you, do it, okay? He had to go through some pretty major training to be where he is, so you listen to him, okay? Stay safe, Kieran. Please."

"Of course," she said.

She collected everything from the table, glad that Declan was too distracted to notice what she'd really been doing. She tucked the rubbing into her pocket, then found Marty and asked to go home. As they passed the table where she'd been sitting with Jimmy, she bent down and pretended to find his phone on the floor.

"Someone will be missing that," Marty said.

"Yeah, but at least I know this guy. I'll get it back to him tomorrow. He's in almost every day."

Marty just nodded.

She took a deep breath and said, "I can't reach Craig."

"He's going through a lot, I imagine. He shot a man. That's a lot of red tape," Marty said.

"I really need to reach him," she said.

"What is it? Can you tell me?" he asked. "I'm not Craig, but I *am* FBI."

She hesitated, then told him what she'd found and how scared she was starting to feel. He nodded and pulled out his phone. The next thing she knew, she was talking to assistant director Eagan.

Eagan thanked her and told her to go home. "I'll send men to that address, and we'll see if anything is going on."

"Better?" Marty asked her when she hung up and handed him back his phone.

"Much."

"Give me a minute. I want to take a look at the street," he said. "Stay inside. That's a cop in the corner there. I'll come back in for you in a minute or two."

She agreed, and a minute later, as promised, Marty was back. He told her to follow him, then did his best to shield her with his own body as they went to the car.

He was equally careful when they got out in front of her apartment.

The minute they hit the sidewalk, the karaoke club bombarded them with an Adele number sung slightly too high.

He grinned at her. "Karaoke! I love it. What a cool place to live."

"Thanks."

He followed her into her apartment and watched as she secured both the bolts. She turned and asked him if he wanted anything.

He shook his head. "Get some sleep," he told her. "I promise, I'm better than a German shepherd. I'll be on the sofa, watching the door."

In her room, Kieran donned her pajamas, though she knew she was never going to sleep.

But she would lie down.

And wait.

It was well past 1:00 a.m. when Craig was finally free of the red tape that came with any shooting and, pending final review, cleared of any charges, in large part because Eagan had stepped in and called on every friend he had. Luckily, there had also been a number of witnesses able to testify to the shooter's rampant disregard for life.

While the engines to clear Craig of the shooting had revved into gear, the dead man had been taken to the morgue. An ID and a twenty-dollar bill had been found in his wallet.

The ID had been proved to be bogus. According to his fake driver's license, he had been one David Thoreau.

As it turned out, his fingerprints told another story. He was really Dean Thiessen, an out-of-work computer expert. He lived alone in Hell's Kitchen—or Clinton, as the area was now called—and had no known family. His prints were in the system because he'd once been arrested on a robbery charge, though the case had been dismissed for lack of evidence.

His gun was sent to the lab, where it proved to be the weapon that had killed Maria Antonescu.

Craig hadn't been able to call Kieran or even Marty, though Eagan had let him know that Marty had filled Kieran in, and then that she'd asked Marty to pass along an address.

The NYPD had staked out the store, but nothing had happened.

Was that because one of the killers was now dead himself?

Craig had recognized the man because he'd seen him sitting in Finnegan's, talking with Jimmy.

Just before Eagan had arrived to give him the all clear, he'd been sitting morosely in the quiet FBI offices when Mike walked in.

"What's that face for?" Mike asked. "You saved my life tonight. Shouldn't you be smiling?"

"Someone's dead, Mike. And I killed him."

"It was either him or me or you. I rather like the way it turned out."

"But if I'd just winged him..."

"We shoot to kill when we're being shot at. You know that," Mike said.

Craig nodded.

"Idiot, thinking he could gun down two agents like that," Mike said.

Craig looked at him with surprise. "What?"

"He came after us."

Craig shook his head. "No, I don't think so. I think he came after Bailey Headley. I think he was trying to stop her from talking to us."

"Could be," Mike agreed thoughtfully. "Wonder if he knew she'd already told us everything she knew?"

"She have any protection assigned to her, do you know?" Craig asked.

Mike nodded. "Mr. Rowe brought her here as soon as the coast was clear, and an agent escorted her home. There are teams watching her apartment 24/7. I don't know how long we're going to be able to watch so many people," he said with a sigh.

"We're close—we're so damned close. Do we have that sketch yet?" Craig asked Mike.

"Yes. And we were right."

"Sylvia Mannerly. Who'd have thought it?" Craig asked.

Mike nodded. "The police went out to bring her in, but she's not at home or the office. She's implicated in this somehow, Craig. I just wish I knew how. Whether she's been supplying information, setting people up—or committing the crimes herself—she's guilty somehow."

"*And* in the wind," Craig said. "We need to put out an all-points bull—"

"It's been taken care of," Mike assured him. "We're lead on this case, but we're not the only ones working it. Mayo has cops out scouring the city for her."

"So the shooter tried to save her ass," Craig murmured.

"You think she was actually at the robberies?" Mike asked.

Craig shrugged. "I think it's possible. She's tall enough—especially if she was wearing boots with lifts. I think that the man I killed tonight was definitely one of the killers."

"We need to speak with Jimmy McManus, too," Mike said. "They can't find him, either."

"What?"

"He was at the pub tonight, but he left early. Mayo sent officers to his apartment, but he's a no-show, too."

Eagan poked his head into the office. "You still here, too, Mike? Go home. Both of you. You can pick this up again tomorrow. We have people watching for Sylvia Mannerly—if that's her real name—and Jimmy. Go on, get out of here."

"So I'm cleared to go?" Craig asked him.

"You're as clean as a newborn babe. You should sleep. I can get someone else to relieve the kid and watch over Miss Finnegan."

Craig shook his head. "I'll relieve Marty," he said.

"Yeah, I figured," Eagan said, studying him.

Craig tried to keep looking directly into the director's eyes. It was a struggle. "Good night, sir," he said.

"Good night."

Craig drove straight to Kieran's. He parked the car and hurried down the street, almost forgetting to watch out for himself. Then something stirred the hair on the back of his neck and he paused, suddenly certain someone was following him.

He turned but didn't see anyone, so he retraced his steps, checking out the entryways along both sides of the street. No one.

He hurried back to Kieran's place and headed up the stairs.

The karaoke club was going late. How the hell did anyone sleep around here?

He paused outside Kieran's door then hurried back downstairs.

Monday night, after 1:00 a.m., and the club was still crowded. He walked inside and looked around. All he saw were groups of college students, a lot of them wearing sweatshirts identifying them as NYU students.

He headed back to the door. It wasn't that the killer couldn't be there and wearing a college shirt.

It was just that he had no way of knowing who might have just slipped in and who'd been there all night.

Back at Kieran's place, he knocked.

Marty opened the door just as Kieran came out of her bedroom wearing panda pajamas. Her eyes were big and blue as they settled on him questioningly, and her auburn hair tumbled around her shoulders in disarray.

At that moment he didn't think he'd ever seen a woman—or an outfit—that was more seductive.

He managed to get Marty out the door quickly, promising to explain everything in the morning, and then he turned to Kieran.

"Craig—"

"Not now," he told her softly. "Not now."

He folded her into his arms, and she seemed to understand instinctively that this was a time for action, not words.

She kissed him hard and moved seductively against him.

They stumbled together back into her bedroom, where they made love. And then they made love again.

And somehow that eased all the tension from him and brought on the exhaustion.

When he opened his eyes again it was morning and she was straddling him, smiling.

"I have a present for you," she said.

He managed a sleepy grin at that.

"I think you gave me the best present in the world last night. Are you telling me you're ready for more?"

"Not yet," she said. "It's a cell phone."

# CHAPTER
# SIXTEEN

Kieran showered, then started coffee and bagels while Craig studied Jimmy McManus's phone. He made a few calls, then joined her.

"So I heard you found an address etched into a table," he said. When she nodded, he shook his head. "The cops sent men to watch, but nothing happened. They've called the store manager to tell him to be especially vigilant. The thieves might have planned to hold it up last night, before one of their own was killed. Or maybe they got wind the police were onto them—who knows? So, does Jimmy know you have his phone?"

She shook her head. "I doubt it. He must know by now that he lost it at the pub, though, so I figured we'd have it back there by this morning and he'd never know."

"Found in plain sight?" he asked her.

"Yes, of course. It was on the floor," she said, waving a hand in the air.

He was thoughtful a moment. "Do you think your bosses will mind if you call in late?"

She shook her head. "I'll tell them I'm with the FBI. Plus I worked on a Sunday."

"Why did you work on a Sunday?"

"Dr. Miro does a lot of work for battered women. She took on a case pro bono, and the woman wanted to open up more, so I went out to Rikers to see her."

Kieran made a point of pouring coffee as she spoke. She didn't like lying to him. She still didn't want to tell him about Tanya Lee Hampton and what she had heard. It was just too dangerous—not for her, but for Tanya.

She still felt uncomfortable lying to him, though.

As uncomfortable as hiding the fact that Danny had stolen a diamond for Julie.

She paused, remembering that Gary had been in the bar the night before.

She set a cup of coffee in front of him and asked, "You haven't said anything about your night. I guess it's all in the line of duty? You're shot at, so you shoot back."

"No," he said, looking at her steadily. "Most of the time we're just sitting around and watching people. Or asking questions. Following leads and clues, and hoping that people will talk to us."

"So we've both been marked for death," she murmured.

He shook his head. "I think they were after a woman who is helping us. Anyway, the guy is dead. And I'm pretty sure you'd recognize him."

He went on to explain, taking care not to throw suspicion on Jimmy, since he was a friend of hers, even though the guy's disappearing act looked like a pretty clear admission of guilt to him.

"And you think he was one of them—one of the thieves?"

Craig nodded. "I'm going to grab a shower before we head in and let my tech guy see that phone. Then I'll get you to work."

"I'll call the office," she said.

Craig showered and dressed at the speed of light. In ten minutes they were out of her apartment and on the way to his office.

"Come on, we're going to go see Wally," he told her, leading the way.

Wally worked in a room filled with cubicles, computers and mysterious high-tech devices. He stood quickly, smiling at Kieran. Craig quickly introduced the two of them.

"Kieran found this phone on the floor at Finnegan's last night," Craig said, not batting an eye. "Can you pull the call records for me? And will that take long?"

"I have the phone in my hand. No time at all," Wally said. He kept smiling at Kieran. She smiled back. "Love Finnegan's."

"Thanks."

"Love the motto, too. 'Any decent person would lend a hand.'"

"Thank you," she said again.

"We have to return the phone this morning," Craig told Wally. "Whoever lost it will probably come back looking for it."

"No problem," Wally assured him.

The phone held a chip. The chip held an address book as well as a listing of every incoming and outgoing call.

Wally gave Craig the list. "There's a number you should note," he said.

"Which one?"

Wally pointed. "That one," he said. "I recognized it from all the paperwork coming through. It's the number for Clean Cut Office Services."

The noose seemed to be tightening around Jimmy's neck.

Craig got Kieran to work, where Marty met them, ready to take on the responsibility of watching her through the day.

He doubted that anyone would be stupid enough to attack her there, but since the shooting attack in the pharmacy, nothing seemed impossible. Still, cops and attorneys were coming and going at Fuller and Miro all the time, and a lot of them carried guns and knew how to use them. It would take a pretty desperate killer to go after her there.

Eagan had seen to it that a search warrant was already being executed on Clean Cut Office Services.

Bailey Headley had described Sylvia Mannerly so well that the sketch artist's rendering could have been taken with a camera.

Just as he was about to head uptown to join Mike at the cleaning company, Craig received a call from Eagan.

"We've found Jimmy McManus," Eagan said.

"Dead or alive?" Craig asked.

"Alive, and about to be released from the hospital. He was the victim of an attack that left him for dead, but luckily for him, the bullet only grazed his head. There was a lot of blood, though, probably why his attacker most likely thought he was dead. It was either a real mugging or meant to look like one. His wallet was stolen, and he wore a Rolex and that's gone, too, along with his phone, a couple of gold chains and a gold ring."

"How did they find him?"

"His name popped up when we screened city hospitals and morgues."

"Who's with him now?"

"The cops are there. You know, even though he knew the guy who shot at you, we don't have any evidence against him."

Craig knew that, and he knew Kieran would be happy if McManus turned out to be pure as the driven snow.

"Are the cops bringing him into the office?" Craig asked.

"They are. Head back here now. Leave Mike in charge of the search at the cleaning service."

"I'm turning around as we speak," Craig promised.

Work seemed to stretch on forever. There was a meeting in which both she and Jake were thanked for being exceptional employees and helping to keep the ethical standing of the company at an extreme high.

She met with Madison Taylor, the daughter of a wealthy industrialist, who had taken up shoplifting. As they talked, Kieran felt that, just as she'd expected, the girl had been making a play for her parents' attention, a play that had failed because they hadn't even bothered to come home from a European vacation when she'd been arrested. They'd simply hired a battery of attorneys and sent her to Doctors Fuller and Miro.

As caught up as she was in matters of life and death, Kieran forgot for a moment that she was practicing therapy and yearned to smack the girl. To Dr. Miro's credit, she'd refused to write a prescription for anxiety drugs and sent the girl straight in to see Kieran, who managed not to strangle her and instead tried to make her understand that she couldn't control other people, only her own reaction to them.

It was a philosophy she tried to live by herself, though not always successfully.

The day continued to drag on. She saw a few more people, but continually found herself looking out the window and wishing she was out on the street.

She didn't even bother suggesting going out for lunch; she knew Marty would never have agreed to it.

She wished that Craig would call. He didn't. She refrained from calling him herself.

At four thirty she gave up on getting anything else done and went out to the lobby. Today Marty was sipping coffee and reading a current-affairs magazine; she could tell by the pile on the table in front of him that he'd already gone through all the entertainment and gossip magazines.

He looked up at her, and she said, "Hey, I'm done for the day. Want to head out when you're done with your coffee?"

He stood immediately. "I'm ready now."

"It's okay—I'm not in any hurry," she told him.

As she spoke, they heard the squeal of tires from down on the street, followed by angry shouting.

"The traffic in this city is crazy," Marty said, shrugging.

But the commotion coming up from the street said something more was going on.

"What the hell—heck?" Marty murmured, then pulled his gun and headed downstairs.

Kieran followed him.

"You should have stayed in the office," Marty told her, dismayed to realize that she had joined him in the elevator.

His gun in his hand, he shoved her behind him when they reached the first floor and the doors opened. She stayed close as they headed for the street door.

A policeman in uniform was already there, ordering people back. She could hear sirens.

As the crowd followed the cop's orders and moved back, she saw the body of a man lying on the sidewalk. His throat had been slit, evident from the widening circle of blood under him and the crimson stain soaking his shirt.

Kieran gasped. "Oh, my God, I know him!" she said before she could stop herself.

He was the dark-haired man who'd been at Finnegan's with Jimmy.

McManus looked like hell, Craig had to admit.

He was also damned lucky. The side of his head was bandaged where the bullet had scraped along his temple just two inches from his eye. He sat in the conference room looking at Craig like a very old lost lamb.

"I didn't know," he said, his voice husky. "You say that David Thoreau was really Dean Thiessen? And that he tried to kill you?" He shook his head incredulously. "He and his partner—tall dark-haired guy—just sat down and started talking to me one day at Finnegan's. They were nice guys, friendly, thought the pub was a great place, so old-school New York. We kept talking—they found out I do some investing, and they told me they were looking to put their money in something that couldn't crash. Something that might go down, like everything does sometimes, but wouldn't crash. Like gold. If you own gold and hold on to it, the value will always go back up, even if it slips. Or diamonds. Quality diamonds. Well, I know a lot of jewelers. A lot of them come to Finnegan's. Years ago, before old man Finnegan died and the kids took over, a lot of the established jewelers had some kind of monthly meeting there, and a lot of jewelers from all over the city still go there. I'm an old-timer, too, and a lot of them are still my friends. I get a big buyer for them and they cut me in. I don't really need to work, but I like to keep my hand in."

"So you introduced the two men to some of your jeweler friends, and then they turned around and learned everything they could from the owners and managers before robbing and killing them?" Craig said.

Jimmy winced and seemed to fold in on himself. "And Bobby," he said with a whisper. "It was them, right? Those guys beat up Bobby and nearly killed him, didn't they? And now they're after me."

"So," Craig said, "how did Sylvia Mannerly fit in?"

"Who?" Jimmy asked, looking puzzled.

"Jimmy, your phone was found," Craig said, but he didn't mention how or when. "It wasn't stolen in the mugging."

Jimmy shook his head. "Son of a bitch, huh? Well, at least the muggers didn't get everything," he said bitterly. He frowned, looking at Craig. "So you have my phone, huh?"

"We don't have your phone. Kieran found it on the floor in Finnegan's. You called a woman named Sylvia Mannerly."

Jimmy looked completely puzzled. "No, I didn't."

"Clean Cut Office Services," Craig said.

"Oh!" Jimmy said. "Yeah, of course I've called there. They clean my place."

"You have an office?"

"My apartment is my office," Jimmy said.

"You knew that the victim at the last robbery worked for the company, and you never mentioned that to anyone?"

"People were killed in a computer warehouse robbery last year," Jimmy said, looking at Craig in confusion. "I own one of their computers. I didn't go to the police."

"Jimmy, a man who was almost certainly involved in a series of robberies and murders is dead. Who's to say that you weren't involved, too, and that's why you were also supposed to die?"

"Sweet Jesus in heaven!" Jimmy said with horror. "Me, involved?" He was suddenly furious. "Have you checked my financials? I don't need to steal diamonds."

There was a knock at the door before Craig had a chance to point out that for lots of people there was no such thing as rich enough. He excused himself and rose.

Eagan was outside. "We've got another dead man," he said.

There was so much confusion on the street that Kieran found herself surprisingly impressed by Marty Salinger's ability to keep her protected while officers spilled onto the sidewalk, sirens wailed and a half dozen witnesses talked at once.

"He was thrown out of the car."

"No, man, it looked like he just kind of fell out of the car."

"It had tinted windows."

"It was like they wanted him found at this exact location." In a matter of moments, chaos became order. The scene was blocked off with crime-scene tape, and officers smoothly separated the witnesses who needed to give statements from everyone who'd been drawn by the scent of blood.

Marty moved toward the group of witnesses, flashed his badge at the cops and explained that Kieran worked upstairs, was under his protection and had recognized the victim.

"You know this man?" an officer asked her.

"I don't *know* him, but I've seen him," she clarified. "He's been in Finnegan's on Broadway, the pub my family owns." She hesitated. "He was there with the man who was killed in that shoot-out yesterday."

The next thing she knew, she and Marty were sitting in the back of a police car, waiting for Detective Mayo.

"Great," she muttered. "I couldn't keep my mouth shut."

"You were honest," Marty said, smiling approvingly.

She leaned back, feeling a chill. The man had been thrown from a car in front of her office. The police were now looking for that car, of course, but not one of the witnesses she'd heard knew anything about the car except that it was dark and had tinted windows.

Naturally, with a body bleeding out on the sidewalk, no one was looking at a license plate.

He'd been dropped there as a warning to her. She was absolutely certain of it.

So both men who had been with Jimmy McManus

were dead, and something on Jimmy's phone had been a red flag to Craig.

"Not possible," she murmured aloud.

"What's not possible?"

"Jimmy is a really old customer," she said. "He's friendly, sure, always talking to strangers, but I can't believe that he's involved with this."

The car door opened, and Kieran jumped.

It was Craig.

Relief rushed through her. She wanted to throw herself into his arms, but she reminded herself that Marty was there and managed to control herself.

"Get out," Craig said. "I'm taking you home."

"I would have done that, but the police want to talk to her some more," Marty said, then turned to Kieran and explained, "We work in tandem with the police. We don't take over cases—we offer our expertise, our manpower and all the resources of our agency to—"

"Marty, come on, get out of the car. You did the right thing, but now it's time to get Kieran out of here. The police can talk to her later."

"Oh, okay," Marty said, obviously relieved.

As she got out of the car, Kieran couldn't help but look toward the dead man again, though at least by now a screen had been put up to shield the body.

"Let's go," Craig said.

She could see Detective Mayo standing behind the body. He looked at the two of them and nodded.

"We've got Jimmy McManus," Craig said as he led her away. "He was attacked."

"Jimmy was attacked?" she asked. "Is he—"

"He's alive," Craig told her. "Let's go."

"Where?" she asked.

"I told you, I'm taking you home."

She shook her head. "Craig, take me to Finnegan's."

"Don't be crazy. Finnegan's is much too connected to everything that's going on. Bobby and Jimmy have both been attacked, and two men who frequented the place are dead. You need to be in your apartment, locks double-bolted, safe and secure."

She looked at him and shook her head. "Craig, nothing has ever happened *in* Finnegan's itself. I need to be with my brothers."

He pulled her away from Marty, who started to follow, then saw Craig's look and backed off. Craig set his hands on her shoulders and looked down into her eyes. "You're the one in the most danger," he told her. "I'm certain of it."

"Right. Tell that to Bobby and Jimmy. And the dead men."

"Kieran, you've got to go to your apartment. Marty will stay and watch you."

"Craig, please, he can watch over me at Finnegan's, and when you're finished for the night, you can join us there."

He looked so torn that she almost relented. God knew she did want to preserve her own life.

But her brothers were part of her life, and she knew that the three of them would be together at Finnegan's, which meant she needed to be there with them.

Craig saw the determination in her eyes and sighed. "Marty!" he called.

"Yes, sir."

"Marty, I'm begging you, stop the 'sir' stuff. Finnegan's. Follow me there. And when you get there, watch over her—like a hawk."

"Yes, sir!" Marty said.

* * *

Craig turned on the Bluetooth as he drove and didn't care that Kieran was listening to him as he called Detective Mayo, who was still at the scene. Mayo told him that he still had cops watching over Finnegan's—two men undercover and two in uniform.

Craig thanked him, then called Eagan and brought him up to speed on what he was doing.

"Just so you know, we sent Jimmy back to the hospital," Eagan told him. "I've got a man watching him. I think they're going to check him in for the night. He started getting a splitting headache. Possible concussion from the gunshot."

"Did you find the bullet or the casing? What was he shot with?" Craig asked.

"They didn't find either one at the scene. The shooter must have taken them while he was mugging Jimmy and robbing him blind."

Craig reached Finnegan's and parked directly in front. "Get out on my side," he said quietly to Kieran. "And stay in front of me."

She nodded, and moments later they entered the pub together.

Music was playing through the speakers, the bar stools were full and so were most of the nearby tables. Some of the customers looked familiar, but there was no one he really knew.

He saw the two cops in uniform at a table near the door, and a couple he pegged immediately as the undercover cops sat drinking coffee at another.

He turned and kept his eyes on Kieran as she left him to join Declan at the bar.

"Kieran. What are you doing here?" he asked his sister.

Maybe Declan could talk sense into her.

Or, knowing Kieran, maybe not.

"I'm here to be with my family, and that's that," she said firmly.

Declan looked up as Craig approached. "Damn, she reminds me of my grandmother sometimes. Sweet little thing with blue eyes and rosy cheeks—and stronger than steel. Hell on wheels once she got something into her head."

Obviously there was going to be no help from Declan.

"Danny and Kevin here?" Craig asked.

Declan nodded, indicating the floor. "Debbie's off, and Mary Kathleen is staying with Bobby, giving Julie a break." He looked at Craig. "I hear Jimmy McManus was attacked."

Craig realized Declan hadn't heard yet about the dead man in front of his sister's office, so he filled him in on that, too.

Declan stared at his sister. "What on earth are you doing here? You should be sleeping in a locked room at FBI headquarters!"

"Declan, they're killing their own. They're scared. Whoever's the head of this thing is covering their tracks so they can take the money and run," Kieran said.

And that was a possibility, Craig had to admit.

They might never find Sylvia Mannerly or even identify the fourth killer.

No, he promised himself. He would be damned before he saw it go down that way.

Marty came up behind him just then. "I'm here," he announced. "I'll be here until the bitter end."

"Nice way to put it," Declan murmured.

Craig turned to Kieran. "I *will* be back. Don't even think about leaving until I get here. That goes for all of you," he said to Declan.

Declan nodded. "Whatever you say."

Craig wanted to take Kieran in his arms, but he couldn't, not with things the way they were. Most of all, he just wanted to stay wherever she was and watch over her himself, but he couldn't do that, either.

He didn't touch her and hardly looked at her, just nodded at the three of them, turned and left.

He drove to the offices of Clean Cut Office Services.

Mike was supervising a half dozen officers as they went through the place.

"Anything?" Craig asked him.

"It looks like our Ms. Mannerly was very careful. Everything of hers—everything personal—has been removed. The way I figure it, she was setting up her thieves with her employees—young, innocent girls, many of them recent immigrants—and getting her employees jobs at the places she intended to hit. You know the address that Kieran found on the table at the pub?" Mike asked.

"Yeah?"

"That store was on a list of new clients. I think it would have been hit soon, but maybe the thieves must have gotten wind that the cops were watching the place, or maybe it just wasn't next on the list. I think Mannerly was smart. She knew the FBI was investigating, so she tried to keep ears and eyes on us."

"Maybe Kieran saved another life," Craig said.

"I heard about the dead man in front of Kieran's office."

"Throat slit," Craig said. "They've got an APB out on the car." He shook his head. "Ice-cold, huh? A guy dies trying to keep Bailey Headley from describing Miss Mannerly, who just disappears nice as can be, and suddenly the guy's buddy is murdered, too. Nice functional work family, huh? Who killed him, do you think? The unknown fourth killer or our Ms. Mannerly—who definitely isn't Ms. Mannerly, by the way. Eagan called me on my way over. She was using a social security number belonging to a woman who died in 1980."

"Figures."

"We're trying to find out who she really is," Craig said.

Mike nodded.

"Anyone search her apartment yet?" Craig asked.

"We would—if we knew where it was," Mike told him.

"She must have an address listed."

"She does," Mike said, and smiled grimly. "It's in the middle of the Hudson River."

Craig swore in frustration. Mike had this covered. Mayo was on the most recent body, which was on the way to the morgue. He wasn't needed here or there.

Mike must have read his mind. "Go," he said. "I'll let you know if anything new turns up. Where are you headed?"

"The street," Craig told him. "I want to find a bullet."

As he drove, he called the office to get the exact location where Jimmy had been assaulted. It turned out to be very near to where Bobby had been found.

Very near Finnegan's.

Craig headed to the address. The bullet had winged Jimmy McManus on the left-hand side of the head.

Craig worked all possible trajectories and searched the buildings one by one, running his hands over stone and concrete, paint and graffiti.

He couldn't find the bullet.

Eventually he gave up and decided to head back to Finnegan's.

But not until he made a stop at home.

At his place, he changed. He was all set to leave when Eagan called.

"May mean nothing," Eagan said once he'd finished talking.

Or it could mean something big.

In fact, Craig was pretty sure it did.

Glad that he had decided to change, Craig left hurriedly and headed to Finnegan's, careful to park his car well down the block.


The night seemed especially long, even for a Tuesday.

At ten o'clock Declan ordered his younger brothers and Kieran to go home.

Kieran, of course, refused. She was waiting for Craig.

Danny and Kevin argued, but they finally agreed, promising that they would stay together, go straight to Declan's place and phone when they arrived, which they did not long after they left.

Danny would return with Declan in the morning, while Kevin had another acting job for the dating service.

Declan shook his head at his sister. "You should have stayed home, all locked in, too."

"No, I would have imploded, worrying about all of you. And now I'm not going anywhere until Craig shows up."

"Well, we're going to close early. We'll lock up and wait for him."

He announced that they were going to close by midnight. The only people left in the place were a few regulars and the cops, so no one objected when the last call went out.

Kieran saw the couple she'd pegged as plainclothes cops stop to speak to the uniformed officers, and then they left.

The two in uniform stayed. "We're here to keep an eye on you all night," one of them assured Kieran.

"I'm waiting for Agent Frasier to get back," she told him.

"Then we'll wait until he does," the second officer said.

Kieran had walked their last customer to the door and was ready to lock it when someone came running toward the door from the street, calling her name.

"Kieran, wait!"

It was Gary Benton. He looked like hell, as if he'd been in a fight.

As if he'd been crying.

She backed away, so surprised by his appearance that she didn't think to protest.

"Gary, what the hell? We closed early tonight."

One of the cops came forward. "If you need us to—"

"No, no," Gary said. His voice dropped to a whisper. "Kieran, please, I have to talk to you. About Julie."

Declan had come forward by then, along with Marty.

She lifted a hand. "It's all right. Give me a minute. I'll talk to Gary in the office."

"Wait," one of the cops said.

"Wait?" Gary murmured. He looked at them and lifted his arms. "Frisk me, if you think I have a weapon."

The cop took him at his word, then nodded at Kieran. "He's clean."

Gary followed her as she led the way to the office, Declan following close behind. The cops and Marty waited at the bar, ready to leave whenever she was.

"Care if I fool around behind the bar?" she heard Marty ask as they walked down the hall toward the office. "I did some bartending in college."

"Go for it, Marty," Declan said. "Knock yourself out." Then he joined her and Gary in the office.

"What the hell is it, Gary?" Kieran demanded, closing the office door behind them. "Because if you're in on these thefts, I'll strangle you myself."

"I'm not, I swear," Gary said desperately. "But I think I know who is. Those guys who were in here with Jimmy."

"We know that already," she said, her tone cold and hard.

"They're working with someone. They talked about their investor when Jimmy and I met with them. They wanted to know all about where I was working. I think… I think they were watching all of you…maybe afraid you saw something, heard something, when you were waiting on people. And then after you helped catch those thieves, they seemed to be watching you in particular. I didn't think that much of it at first. I mean, guys watch you all the time. Then—then there was the subway thing. Kind of fishy, I thought. But then tonight

I got a call. It was a raspy voice. I don't know if it was a man or a woman. And they seemed to think that I knew something, too! They said they had Julie, and that they'd kill her if they couldn't talk to you."

"Kieran isn't talking to anyone," Declan said.

"They're going to kill Julie!" Gary said.

"Like you care," Kieran said. She was terrified for Julie, but she knew, too, that if she went anywhere near whoever had made that call, she would be dead herself.

"Yes, I care, damn you!" Gary said. "Yes, I was a bastard! She's hugely successful in her career, everyone loves her—and she loves those damned dogs. Yeah, I thought I wanted something else, some excitement, someone who was into me. But I was *married* to her, and whether you believe me or not, I still love her. Kieran, I'm scared. I was on my way here to talk to you when someone in a mask and a frigging cape caught up to me just outside my building. Slammed me against the wall and put a knife to my throat. Told me they had Julie, and that if anyone ever wanted to see her again, I had to get you to meet up with them."

"Where? When?" Kieran asked.

"They're going to call. They told me to get here, to find you and then they'd call."

They suddenly heard a loud crash from behind the bar.

"I knew that guy wasn't a bartender," Declan muttered. "Stay here," he told Gary and Kieran. Then he met his sister's eyes. "And don't you do anything—*anything*—until I'm back."

As soon as Declan was gone, closing the door behind him, Gary lunged across the desk.

He was reaching for Declan's letter opener.

# CHAPTER
# SEVENTEEN

Craig sat on the sidewalk just down the street from Finnegan's, an empty cup from a fast-food restaurant at his side.

He had a ukulele with him that he'd gotten as a gift when working a case in Hawaii seven years ago. He couldn't play it, of course. He only knew the practice notes that came out "my dog has fleas," the way he'd been taught to play.

He wasn't sure if he was flattered or insulted that a fair amount of change, and even a few dollar bills, had been tossed into his cup.

He continued to strum the ukulele, singing ridiculous songs and pretending to be very drunk.

And watching.

Always watching.

He watched as Declan started to close the place and the customers left, and he nearly jumped to his feet when Gary went rushing past him.

But he saw the cops at the door and forced himself to wait, still watching.

Gary hadn't been there five minutes before a couple walked by him, their faces hidden, the man's by a hat pulled low over his eyes, the woman's by her hooded cape.

They went straight to the door of Finnegan's, which he knew was locked at that point, but then the man took something out of his pocket.

A key?

Who the hell had a key to Finnegan's except for a Finnegan?

Craig leaped to his feet, but the couple was already inside. And the second they were in, he heard a sound he knew all too well: gunfire. Muted by a silencer.

Craig raced inside, trying to assess the situation. The couple, both of whom were carrying guns, had taken everyone by surprise. He still couldn't make out their faces, but he was sure he knew who they were.

The gunmen were ordering the cops and Marty to lower their guns. Just as they started to comply, Declan came hurrying out from the back office, and both guns swung in his direction.

Craig started to talk, slurring his words as if he were drunk. "Hey, what is this place? A pub or a movie set? Hey, lady, you look like that actress—what the hell was her name? Betty Grable? No, no… Clark Gable? Hell, no, he was a man."

He succeeded in confusing them, if only for a moment, and that would have to be enough.

"Shoot the damned drunk," the man snapped.

Jimmy McManus. Jimmy, who had shot himself for

effect, then dismissed his bodyguard and left the hospital without being discharged.

Craig poured on the speed and crashed into the woman, taking her totally unaware. They crash-landed in a pile right in front of the bar. Her gun went flying beneath a stool.

One down, one to go.

A shot was fired, but Craig realized with relief that it went straight into the air.

"Someone get that stupid drunk out of the way!" Jimmy ordered. His voice was different from his usual friendly tone, cold as ice. "Now—or I start killing people. I want Kieran. I want her out here *now*."

"McManus, you can shoot everyone in here, but I will not let you kill my sister," Declan announced.

"You can't kill all of us," Marty said boldly.

Another shot rang out, and Marty screamed as blood oozed from his shoulder.

"I'm a crack shot, and yes, I *can* kill all of you," Mc-Manus said. "Now drag the drunk back there with the rest of you and get Kieran Finnegan out here."


"Gary, you bastard," Kieran snapped, slapping her hand down on the letter opener before Gary could reach it. "You bloody bastard."

He looked at her, tears streaming down his face. "I wasn't going to use it on you. I was going to use it on myself."

Looking into his eyes, she believed him.

But before she had a chance to tell him to stop being a drama queen, she heard shouting and then…gunfire? Adrenaline raced through her as she realized someone was shooting up the bar!

She hurried out to see what was going on and froze.

It was like something out of *The Godfather* crossed with the Three Stooges. A man in a fedora was standing there with a gun trained on Marty and the cops. Then he looked straight at her and she gasped.

Jimmy McManus.

Meanwhile Declan was trying to help some drunk off a woman in a cape.

None of which mattered because Jimmy was staring at her with hatred, and his gun was aimed at her heart.

"Kieran, precious Kieran, pride of the entire Finnegan family—and the stupid bitch who ruined everything," he said.

"Jimmy, you piece of dirt. I don't know how I ruined everything for you, but I'm glad I did."

"My gun," the woman on the floor muttered. "Where's my gun?"

Jimmy didn't even seem to hear her. He was completely focused on Kieran. "You knew...you heard things—you fucked everything up."

"I *wish* I had heard things. Then you could have ended up behind bars sooner," she told him.

"The other guys would have been caught and blamed—even with their ridiculous squirt guns—but no. Who the hell wouldn't think that they killed sometimes and not others, once they were caught red-handed? You went to the damned holdup. On purpose. You heard them talking—you went there to stop it and you did. You're a little snoop, eavesdropping in here all the time. And you think you're a superhero! Any decent person, well...no. Some people know that there are consequences for their actions!"

* * *

The scene had become actively surreal, Craig thought, but he was finally beginning to grasp the truth, or at least what passed for truth in the deluded mind of Jimmy McManus.

McManus had somehow decided that Kieran, not the FBI, had stopped the robbery.

But this wasn't the time to tell McManus that he'd lost his mind, not when he had his gun trained on Kieran.

"Hey, lady, you lost your gun?" Craig said, still using his best drunken slur. "I'll help you find it."

He pretended that he was reaching under the stool.

Instead, he took a calculated risk.

He made a dive for Jimmy.

McManus's gun went off, and Craig hit the floor.

Kieran heard a loud scream, then realized that it was hers.

But she was only paralyzed for an instant. Then she raced toward the drunk lying on top of Jimmy McManus. The impact had knocked the gun from Jimmy's hand, but it was still within reach, and the bastard was already reaching for it.

The woman was making a dive for it, as well, but Kieran saw that Marty Salinger and the cops had sprung into action, too.

She slammed a foot down on Jimmy's hand just as his fingers started to curl around the grip of the gun.

It looked like a big gun, too, and then she realized that half of it was a silencer.

What the hell difference did it make what kind of a gun it was? It shot bullets that killed people.

One of the cops was already tugging on the drunk's body, rolling him over.

The other was wrestling Jimmy onto the floor and putting cuffs on him.

Marty, by the book, was reading the woman her rights as he put the handcuffs on her.

As Kieran heard the first cop call for an ambulance, she hurried over to the drunk, praying that she could do something to save the life of the man who had saved all of theirs.

The first thing she saw was that there was no blood.

How? He'd been shot point-blank in the chest. And then she saw that a patch of facial hair was coming off.

"Craig!" she cried, tears springing to her eyes. "Craig, oh, my God…"

He blinked and looked up at her.

He was alive, but he gasped wordlessly as he tried to talk.

"Get the vest off him. The bullet is in the vest," Marty told her.

She ripped at Craig's clothing. When she got to the vest he winced.

"Broken…" he whispered.

"You're alive, and there's an ambulance on the way," she said. She could tell she was going to cry and betray all the fear she was feeling.

"Broken ribs," he managed.

"Lie still," she said.

"Hey!"

Everyone went still.

Gary had made an appearance.

"Julie!" he said. "What about Julie?"

Kieran didn't even have a chance to get up. Declan walked over to Jimmy, grabbed the man by the lapels and said, "If anything has happened to Julie Benton, I don't give a damn about the law. I'll skin you alive. You're lower than a rat, a roach. You're the worst fucking piece of crap in the world."

McManus stared back at Declan with hatred in his eyes. "Don't be an ass. Gary is so fucking stupid, he'll believe anything. All I needed him to do was get in here and get Kieran on his side. We watched him flip out and waited outside until the time was right, and then we were going to take care of you and get out of here for good." He looked over at Kieran. "She ruined a perfect plan. I wanted her dead."

Kieran felt a chill sweep through her. She rose and walked over to Jimmy McManus. "You used Finnegan's. You used this place, our hospitality—you used our friendship. You made us a part of killing people. I hope to God someone knifes you to death in prison."

"He could get death. This might be a federal case, since it crosses state lines," Marty pointed out.

"I'm fine if he's just locked away to rot slowly, thinking about the fact that I'm alive and well and enjoying my life," Kieran said. She was shaking, and she felt sick. Jimmy had been a customer forever.

He'd probably been using them forever, too, learning things to help him cheat and steal—and kill.

She was glad she didn't have a weapon, because she was afraid she would have used it, she was so angry.

She spit on him instead.

"Did you see that?" McManus demanded. "I want her charged with assault."

"You have to be kidding," one of the cops muttered.

"I didn't see a thing," the other said.

"You know what? I didn't see anything, either," Marty said, and he grinned down at Craig, who smiled back at him, then started trying to get up.

Kieran watched her spittle drip down Jimmy's face, then went back over to Craig and knelt down beside him. An ambulance was coming.

She would be in it with him.

As she took his hand, she looked at the woman, who was staring angrily at McManus. "You are a moron!" she said. "If you hadn't had such a stick up your butt about this stupid girl—"

Marty jerked her cuffs, and she cried out.

"Oh, sorry," he said, not looking sorry at all.

"Who the hell *is* she?" Kieran asked Craig.

He managed to smile at her and squeeze her hand. "I believe she's about to be an inmate at a federal prison."

"He did it! He killed them all!" the woman cried.

"Bitch!" Jimmy said. "You were the one who wanted Maria dead!"

Detective Mayo and assistant director Eagan walked in just then, followed by a pair of EMTs, and suddenly the night was alive with people and action.

Kieran followed Craig into the ambulance, but before the doors could close, Declan put out a hand to stop them.

"Only one escort, I'm afraid," the EMT said.

Assistant director Eagan stepped up and said, "I think we can make an exception."

The EMT, clearly faced with a power greater than his own, gave in.

Declan climbed in and hunkered down on the floor while Kieran held Craig's hand and the EMT checked his vitals.

The siren blared as the ambulance raced through the late-night streets.

The impact of the bullet had caused three fractured ribs. Other than that, he was fine, and happy to vent his annoyance at being forced to stay in the hospital overnight.

Kieran told him that he was a horrible patient, but really, it wasn't so bad. Julie and Mary Kathleen and the Finnegan men all stayed at the hospital through the night, going from his room to Bobby O'Leary's.

Even Mike came, and Craig was glad to have him there to field questions about the case and explain what they knew about Sylvia Mannerly and Clean Cut Office Services.

When morning came, they learned that Sylvia and Jimmy had actually met online through a dating service, of all things.

They'd discovered how much they had in common. As in a desire to pull off enough robberies to get rich enough to retire to the tropics.

They'd agreed on copycatting the original gang but going further and killing witnesses, because witnesses could get you caught.

But when Kieran had become involved and that involvement had led to the original thieves being caught, Jimmy had been convinced that she knew something, that she'd overheard something and was going to get him caught, too.

From there it had just been a short step to him deciding she had to die.

The next day, Craig was let out of the hospital, but he was, as Mike had been, forced to take medical leave.

And that meant he was free when Kieran asked him to go and see someone with her.

The someone was Tanya Lee Hampton. They met her at a small duplex in the Bronx with a little playground in front. Her two toddlers were there, and they were delighted with the presents Kieran had brought them. They talked about Tanya's legal situation, which was looking up. Her lawyer had made a deal with the district attorney's office; she was on probation and would do community service. But Dr. Miro had also found her a job that she could do with her children. She was going to become a secret shopper, testing out restaurants and stores that that were geared toward kids and families.

When it was time to go, Kieran and Tanya hugged tightly, and Kieran thanked her as they exchanged a speaking look.

"What was that all about?" Craig asked her as they walked back to his car.

She was thoughtful and then turned to him.

"We have to accept that sometimes we're going to have secrets. It comes with our jobs. Like the other night. I'd never even heard of Sylvia Mannerly or whoever she really is. You can't tell me everything all the time. And in my line of work, people have to be able to talk to me and expect confidentiality."

He couldn't deny the truth of what she said.

Whatever lay between the two women, he thought, it had obviously ended well, and he would let it lie.

He smiled at her. "You know, I have some time on my hands. Time I could use to do some traveling."

"And I have a job."

"I'll bet you could take some time off if you wanted to."

She laughed, and he realized just how much he loved the way her whole face brightened and her beautiful blue eyes sparkled.

"Special agent Frasier. We haven't even known each other a full two weeks and you're asking me to go off with you already?"

"There's this lovely place in the Poconos," he said. "After everything you've been through, I bet your bosses would be happy to see you get a little rest and relaxation. 'Any decent person would lend a hand,' right?"

"Or take a bullet," she said, searching out his eyes.

He shrugged. "I was wearing a vest."

"A point-blank bullet."

"What do you say?" he asked.

"I don't know, Craig. The pub is so busy. You'd think people would stay away after what happened, but it's been crazy busy. Declan has had to hire on two more people."

"He would tell you to go," he said.

"Should we go find out?" she asked, leaning against him.

He laughed softly, pulling her closer. "It's funny. I'm with this lovely young woman," he said softly, "and yet I seem to be dating an entire family."

She smoothed back his hair, watching him anxiously. "Do you mind?"

He shook his head. "I'll take a Guinness," he told her.

She smiled and took his hand.

They would head to the pub, he thought, and then home. Where she would make very careful love to him.

Life was good, he thought, and he pulled her closer still, then kissed her thoroughly.

He wondered what else the future might hold.

\* \* \* \* \*

# EVERYONE GOES
# TO FINNEGAN'S

Kieran Finnegan, five years old, curled up on her mother's lap. She waited with anticipation; it was a precious time.

Sunday night was story night. Her da had her three brothers, and it was her all-alone time with her mother. Of course, each boy had his time alone with Mum, too, and Kieran had her alone hours with her da, but this was her night, and she loved the stories, even when she heard them over and over again.

What Mum called the "first story" was her favorite. It was about how the Finnegan family had come to own the pub, and she loved it. There were pictures, too, old photographs of the family; they went with the story, and it was quite wonderful.

"So…" her mum said. "What will it be tonight? Ah! I know! The day the president of the United States came to Finnegan's!"

"No!"

"No? Not the president?" her mother teased.

"No."

"Ah, what about the great Irish actress who visited?"

"No!"

"Ah, okay…the first story, right?"

"Please, yes, please!" Kieran said.

And so her mother began. The story took them back, way back to the 1850s and '60s, a time when many Irish were new to the country, fresh off the boat—and, often, out on a battlefield…

A time when life itself could be a struggle…

But goodness could still prevail.


A cannon ball hit the ground and exploded, far too close to the hospital tent where Caitlin Adair worked at the side of a wounded soldier, pressing hard on the bayonet wound, just the way she'd been taught. Earth spewed; men and horses screamed.

Caitlin barely flinched.

The war had been going on far too long.

"Sir!" she cried, looking over at Captain Mulligan, surgeon for the Irish brigade.

"Doesn't matter, Caitlin," he called back. "Hold!"

So she did. Once again, almost in the center of the camp, a ball exploded. Captain Mulligan hurried to her side as the dust and black powder rose around them, all but blinding Caitlin and everyone else in the area.

She held tight, keeping pressure on the wound.

"I've got it, lass," the captain told her. "See if you can help with…any living."

Battle had commenced. Caitlin didn't believe the medical tents were being targeted with any intent; they were just too close to the camp where the soldiers had been awaiting the coming battle. But whether they were being attacked on purpose or not, it was all becoming a melee, and some men were down while others were rallying to fight.

She rushed into the center of the camp, ducking here and there to check on the men who lay on the earth, most already being dragged into piles of the dead, others being helped by friends. She saw one man off at a distance, with no friend to lend assistance, and she hurried over to him.

*Dead*, she thought.

The war was nearing an end. She'd been working with Captain Mulligan as a nurse from the beginning—ever since Danny was killed at the first Battle of Antietam in September of 1862. There, the New York Irish had covered the retreat after the horrific thrashing the Union had received at the hands of the Rebels—many of them, Yankees and Rebels, had been comrades just a few months previously.

Caitlin hated the blood and death, the dismemberment, the cries of the wounded and the dying, those who were stoic and those who cried to heaven.

But she'd never failed in her duty to help. Right after the first battle of the war—and right after receiving word of the death of her fiancé—she'd met Mary McNally. Mary had been with Danny at the end; she gave Caitlin Danny's crucifix, his cards, his wallet, all that had remained, and she'd told her how he'd been strong to the end, how she'd held his hand, and he had talked of his love for Caitlin.

Caitlin believed that Mary McNally had made death easier for Danny—and life without him easier for Caitlin.

Hunkering down by the fallen soldier, she looked

around, silently praying that the barrage of cannon fire had ended. She could hear shouting and gunfire on a distant hill, and she thought the Rebels had expended what fire they had. She was safe.

"Caitlin! Miss Adair!"

It was young Ethan Delaney calling to her. He moved through the mist and black powder, hurrying along with a stretcher.

"I'm here to help!"

"Thank you, Ethan. This young lad… I believe he's beyond our help."

Caitlin laid her fingers against the man's pulse. As she'd feared, he was dead. She studied his face. So young, not a bit of stubble on his chin. Blue eyes, sightless now, stared up at her.

She closed them gently.

"There are more men farther afield, a wee bit!" Ethan said.

"Aye, we'll seek them out, shall we?" Black powder was one of the most deceptive weapons of war, Caitlin thought. It darkened the air with stark certainty— blinded so many. Now, it mixed with an eerie fog, almost as if God wept dark tears as His children tore one another to shreds.

She started to speak, to tell Ethan they had to go back. They seemed to have moved beyond the rain of death that had fallen upon their camp, and there was no sense in going on. But she fell silent, certain she heard a soft moan.

"Ethan?"

There was no answer. So much for assistance in that direction; they'd already lost each other in the murk of the day.

Out of nowhere, she felt someone behind her. And suddenly, she was swept hard against a man's hot, living chest, a hand clamped tight over her mouth.

"Not a word, lass, not a word. I'd not hurt you. I'd not hurt you in any way, do you ken? Do you understand me, lass?"

It was a man who spoke in the thick brogue of the mother country.

*He was from the South of the Old Country,* she thought. *Not from Dublin. She knew that accent well enough; she'd been eight years old in 1850 when her own mum and da left after the Great Famine of 1845 saw more than half the Emerald Isle starving.*

Yes, he was an Irishman. Holding her tight as if she were an errant lamb, acting the lout and the fool.

She should be afraid, she knew. Not every soldier was a good man.

And, she realized, somewhat surprised, this one wasn't even a Yank.

She didn't think. Later, she would ponder that foolishness. But, at the moment, she didn't think. She just felt a rise of temper.

And she bit him. Bit him hard, teeth tearing into the hand over her mouth.

He grated out something, a wicked cry of pain.

But he did not release her. Nor did he harm her.

"Well, now, I'll be havin' an injury greater than the one I wish to cure!" he muttered. "Now, stop and behave like a lady, lass. Me sainted mother would have me hide were I to grow too rough with the likes of you. Yet I'll not have this man die! You will help me."

The grip he had on her was strong; if he chose, this man could certainly snap her neck.

He didn't mean her harm. He was speaking about an injured man. She had sworn—just as Captain Mulligan had—that she'd let no man die without offering the best care she could, whether he was Yank or Rebel, black or white, Irish or English.

"You understand me, eh? You will help?"

His hold on her eased.

"Aye, you great ass!" she told him, jerking free and spinning around to look at him.

He was tall, lean—almost gaunt—and yet his shoulders were broad and strong. His face was truly fine, with high cheekbones, a generous mouth, straight nose, well-set eyes. They were a startling blue-green, something she saw easily against the dark soot that seemed to cover most of his face.

"This way," he said, reaching for her hand.

She could still hear the sound of the battle; the New York Irish Brigade fighting with its fierce battle cry, "Faugh a ballagh." Or in Irish, "Fág an bealach," meaning "Clear the way!"

And she could also hear, now and then, a bone-chilling Rebel yell…

He caught her hand, and there was no escaping his grip.

"You needn't jerk," she snapped. "I will help any man. I care not that he's of your ilk!"

"Of my ilk! And what would that be, luv?" he asked drily.

"Traitor!"

"Traitor?" he repeated, and laughed. "Ah, lass! Was Hancock a traitor? What of Patrick Henry? Ah, never you mind. History will call us hero or traitor. We shall see."

"You're Irish!"

"Indeed. Unless I've gone deaf—not unlikely with all the noise about, one might say—so are you!"

"But…you're not with us!" she said. "Not with the Union!"

"What, lass? Did ya think every Irishman in this damned no-man's land was a bloody Yank? Lord a-mighty, my girl, but we've moved here, there and everywhere within this great country. God help me, I'm not even sure exactly what I'm fighting for, 'cept the boys I've come to know from Virginia. But, fear not, fair lady. 'Tis a Yank I'm bringing you to fix!"

He could see better through the darkness than she could. They suddenly came upon the entrance to a cave, all but hidden not by powder but by the richness of the coming spring: thick bushes and rich vines grew all about the stone. He lifted the drapery of nature and urged her in. And there she found a man lying on a horse blanket. He had a bandage—created from the ripped sleeve of a man's shirt—around his leg. The Reb had brought what supplies he could in his saddle-bags and set them up around the man. And, Caitlin realized, the man was part of the Irish Brigade, the "Fighting 69th."

She looked at her captor.

"Water, fresh from the brook," he told her, pointing to a canteen. "Whiskey, there in the flask. A knife—burned the end of it good, but I'm afraid of trying to get out the bullet myself. I'll have a new fire burning in a wink."

She stared down at the man on the blanket that lay on nothing but a pallet of earth and leaves.

"Who is he… Why?" she murmured, confused.

"He is my cousin, and he is a man, living but injured. And, as I've told you, I'm afraid to go for the bullet myself. I've spent too much time firing the bastards, and not near enough time getting them out of the flesh they've torn apart."

Caitlin went down on her knees next to the man. Carefully, she removed the bandage. She was glad to see the wound wasn't festering and that it clotted; her patient would not bleed to death before she had a chance to even pray that she might save his life. She reached for the whiskey and poured it over the wound. "I don't have a bullet extractor. We really need to get him back to the medical tent," she said.

He hunkered down beside her, reaching into the pocket of his gray uniform jacket. To her astonishment, he produced a probe. "Will this do?"

"An extractor would be better," she said. "But, yes..."

He had matches. She saw that he'd had a fire set to go, and he lit it then. "I'll hold his leg. You need to get out the bullet." The fire burned, spreading warmth and light.

He held the patient down.

Caitlin inhaled, exhaled, prayed—and went for the bullet.

Her hands were tiny, her fingers long and slim. An extractor would've been better, as she'd said, but using the probe as leverage, she managed to get the bullet out. They applied pressure together. She bathed the wound with the whiskey again.

And then she saw the patient looking at her. He managed a smile. "Whiskey!" he breathed. "A touch in the mouth, eh, for the pain?"

She gave him the flask.

"Not too much. We may yet need some of that drink, good sir," she told him.

He swallowed deeply. "Gentle touch, lady! A sweet and gentle touch." He turned to the man by her side. He was silent for a long moment, and yet she saw in his eyes that there was a tremendous warmth between the men.

"Sean, you bastard! What, did you kidnap the lass?"

"Ah, cousin! No kidnapping, sir! Just a-borrowin'! She's free to leave now she's done. But I reckon I'm the one who has to be going. She'll see to it you're safe. Back in the arms of your brethren."

"Stay, Sean. It is obvious to all since Gettysburg. The South is losing now, despite the genius of you bastards at war." He swallowed hard against his pain once more and gave his attention to Caitlin. "Lieutenant Colonel Michael O'Brian, Miss. And the scruffy lad is Sean Finnegan. We are in your debt."

"Sir, I'm in this to do what I can," Caitlin said softly. "And, you, sir, need real medical care. I've done what I am able—"

"Ah, lass, best we lie here, as we are, eh? Fierce that battle raged! The dead and dying will be all about, and if a surgeon were to come upon me now, well, he'd say the leg was a goner, and I think you might have saved it for me," Lieutenant Colonel O'Brian said. He shuddered and asked, "Might I have another shot of that whiskey, lass?"

Caitlin glanced over at Sean Finnegan, not certain what his plans were—and wondering as well if they needed to save the whiskey.

But Sean nodded at her. "Aye, ease his pain!" he said.

Caitlin did so, but as she handed O'Brian the whiskey, she nearly jumped out of her skin.

She thought the most horrific cannon fire of all had gone off!

It had not.

She was startled to feel a gentle hand on her shoulder. Sean Finnegan. "Thunder and lightning. God Himself in a rage over the blood we're spilling, I dare say."

"Then why spill it?" she whispered.

Sean Finnegan didn't answer right away. He looked down at their patient, his cousin, and sighed softly, seeing that Michael O'Brian had either passed out or fallen asleep.

He shrugged. "I made my new home in Virginia. I went with my state, Miss…?"

"Adair," Caitlin told him. "Caitlin Adair."

"Not quite a hundred years ago, the states gathered together as colonies, but they were still separate entities. Virginia is a sovereign state. She wanted to secede. There are different ways to view this tragedy. The victor shall declare which way was the right way."

"But, there's the issue of slavery!"

"Yes, an institution that must end and, I believe, time would have seen to it. I'm fighting here, Miss Adair. I do not own slaves, nor do I condone slavery. But I did become a Virginian." He paused, looking out the entrance to the cave; the rain was coming down in torrents now. "I do believe the South will lose the war. I, like my company, will see it through to the bitter end, and then we will all pick up the pieces. And so, what are you doing here, Miss Adair? Have you no husband, no fiancé, who might be worried or offended that you spend your days nursing wounded men?"

"I have no husband. My fiancé died at the beginning of the war. At Antietam. But, had he not, he wouldn't have objected to me helping the wounded. And, frankly, I'd not love any man who would object to whatever care I might offer those in pain," she said.

He smiled slowly at that. "Bravo, Miss Adair!"

"And what of you, sir? Do your wife and children await you in Virginia?"

"We did not have time for children," he told her.

"Your wife?"

"She died in Petersburg. She was a civilian casualty."

"Oh, my God!" Caitlin breathed, horrified. "I'm so sorry. I—"

"My dear Miss Adair, you needn't be afraid of me, of my seeking vengeance. No one sought to kill her. I don't hate Northerners because of her death." He paused. "I will admit that at first, I hated everyone. I hated the fact that so many of us had been starving, and we'd fled Ireland. I hated the Yankees for fighting and I hated the Rebels for seceding. But I like to believe I'm a sane man. I hate this war. I hate all war. I will always hate war. Moira was killed by accident. A building collapsed during the siege. She was doing as you're doing—helping out in a state building turned hospital and it was hit by shells…and she was crushed with dozens others inside. I received a letter from the Yankee surgeon who tried to save her. He must be a very fine man. I hope to meet him one day. And I believe that there will be peace, and perhaps I will have a chance to thank him proper." He reached for the whiskey flask and took a long swallow, and then lifted the flask to her. "I want to believe there will be a day, once again when we can waken each morning to live rather than to kill. What about you?"

She hadn't thought much about her life. She hadn't thought much about anything beyond the war.

"Have a swig. It can help."

"Ah, yes, a lady drinking whiskey."

"Ah, lass! You are the finest lady I've met. Silks and satins and drawing room manners do not save men's lives. To you, Miss Adair!"

She accepted the flask and gulped some down. Then she returned it.

The rain was heavy; the dirt by the entry to the cave was beginning to soak from the overflow.

"We need to move him further back," she murmured.

"Indeed. He's on my saddle blanket. We each need to get a grasp and pull," Sean said.

She took one end of the blanket, while he took the other. They carried their patience deeper inside the cave. Little effort was required from Caitlin to put forth; Sean Finnegan had a solid grasp and, while he was lean— Confederate rations were very low, she knew—he was wiry and strong.

The fire Sean had built glowed near the entrance. Caitlin closed her eyes and imagined the battlefield. She wondered if Captain Mulligan was looking for her, and what had happened to Ethan Delaney. But she wasn't afraid at all. She felt strangely warm in the cave; it was as if she'd stumbled upon an oasis in the midst of all the carnage.

Lieutenant Colonel Michael O'Brian lay silent, sleeping or passed out.

She and Sean Finnegan leaned against the rough wall, watched the orange and blue dance of the flames, and listened to the rain thundering outside.

"So. Where is home for you?" he asked.

"It was Washington, DC," she said. "My family came to America and we lived in New York, but my mum died of pneumonia and my father of a heart attack not long after. I was working with an old family friend as a writer for the Smithsonian museum. Danny, my fiancé... Danny was with the military. We would have wed—" She broke off, shrugged and looked at him. "When the war is over, I'm going back to New York, I believe."

"Ah, yes! New York. Where the Irish gangs run crazy, politics are corrupt. And yet you can almost understand the reason for the gangs because business owners have signs on their doors that state 'No Irish!' and the Five Points area is brutal as all hell."

"Aye," Caitlin said and smiled.

"You're smiling!"

"It's a great city. We have to fight to find our place within it, but we *do* fight—with words and newspapers, far more important than fists!—and we watch it grow and change. My cousin bought a place downtown near Trinity. He's opened it as a rooming house and is making good money in a completely legitimate way!" Caitlin told him. "And I have a friend who has a cigar shop now. And another who runs a coffee shop. I may be a fool, but... I believe in the dream."

"My cousin bought a place by St. Paul's," Sean said, smiling, too, as he leaned back. "It's not much now, but I know Michael. It will be a grand pub one day. There will be a long line of taps. There will be a comfortable room for women and children. There will be fish and chips served along with bacon and cabbage and fine pies... Michael will show them all!"

"You've seen this pub?" she asked.

"Of course. I was going to come and work it for him," Sean replied.

"But…it's in New York."

He laughed softly. "Yes, New York. Well, our plans were all made before the war, you know."

They were both silent.

The rain continued to pound.

"Perhaps…" Caitlin murmured.

"Perhaps?"

"I was thinking you should…go. Leave this place, I mean. Now. We're not sure of what is going on. I don't know what your fate might be if you stay."

He laughed, then smiled at her again, and she quickly looked away, disturbed by the way his smile made her feel. Danny had been dead a long time. She couldn't believe that her heart—and her senses—were suddenly being awakened by a man who was essentially an enemy.

"You are assuming the Yanks will take the battle," he said.

"I do assume the war is drawing to a close," she responded quietly. "The South is starving. The ports along the Mississippi River have all fallen. I…"

"You fear for me?" he asked, his smile deepening.

"This battle… You were outgunned, and outnumbered. They're going to take you!" Caitlin said. "Don't you realize? They're going to take you. You'll be a prisoner. Prisoners don't…fare well."

Her hand lay on the ground, and he set his over it gently. "I won't leave yet," he told her. "Night will fall, and God knows who or what else lurks in these woods. Come the dawn, I will leave you and my cousin. But I will stay with you through the night."

Night came, and they sat there, speaking from time to time.

Michael O'Brian awoke, restless. Sean found some hardtack and dried beef in his saddlebags. He disappeared into the driving rain and returned with an armful of twigs and branches, feeding the fire and making a meal of dried beef and the hard bread in a small tin from his mess kit.

While the storm waged on, they had something that resembled supper, and they talked—about Ireland, about the United States and even about the Confederate States.

Then Michael slept again, and Caitlin felt good; his wound seemed to be healing well already.

She leaned against the cave wall. And, eventually, as sleep claimed her, she leaned against the shoulder of the Rebel at her side.

Caitlin awoke startled, but not sure why.

Lieutenant Colonel Michael O'Brian still slept.

Sean Finnegan was gone.

And then she knew why she'd awakened.

The rain had stopped, or petered out to just a drizzle. But she could hear movement outside, like a rustling in the bushes. She stood, grabbing one of the tree branches Sean had brought in for the fire. She didn't know why she was afraid. If Union forces had won the battle, she was safe, and Lieutenant Colonel O'Brian would be well-tended. And even if the Rebel troops had taken the day, she wouldn't be hurt. It would go badly for O'Brian, though, simply because the Southerners really had nothing left. They couldn't feed their own people, much less prisoners. And as for her…they'd send her back.

Despite that, she *was* afraid. Very afraid. Something felt…wrong.

Then she jumped back. A man walked in. Crouched low at first to clear the entrance at the cave's mouth, then straightening and calling to a friend, "Well, will you lookee here! Wow, we've got a treasure in the night!"

"What are you going on about?" another man asked, stepping in.

Caitlin didn't know if they were Northerners or Southerners—their clothing was such a mix. Their jackets and boots had probably been taken from dead soldiers they found along the way.

Both men stared at her. And both smiled.

"She's tending a Billy Yank, there," one of them said. He was the first one who'd entered. He had the worst set of teeth Caitlin had ever seen. And he wielded a knife. She wondered why the state of the man's teeth seemed to bother her more.

"He don't look like he can put up much of a fight," the other said. His teeth were fine. He had scraggly brown hair and a look in his eyes that was worse than the other guy's teeth.

"We're supposed to be finding food and arms," Bad Teeth said.

"Ah, but a prize like this…" Shaggy Hair muttered.

"Share and share alike," Bad Teeth reminded him.

"Share with our fellows?" Shaggy Hair asked, and laughed. "There not sharing with us at the moment. They're busy cleaning up whatever goods they can find and 'confiscate' back at the old Hartford farmhouse near the battlefield. They'll be needing to share with us later. Right now, with what we got right here, you and me, we just share first."

"What about Billy Yank on the ground there?"

"We throw him out."

"Touch him, and you die!" Caitlin said ferociously. How she was going to make that happen, she didn't know. She'd go down fighting before either of them touched her or Michael O'Brian.

Bad Teeth lunged for her. She swung her branch for all she was worth. Even as she caught him in the middle and he yelped like a hyena, Shaggy Hair came after her.

She was about to go down. Visions of assault and rape flashed through her head, along with dying naked on the ground with Michael O'Brian.

But none of it ever happened. No one ever touched her.

Sean Finnegan burst back in. He managed to capture both men, grabbing them by the back of their necks— and cracking their heads together hard. They fell without a whimper.

Sean stepped over them, hurrying toward her. He pulled her close, smoothing back her hair as her face rested against his chest.

*He was warm, powerful, so vital. She wanted to stay there forever. To touch him and know more of him, know all about him, stay... Just stay.*

He drew back, studying her anxiously.

"I'm fine," she assured him. "I'm fine. Thank you."

"I heard you talking to them. You were very fierce. You're a fighter. But...you're really not that big."

On the ground, one of the downed men stirred.

"I'll be back," Sean promised.

He picked both men up by their arms and dragged them outside.

He didn't come right back; she didn't know where he'd gone. And then…he did return.

Once more, he took her anxiously into his arms. She realized she was shaking. She reached up to touch his face, her palm against his cheek.

"May I?" he asked softly.

She nodded. And he kissed her. Their kiss was deep and warm and exciting and stirring and somehow reassuring. It was a promise, an acknowledgment of a night that had been like a lifetime.

And somehow, it was hope.

Sean drew away and said huskily, "I have to go. But I swear you will be all right. I swear."

Then he was gone.

Moments later, she heard voices, and she raced to the entrance of the cave. She saw that a ragtag team of the Irish Brigade was coming toward her.

Captain Mulligan, followed by Ethan Delaney, was at the head.

She called out to them, waving her arms.

The storm was gone; the morning had dawned with a golden glow, as if all the sins of the world had been washed away.

"Thank God!" Mulligan cried. "Ethan was afraid you'd been taken!"

"Well, I was taken, but to tend to one of our own," Caitlin said. "Lieutenant Colonel Michael O'Brian lies within. I believe he will do well. Clean wound and the bullet is out."

"I'll see to him, sir!" Ethan said, rushing into the cave.

Mulligan studied Caitlin. "You're quite all right?" he asked.

"Indeed, I am."

"Thank God, lass, thank God. This war is drawing to a close. We have feared our enemies all these years. Now, once again, we will be one country, and that country will be filled with good men—and, inevitably, with bad men. It will not matter if they hail from the North or South. There will always be those who take advantage. They will show their true colors." He hesitated. "The Hartford farmhouse up a ways... It was attacked last night. By a band of deserters, North and South. The house was robbed, the house was burned to the ground. We—we don't know what happened to the family, but... well, at least we believe we have two of the men who did it. Strange—they arrived outside the medical tent as dawn broke, trussed up like a pair of sows for market. So...thank God! Indeed. Thank the good Lord above that you're okay!"

She *was* okay; Caitlin was okay.

But she was shaking. When she started to sink to the ground, Captain Mulligan caught her and held her up.

"Caitlin?"

"Captain, I'm safe. Thank you!" she told him fervently.


The war did draw quickly to an end. The battles of Bentonville, Five Forks and Sailor's Creek were hard fought.

Then General Robert E. Lee arranged a surrender at Appomattox Courthouse, and while a few skirmishes would still occur, the war was, for all intents and purposes, over.

It had actually ended for Caitlin a while before. Lieutenant Colonel Michael O'Brian had needed a nurse to get him north for his convalescence, and Caitlin had agreed to accompany him. She could see her family; she could plan something of a future. The two of them became close. He told her once he knew he could never be her father, but he would be happy to look after her the way a father should.

She told him she was pretty good at looking after herself—but that she was truly glad to have a friend.

As it happened, she was able to see the pub Sean Finnegan had talked about. Michael O'Brian had rooms over the pub, and she was welcomed to visit one of them.

Of course, sadly, the place had gone to rot and ruin while O'Brian was gone. Caitlin set to cleaning out the trash that had accumulated. Friends and family helped, and they managed to get the taps cleaned and the tables polished. O'Brian was, of course, deeply grateful, and offered jobs as cooks and bartenders, bookkeepers and more, to her friends and family. But it would take a bit of effort to get it all going.

Caitlin sat with Michael O'Brian one morning, sipping coffee and describing how the place could be arranged when they were ready to reopen. He reminded her that he'd been a pub keeper before the war, wagging a finger at her and laughing. And then, suddenly, much like her own father, he keeled over where he sat.

She summoned the doctor; it was too late.

Michael O'Brian was gone.

Three days later, Michael was buried with full military honors at a Catholic cemetery in the Bronx.

Caitlin remained in shock, but she stood in the middle of the pub, looking over at the friends and family who were hoping to make a living at the pub.

"I'm afraid I don't know the fate of the property," she said. "We'll just have to wait and see. Until then…"

The doors to the pub swung open. She was surprised to see a dapper man with a handsome frock coat, a high bowler and a cane enter, followed by what had to be two of the best-dressed thugs she'd ever seen.

"Ah, Miss Adair, I do believe!" the man said. "I'm Franklin Henderson, and I'm sure you've heard of me. I own a great deal of the property in this area."

Perhaps she'd never manage not to be a bit of a sass; she couldn't help herself. "Ah, sir! I believe you are mistaken. Trinity Parish owns a great deal of property in this area!"

A flash of anger seemed to touch his face, but then his polite smile deepened. "I have excellent lawyers, Miss Adair. If the property isn't claimed by the rightful heir—a man believed to have perished in the war—the bank retains ownership and I will be taking it from the bank. I'm here to politely inform you that you have just days to vacate."

"And if we don't? Sure, I can afford a lawyer of my own? I'm certain that Michael O'Brian left other papers," Caitlin said.

One of the thugs was carrying some kind of strap. He made a point of creating a beating sound with it.

So she was left to stand there staring back at him—and to feel ill, wondering what would happen to them all.

Then the Broadway door to the pub burst open again, and a ray of sunlight streamed through.

To Caitlin's disbelief, *he* was there.

Sean Finnegan.

"Caitlin!" He called her name. He hurried down the room toward her, sweeping her into his arms. He set her down, smiling, then turned toward the others. "How do you all do? Forgive me. I'm Sean Finnegan."

He spun on the men who had come. "Sean *Finnegan*!" he emphasized, as if he knew why they were there. "I've just been to the bank. I am the rightful owner of this fine establishment."

He walked back toward the men. "And might I suggest that if my fiancée, Miss Adair, is ever *politely warned* or otherwise addressed again, I will be seeing to the reply."

He was, of course, ridiculously tall, and broad-shouldered, and he'd filled out nicely. And bathed.

In truth, he was quite beautiful.

A cheer went up.

Franklin Henderson looked very angry. He pointed his cane at Sean Finnegan. "Sir, trust me. This is not over. You will sell me this property."

"Sir, I will not. And I do suggest you leave!"

The men stormed out, and another cheer went up. Sean turned to Caitlin. "I…uh, well, I'm afraid I presumed a great deal there. You mustn't feel obliged. But, well…you're alone, I'm alone, Michael loved us both. You barely know me, but I know you. I know who you are, and how you think. I know your heart and your courage. I—"

She wasn't in the least proud. She threw herself at him, into his arms, hopping up and winding her legs around his waist.

Finding his lips. And they kissed and kissed…

Hope fulfilled.

"We'll make it one of the best pubs in the city!" she whispered, her lips breaking from his at last.

"You know," he told her seriously, "you don't have to marry me. Michael would've wanted you to have the pub. He worked hard at it before the war. You've gotten it going since then. You saved his life."

"You might have saved mine."

"Ah, lass! You're the strongest, most fearless girl I've ever met. You'd do just fine, with me or without me."

She smiled at him. "I'm okay tough, huh?"

"Okay tough! Indeed!"

She smiled and she couldn't help herself; she kissed him again. "We've a wedding to plan!" she said happily. "And the pub to get going! Ah! Yes, we'll open with a celebration…and we'll call the place… Finnegan's!"


"Finnegan's!" Kieran said, clapping her little hands together.

"And so it has been. Family members have come and gone from Ireland, but since that day, the pub has been Finnegan's. And so it will remain."

"And you and Da will run it forever now!" Kieran said.

Her mother smiled and smoothed back her hair.

"Family will run it…forever, we hope!"

Kieran felt her mum's kiss on her forehead. And she smiled up at her and promised, "One day, I will tell the first story to my daughter!" she promised.

Kieran's mother closed the book.

"Mum?" Kieran said worriedly.

"None of us knows, sweet child, what the future will bring. But I do believe that you'll always have love. You have me and your da and your brothers and Finnegan's and...."

"And?"

"You're Irish! Lucky enough! And now, to bed!"

To bed.

The future was always ahead of them, still to come. And so it would be with Finnegan's.

\* \* \* \* \*

*Keep reading for a special preview
of the next thrilling novel in the*
NEW YORK CONFIDENTIAL *series,*

*A PERFECT OBSESSION*

*Coming soon from*
New York Times *bestselling author
Heather Graham and MIRA Books*

# 1

*"Horrible! Oh, God, horrible—tragic!"* John Shaw said, shaking his head with a dazed look as he sat on his bar stool at Finnegan's Pub.

Kieran nodded sympathetically. Construction crews had found old graves when they were working on the foundations at the hot new downtown venue Le Club Vampyre.

Anthropologists had found the new body among the old graves the next day.

It wasn't just *any* body.

It was the body of supermodel Jeannette Gilbert.

Finding the old graves wasn't much of a shock—not in New York City, and not in a building that was close to two centuries old. The structure that housed Le Club Vampyre was a deconsecrated Episcopal church. The church's congregation had moved to a facility it had purchased from the Catholic church—whose congregation was now in a sparkling new basilica over on Park Avenue. While many had bemoaned the fact that such a venerable old institution had been turned into an establishment for those into sex, drugs, and rock and roll, life—and business—went on.

And with life going on...

Well, work on the building's foundations went on, too.

It was while investigators were still being called in following the discovery of the newly deceased body— moments before it hit the news—that Kieran Finnegan learned about it, and that was because she was helping out at her family's establishment, Finnegan's on Broadway. Like the old church/nightclub behind it, Finnegan's dated back to just before the Civil War, and had been a pub for most of those years. Since it was geographically the closest place to the church with liquor, it had apparently seemed the right spot at that moment for Professor John Shaw. They'd barely opened; it was still morning, and it was a Friday, and Kieran was only there at that time because her bosses had decided on a day off following their participation in a lengthy trial. She'd just come up from the cellar, fetching a few bottles of a vintage chardonnay for her brother that had been ordered specifically for a lunch that day, when John Shaw had caught her attention, desperate to talk.

"I can't tell you how excited I was, being called in as an expert on a find like that," the professor told Kieran. "They both wanted me! By they, I mean Henry Willoughby, president of Preserve our Past, and Roger Gleason, owner and manager of the club. I was so honored. It was exciting to think of finding the *old* bodies—not the new body. But then...opening a decaying coffin and finding Jeannette Gilbert! And the university was entirely behind me, allowing me the time to be at my site, giving me a chance to bring my grad students here. Oh, my God! I found her! Oh, it was…"

John Shaw was shaking as he spoke. He was a man who'd seen all kinds of antiquated horrors, an expert in the past. He fit the stereotype of an academic with his lean physique, his thatch of wild white hair and his little gold-framed glasses. He held doctorate degrees in archaeology and anthropology, and science and history meant everything to him.

Kieran realized that he'd been about to say once again that it was horrible, like nothing he'd ever experienced. He clearly realized that he was speaking about a recently living woman, adored by adolescent boys and heterosexual males of all ages—a woman who was going to be deeply mourned.

Jeannette Gilbert. Media princess. The model and actress had disappeared two weeks ago after the launch party for a new cosmetics line. Her agent and manager, Oswald Martin, had gone on the news, begging kidnappers for her safe return.

At that time, no one knew if she actually *had* been kidnapped. One reporter speculated that she'd disappeared on purpose, determined to get away from the very man begging kidnappers for her release: her agent and manager.

Kieran hadn't really paid much attention; she'd assumed that the young woman—who'd been made famous by the same Oswald Martin—had just had enough of being adored and fawned over and told what to do at every move, and she'd decided to take a hiatus. Or it might have been some kind of publicity gig; her disappearance had certainly ruled the headlines. There were always tabloid pictures of Jeannette with this or that man, and then speculation in the same tabloids that her manager had furiously burst into a hotel room, sending Jeannette Gilbert's latest lover—gold digger, as Martin referred to any young man she dated—flying out the door.

In the past few weeks the "celebrity" magazines had run rampant with rumors of a mystery man in her life. A secret love. Kieran knew that only because her twin brother, Kevin, was an actor—struggling his way into TV, movies and theater. He read the tabloids avidly, telling Kieran that he was "reading between the lines," and being up on what was going on was critical to his career. There were too many actors—even good ones!—out there and too few roles. Any edge was a good edge.

While all the speculation had been going on, Kieran couldn't help wondering if Jeannette's secret lover had killed her—or if, maybe, her steel-handed manager had done so.

Or, since this was New York City with a population in the millions, it was possible that some deranged person had murdered her. Perhaps this person felt that if she was relieved of her life, she'd be out of the misery caused by being such a beautiful, glittering star, always the focus of attention.

It was fine to speculate when you believed that someone was just pulling a major publicity stunt.

Now Kieran felt bad, of course. From what she *knew* now, it seemed evident that the woman had indeed been murdered.

Not that she had any of the facts other than that Jeannette had been found in the bowels of the earth in a nineteenth-century tomb, but it was unlikely that Jeannette Gilbert had crawled into a historic coffin in a lost catacomb to die of natural causes.

"It was so horrible!" John Shaw repeated woefully. "When we found her, we just stared. One of my silly young grad students screamed, and she wasn't the only one. We called the police immediately. The club wasn't open then, of course—except to us, those of us who were working. I was there for hours while they grilled me. And now…now, I need this!" His hand shook as he picked up his double shot of single-malt scotch to swallow in a gulp.

He was usually a beer man. Ultra light.

It was horrible, yes, as Shaw kept saying. But, of course, he realized he'd be in the news, interviewed for dozens of papers and magazines and television, as well.

After all…

He'd been the one to find Jeannette Gilbert dead. In a coffin, in a deconsecrated church now turned into the Le Club Vampyre. Well, that was news.

The pub would soon be buzzing, especially since it was on the other side of the block from Le Club Vampyre.

The whole situation, aside from the grief of a young woman's untimely death, was interesting to Kieran. In her "real" job during the week she worked as a psychologist and therapist for psychiatrists Bentley Fuller and Allison Miro. But, like her brothers, she often filled in at the pub; it was kind of a home away from home for them all. The pub had been in the family—belonging to a distant great-great uncle—from the mid-nineteenth century. Her own parents were gone now, and that made the pub even more precious to her and her older brother, Declan, her twin, Kevin, and her "baby" brother, Daniel.

So, while Declan actually managed the pub and made it his life's work, Kieran was employed by Doctors Fuller and Miro, Kevin pursued his acting career and Danny strove to become the city's best tour guide. And they all spent a great deal of time at Finnegan's.

The tragic death of Jeannette Gilbert would soon have all their patrons gossiping about this latest outrage regarding Le Club Vampyre. They'd been talking about it now and then for six months, ever since the sale of the old church to Dark Doors Incorporated. Patrons had become extremely glum when the club had opened a month ago. A club! Like that! In an old church!

The club had also, of course, been the main topic of conversation yesterday, when the news had come out that unknown gravesites had been found—and Professor John Shaw had been called in.

Of course, people were still talking about the old catacombs today. Not that finding graves while digging in foundations was unusual in New York. It was just creepy-cool enough.

Creepy-cool was fine when you were talking about very old gravesites.

Because they were old—they were the site of the earthly remains of people who'd lived and died long ago.

Not the newly deceased.

At the moment, though, Kieran was one of the few people who knew that the body of Jeannette Gilbert had been discovered. Kieran had been among the first to find out; that was because she knew Dr. John Shaw—professor of archaeology and anthropology at NYU, famed in academic circles for his work on sites from Jamestown, Virginia, to Beijing, China—very well. He and a group of his colleagues had met at Finnegan's Pub one night a month as long as she could remember.

When she'd see him looking so distressed, she'd ushered him into one of the small booths against the wall that divided the pub's general area from the offices. She'd gotten him his scotch—and she'd sat down with him so she could try to calm him down.

"Oh, my God! I can just imagine when it hits the news!" he said, looking at her with stricken eyes. And yet, she recognized a bit of awe in them...

Of course, he hadn't known Jeannette Gilbert. Kieran hadn't, either. She'd seen her once, on a red carpet, heading to the premiere of a new movie in a theater near Times Square.

Sadly, Jeannette hadn't been an especially talented actress. But she'd been too beautiful for most people to care.

"I'm so sorry you're the one who found her," Kieran said. That should've been the right thing to say; usually, people didn't want to find others dead. Though John Shaw was going to be famous in the pop-culture world now, as well as the academic world.

But it was obvious that he was badly shaken.

He was accustomed to studying bones and mummies—not a woman who'd been recently murdered.

"I was—I am!—very excited about the project. I don't understand how the church could have lost all those graves. Can you imagine? Okay, so, you know how they built St. Paul's to accommodate folks farther north of Trinity back in the day? Well, they built St.

Augustine's for those a little north of St. Paul's. And, according to my research so far, the church was fine until about 1860, when way too many people went off to fight in the Civil War. It wasn't deconsecrated—just more or less abandoned because the congregations were so much smaller. Then, according to records, Father O'Hara passed away, and it took the church forever to send out a new priest. Apparently, there was structural damage by then, which closed off that section of the catacombs. You see, there was, until about seventy-five years ago, an entrance to the catacombs from the street, and I suppose everyone—church officials, city organizers, engineers, what have you—believed all the graves had been removed. Of course, most of the dead were buried then in wooden coffins, and in the ground area outside, most of those became dirt and bone. But there were underground catacombs, too. Coffins set upon shelves... Some of the dead were just shrouded, but some were in old wooden coffins, and they were decaying and falling apart and I had workers taking them down so carefully—and then there she was!"

He sipped his scotch again and looked at her intently. "Kieran, you're not to say a word, not yet. The police... they asked me not to speak about this until...until some-one was notified. I don't think either of her parents are living, but she must have family..." His voice trailed off. "My God. It was ghastly!" he said a moment later. "Gruesome—ghastly!"

This time, he didn't sip his scotch. He swallowed it down in a gulp.

Kieran wasn't sure why she turned to look at the front door when she did; it was always opening and closing. Maybe she wanted to look anywhere except at John Shaw. She was a working psychologist, and yet she wasn't sure what to say to the man.

She glanced up just in time to see Craig Frasier come in and blink to adjust to the light.

She wasn't surprised Craig was there; they were seeing each other and had been since the affair over the "flawless" Capeletti diamond. They were talking about giving up their current situation, in which they each had dresser drawers at the other's apartment, and moving in together.

But while she had truly fallen in love with Craig, she was a little hesitant—and a little worried about the fact that the man she believed to be her soul mate also happened to be a special agent with the FBI. Her family was striving to be legitimate now, which hadn't always been the case. Growing up, her brothers had had a few brushes with the law.

And trusting her beloved brothers to behave wasn't easy. They were never malicious; however, their ways of helping friends out of bad situations weren't always the best.

Then again, she'd met Craig because of the Capeletti diamond and Danny's determination to do the right thing…

And because of some criminal clientele.

"Excuse me," she murmured to John, assuming that Craig had come to see her.

The door was still open; he stood in a pool of light and her heart leaped as she saw him. Craig was, in her mind, entirely impressive, tall and broad shouldered, with extraordinary eyes that seemed to take everything in.

But he had not, apparently, come to see her.

He greeted Kieran with a nod, held her shoulders for a minute—and then offered her a grim smile as he gently set her aside so he could move past her.

Something was up. Craig spent his free time here with her and her family. Her friends, coworkers and the usual clientele all knew that Craig and Kieran were a couple.

Today, however, there wasn't even a quick kiss. Craig was being very official.

He was heading straight to the booth where John Shaw was seated.

Kieran stood there for a minute, perplexed.

Of course, Craig was FBI. But a local woman had been killed, and no matter how famous she'd been, it should've remained a matter for the NYPD. And John Shaw had left the old church/screaming-hot nightclub less than an hour ago.

Why would Craig be here so quickly? And more to the point, why was the FBI involved?

She didn't get a chance to slide back into the booth and find out what was going on; she felt a tap on her shoulder and turned around.

Her brother Kevin was next to her. Kevin was a striking man—in *anyone's* opinion, she thought. He was tall and fit with fine features, dark red hair and deep blue eyes; their coloring was the same. They were twins, and it showed. She loved her brother and she felt that acting was the perfect career for him. Like all of them, however, he worked at the pub when he could.

"I have to talk to you!" he said urgently.

"Sure," she said.

"Not here. In the office," he told her. To her surprise,

he glanced uneasily at Craig—whom he liked and with whom he was pretty good friends.

Her brother whirled her around and headed her down the entry aisle toward the bar and then to the left and down the hallway to the business office. He peered in, as if afraid their older brother might be there, since it was, basically, Declan's office.

He closed the door behind them.

"She's dead, Kieran! She's dead!" Kevin said, looking at her and shaking his head with dismay and anxiety.

She stared at him for a moment. He couldn't be talking about Jeannette Gilbert—no one knew she'd been found at the church yet, not according to John Shaw.

Her heart quaked with fear. She was afraid he was talking about an old friend, or a longtime customer of the pub.

Someone he cared about deeply.

"Kevin, *who*?" she asked.

"Jeannette."

She frowned. "Jeannette Gilbert?"

He nodded.

"Okay," she said slowly. "*I* know that, because John Shaw just told me. But he only found her a few hours ago. The police asked him not to say anything."

Kevin took a deep breath. "Well, John Shaw might not have said anything, but one of the workers down there—a grunt? A student? I don't know—came out and told people on the street, and the story was picked up, and there are already media crews there."

She studied her brother. "Kevin, it's terrible. A young and beautiful young woman who was very popular has—I'm assuming—been murdered. But, Kevin, I'm afraid that terrible things do happen. But…we didn't know Jeannette Gilbert. Not personally."

"Yes," he said. "We did."

"We did?"

"*I* did," he corrected. "Kieran, I was the so-called 'mystery man' she was dating! I might have been the last one to see her alive."

The NYPD had been called in first; that was proper protocol, since New York City was where the body had been found.

Jeannette Gilbert hadn't been kidnapped in another state and subsequently killed in New York. She'd last been seen by her doorman entering her apartment; she was a longtime Manhattan resident. She had, in fact, grown up in Harlem, a little girl who'd lost both parents and gone on to live in a household filled with children and an aunt who hadn't wanted another mouth to feed.

At the age of seventeen, however, she had an affair with a rock star.

While the rock star denied any kind of intimate relationship with her at the time, he'd gone on to put her in one of his music videos soon after.

An agent had picked her up and it had been a classic tale—little girl lost had become a megastar. By twenty-five, she was gracing runways and doing cameo spots on television shows and even appearing in small roles in several movies. She was considered a true supernova.

Because Jeannette's physical appearance had been called *perfect* by every critic out there.

She could walk a runway.

She had beautiful skin, luscious hair, long legs and a body that didn't quit.

Craig Frasier had learned all this about Jeannette in the past few hours. Before that, she'd been a face he might have recognized on a magazine cover.

But he'd made it his business to read up on her quickly.

Because her death had suddenly become the focus of his life.

He'd been in his office, reading paperwork from witnesses about the murder of a known pimp, when he'd been summoned, along with his partner, Mike Dalton, to Assistant Director Richard Eagan's office.

Craig and Mike had been partners for years. Craig had been assigned a young, new agent when Mike was laid up on medical—a shot to the buttocks—about a year ago. He'd learned then how much he appreciated his partner; they knew each other's minds. They naturally fell into a division of labor when it came to pounding the pavement and getting the inevitable paperwork done.

And there was no one Craig trusted more to have his back, especially in a shoot-out.

Eagan, a good man himself, was hardcore Bureau. His personal life had suffered for it, but he never brought that into the office. He was the best kind of authority figure, as well—dignified, fair, compassionate. And efficient. He never wasted time. There were two chairs in front of his desk, but he hadn't waited for Craig and Mike to sit down. He'd started talking right away.

"I had a back-burner situation going on here," he'd told them. "We'd been given information, but the local police down in Fredericksburg, Virginia, were handling the case. A girl—a perfect-looking girl, an artist's model—disappeared about six months ago. A few

weeks later, her body was found in a historic cemetery outside Fredericksburg. She'd been stabbed in the
heart, then cleaned up, dressed up and laid out in a
family mausoleum. She was discovered when the family's matriarch died, since she'd been put in the matriarch's space. As I said, it seemed to be a local matter,
and the Fredericksburg police and Virginia state police
had the murder. We were informed because of the unusual aspects."

Eagan had paused, running his hands through his
hair. Then he'd resumed speaking. "We're all aware of
the high-profile disappearance of Jeannette Gilbert."

Mike had nodded. "Yeah, we were briefed with the
cops about her disappearance when she went missing.
We weren't really in on it, as you know. But we were
on the lookout."

"Ms. Gilbert's been found. An archaeological dig at
old St. Augustine's."

"You mean—" Mike began.

But Eagan had cut him off. Yeah, he meant the new
nightclub. Eagan wasn't a fan. He'd gone on and ranted
for a full minute about old historic places becoming
nightclubs. In his opinion, that suggested New York
City had no real respect for the past.

Craig knew Mike hadn't been asking his question
because of the club; he'd been trying to ascertain if
she'd been found dead.

Mike had glanced over at Craig; Craig shrugged.

They'd both just let Eagan rant, figuring it was obvious. The poor girl was dead.

It had ended with Eagan saying, "Yes, she's dead.
And it is bizarre—as bizarre as that earlier case, maybe
even more so. Because in this case, the perp had to

know she'd be found quickly. He'd placed her in a historical site where anthropologists and archaeologists were expected to arrive imminently. Later, you can go over the info on the Virginia case, do some comparisons. We're part of the task force on this, but we're taking the lead, and you two are up for our division. Because, gentlemen, I believe we have a serial killer on our hands."

They'd asked about the security tapes.

Techs were going over those now.

"That's a bitch!" Eagan had exclaimed. "Try looking for something out of the ordinary when every damned customer in the place is like an escapee from a Goth B flick or worse! Not to mention that the club closed down when the body was discovered. There's no club security at night other than the cameras, but cops have been patrolling the place since the historic folks stepped in."

From the office, he and Mike had gone straight to the church. The ME on duty was Anthony Andrews, a fine, detail-oriented doctor, but he hadn't really started yet.

Photographers were still taking pictures, trying to maintain the scene just as it had been after Professor Shaw had opened the first coffin—and had seen Jeannette Gilbert.

A half-dozen members of a forensic team had been moving around, but Dr. Andrews had delicately stopped the photo session to show Craig and Mike what he'd discovered. Gilbert had been killed in another location, stabbed through the heart, and then bathed and dressed and prepared before being placed in the old coffin.

Seeing her had been heartbreaking. He hadn't known the young woman or really anything about her until today, but she'd been young and beautiful and her life had been brutally taken. She lay in the old coffin, dressed in shimmering white, a wilted rose in her hands. With her eyes closed, it looked as if she slept.

Except, of course, she'd never wake again.

"Defensive wounds?" he'd asked Andrews.

"Not a one. She was taken by surprise. Whoever killed her stood close by—had to be someone who seemed trustworthy. Maybe someone she knew," the ME had speculated. "Or she could've had some kind of opiate in her system. Anyway, she didn't expect what was coming."

"Time of death?" Mike had asked. "She's been missing about two weeks."

"I'm thinking one to two weeks," Andrews had replied. "If she was abducted, perhaps soon after. And I don't believe she's been embalmed—but she was somehow preserved. Maybe in a freezer while he worked on her or made arrangements or…" He'd sighed. "I need to get her on the table."

Two patrol officers, the first on the scene, had closed off the area. Luckily, the club was closed, pending the investigation of the newly discovered crypt. Detective Larry McBride with the major crimes division had been the first to arrive. Craig and Mike had worked with him before. He was particularly mild mannered but he had a brilliant mind and nothing deterred his focus.

"Glad you guys are lead on this," McBride had told them. "This is… Well, I believe we definitely have a real psychopath on our hands. Bizarre! Wherever he killed her, he washed away the blood. I've got officers who'll be doing rounds with pictures of the dress. Pending notification of the so-called aunt who raised the girl, they'll be asking all her friends if she owned the dress, or if the killer obtained it."

"Checked the label," Andrews had said. "It's from Saks."

McBride had nodded. "Nice dress. She looks like a princess." He paused. "I have a daughter her age… So, anyway, no inside security by night—but cops watching on the street. The men on duty swore no one went in until Roger Gleason opened it up to wait for the archaeologists. Gleason says he comes in every day, even though the club's closed for a few days. I interviewed him and he seems to be on the up and up. Says he's personally not that interested in the historical stuff but seeing that the work goes well will actually make his club more famous. He's not one of those guys who lets his own property go unattended. He was working up here and heard Shaw's screams. Shaw swears there was no one down there the time but him and a few of his grad students. I have names, et cetera, which I've emailed to you already. They were all questioned. I don't think they had anything to do with Ms. Gilbert's death. The mystery here is, *how the hell did the bastard get in with the body?* Anyway, the security footage is down at your office now. And, of course, we're hoping Forensics can come up with something. This killer…well, they're calling in shrinks. You know, profilers. The murder was cold, swift and brutal. But then he takes all this time with her. He comes in like a shadow— and then leaves her on display, waiting to be found. I talked with Eagan, and I've been hanging around for you guys. Actually, I'm almost afraid to leave. It's a media frenzy out there."

By then the frenzy on the streets had involved more

than just media. Word had spread; dozens of celebrity stalkers and those inclined to the macabre had congregated outside the club.

Craig had questioned Gleason himself before leaving. He seemed like a Wall Street type—and although his club might be Goth, he was far more prone to the elegant in his manner and dress.

New York City's finest were dealing with the facility and crowd control.

"I need to talk to Shaw," Craig had decided.

But Shaw wasn't there. They'd heard that when he'd first gotten up close and personal with the body, he'd screamed like a banshee.

And Allie Benoit, John Shaw's grad student and assistant, had told him that Shaw had spoken with the police, and then freaked out and fled. Allie was pretty sure he'd gone to the pub—the pub whose back wall abutted that of the old church-turned-nightclub.

And that *was* exactly what John Shaw had done.

*Finnegan's!*

Craig had sworn, walked around the corner and reached the pub.

The damned man just had to go to Finnegan's!

The pub had stood there almost as long as the church. It had seen the New York draft riots during the Civil War, and the violence of the Irish gangs that had once held huge sway in a city where immigrants poured in daily from around the world.

The pub had witnessed so much history.

Including the recent history of the diamond heist that had nearly cost Kieran Finnegan her life.

"She won't be involved!" he'd said firmly, speaking aloud.

But before he'd entered, h[...]
his gut, that the die had alread[...]
*Of all the pubs in all the worl[...]*
*Finnegan's.*

...he'd entered the pub, Craig's attention was all for his search. With luck, Kieran would be at the office today or—

Naturally, she'd walked directly over to him.

And he hadn't been able to do what he wanted to do—tell her that she wasn't to have the least interaction with *anyone* connected to the murder.

He didn't have the right to make that kind of demand.

And since she was here, she might have already served John Shaw, and John Shaw would've talked to her...

At the moment, though, he needed Shaw. She'd understand that; he never had to explain himself or his intentions to Kieran.

She knew what he did for a living; he knew about her professional work for Doctors Fuller and Miro. They respected each other's professions and discussed things when they could—or when the other might have a useful insight. Or when, as occasionally happened, they became involved in the same case.

Fuller and Miro worked with the police and the FBI. They often gave their opinion of a suspected criminal's state of mind or behavior.

They'd been involved, all four of them together, in a situation before—the so-called Diamond Affair.

But now...

He wanted to hold her and yet he couldn't; he was here professionally.

Even as he approached the booth where John Shaw was seated, he was still hating the fact that the church where Jeannette had been found was directly behind Finnegan's. He'd come to terms with being in love with Kieran—and the fact that she, too, dealt with criminals.

However, it was still difficult for him to accept that she was sometimes too quick to put herself in danger in defense of others.

*Yes, it seemed to be a* Casablanca *moment.*

*Of all the old abandoned dug-out holes in Manhattan....*

*The damned catacombs just had to be close to Finnegan's!*

Too close... This place was too close to where a young woman lay dead, where her body had been stashed with the bones of those long forgotten.

Craig knew John Shaw, and Shaw knew him; they'd met at the pub several times when Shaw had come for his professional meetings or get-togethers—or when he just wanted to sip one of his ultralight beers and chill.

"Craig!" John said, looking up at him with surprise. "I—oh, my. You're coming to see me. So I guess it should be Special Agent Frasier. Not Craig. Look, I'm not sure what else I can say to anyone. All I know is that we opened that coffin and...and there she was."

Craig slid into the booth and smiled at him. "You must be pretty rattled."

"Yes. You're here officially? The police told me not to say anything yet. They need to contact the poor girl's family. I mean, that's why you're here—coming to me and not Kieran, right?"

"Yes, John, this is official. The NYPD detectives are on the case, of course, but we're taking part, as well. We've put together a task force. This as a very high-profile murder."

John nodded, his white hair—something of a strange mullet cut—flapping beside his ears. His glasses slid down his nose with his effort and he pushed them back with his forefinger.

"Of course. This needs to be solved fast," John said. "But..." His expression grew even more perplexed. "I don't know how I can help anymore. I don't know how I can help, period. Professor Digby—Aldous Digby, one of my associates—and I were there, and three grad students. Oh, and two of the construction guys. The guys were watching—waiting to get back to work. I didn't let them touch the coffin. Nice guys, but, you know, that coffin might be two hundred years old—well, you need to have a delicate touch. And Ms. Gilbert. The second I saw her... I have to admit I screamed. I was rattled, as you said. But I made sure everyone got out. We did and then went up to the church, the—the club area, to wait for the police."

"Right. So there were seven of you. I have the names," Craig said. He was certain that the meticulous Detective McBride had sent his email.

He'd also seen Jeannette Gilbert's body at the site.

He winced, the picture of her still so clear in his

mind. Her lovely, pale, perfect face. The white dress. The red rose.

John nodded. "Seven of us were in there—and seven of us got out quicker than a flash. And we were all interviewed." He sighed loudly. "Hell of a thing for the owner of that place. They've barely been open, what, a month or two? Then they have to stop work and close up because an engineer finds the coffins in the dirt and then the catacombs. They bring us in, and... Sad. So sad. By God, she was beautiful! Poor thing."

"Just to confirm, you were there yesterday?" Craig asked him.

"Of course. I was there as soon as the situation was reported." He paused. "Did you know that the land where the Waldorf Astoria sits was once a potter's field? Think of how old this city is. A number of the parks we enjoy today were originally cemeteries. I worked the old slave cemetery they discovered a few years back, so it was natural that I'd work on this one, too."

"You started on the church yesterday?"

"Yes, I did. I was called yesterday morning and I made arrangements to get there as fast as possible."

"And then?"

"I assessed the location. I called in Digby and my assistant, Allie Benoit. You don't pry apart ancient caskets willy-nilly. We researched church plans, but the original architect's plan is long gone." He shook his head. "You must be familiar with what happened. The church sold the property to the club people. There was an outcry, not that it made any difference. But the building is so historic. Everyone wants to shop Fifth Avenue, see a show, bank on Wall Street. They forget that Wall Street *was* a wall. Canal Street was a canal—or a cesspool, really. Those are all part of our city's origins and we need to preserve history!"

Craig nodded, although he wasn't convinced they'd needed to preserve the cesspool that had been Canal Street. He spoke quickly, not wanting the academic to bluster endlessly. "What time did you get in there?"

"Let's see... They called us right around ten in the morning. I was there within the hour."

"So, who was there then?" Craig asked. "Besides you and the colleagues and workers you've mentioned."

"Oh, lots of people. The manager—owner, too, I think—Roger Gleason. He'd been working down by the construction area. They stored their booze down there—in the old crypt they knew about, I mean, with the coffins and bodies all gone now. It's a foundation, a basement. The basement—the *crypts*—were far more extensive than people realized. The wall had hidden some of the old coffins and shrouded corpses, so when some of the corpses were moved, the 'second' crypt was missed."

"Okay. Anyone else know what was going on?"

"At least two construction workers and one of the barmaid-slash-dancers. Have you seen what they do in there? She was dressed up in a little black bra and skirt and wearing some wicked makeup. The girls dance on tables when they're not handing out booze."

"So, employees, construction workers—anyone else?"

"Oh, yeah, the rep from the historic preservation group. Henry Willoughby. Loves history. He's not a scientist, but he's a great hands-on guy, ready to protect the past and help out if he can. The man loves New York and studied history and architecture. His wife passed away a while back, and now he gives all his love to the city. He stayed long enough last night to check in with us, make sure we were ready to catalogue the bodies and the artifacts we found. I would've brought in more crew, but—"

"Who stayed, then? Who was actually there when you kept working?"

"The seven people you know about—me, Digby showed up, my grad students—plus a structural engineer and a construction worker, all to see that we didn't bring down a wall, I assume." He cleared his throat. "Of course, after I initially went in yesterday, the construction guys created a kind door for us."

"How long were you there yesterday?"

"Oh, it was almost midnight before I left! I didn't touch or open anything. I stepped over the hole—where the wall broke when they working on the foundations— into the crypt beyond. We make drawings and assessments and plan before we start the actual work, so, yes, I'd say it was midnight. By then, of course, the vampire dancers were gone and all the club people had been told to go home. Once they'd made the find—the second crypt—they closed down, of course, but people were hanging around. It's…it's history being reclaimed! Roger Gleason, the owner, seems like a nice guy. He has a conscience and some perspective on what's important. We didn't have to get court orders or anything. He simply agreed to close for a few days. They had patrol officers covering the place, making sure that once the news about the crypt got out, some Goth or necrophilia-pursuing freak didn't try to break in."

Craig nodded. He knew the answers to most of what he was asking; he just wanted it from Shaw and he wanted to ensure that their facts were straight.

"Yesterday," Shaw said, "you understand, it was *discovery* day. I planned where to put some lights. I judged the space for people and decided on equipment. I did all the assessments, got my ducks in a row, you know what I mean?"

Craig nodded again. "This morning when you arrived—were things exactly as you'd left them?" he asked.

"What?"

"Had anything you'd done been changed? Were tools missing, anything like that?"

Shaw frowned. "I... I don't think so. I don't get it. I'd roped off different areas in the basement for my people. We had our little brushes and chisels and... no, I'm positive that our work tables were as the way we'd left them," he said. He leaned forward. "Didn't Ms. Gilbert disappear about two weeks ago? She didn't look as if she'd just been killed. She...she was beautiful as she lay there, but some decay had set in. I guess down there, with the cool temperature, natural decay wouldn't be what it would up here." He briefly closed his eyes. "If she was embalmed, she wasn't embalmed really well, but she was...dressed up. As if she'd been prepared for a viewing. Seeing her... It gave me chills! Chills! And I work with the dead all the time. When... when did she die?"

"The medical examiner is estimating her death to have been between one and two weeks ago. He'll tell us more definitively when he's done the autopsy."

"So, you think that..."

"I don't think anything yet," Craig said. "We need more information from the experts before I can even speculate. Go on, please, tell me about this morning."

"Oh. Oh," John said. "This morning." He looked longingly at his whiskey glass.

It was empty.

"You want another?" Craig asked.

"Yeah," John said huskily. "Yeah. The long dead are one thing. Fresh corpses…or not so fresh corpses…"

Craig knew what he meant.

He scanned the bar area but didn't see Kieran. Declan Finnegan, however—looking like an old-time Irish bartender as he dried a glass, decked in a white apron tied around his waist—was behind the bar.

Craig walked over to him. Declan, he knew, had been fully aware that Craig was in the pub and that he was talking to John Shaw.

"You want another whiskey for him?" Declan asked.

Declan was the eldest of the Finnegans; he wore his sense of responsibility and dignity well. All the Finnegan family were attractive and charming people with different degrees of red in their hair, and they all had eyes in varying shades of blue. Even a casual observer had to note that they were related.

Declan tended to be the most serious in demeanor. He didn't ask questions, not of Craig; he knew he'd learn what was going on if and when it was appropriate.

"Thanks," Craig said. "Any idea where Kieran is?"

"She and Kevin were helping out. I'm not sure where they went. Sorry you had to come to the bar. Anything for you?"

"Soda water?"

Declan quickly poured him a glass from the fountain, and Craig returned to the table. Where the hell had Kieran gone?

She was helping her brother out today, which meant

she was working here somewhere. If he was going to start worrying every time she wasn't in sight, he'd have to get a psych evaluation himself.

John Shaw took the whiskey from him; it looked as if he was going to gulp it down. Craig set a hand on his. "Hey, that's prime stuff, my friend. Sip it."

"Yeah, yeah, of course," Shaw murmured.

"Okay, so, you got in today—"

"Early. Just after seven. This is an important true find. The historical value is immense."

"Of course. I understand," Craig assured him. "So, today. You haven't opened any of the other coffins in the catacomb, have you?"

"No. Some of the coffins have disintegrated, and the remains are down to bones and dust and spider webs. Remnants of fabric… Belt buckles, shoe buckles…" John said, studying the amber liquid in his glass.

"But you found Ms. Gilbert in the first coffin?"

Shaw nodded glumly.

"What made you open that one first?" Craig asked.

The question seemed to confuse Shaw for a minute. "It seemed to be the best preserved…" He paused, staring up at Craig. "Actually, it was at an odd angle on the shelf. As if it had been moved. Oh…that was obviously because someone had been there! They'd put her body in it!"

"Do you remember it being that way the day before?"

"No! That must've been it. There was something different!" John Shaw said. "I didn't realize it immediately. It was such a…subtle difference. The thing is, I thought I'd start with the best-preserved, but so did…" He frowned at Craig. "It was definitely the best preserved. And someone else knew that, too. Her killer."

Jeannette had been dead at least a week, possibly two. But she'd been placed in that coffin in a forgotten crypt much more recently than that.

The killer had learned about the archaeological find—he'd made use of it for his own designs.

"Excuse me," Craig said abruptly. "I'll be right back."

He wanted to see where Kieran was; it suddenly seemed important.

She wasn't at the bar. She wasn't on the floor.

He hurried down the hallway to the office and pushed open the door, not bothering to knock.

Kieran was there, and Craig let out a sigh of relief.

But then he saw that she wasn't alone. She was sitting on the sofa in front of the desk, talking earnestly with her twin brother, Kevin.

They both looked up at him, startled—and their expressions could only be described as guilty.

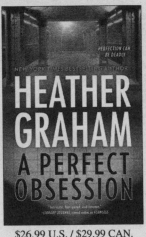

# Turn your love of reading into rewards you'll love with

# Harlequin My Rewards

**Join for FREE today at**
**www.HarlequinMyRewards.com**

Earn **FREE BOOKS** of your choice.

Experience **EXCLUSIVE OFFERS** and contests.

Enjoy **BOOK RECOMMENDATIONS**
selected just for you.

**PLUS!** Sign up now
and get **500** points
right away!

Earn
FREE
REWARDS
HarlequinMyRewards.com
Join
Today!

MYR16R

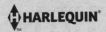

# INTRIGUE

## EDGE-OF-YOUR-SEAT INTRIGUE, FEARLESS ROMANCE.

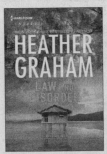

## Save $1.00

on the purchase of
LAW AND DISORDER
by *New York Times* bestselling author
HEATHER GRAHAM,
available January 17, 2017,
or on any other Harlequin® Intrigue book.

Available wherever books are sold, including most
bookstores, supermarkets, drugstores and discount stores.

--- ✂ ---

# Save $1.00

## on the purchase of any Harlequin Intrigue book.

Coupon valid until April 30, 2017. Redeemable at participating outlets in
the U.S. and Canada only. Not redeemable at Barnes & Noble stores.
Limit one coupon per customer.

52614431

5 65373 00076 2 (8100)0 12234

HGCOUP1216

# REQUEST YOUR FREE BOOKS!

## 2 FREE NOVELS FROM THE PARANORMAL ROMANCE COLLECTION, PLUS 2 FREE GIFTS!

**YES!** Please send me 2 FREE novels from the Paranormal Romance Collection and my 2 FREE gifts (gifts are worth about $10). After receiving them, if I don't wish to receive any more books, I can return the shipping statement marked "cancel." If I don't cancel, I will receive 4 brand-new novels every month and be billed just $24.76 in the U.S. or $27.96 in Canada. That's a savings of at least 29% off the cover price of all 4 books. It's quite a bargain! Shipping and handling is just 50¢ per book in the U.S. and 75¢ per book in Canada.* I understand that accepting the 2 free books and gifts places me under no obligation to buy anything. I can always return a shipment and cancel at any time. Even if I never buy another book, the two free books and gifts are mine to keep forever.

237/337 HDN GLDY

| | |
|---|---|
| Name | (PLEASE PRINT) |

| | |
|---|---|
| Address | Apt. # |

| | | |
|---|---|---|
| City | State/Prov. | Zip/Postal Code |

Signature (if under 18, a parent or guardian must sign)

### Mail to the **Reader Service**:
**IN U.S.A.:** P.O. Box 1867, Buffalo, NY 14240-1867
**IN CANADA:** P.O. Box 609, Fort Erie, Ontario L2A 5X3

**Want to try 2 free books from another line?
Call 1-800-873-8635 or visit www.ReaderService.com.**

* Terms and prices subject to change without notice. Prices do not include applicable taxes. Sales tax applicable in NY. Canadian residents will be charged applicable taxes. Offer not valid in Quebec. This offer is limited to one order per household. Not valid for current subscribers to Paranormal Romance Collection or Harlequin® Nocturne™ books. All orders subject to credit approval. Credit or debit balances in a customer's account(s) may be offset by any other outstanding balance owed by or to the customer. Please allow 4 to 6 weeks for delivery. Offer available while quantities last.

**Your Privacy**—The Reader Service is committed to protecting your privacy. Our Privacy Policy is available online at www.ReaderService.com or upon request from the Reader Service.

We make a portion of our mailing list available to reputable third parties that offer products we believe may interest you. If you prefer that we not exchange your name with third parties, or if you wish to clarify or modify your communication preferences, please visit us at www.ReaderService.com/consumerschoice or write to us at Reader Service Preference Service, P.O. Box 9062, Buffalo, NY 14269. Include your complete name and address.

# HEATHER GRAHAM

| | | | |
|---|---|---|---|
| 32928 | THE PRESENCE | ___ $7.99 U.S. | ___ $9.99 CAN. |
| 32815 | GHOST NIGHT | ___ $7.99 U.S. | ___ $9.99 CAN. |
| 32796 | GHOST MOON | ___ $7.99 U.S. | ___ $9.99 CAN. |
| 32791 | GHOST SHADOW | ___ $7.99 U.S. | ___ $9.99 CAN. |
| 31948 | DARKEST JOURNEY | ___ $7.99 U.S. | ___ $9.99 CAN. |
| 31945 | DEADLY FATE | ___ $7.99 U.S. | ___ $9.99 CAN. |
| 31895 | HAUNTED DESTINY | ___ $7.99 U.S. | ___ $9.99 CAN. |
| 31799 | THE SILENCED | ___ $7.99 U.S. | ___ $8.99 CAN. |
| 31789 | THE FORGOTTEN | ___ $7.99 U.S. | ___ $8.99 CAN. |
| 31758 | THE HIDDEN | ___ $7.99 U.S. | ___ $9.99 CAN. |
| 31750 | THE DEAD PLAY ON | ___ $7.99 U.S. | ___ $9.99 CAN. |
| 31656 | THE BETRAYED | ___ $7.99 U.S. | ___ $8.99 CAN. |
| 31637 | THE HEXED | ___ $7.99 U.S. | ___ $8.99 CAN. |
| 31601 | LET THE DEAD SLEEP | ___ $7.99 U.S. | ___ $8.99 CAN. |
| 31507 | THE NIGHT IS ALIVE | ___ $7.99 U.S. | ___ $8.99 CAN. |
| 31429 | THE UNSEEN | ___ $7.99 U.S. | ___ $9.99 CAN. |
| 31416 | THE VISION | ___ $7.99 U.S. | ___ $9.99 CAN. |
| 31370 | THE UNINVITED | ___ $7.99 U.S. | ___ $9.99 CAN. |
| 31349 | THE UNHOLY | ___ $7.99 U.S. | ___ $9.99 CAN. |
| 31318 | PHANTOM EVIL | ___ $7.99 U.S. | ___ $9.99 CAN. |
| 31303 | GHOST WALK | ___ $7.99 U.S. | ___ $9.99 CAN. |
| 31242 | SACRED EVIL | ___ $7.99 U.S. | ___ $9.99 CAN. |

*(limited quantities available)*

| | |
|---|---|
| TOTAL AMOUNT | $ _____ |
| POSTAGE & HANDLING | $ _____ |
| ($1.00 for 1 book, 50¢ for each additional) | |
| APPLICABLE TAXES* | $ _____ |
| TOTAL PAYABLE | $ _____ |

*(check or money order—please do not send cash)*

To order, complete this form and send it, along with a check or money order for the total above, payable to MIRA Books, to: **In the U.S.:** 3010 Walden Avenue, P.O. Box 9077, Buffalo, NY 14269-9077; **In Canada:** P.O. Box 636, Fort Erie, Ontario, L2A 5X3.

Name: _____
Address: _____ City: _____
State/Prov.: _____ Zip/Postal Code: _____
Account Number (if applicable): _____

075 CSAS

*New York residents remit applicable sales taxes.
*Canadian residents remit applicable GST and provincial taxes.

**MIRA®**

MHG1216BL